51 Pegasi

– Black Mac

ISBN 9816853-3-1

This is a work of speculative fiction. As such, there are real and fictional people, places, and events applied as background, but this tale is fiction; every character is fictional and does not or should not reflect on the real lives of anyone. This book is not designed to apply judgment but to look at these events through the lens of an assortment of diverse characters. If I did it right, you will hear several voices, not just the narrator.

Published in the United States and distributed to the world from the U.S. and the United Kingdom

Distributed by Amazon.com and Cowboy Logic Press at

www.cowboylogic.net/51pegas

Edited by Annie Vialle and Roger Haller

I dedicated this book to my direct Next Generation, Steve, Becky, and Matt, whom I helped initiate, and Bill, Eric, Cory, and Jamisyn, whom I've had the opportunity to influence. To their spouses and children, who make me proud of my path every day, and to my circle for keeping me real.

I hope this book inspires them to make a positive difference in their world.

Cover Illustrated by Roger Haller

Special Thanks to Joni Haller, Ken Sharp, Becky Haller-Fry, and Liudmyla Sovetovs for beta reader feedback.

51 Pegasi -Black Mac

A Second Chance

What happens when outcasts get a second chance to get it right for humanity?

By

Roger Haller

Mac's map of the explored regions of the new world

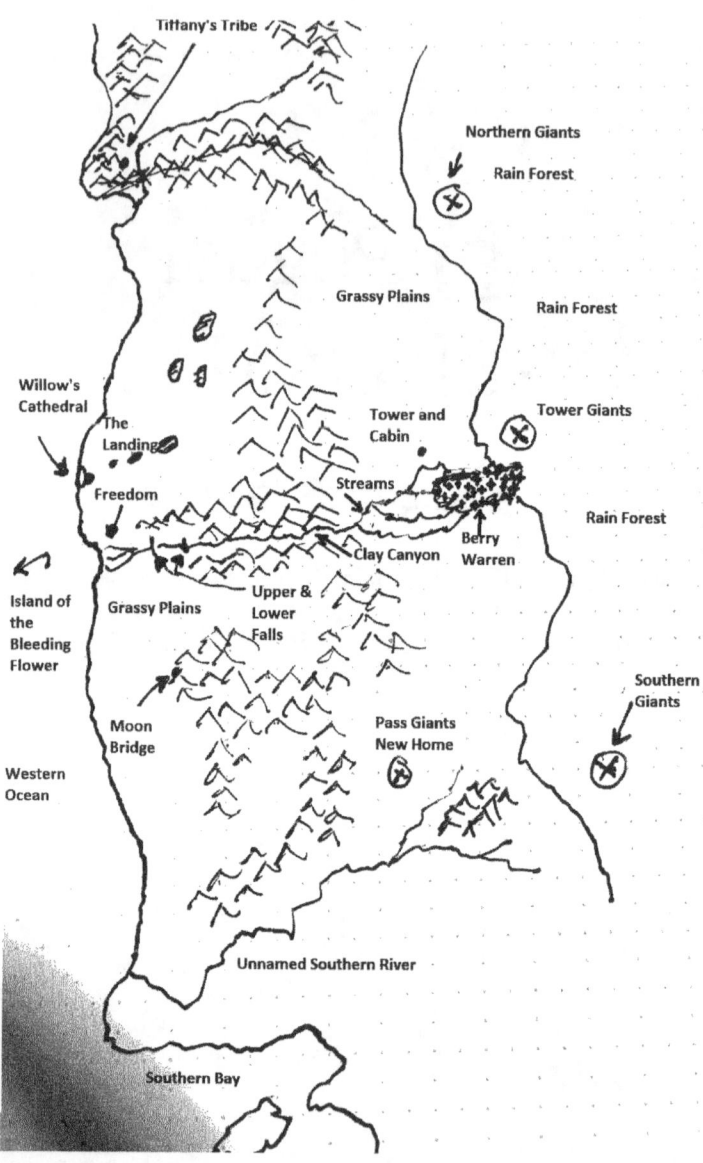

Chapter 1

Tucson

I had been drinking too much over the last couple of months. Not because I needed to kill my past so much as I had nothing better to do. That may sound strange.

Perhaps I should have been drowning my pain over losing Margo, but I had very little emotion. I was numb. Nothing felt necessary in this twilight zone of grief.

Sure, there had been stages of grief. First, I remember the denial when the police came to my office to tell me. Then there was the bitter anger when they asked me if we had been fighting and revealed that a 'male friend' I didn't know had died in the accident with her. Finally, when the cops left me, I bawled my eyes out and pleaded with a god I doubted to help me understand.

When I had no more tears, I reread the accident report but was amazed when I noticed all my emotions had drained; my feelings had turned off. The sadness was a wet blanket that I felt would never lift. I had been dealing with some nefarious competition lately in my professional life, but nothing the business and I couldn't handle. Margo and I were drifting apart, but I felt we just needed to vacation more to rekindle.

The accident report was black and white, and my next days were too.

They turned into business transactions with insurance agents who always dealt with this and had to fake the emotions in their hollow condolences. I still dealt with waves of doubt and what-ifs, but it was almost third-party. I felt I was looking at someone else's life. Reflecting on the blur, perhaps I never left the denial stage. Hours of self-analysis were not making my life come together.

The next few days magnified the reality of my marriage and my sanity's last hours. My tailspin began when my wife and her friend died in a wrong-way head-on crash. All because a terminal cancer patient missed the concrete overpass pillar by inches; he struck my wife's Volvo instead.

My business was running itself; my people knew what to do, and they didn't need my attention to keep the ship afloat. I had a team invested in dealing with the unscrupulous competitor. Abbot Logistics was playing dirty with my customers. This Bruce Abbot guy was also beginning to show up in my circles. Something was ringing alarm bells, but I couldn't put a finger on it in my state of mind. My team had run a SWOT analysis on them and had countermeasures ready to launch.

Trade with Mexico was healthy, and the trucks rolling back and forth between Tucson and Hermosillo supported many lives and made me wealthy. It meant nothing today. I took a month off, then six months, while reflecting on my personal life.

I tried to check in with Tony and My dad.

Dad was never easy to find, and my red-headed brother had quit his job in Detroit and was figuratively following in our father's footsteps. Now, he may have been literally tracking him down. The last I heard, he had been in a logging camp in Northern Ontario.

Dad was home from time to time while we were young. At least once a month but sometimes averaging every couple of weeks. We never knew what he did for a living, but we always had food and clothing and lived in a modest, comfortable single-floor home on the outskirts of Reston, Virginia. My mother had been gone since I was in my 'tweens.' I hadn't known her well. She was always gone when I was a small child until she was just... gone.

My older brother, Tony, and Carmela, were my life constants. She was our live-in nanny, maid, and cook and was the most constant parent we knew. Carmela left with a health issue when I was seventeen. She left me with a rudimentary Spanish and a deep respect for family.

I knew from early life that my brother was a step-brother. Tony was two years older than me and had experienced the disappearing mother scenario before I came along, so this was simply a shoulder shrug for him. He told me he didn't care much for her as a small child because she didn't seem interested in him. His only relationship was a small toy once a month when she would drop by until he was about four or five. She would not be in the house simultaneously with my mother.

He left home at sixteen to find his path, and I didn't hear again from him until I graduated high school. He was the only one to show up for my ceremony.

I had no idea how he knew, but he made that day for me. He spent a week catching up with me before hitting the road again.

He gave me five hundred dollars and a tuition certificate for community college as a graduation present and told me to turn it into a future.

I turned it into an old pick-up and started a delivery business while I took night school classes to earn my pre-grad degree in macroeconomics.

Now, in the present, I didn't expect to see any of them soon, so I was alone. I did nothing constructive while contemplating, so I called an office meeting and offered to sell my company to my employees. I presented a plan to finance their purchase and have them keep me in an income from equity payments and shares for the rest of my life.

It took another six months to make all the connections, sign all the papers, and shake all the hands, but it was all shadow. I felt none of it.

I then sat with the lawyers, arranging the shares to help set up the equity to make this happen. I also set up a bank account and accounting firm to manage the transactions to and from the company for my personal stake. I gave the head accountant power of attorney to make decisions.

Finally, I decided to find myself and see how I might re-invent myself in a way that could do some good for society. With all my loss, I felt mortal. I thought I had not reached my human potential and would not leave a valuable legacy beyond a few people in a comfortable business.

I must be able to make a difference or at least feel helpful. I finished my last duties at the CEO desk I had cleared last week and took all my belongings to my desert home in the Catalina foothills. I took one last look around the office I had built from a one-room storefront 12 years ago and looked out the windows at the unprecedented desert downpour.

My train of thought came back from memories with a flash of lightning and the pounding rain on the dark vista outside my window.

The reflection of my skin seemed gray and washed out. I grunted in irony as the rivulets running down the window panes seemed to be tears on my face. I vaguely wondered if Tanque Verde Creek would be raging, but the thought didn't stick.

My hair had grown much too long, my natural afro was in full bloom, and I had a two-week beard. I had better hit the barber tomorrow.

Nothing was sinking into my idling brain and dulled senses. I couldn't get traction as the anniversary of my empty life brought me constant memories of my family. It all seemed like yesterday and a lifetime ago at the same time.

I spun slowly on my heel to head for the elevator.

***

Chapter 2

Caged

Cage Log - 11/02/2006

I've been getting acquainted with my new reality for two days but have no idea how I got here, where 'here' is, or what fate lies in store for me. I am in a jail... or a cage with no facilities. There is no food; the only water is the puddles left at the weather edge of my cell from the constant warm rain.

My last memory before this predicament was leaving my desk and heading for the elevator. I flipped my raincoat on my arm, grabbed my fedora, and grabbed my laptop. It didn't happen in Tucson often, but it looked like a storm was coming in. So, I woke naked, using my raincoat as a blanket and pillow. There wasn't much I could do with my hat.

Thinking hard, I decided I had better document what was happening. A journal may or may not make sense, but it gives me something to do as I figure out where I am and what is happening. So now I log everything that happens on my laptop. After some thought, I repeat my efforts here with a fine point Sharpie from my computer case on the back cage wall, which is the only solid one.

I won't have a computer battery for very long, so the wall will, I assume, last longer.

Hopefully, someone will read this sometime and discover what happened to me.

Then again, I suppose it means you will be in my predicament. I'm so sorry.

I need to eat soon and have taken to chewing on the nametag on my computer case. It's not very satisfying, but it's not so bad.

Writing these words seems strange. I suppose I should be writing my will. Right now, I'm just not in the mood to figure out who should take possession of my home and car.

I'm not sure what to expect. I've lost weight but still have energy from the water and feel light and agile. I can jump and touch the ceiling, which must be ten feet from the floor. At home, my two hundred-and-twelve-pound frame was lucky to get off the floor in a mighty jump—some crash diet.

Keeping the front edge of my cage for puddles of drinking water, I used a back corner for my toilet. I decided to do my body business in the rain-soaked corner and scraped it out between the bars with a small tree limb the wind supplied, but I hadn't needed it today. The rain was removing the evidence quite nicely.

Night comes suddenly in this place, and it seems to come more often. I expect incarceration and starvation to make the days drag, but I can watch the shadows of dull daylight crawl across my cage, and night is with me again.

The night is never quite dark as an eerie blue night light seems to emanate from under some nearby bramble bushes.

I think I could see some basketball-sized berries grow-ing,

There is nothing else to do but think; I lie down and try to sleep. Maybe I'll dream about Margo tonight.

We did have a comfortable history, and those events seemed to rise to the top of my memories now.

I will keep the Sharpie from my case in my raincoat pocket for easy access.

My skin feels pruned and wrinkled as I rub my hands under my coat. Sleep is getting easier now because of my weaker body. It seems my only retreat.

***

Cage Log - 11/03/2006

I woke sliding up against the bars near the front of my prison. I grabbed at my computer bag as it sought freedom between the bars. I missed it.

I may have whimpered some then, but I don't remember well. My memory stings still with the picture of my fate as beside me swung two huge fur-laden legs in a fore and aft ballet while my jail bounced up and down, causing my head to bob like a carried chicken.

I had pressed my head to the bars to peer up at the tower in charge of my journey.

A three-story biped that looked much like Discovery Channel's version of a Neanderthal but with far more hair.

More precisely fur.

I decided it might be a good time to be quiet, so I worked my way to the back wall. With my coat on and my fedora perched in a most business-like manner. Next, I used my shoelaces to tie my Sharpie to the bar nearest my journal.

I braced my forearm firmly against the wall and continued the journal you read now.

I just checked the time and date on my watch, carefully wrote every word you are reading now, and I'm working my mind into thinking I am not the type that gets seasick. I...

I'm back.

The floor had lurched, and I launched to the front of the cage

I lost a couple of ounces of bile through the bars and down the leg of my captor. It wasn't pleased, so the jail and I had come to rest on a huge boulder.

The beast took time to wipc down its glossy brown fur before dropping its ape-like face to my level to study its trinket.

A colossal fist came into view with an index finger like an eight-inch log, pointing directly at me. In stunned horror, I watched as it slid happily through the bars to bunt me in the belly. The tap was hard enough to double me over and collapse me on the floor.

It tried to communicate with grunts and deep rumblings in its chest, then settled in to pet me with two fingers as a child would a scared baby rabbit. I felt the part.

With another grunt, it stood, and my journey continued.

I crab-walked back to the journal, and here I am again to work on my log, no better for being sick and sore from bruised ribs.

The shadow is deepening toward night again, and my giant keeper settled my cage into place across from several others.

Most containers seem empty, but I see another human in the same predicament, one cell across from me.

...Back in a minute.

Okay, get a load of this. I had a conversation with a human. I'll spell it out as best I can remember below. I called out to the woman across the way in the waning light. She stood from kneeling and ran to the bars at the front of her cage.

"Do you speak English?" she asked.

I could not stop shaking as I called back. "Yes, I do; my name is Tom MacAdams from Tucson, Arizona."

"I'm Sharon Rowlands from Eugene, Oregon... Canyonville, actually, but the closest big city is Eugene. Do you know where we are? Do you know why we are here?"

"Not a clue. All I know is I'm starving, wet, hot, and so thankful to hear another human voice."

Below us, I now heard rustling, and a new voice joined the conversation.

"Je suis français, parlez-vous français?"

I knew enough that I could not talk with this guy well.

"Non, pas... très bien"

"Okay. I ...try English...some.

Je Suis...Uh, I am Jean Belanger, Oui? Je... I am... uh... from Besancon beside riviere du Doubs... beside Jura Mountains...France."

"Hello, John, I am Tom, and that is Sharon. How long have you two been here?"

Sharon replied

"I was just dumped here."

"Oui, Je..., Me too. Also, my name is Jean, J.E.A.N., not John."

"Ah, I get it. Sorry, Jean. Most people call me Mac. I should point that out, too."

"This is not a problem, Tom..., Mac."

Our chat fest was interrupted by a flurry of fur between us. Bits of raw meat that reminded me of turkey, celery, or rhubarb-type stock of vegetation. Also provided were a few large, royal-blue berries I recognized from our surroundings were pushed through all our bars by massive fingers.

I could see no gain in holding out for a Big Mac, so I dug in. The giant produced large water containers, and the creature seemed pleased to see us eating.

The giant's lips curled up over crooked teeth in a mustached smile, and judging by the canines, that mouth also ate meat.

The captor lifted my cage high in a tree and fastened it somehow from the roof.

I was eating, swaying in front of an interested set of curious black eyes.

The giant's quizzical look left me wondering if it would respond to an attempt at communication. I stopped for a moment and moved to the front of the cage. I held out my arm with my palm up and spoke.

"Hello, I'm Tom... Can you understand me?"

The beast growled something low and grinned. It held its hand as I did. I reached a little farther, and it responded by putting its finger within my reach. I gently tapped the finger and nodded, pointing at the food.

The creature nodded, pointed at my raincoat, and held its hand to me, palm up. I assumed it wanted to know why I had removable skin.

I peeled it off and held it to the cage.

The creature took it between two fingers and tossed it at the berry warren. It lifted my cage from its perch, set me back on top of Jean, and moved to the others.

I made my way back to the wall to record this fantastic day. Disappointed by losing my last vestige of clothing, I was, at least, equal with Jean and Sharon now.

I had been feeling guilty owning some modesty while my companions went without.

I had planned to give it to Willow when I had the chance, but that chance never happened.

I struggled to understand how I arrived with some clothing, a computer, and a hat while my neighbors arrived naked and without accessories.

I now know how important it is to learn to communicate with my captor. My life probably depends on it. If you are unfortunate enough to read this, I expect this will be the information you need most. I am going to sign off now and study.

***

Cage Log - 11/10/2006

A primarily uneventful week has passed with regular food and water.

I got to know Sharon and Jean better than I wanted to, seeing I was in full, unclothed view of Sharon at all times as she was with me, and poor Jean lived directly under my "toilet."

We agreed to use the same corner, and Sharon and I decided to turn when necessary. I did notice; however, we were all getting used to living in full naked view of each other. I was amazed at how quickly social norms could wear off when conditions dictated the rules.

I noted that this social rule was beginning to fade naturally as we subconsciously adapted to this new way of life.

Communication with the creature continued; today, we hit a new milestone.

I now understood the Giants used a written language as they placed a huge sign over the cages. When I could, I duplicated the characters on a piece of notepad paper with my Sharpie and showed the beast.

My efforts impressed my giant Sasquatch considerably. With motions at the cages, the sign, and hand-to-hand, I learned it was a for-sale sign.

Today, I was surprised by the arrival of another of these creatures. This creature had a lighter shade of brown, high-lighted by golden tips on each hair. The effect of the tint created a sheen overall and was most impressive.

The two communicated briefly, and the new one began my training. I had no hope of parroting these giant creatures' sounds when they spoke, so I concentrated on their written language. I reached an epiphany when I recognized a pattern in the characters.

Putting the characters together, I experimented with rudimentary words.

The golden beast made clear a particular set of characters referred to us as three captives.

Then I found a slight variation that differentiated between Sharon and us men. This fact meant these beings understood our different sexes. My understanding of these words was not all pleasant; I now understood those signs.

This day has been a tremendous spike in my learning, but I can no longer see what I write on this wall, so I will continue tomorrow.

***

Cage Log - 11/11/2006

This morning was an awakening. In more than one way.

Shortly after the giant fed us, the giant opened Sharon's cage from the top and gently plucked her out, dangling and screaming.

She was three stories in the air. Next, the creature lifted my roof and placed Sharon in my cage. Once let go, she ran to me, and I held her as she shivered in fear.

The roof of my cell was replaced and clipped, and that fur-covered face studied us as we huddled in the center of my prison. The creature wagged a downturned finger at us a few times, which made Sharon cling tighter and, in turn, made the creature grin. Then, with no more than a scared huddle to entertain, the creature showed us what it wanted.

First, Sasquatch carefully removed the cage roof, using only two fingers and a thumb; it placed my petrified guest on her hands and knees.

I was then placed on my knees behind her with my arms on her shoulders.

When we stayed where the creature had placed us, he settled the roof back on our cage, clipped it shut, and the curious face was again at eye level with us, its eyebrows lifted in a hopeful gaze. We were breeding stock.

The strange scene made me think I needed to write this down later because readers of the journal must know what the Giants expect of them should they come upon my words. It may save their life. Sharon looked around at me, so my attention returned to the situation.

"Sharon, do you understand what that creature wants?"

"Yes... What are you going to do?"

"Play along with me... First, I will convey that we know their expectations and then communicate that we want privacy."

"But I don't want...."

"I know, but I need to try and buy time. I will pretend I am uh...you know...mating with you. Please play along, and I will pull you to the back of the cage, cuddle, and look over our shoulders at the beast in hopes it gets the idea that we don't want an audience. Are you with me?"

She hesitated a moment. "Yes... Okay."

I made the expected motions, but I must admit, it was not as unpleasant for me as I supposed it was for Sharon. Shortly, I pulled back, stood, helped Sharon up, and moved her to the back of the cage. We knelt huddled and looked over our shoulders at the smiling creature.

It left, seemingly satisfied we were going to mate.

Sharon pulled her head back from the huddle.

"Now what?"

"I don't know, but I feel it will not settle for pretend. I think it wants to raise pet humans... or I hope it wants pets."

"What do you mean by that?"

"I simply don't like the alternative."

I was silent momentarily, and her gaze rose from her hands on my sides to my face. Her eyes grew wide along the way.

"No!"

"Look, it won't make us a flea's pimple of good to worry about appearances. We need to think like we are going to stay alive. We are in no position to dictate our fate at present. The way I see it, we must become pets to survive. We need to be cute, entertaining, and endearing. And with lower security, we need to plan our escape."

Sharon's horror leaned a bit toward hope as she caught my drift.

"What do you suggest?"

I was silent for a moment while carving up this reality. Then, I pulled Sharon gently closer. My voice lowered.

"We have to, mate. Can you bear children?"

"Wha...."

"Look, if we don't, they will assume I am a dud, and you will be placed with Jean to try harder with him.

It's your choice, but you will have to mate with one of us or both, or all of us will be expendable."

Sharon glanced at the floor momentarily and said, "I've had my tubes tied."

She looked up again.

I looked into her eyes as she absorbed the insanity of discarding human games and embracing the animal side of our nature. At least she wasn't screaming at the idea.

Sharon was past the twenty-something prime a bit, and so was I. Of course, neither of us was part of the elite in human social politics, but she certainly had her charms, and I would have no trouble with the arrangement.

"Okay. That means this ploy will not last very long." I looked in her eyes.

"We need to work the ruse as we plan our escape. You may also be mated with other men if this takes a while. I suppose it depends if there are more where we came from and how we impress with our attempt."

Her head shook from side to side in a dazed arc, but she looked me over and rested her eyes on my face.

"Have we met? You look familiar, somehow."

I looked closely at Sharon now, and I liked what I saw. "No, I don't think so. I would have certainly remembered you."

She smiled, and I knew I would have remembered that smile.

Tom, you aren't Brad, and I'm not Angelina. If we must do this, you most certainly will do in a pinch." She delivered the line with a smile, so I supposed we were an item.

"The fur-ball is going to expect a show, isn't it."

I pulled Sharon tight and held her and we talked as the sun went down. She felt it wise to get to know each other if we were going to be mates. I found out her father's family had immigrated from Scotland in the early 1800s.

Her mother's family started in Oregon from a French-Canadian trapper and a local Native American. She learned about my mixed family.

***

51 Pegasi - Black Mac

Cage Log - 11/12/2006

Today, we performed for our captor, so it ran for its companion, and suddenly our audience grew. I had trouble concentrating when it became apparent five creatures were getting a charge out of two small naked animals mating. We kept it rudimentary because we didn't think it would understand or appreciate foreplay or the gentle attention that comes with love. That may have been a wrong assumption, but for a stage performance, it fit.

A complicated conversation grew outside our cage.

The Giants moved Jean to Sharon's former home and changed the sign above it to what I now thought to be "Sold." Jean was not a mating pair, but someone or something paid the price for him.

We need to get out of here.

***

Chapter 3

Escape to the Briar

Keeping my experience documented on a cage wall was my attempt to paint some reality around what I was going through. Of course, my log probably wouldn't be the first instinct for most people, but I showed up in this world with my office in my hand and nothing else. I started working. Once my reality started to sink in, I wanted to begin my legacy with a warning to help prepare anyone following.

Right now, Sharon, Jean, and I needed to escape. Our chance came during our next evening.

Taking Sharon by the hand, I moved to the bars facing Jean. He curled in a ball in a far corner. You might imagine the thoughts running through his mind as he watched our life unfolding across from him.

"Jean," I called softly, "Are you awake?"

"Oui – yes!"

"Jean, do you understand our situation? I think, more than ever, we need to break out and take our chances in the wild."

"I agree. We cannot live like dis much longere. I waz hoping to parley about dis.

I tink I may have ze way out, bat we need to be together in dis cage. I have found a looze bar and haf been able to move it on de floor far enough to get trough.

Ma-be dere is de flaw in your cage as well, no?"

"Great news, Jean, but I have worked on every corner of this cage and everything between and have found no flaw. I have been thinking of the cap, but it suspends us, and when it is disconnected, we will crash to the ground.

I haven't given up on that yet, but I prefer floor-to-ground distance to roof-to-ground. So far, I think our best bet is to join you in your cage."

"Oui, that would be best."

Sharon joined our thoughts. "Guys, I noticed a tree re-sembling a willow under Jean's old cage. The branches seem long and flexible, reaching the bottom of the cage.

I often wished I could squeeze out and take my chances on one of those branches."

I smiled. "Sharon, you are smarter than both of us guys together. Jean, could you reach one of those long willow switch-es?"

Jean stood up with eyes wide and hurried to his loose bar. We watched him pull it aside and lay on the floor at the gap. Jean reached out and grabbed a switch that was as big around as his arm.

It moved easily in his grasp as he slid it along the side of his cage. Excitement lit up his face in the gathering dusk. "Etonnant!... Amazing!"

I was thrilled. "Team, if you are ready to escape, I may know how to get us all in that cage. It may backfire and get us over here, but I can do it.

If it works, we will be on our own in the elements. Are you with me?"

Jean quickly gave me a thumbs up, but Sharon thought for a few moments. "Yes, I want my freedom more than I want my life. Let's make this work."

"Okay, here is my plan. I have learned to communicate well enough to get my message across, but I will try to convince our captor that we both want to breed with Sharon to give the best chance of conception."

This statement caused silence for a few moments, but as the darkness had dropped and we could hardly see Jean anymore, Sharon nodded and said, "Yes, that may work." Jean agreed.

The next day at feeding, I made my pitch using signs and limited text. The giant considered without comment while we ate, but in a few minutes, it lowered our cages, lifted the lids, and carefully placed Sharon and me in the cage with Jean. We made no moves for the tops of the walls, so the giant hung us back in position, and before it left, I requested a cover of some kind with signs that we wished for privacy. This request resulted in a skin "tarp" tanned to a soft, luxurious texture. I wondered why the Giants hadn't offered them earlier, but I only replied with gratitude.

After finishing our daily ration, we convened under the chamois to make movements, suggesting to our captors that we were attempting to serve their request.

We also talked at great length about what we would do when we hit the ground.

I grunted and moaned, rolled my eyes, pointed upward to our censored audience, then said, "Those berries seem to grow in the brambles around us.

The bushes grow taller than a house, but I think I've seen some trails in and out of them and may have seen movement. Perhaps something like rabbits live in them, and I hope we can too. We need a haven close by as I feel those Giants will be avid hunters and trackers.

Also, the berries can help us stave off hunger until we can supplement with protein."

I received nods from both, and Sharon followed with, "I hope we can take the hide with us. I have never valued anything as much as this thing since I've been here..., except, of course, you two." We chuckled quietly as she poked at our blanket to prove we were still having a good time.

Jean said, "Oui, Je... I have been watching the bushes, too. I see a small animal like a petite porc..., how you say...pigglette, no?"

"That would be very handy, Jean," I replied, "We will need to figure out traps and weapons as we go."

"I am a state champion archer." We both turned to look at the willowy woman between us. "I competed since I was nine and had a room full of ribbons and plastic trophies at home. I may be able to make a willow bow if I find something for the string."

Jean smiled at me as he pointed at Sharon. "She eez our Willow Warrior, No?"

Again, we chuckled softly. We were all feeling hope for the first time since we arrived, and no matter how it turned out, we gelled as a team and enjoyed our first natural bond in a new life.

Princess Willow, the Warrior, said, "I think it's getting dark."

***

Indeed, the giant had left us to our resources, and we lost no time moving to the loose bar in the cage. I rolled up the hide as Jean worked the lower end of the bar over a scratch mark on the floor, he had made from working the bar loose.

"Let me go first so I can test. D'accord?"

I nodded, and Jean slipped out, feet first, to a sitting position, grabbed a firm hold on the willow switch, and leaned out. The branch lowered him gently to the ground like an elevator. He pulled it around in an arc before letting it go so it would flip back up alongside the cage instead of slapping it and making a loud noise. Brilliant!

The switch snapped back into its original position without complaint. Our newly named Willow copied the procedure but landed on her tiptoes. Jean helped her reposition the switch before letting go, and the elevator was delivered crisply to the top floor again.

I dropped the hide to Jean, pulled myself into position, and pulled the loose bar back as close as possible to the position behind me.

Then, as I leaned out, I pulled it a little farther to get it as close to normal as possible. Finally, I was deposited quietly on the ground. I repeated the reset procedure invented by Jean, and we headed for the closest bramble with a soft blue night light reminiscent of a 1970s black-light disco.

The brambles were handy for animals our size. With due attention to the oversized thorns that spanned anywhere from two to six feet long, we were soon deep in a briar patch that would easily span three city blocks. The air was cooler than the jungle heat, and we soon saw the source of the soft blue light.

There were nodes of luminescent blue fungus that delivered just enough light to make our way. Jean was the tallest of this little tribe, so he had to bend in places. I also had to bend over much of the time to avoid thorns pointed down into the warren.

We decided to rest to ensure we had some strength left for tomorrow's light and the fight to stay out of the reach of the pursuit.

None of us had any doubt we would not survive the anger of the Giants if they were to capture us. It felt good to feel free and somewhat safe for the first time since understanding our original purpose in this nightmare.

We found it wise to try to get off the floor of the warren for the night and, with a bit of work, were able to secure a hammock perch above the trails. We found this quite helpful as the trails through the briar become a highway. We discovered that many creatures traveled out to graze the grasslands around the brambles through the cover of night.

The most significant population were strange little quadrupeds that seemed to be a cross between a piglet and a reptile, with a hunched back like a startled cat.

We suspected we might have already been eating the meat from these critters, but we had also eaten something white and stringy with much longer muscles. The meat tasted like turkey or poultry that seemed to have come from a more oversized frame.

Morning found us sampling the berries, and we had to laugh at the mess made by the juicy berries as we had no manner of cleaning up. We did manage to eat our fill, however, and Jean even attempted a small bite of the blue mushrooms to see if he would get a reaction.

By mid-day, the heat was reaching down into the warren, but it was subdued nicely by the deep shade, and we felt much more comfortable than we had been in the cages.

However, a heart-stopping roar back where our trail had started smashed our comfort. The Giants noticed our absence. The explosion of noise subsided, but we heard activity and communication from every direction during the day. The Giants did not attempt to enter the brambles. We were missed, but not to the extent they would deal with the thorns.

I felt the protective bramble spears would be critical to our future and salvaged a few dried ones from the floor of the briar. These made handy weapons as they were light yet highly durable.

No amount of chipping at them with rocks could carve or whittle them to shape. Willow and I tried everything in our imagination to no effect.

Meanwhile, Jean had been working to free a living thorn from the brambles, and he could mark it and chip at the green fiber enough to notch and carve the raw material. He found that he could break the weapon from the vine with pressure with the lay of the grain of the thorn but had no chance when striking and pushing against the grain.

By the end of the second day, we had three spears with barbs. Willow had found a few dropped thorn buds that fit in our hands but had amazingly sharp hooks with knife-like inner edges sporting ridges that, when held right, could slice a neat gash down a vine.

We were becoming armed. That night, we hunted for the first time with a green, barbed spear thrust downward on a scurrying animal. We were successful, and the slicing buds allowed for skinning and butchering. We now ate familiar meat with our berries.

The three of us were confident we were no longer on Earth by comparing our observations. Not only were the flora and fauna alien to our experience but there were also other clear signs the known laws of physics no longer governed us. Our days were shorter.

None of us managed to keep a watch on our migration, but our body clocks were stunned by the short day-night cycle. We were all much lighter on our feet. We could jump higher, run faster, and carry what we felt was more weight.

Gravity was not as strong as we engaged with the environment in this place.

We did, however, notice similarities to Earth.

We felt the planet's rotation was like Earth, where we saw the sunrise in what we felt was the East and set in the West. We assumed from this that the planet rotated on an axis based near the North and South poles.

We felt we were much closer to the equator than the poles because of the heat and the short dusk and dawn time frames. Now that we were out from the cover of the dense canopy, we began noticing our sky.

Much as Earth was, our sun appeared the same, but we had a new set of stars at night, and the kicker was a pair of moons. We had hints of a wider moon path in the jungle but never saw the sun's or moon's direct light from our cages.

With our assumptions, we discussed our observations of this new world. We decided something allowed biology to build bigger packages on this planet. The Giants tucked us into a tropical environment that we imagined was like the Brazilian rainforest. We noted the size difference between the creatures and the berry thicket where we now lived.

The fruit's size and the trees' height were all magnified from what we were used to at home. From under the berry bush, we observed it was much lighter to our West than our East and discovered that the forest where we had initially been captives gave way to grassland to the West with a mountain range rising beyond the grass. Looking off to the East, we could see nothing over the massive forest.

Although the reaction to our escape seemed to settle back where we entered the briar patch, we sometimes heard the giant's unmistakable grunts to the East.

So we migrated farther to the West in our warren until we could no longer hear them. It seemed they might be harvesting berries, and we felt it better to put as much distance as possible between us and captivity.

We were peering out from under the Western limit of our bramble cover in a couple of days. Then, a new world of waving grass appeared. The grasslands continued unhindered until a mountain range rose to the West. The grass rose well above our heads in places and often at eye level, but we had no illusions the grass would hide us from above.

The grass cover would work well from a distance but not from the air.

If we could get far enough from the Giants, we felt we would have the cover to get to the mountains, and from there, who knows. Freedom? More Giants? New threats?

Or possibly a haven to live out what we have left of our lives. The exception to the dry grass prairie stretching to the South and West was a meandering snake of silvery green with small trees and blue-tinged shrubs.

This vista was beckoning with the promise of water for an escape trek.

I noticed my partners peering around me at the waving scene shimmering in the heat. I pointed out across the prairie to the Northwest at a dead tree. Well over a hundred feet tall, the foreboding skeleton of wood stood as a warning of what could happen if you moved away from the massive rainforest wall.

We could see the dark wall rise to the East, along the edge of the drying bramble sanctuary. The tree was not far from the brambles but was a long way from the forest.

We could see a few other straggler trees in the direction of the forest, but all they could make out were dead and dry. A few lay on the ground, but none stood West of this landmark tree. What did appear West of the tree was a massive metal tower that stood much taller than the tree—possibly a cellular tower with a small cabin at its foot and a nearby creek.

"Regarde ca... look!" Jean headed out.

"Just a minute, Jean. Listen." Standing just outside the warren, I cupped my right ear with a hand and raised my left hand slightly. They went silent. Lightly at first but stronger now that they were focused, they could hear far-off screams.

At first, we thought someone was in trouble, but when we listened carefully, the screams sounded excited or angry. Finally, Willow pointed to the sky, and we watched a flock of enormous birds flying in our direction.

Amazed, we watched as the birds grew larger as they drew nearer. Suddenly, we understood we were targets and re-alized the massive size of the flying raptors. We dove quickly back under cover.

With stunning ferocity, the entrance to the briar tunnels exploded with three-foot claws and horrific, curved beaks emitting mind-numbing screams designed to remove the ability to think. We scrambled deeper into the barbed sanctuary with no thoughts but to survive.

Thankfully, the thorns did their job, and the massive raptors lost interest and moved on to find more available prey.

Instinctively, we knew better than to investigate the quiet scene immediately.

***

Chapter 4

The Tower Cabin

Our small team stayed in the thicket for most of the day, but as the light faded, we worked our way back toward the thrashed trail exit. The scrub had been quiet, but we now heard the briar citizens beginning to stir.

"Regardez!" Jean motioned that he was listening. "Nous apprenons...we learn des locals, non?"

"I understand, Jean. Good idea. These critters have lived with the Giants and the big purple chicken hawks all their lives, so they know when it is safe to go out."

I looked at Willow, and she nodded. The panic from earlier became a concern, and I felt that was a healthy habit for our survival in this world. We listened to the rustle, squeaks, and grunts around us and watched as the small, humped-back creatures began filing out into the grasslands. Granted, they were a lot harder to see in the tall grass than we were, but evolution had allowed them to survive as a species in a role in the middle of the food chain. There was still enough light to see the tree and tower, and the migration had begun, so we felt this was our chance.

"Do you think we should make that building at the tower's base our next home?" Willow seemed worried but resolved.

"Yes and no.

For what it's worth, we could live in the warren for the foreseeable future, but it is too close to the Giants and those purple raptors for me. So, we need to get to those mountains; that tower and that cabin are the first step in that Journey. I like that the small river seems to come from those mountains. It may be our safest path to safety."

Jean nodded and headed out into the grass. We carried as many long weapons and knives as we could. We also found space for the coveted hide we brought from the cage. Willow and I followed with our eyes focused on the popcorn clouds as much as where our next footstep would be in the blind trek through the grass. We had many small trails to follow and kept the old tree and the tower beyond in line. We had our landmarks to lead us as long as we had light.

Unfortunately, we found we didn't have the use of the blue fungus for light.

By the time the dusk was fading out, we were only getting to the old tree. Luckily, the first moon began to lift over the horizon behind us. Within a few minutes, we saw that the moon lit our path quite well. We could still make almost the same cadence we had in the waning sunlight, and the evening was a bit cooler, so the trek was more comfortable.

We were awed by the size of our close-up view when we reached the tree. A few dead limbs were lying around the base that were taller horizontally than I was vertical. Brambles surrounded the bottom of the tree, but they had died some time ago.

Time had reduced the dry briar to a dangerous mound of spears and crackling dead vines that protected the tree's base from intruders.

Stepping up on one of their smaller branches, I could scramble up and look back at where we had come. Willow and Jean followed me. In the moonlight, I could make out the massive black wall to the East that stretched to the horizon, both North and South.

We could see the ocean of berry bramble stretching back to the black mass from that wall, just North and East of us. From here, we could see how extensive an ecosystem it was.

Through the middle of that thicket emerged the stream we had noted, and we could see it winding through the grass, past a few sentry trees on the way to our new host, and we could see it wander across our path a hundred yards or so toward the tower. But we would have to ford that stream to get to the metal structure we could see now, reflecting the moonlight.

The tower was much closer now, and we could make out the dark form of the cabin at its base. There was no light from either, but it was possible that we were not the first humans to visit this place. Perhaps, I thought, we would learn where they were and how to connect with them.

"Let's get to that cabin, team. I bet we can be there in an hour." I laughed at the thought of an hour, as that unit of time didn't make any sense here. Willow understood what I was laughing at and chuckled along. A moment later, Jean got the joke and joined in. "Perhaps we need a new clock, oui?" Willow replied, "Undoubtedly," as we hopped down from our perch and headed for the stream.

Almost immediately, we could hear the burble of the stream, and in short order, we were on its banks.

Suddenly, there seemed to be a spotlight on our scene, and looking back, we could see the second moon had risen and added another layer of light over the vista.

Finally, we had enough light to see the strange little footprints of the Humpbacks.

We now know they ventured out this far. We noticed a lot of shrubbery and small willow-type trees on the river banks and noted this would be handy for cover when needed. However, we agreed it was not nearly as safe as the briar warren. We waded into knee-deep water in a wide spot in the stream.

"Mac, dis rivière, she go de wrong way, non?"

We all directed our attention to the flow. To the West were mountains. We would assume this stream would come from them. Two things struck me. The size of the stream suggested no major tributaries, and since the flow was to the mountains, there had to be a deep pass or way around the craggy sierras to allow it to go to its final destination.

There could be a lake, but that didn't seem likely. With a dry view of the base of the mountains to the West suggested a pass. We had a lot to ponder.

The cool water felt refreshing, so Willow found a slightly deeper pool near a bend, sat deep in the water for a moment, and then ducked under to bathe. Her initiative looked like a great idea, and Jean and I were soon splashing and giggling like children with her as we enjoyed our first bath in this world.

Soon, we were refreshed and rejuvenated and were quickly on the last leg of our trek to the tower.

The building at the bottom of the immense frame stood as an iconic silhouette with a glinting glass window reflecting twin moons from a flat black rectangle.

As we approached, we could make out a very human-sized door. We noted unremarkable, unstained wood sheeted the structure. It appeared dry and weathered.

The building looked very much like a ghost town in North America. As we stepped up, we saw no security, fence, barriers, or locks on the single, unadorned door. But we did see a wooden latch and dark steel hinges you could find in a hardware store back home.

Our rag-tag team looked at each other, and wordlessly, Willow stepped ahead and opened the door. The interior was stark but presented a table, two chairs, two cots, and shelves on three walls. One wall sported the door and window. On closer inspection, some lower shelves contained cooking pots and eating utensils. There was also a pail for water, a small propane bottle, cable, a single burner stove, and a tea box. Another wall supplied clothes. There were Jeans, shirts, a stack of light blankets, and a few assorted pairs of sandals.

The moonlight through the open door displayed the table, where a wooden, rectangular box with a single metal button stood.

I carefully lifted the box to see if he could see a label with any letters or numbers to indicate what we found. I found the box light, so I took it to the door to get better light.

"Any idea what it is?" Willow looked around my left arm.

"Wood?" Jean asked.

"No idea. There is nothing to tell me what I'm looking at." I turned and gently replaced the box on the table. Then, I gingerly reached out and pressed the inconspicuous little button.

A slight fizz announced my departure, and suddenly, Jean and Willow were standing alone in panicked silence.

***

Willow told me later that instinct kicked in, and they both ran out the door but stopped to stare back at the lonely cabin in shock.

"Mon Dieu!"

"What Happened?" Willow's voice quivered as she called out, "MAC!!"

Jean shushed her. "Shh. Maybe many ears."

Willow turned to him with tears of fright, rimming her lower eyelids. "But... We have to find him."

Jean nodded and started back toward the cabin. On his second step, they heard the fizz sound again, and a moment later, I stepped out of the cabin door. Slightly amused, I waved them back to the cabin.

"I've been on an amazing trip. I think we have found how we got here. I was transported to a laboratory somewhere. All the makings of a regular human lab, with lights, wires, tubes, microscopes, you name it. It was nighttime, so luckily, there was no one around.

I don't think we would be welcomed there. I saw more of these boxes—about a dozen, and a bin full of crystals. They looked like diamonds. Computers lined up on a counter, and most were running programs. There was also an electronic map of the world with several landmarks. I brought three boxes and a jar of the crystals back."

I pointed to the table where the boxes lay.

"I figured you two would be panicked by now because I've been gone a couple of hours, but I wanted to understand as much as possible before I pushed the button on the box again. I had no idea if it would send me back, but I had nothing to lose... except my life."

"Mac, you have only been gone seconds." Willow looked back and forth between me and the equally amazed Frenchman.

"Oui, yes. You melt and gone. We run outside." Jean snapped his fingers, "Den you back."

The relevance struck me, and I was silent for a few moments. My partners were as well—each deep in our realizations.

"I have to go back."

"No! Don't leave again! That freaked me out." Willow's eyes were wide and pleading.

"I have to. These are the machines that brought us to this planet. As you know, you two arrived naked with nothing you were wearing or carrying.

It seems I was supposed to be delivered the same way. This time, I was able to bring cargo back. We can configure the machine to bring what we need.

There are manuals written on the process and settings for these boxes. If we set up a home here, we need to know how to use these things without unknowingly killing, maiming, or sending each other somewhere that would not be pleasant. Of course, you are welcome to come if you want. At least I now know how to get back here."

Willow looked deep into my eyes. "I will die before I push that button."

Jean just nodded.

"Okay, please try to make yourself comfortable here in the cabin. Perhaps we can use a bucket of that creek water. We may need to hang out here for a bit while we learn. I will be back as soon as I can." I reached for the button.

"Wait!"

I turned back toward Willow, and she reached around me and hugged me. "Please be careful, and please come back." She hid her face in my chest for a moment, then stepped back.

I turned in the dark room and pushed the small white button.

I came to, lying on the floor in the lab. A bit dazed, I pulled myself up, wiping something wet from my chest. At first, I feared I was bleeding, but on closer inspection of my fingers and chest, I realized that Willow had been crying. I was surprised at my reaction.

Her tears moved me far more than I would have expected. Willow had come to mean a great deal to me. I supposed mating was a rather bonding event.

Wow. I shook my head and reached for the folder of documents I had seen on my last trip. I opened the folder and found a specifications document, a thumb drive, and a user's manual.

Although I noted that the folder had a label on the outer tab that read, "Howard Thom," I noticed a printed scientific paper from the "Society for Scientific Exploration by Elisabeth Rauscher and Russell Targ" with a Post-it-note stuck to the front that said, "The Nonlocal Universe." I slipped it into the folder, hooked a couple of ball-point pens inside the cover, and tucked it under my arm.

I froze.

The sound of a door closing, something on rollers moving across a floor in an adjacent room, and a hint of lighting through the windows, high on the lab walls, told me it was time to go. I tightened the folder under my arm and pushed the button.

I woke to cold water flowing down my back.

Instinctively, I held the folder away from my body.

I turned to see Jean folded up on the floor by the propane tank with the water pail in his lap. It seems I tried to take his space in this new world when I arrived and displaced him to the floor rather abruptly. As soon as we knew no one was hurt, we all laughed till we teared up.

"I guess we must declare a landing zone in front of this box." With my finger, I drew an imaginary circle in front of the table and stumbled to my feet. "I need to study these papers in the light tomorrow.

That's probably enough for one night." I noted that the twin moons were close to the horizon, with the first almost there. It occurred to me that someone from the lab may show up, so I changed my mind and pulled the manual out to read by moonlight on the cabin stoop while Jean went for another bucket of water.

I found the coordinates instructions, removed the back of the teleporter box by removing four screws, found the location calibrators, Saved the original coordinates to the inner jacket of the folder. I went back and copied the launch designation to the destination designation. The next person to push the button in the lab will wake up on the lab floor. I used my own transporte to go back to the cabin

Before they can use this cabin landing again, they will need to land somewhere else and bring a new transfer box to the cabin. With that in mind, I made sure Willow and Jean used the cots, but I had too much on my mind to sleep for most of the night.

I finally settled down on a pair of blankets. It was still much too warm to sleep with cover, but the chance to sleep in a shelter was surprisingly calming and comfortable.

In the light of the next day, we sorted through the goods in the cabin and found the layer of dust. That meant it had been a long time since anyone had been here. These facts made me think the Giants had a handy receiver in their camp.

I made a mental note of that fact for the future.

I spent much of the cooler part of the day reading the documentation I had scooped from the lab and was pleased to see the format of locations on Earth and this planet.

I could see the technology used advanced artificial intelligence and planetary sensors to work out surface locations, designated "safe" landings, land mass, water, and other environmental considerations. I noted that the large tower outside was the original off-planet antenna for the lab on Earth, but the technology had advanced to much tighter signals that required less antenna.

The documentation also provided a longitude-latitude address index for Earth.

A similar document served 51 Pegasi d. So, I now knew where we were. Earth astronomers had not yet identified planets smaller than Pegasi b, a giant, hot, gas planet they could see. These scientists had used something far more productive than telescopes. The end-point configurations also allowed for date and time settings for Earth and 51 Pegasi d, so I could set trips to coordinate with local times. They could even calibrate street addresses on Earth.

Then I found out why we always seemed to travel commando.

Settings for accessories to the body accounted for a lot more detail in the configuration, bringing proximity and cellular make-up of the accessories. Clothing, paper, simple materials like wood, steel, or other popular materials, and even the transporter boxes had several presets. Still, weeks would need to go into the calibration for chemicals or composites.

I had an epiphany about my journey to 51 Pegasi b. *The bad guys that sent me here must have been experimenting with transporting proximate material when they plucked me from Earth.*

I decided I would like to meet that person or people one day.

I also found the crystals were diamonds. They were the kinetic fuel that powered this technology and came from this planet. I imagined the people who designed this enterprise on Earth were wealthy. There was a reference to an island not far from this tower. I decided I needed another trip to the lab. I needed some connections and address coordinates on Earth.

I explained my plans to my crew, but not as convincingly as I'd have liked. First, I tried on a pair of pants and a shirt from the cabin that was tight but made me acceptable to the casual observer on Earth. Next, I slipped on some sandals that stuck my big toes out some but would not cause too much issue in Arizona. Then I set coordinates on the box for the courtyard behind my office building in Tucson and tucked another box under my arm. Finally, I pushed the button on my reconfigured transporter.

A little dazed, I scrambled off the fake lawn to sit on the wooden bench beside the smoker's table. I heard a startled "Oh!" and looked up to see Lisa, my former office manager, coming from the back door of the building.

***

Chapter 5

Family Reunion

"What are you doing back here? Oh..., Mac?" Are you okay?"

"Lisa. So good to see you. 'Just passing through and need a couple of addresses. Do you think I could borrow a Google map and a cell phone? I'd like to see if I can connect with my brother. I'm afraid I haven't been near a phone for some time now."

"Mac, it must be nice to be phoneless. You're looking a little radiant. Have you been hanging out South of the border?"

"Yes," I replied, looking down at my clothes, "I haven't needed so many clothes where I've been hanging out."

"I see. Would you like me to scrape up a set of state-side threads for you now that you are back? I still have your measurements in my One Notes."

"Thank you, Lisa. No wonder you get the big bucks around here, but this is just a stopover. I'm heading back to paradise as soon as I finish my business here."

"Okay, let's get you some tools." Lisa led me to the elevator and the third floor, where she sat me down at her reporting laptop and logged me in and handed me her phone.

"What's in the boxes?"

"They're Teleporters."

Lisa laughed, took that hint, and went off to make a coffee. I'm pleased she didn't press the subject. I then dialed my brother's number. He picked it up before it rang the second time.

"Hello?"

"Tony, it's Mac."

"Holy shit!"

"Are you still in Ontario?"

"Not one to shoot the shit, are ya, straight to the point. I'm in Fort Sevren." Tony laughed. "Good thing y'called. Say Hi to Dad. I have ya on speaker."

"Wow, how did you manage to corner that old trade wind?"

We all laughed, "He was passing through on his way to Seattle."

"How in hell can you be passing through Fort Severn?"

Evan Macadams came on then, "I was taking my yearly mineral bath up in Reykjavik if ya need t'know.

"I ain't stayin' here, though, Tommy. Dad just won a fishin' boat in a poker game, and it's waiting in Seattle. He talked me into fishin' for a season to try it out. I've had enough of polar bears and ice-cube mountains for now. I love the view, but I'd rather visit than live here."

"Okay, hang on. Do you have an address in Fort Severn?"

"Actually, no, but if you can find the post office, I'm staying in a cabin next door to the post office to the South. But by the time you send anything here, we will be gone."

"Will you be there tonight?"

"Well... Ya..."

"Okay, you two, don't go anywhere tonight. I've got a story you are going to want to hear." I hung up.

When Lisa heard me hang up, she discreetly returned to the room. "Can I get you anything, Mac?"

I smiled widely, "Lisa, I've changed my mind. Can you wrangle up a winter coat, socks, a sweater, and a pair of boots that would do well in the snow... maybe a pair of gloves?"

Her jaw dropped. "Mac, are you losing your mind?"

I laughed. "No, just an unexpected trip."

"This is Tucson. When was the last time you saw snow boots here?"

She smiled. "Never mind. We have a shipment from Chile bound for New York this fall. I'll get you something. How soon do you need them?"

"How soon can I get them?"

"1 hour. Maybe forty-five minutes if they are where I think they are."

"Brilliant. Thank you. Do you have an empty room, a Philips screwdriver I can borrow to adjust my teleporter here, and perhaps a short nap?"

Lisa rolled her eyes, tapped the bottom drawer in the desk I was sitting at, and pointed to my old couch in the back of the room. I replied with a grin, a wink, and a "Thank you so much."

I opened the box and found it to be surprisingly simple. I also noted that all the edges fit together in rubberized slots to make the boxes water-resistant, if not waterproof. They designed them to work as well outdoors as inside.

When Lisa returned, I had my traveling box recalibrated and new coordinates in the spare box. She laid out a new set of jeans, a flannel shirt, a pair of long underwear, top and bottom, thick socks, a parka, aggressive-soled hiking boots, and winter gloves.

"Need some snowshoes?"

I laughed. "No, thank you. You are, indeed, more amazing than ever." I handed her a post-it note slip with the name and number of my accountant and said, "Please bill Andrew and show him my signature below. That will compensate you at retail for your products and time."

Lisa looked me in the eye and replied, "Mac, do you remember carrying the tuition for my sister to get through medical school?"

I nodded.

"She is a gynecologist now, with a nice place in Green Valley and a college fund for her son. So, the bill is well paid."

I hugged her tightly as my eyes welled up. "Thank you,

Lisa. You are a blessing in my life. I see it's dinner time, so you get home to the family. If you let me hang out here this evening, I'll clean up as I leave."

"When will I see you next?" She was a bit misty, too.

"I'm not sure, Lisa.

My adventure has me bouncing around like my brother and dad, but I owe you a nice dinner and chat when I can catch my breath."

"Pinky-swear?"

"Pinky-swear."

Lisa grabbed her laptop case and headed out. I gathered my wardrobe, looked around to ensure I had cleaned up as promised, turned to the desk, and pushed the button on the box.

***

Damn, it was cold.

I sat up in a snowbank, pulled my parka around me, and stood up to get my bearings. Heavy snow was falling through porch light pyramids on the red-brown walls of the post office, and I was looking at the general store. Then, as I spun around, I noted a weathered cabin with a shiny white door and a huge satellite dish. I stepped up and knocked on the door.

"Holy shit!" My brother answered the door. He just stood there amazed.

A fantastic smell wafted from the cabin, and it made me hungry. "Aren't you going to welcome me in?"

He turned sideways and pointed into the kitchen. To my right was a white-haired old Scot with his mouth dropped open.

"So happy to see you guys too." I laughed as Tony closed the door, and I stepped over to hug my crazy old Dad with one arm while balancing my transporters in the other.

"Can I set these down somewhere?"

Tony started to come to. "Ya, here." He pointed at the table and moved a couple of old coffee cups out of the way. I sat at the table as I deposited the transporters, then waved to my father and brother to join me.

"Did I miss dinner?"

"Caribou stew is ready if you are."

I moved the transporters to the coffee table, along with my parka and gloves, while Tony placed the simmering pot on an old glove in the center of the table along with a ladle, three bowls, spoons and forks, and a steaming teapot. He added a coffee cup for me as it seemed he had no teacups. A father and two sons sat down for the first shared meal in over twenty years. Three men chatted happily as we connected lives in the Northernmost settlement in Ontario.

"Okay, you guys, how did it pass that two of the most randomly orbiting adventurers met in Fort Severn? I know about the trip to Iceland and the boat in Seattle, but Tony, last I heard, you were logging, and there are no trees here."

He laughed. "Logging has slowed way down, and I heard about a government project to get isolated villages connected to the internet with satellites.

They needed crews to install big dishes in places like this. So, I called Dad to see if he wanted to make some money. He didn't but did want to see this place, so here we are."

Evan chuckled. "I also needed to recruit a crew for my boat."

Between bites of amazing stew, Tony pointed at me. "Your turn, Tommy."

I was silent momentarily while chewing a generous chunk of potato. "Dad, you may want to sell your boat. You might say I've been on a foreign adventure; you need an open mind to hear my story, and I need you guys to help me on a life-and-death mission."

It seems I had their attention. In true Scottish tradition, I had two sets of bushy eyebrows zoned in on me. Each set had one eyebrow stretched perilously high. The wild white set of eyebrows relaxed, and Dad said, "Do tell."

I told my family what had happened to me. I led them along the path my life had taken since losing Margo. When I concluded with the crew in the cabin and the transporter boxes, all eyes went to the boxes on the coffee table.

"I have a transporter lesson for you both when we are done here. If you agree, one of these boxes will stay with you." We brought the conversation back to each other, but it disintegrated into small talk as the interest was on the coffee table.

Finally, we finished our meal, cleaned the kitchen, washed dishes, poured the last of the tea, and retired to the living room for the teleporter training.

With the help of Tony's screwdriver, I pulled the back off the teleporters, pulled instructions from mine, and had Tony copy instructions into a notebook he had. Two hours had passed by the time we finished, and Tony and Dad were confident they understood.

They both concluded that the fishing season was off, and they needed to explore this new planet, 51 Pegasi d. We decided it was time for rest as tomorrow would be very busy.

Tony had two small bedrooms in the rented cabin, but the couch was more comfortable than I was used to.

The oil furnace ensured the house was comfortable. We all slept till daylight.

Morning brought planning. Dad and Tony would tie up business in Fort Severn, then off to Seattle to deal with the boat. They would set up a transport between Seattle and this new planet in an out-of-the-way place where Giants and huge purple eagles were absent. Tony said he wanted somewhere with fresh air. So, they would connect with me in Seattle soon to coordinate and catch up.

We all knew this was dangerous, and we would likely lose someone at some point, but we all agreed how important this work was. Many lives were at stake, perhaps an opportunity for humanity to spread out and save two planets. Dad supplied the address and key code for an old packing house he had bought in Seattle. This location would be our connection base. There would always be a pair of unlocked cell phones plugged in and charged in an office in the building.

Each with the contact info of the rest and any others the family would have if we were on Earth together.

51 Pegasi - Black Mac

We hugged each other and wished each other safe journeys until we could meet again, then I tucked my transporter under my arm and pressed the button.

***

Chapter 6

Shiv

"Where the hell have you been?"

I sat up in the middle of the brightly lit cabin with Willow pointing at me from one of the cots and Jean grinning from a chair at the table.

"How long have I been gone?"

"Just kidding, it must have been five minutes."

I laughed at the absurdity of experiencing that much adventure in five minutes. Willow and Jean were laughing at the absurdity of my attire. As I caught on, I explained that I had just come from Northern Canada. I quickly discarded my layers of clothing to allow air to get to my overheating body.

"Team, even as this cabin is beginning to feel like home, we must move on. Bad humans will soon be here to repair and maintain this technology, and they and the Giants will notice that we have disrupted their supply chain. So, this place is about to get busy."

"What's the matter with their technology?" Jean was puzzled as he had just seen me use it.

"We're taking it."

They both got it now, and Willow asked, "Where do we go?"

I saw worry spread across Jean's face, and Willow also showed concern. She went to the door, opened it, and peered out. A rush of hot air came past her into the cabin. "Since we have been here, there has been a ringing or a hum that started very soft but is getting louder. I'm not sure I could live with that much longer."

"I noticed it too, and you're right; we need to get away from it."

I saw no disagreement from Jean as he shook his head and covered his ears.

"We need to hide what we can't carry and blend in. I feel those purple sky chickens have the eyesight of an eagle, and the hairy Giants can see very well. I feel the transporter boxes may be safest under the cover of the briar patch. We must try to cover them from the elements, from prying eyes, and where we have some relative safety to retrieve them."

"Back to the Briars?" Willow's question confirmed she knew what I meant. Jean nodded.

"We succeeded in the cover of darkness. I think that is our safest bet going back."

They both agreed, so we spent the rest of the day packing blanket packs, and by dusk, we were ready. Our day had been quiet, and we had been scanning for squadrons in the air. We listened for screams, but all seemed quiet. We were across the creek when it was dark and headed for the tree.

We took the time at the tree to allow the moons to rise, and then we had the light to get us back to the brambles.

The rest of the trip was eventless, but we were happy to see the blue mood light and safety as we entered the spiny thicket.

The next couple of days saw us explore the Northwest section of the briar patch for suitable trails, and we found the spot where the stream left the brambles and wandered temptingly to the West. We found several dead ends in the berry patch trails between the exit that the screaming raptors had smashed and the exit where the creek had begun its journey West. I felt this was natural as the brambles grew around old tracks.

Once we became more intimate with this part of the warren, we found one well-hidden but easy enough to see when we returned. We used the spears of dried thorns to build a floor a couple of feet above the ground by weaving in low-level vines.

We then stacked transporter boxes, clothing, bedding, and valuable paper in a protective pack and covered them with the coveted chamois we had collected from the cage. The wonderful raptor skin was the hardest thing to leave behind but probably the most important for the cache.

"Well, my friends. We can't stay here much longer. So, I feel it is past time for us to move."

Jean and Willow looked me in the eyes.

"There may well be humans following us through the brambles once they know we have destroyed their teleporter and they have no more delivery service for the Giants. So, first, we must clear evidence of our trail into the cache.

Then we need to retrace our tracks back to the creek, then head West in the stream so the only tracks they see are to and from the cabin.

"The next evening, we were again on our way to the tiny river of freedom. This path appeared to be working well. We had heard the purple screamers occasionally and were constantly scanning the skies.

We harvested a Humpback and carried a small corner of our skin tarp to use as a bag for dried meat and berries. Finally, we climbed out of the water at night to dry out, eat, and sleep.

The mountains were getting closer now, but on the last day, we tucked motionless under a silvery, willow-type bush overhanging the stream from the Southern bank. Screamers had been hunting above us. We had witnessed the end of a few Humpbacks that had strayed too far into the grasses.

The last one was too close. Suddenly, a cacophony broke loose as a monster bird tumbled from the skies, a gigantic arrow restricting its wings. A massive shadow flashed over us as we tried to disappear. A dark-colored giant had jumped the stream to collect the bird while a brown, golden-tipped mate jumped, looked back, and roared.

Moments later, the three of us were three stories in the air, held roughly in the palm of this giant's hand. I recognized one of our former captors. Although I suppose, former is now the wrong word. The giant displayed us to the other beast with great joy. We meant a lot to these two Giants. In short, they returned us to a new cage, not the broken one, and an adjacent camp.

***

We did not recognize the surrounding trees, and there seemed to be more of them. This undergrowth was thicker. They didn't feed us, but we watched as the massive bird was skillfully stripped and processed below us.

The Giants left us to our own devices through the night. We didn't have much to say to each other. Fear was our strongest emotion, but we huddled together and sat contemplating our lives in the corner of the cage till dawn.

It seemed we had lived a lot of life in the last few days for it to end.

Morning came too soon, and the gold-tipped giant lifted our cage to the ground and bound us with a braided rope too small to have been crafted with those big hands. The giant wasn't gentle but didn't harm us either. We were then attached to a larger rope slung over a shoulder like a royal sash. There was also a massive wooden stake slung across its back.

The massive ape loped off to the edge of the grasslands, where its black partner met it and handed it one of the two bows it was carrying and a quiver of 12-foot arrows. The pair seemed excited and happily communicated with grunts and gestures as they loped through the grass.

From our bouncing vantage point, I could see the grasslands were like running across a lawn for them. They seemed young, fit, and up for adventure. This excitement was concerning, but so far, it wasn't the imminent end of the human cargo.

The giant's pace slowed, and I could see we had long passed the end of the berry thicket and were now moving beyond where they had captured us at the river.

I could also hear distant screams and noted that Willow and Jean watched the skies as I was.

The stream passed through a small set of hills at this point, so it narrowed and widened as it was squeezed and then opened up, and I noted that the stream nourished a wider swath of bushes, shrubs, and small trees. The small hillsides were lush and offered more cover. I wasn't sure what good that did for the giant apes, but it raised my hopes. Then, our captors stopped and pulled us dangling from the rope while the other giant pounded the stake into the ground. They then tied us to it.

We were bait.

The apes retreated to the hillsides, among the shrubs, and sat down. The flock above had seen all this, and their excited screams were trumpeting doom. They began circling high overhead like vultures. Then, one would dive at us and break off about 200 feet above to launch back to the flock.

They got braver and closer until one of the Giants let loose.

An impaled, screaming raptor tumbled to the ground with an arrow draining its life. Another raging purple screamer dove and grabbed at us with slicing talons. One flashing claw hooked on the rope to our anchor and almost pulled us loose. A massive arrow missed this bird and sailed off over the prairie.

The gladiator battle raged on for what seemed like an eternity but measured in minutes, and more close calls had us fighting to break the bonds. Finally, I had one arm free, and Jean did too, but we had no time to work the knots. Through the panic, we noticed the walking raptor working its way through the shrubbery from the South.

The Giants were focused on aeronautics and were not noticing this one. We screamed and pointed, but they were oblivious.

The light of day was fading, so we weren't quite as visible. They thought, rightly so, that we were panicked. We had hardly noticed a giant berry leaf floating in the water, directly in the path of the raptor as it stepped into the water. Its eyes focused on us; its massive curved beak was open, and suddenly its eyes closed. The Screamer sank quietly into the water as we saw another raptor pinned with an arrow above us, as it screamed and tried to fly away.

Suddenly, a bald, scowling human appeared in the quickening dusk, slicing through our binding with a thorn bud used as a knife. He nodded to the stream and dove under the bird's plumage floating downstream. We joined him under the luminescent purple feathers as the melee continued overhead.

We moved faster once we floated past the small hills and picked up another small tributary to the stream. Finally, I felt it was time to thank our savior. "Sir, I hope you speak English because we want to ensure you understand how grateful we are."

"Glad to be at your fuckin' service. Mac, Sharon, and Jean, the Stud, right?"

"Uh... yes". Willow replied softly first.

"Oh, pardon my fuckin' French, oops, I'm not winning here. Sorry, where I come from, people talk a little closer to the Earth. I'll try to remember a lady's presence and a Frenchman."

Jean chuckled softly. "No problem. Saving our lives does not require, how you say... good grammar."

This new arrival left us with more questions than answers, but the situation was liquid, and we all felt it wise to stay quiet for now. Formal introductions could come later when we were not in so much danger.

***

Chapter 7

The Canyon Pass Tribe and Friendly Giants

Daylight found us four still hanging to the bottom of the floating bird, but we knew we had to break from our cover. The bird had lost most of its buoyancy and was beginning to sink in the rushing water.

Since our escape, we water-wrinkled swimmers had passed several tributaries, and the stream we started in was now a roiling river.

I pointed at a beach downstream and made it clear I was heading for shore. With a nod from the others, I swam from the bird with a determined stroke, and Willow followed. With some hesitation, the Frenchman joined, and Shiv brought up the rear. He was the strongest swimmer. I could tell almost instantly there was little doubt two of them would need Shiv and me to get to shore.

We had all been under full steam for some time now, with no opportunity to rest. I was strong enough, which gave the others incentive, but I often turned to see how it was going. Shiv could tell I needed his help with the others. Willow began to struggle, so I got her to hook her arms around my neck and swam harder to let her rest. Thirty yards more, and we would be on land.

I looked back again in time to see Jean go under the current. With the same glance, I saw Shiv take a quick sweep, grab Jean's hair, and pull him up. This admission to needing help pissed Jean off enough to find new strength to scream. he found power to dig harder, but I put a finger to my lips, pointed at the brightening sky, and swam on.

Jean understood and followed with inspired effort.

Our wrinkled crew finally made shore, and we sagged onto the pebbles, but Shiv and I had to sit with our heads between our hands for a good minute, convincing our frayed muscles to stop quivering in exhaustion. Willow and Jean stretched out flat, and we all worked to get our breathing back to normal.

A few minutes later, when we started stirring, I suggested some grasslands off the beach where we could stay out of sight and gain strength. I didn't need to convince anyone.

"Let's take a few minutes to get to know our hero, crew. I'm Mac", I said to the powerful, built man looking us over. "Black Mac, to most.

I said, "This is Jean, or Etalon as the Giants called him," pointing at the pale man struggling to sit, "Etalon is French for Stud. They considered him a stud for breeding when they decided we might make good pets." Shiv grinned wide, and Jean glowed red. "And this is Princess Willow, or Willow... or Sharon from the old world."

Still grinning widely, Shiv nodded, "I'm Shiv. My birth certificate says Dmitri Shankov, but I have been Shiv since I was 14." Four naked people sat in a circle, looking at each other and sorting out their feelings. Shiv grinned wider, "This is fuckin' strange, sitting around talking with naked people."

We looked around, and I laughed, and then we all burst into belly laughs as we flushed the adrenalin we needed for the last effort. "You'll get used to it. We have all been plucked from our lives on Earth by these fuzzy Giants. We believe we know how they did it, and I'm pretty sure its beginning had something to do with that tower back there. "

"We all woke up in jungle cages without explanation or reason. The only thing I can think of is they harvested us for food."

Shiv shrugged. "Man, that's some crazy shit. I don't have any better explanation, though. I was in a maximum-security prison shower. Suddenly, I'm in some fuckin' jungle cage with a forty-foot Sasquatch checkin' me out." He looked around the group. "I got to know you from the story on the cage wall! You're Tom Mac... something. You're Sharon", he said, pointing at Willow, "and you... You're the Frenchman, Jean. And now I get the Etalon bit!"

Willow shrank back, and the Frenchman was now watching Shiv much closer.

Seeing the unease, I continued to explain, "We're all in a state of shock. We all came from times when we didn't feel wanted, needed, or belong. There is a trend here that may need some more study. Perhaps we're all troublemakers. Perhaps someone needed us out of the way."

My theory broke the tension in the discussion, and Shiv just shook his head and grinned.

I continued. "One thing I do know is we are no longer on the Earth we knew as home."

"How the hell do you know we are not on Earth?" Shiv was shocked as he thought of this possibility for the first time.

I raised an eyebrow. "Have you noticed how high you can jump or how much energy you have here? Have you noticed how fast a day goes by?

When did you hear about a forty-foot Sasquatch or a twelve-foot-high purple eagle with a twenty-foot wingspan?"

Shiv was silent for a moment, "Good points. I did some surprising calisthenics when I escaped past the giant ape. I still don't know how the hell I moved like that, and I had to learn some crazy moves in the pen."

"Willow, Etalon, and I have been pets for almost a month. The 'Sasquatch,' as you call them, are highly intelligent. They have a written language, but there is no way in hell we can reproduce their spoken language. I learned to write their language, so a juvenile who figured we were cute saved us three from the cooking pot. He sold Etalon but saved him from the cooking pot again and brought him back to live with Willow and me."

"If they're so fuckin smart, why are they eating people?"

"Because they are big and hungry. Haven't you eaten chickens and pigs?

"Of course, but they ain't smart."

"Okay, then you are qualified to judge what is fit to eat by how smart it is, right?"

"Ya, I guess so."

"So are the giant cavemen."

Shiv was silent momentarily as he restacked his way of thinking about his diet. He decided to change the subject.

"I get your drift. How did you escape?"

"The Giants didn't know how smart we were or how capable we could be. They put us in a cage with a broken bar and left us alone all night. We headed for the massive thorn bushes where they couldn't follow. We had been free several days before they found us trying to leave the berry thicket.

They stumbled on us while they were hunting those purple screamers. They had no love for us by then but decided to use us as bait, and you turned up like Superman just as our history was about to end."

Shiv smiled at that. I think he liked the role. "If they kept you as pets, what was the hurry to get out?"

"Shiv, we saw several people go by in cages near us. From the market signage, I found we were indeed food first. Imagine rabbit hutches back home, where some were pets, but some were food and hides. So not only do we need to get away, but we also need to break this source from our world and close the supply chain for good."

Shiv dropped his head, "Ya think?"

Willow used the silence following his statement to join in,

"I'm pleased to meet you, Shiv. We are trying to get far enough away from these beasts to set up camp, then come back and save people. We think we have figured out how they do it, and Mac has learned a lot about their technology.

But of course, we need to find out where all this is happening and stop it, too. We think many more of us have escaped, and we hope to find the brains and muscle to make this our safe and comfortable home. The three of us have no need to go back and live on Earth."

"Glad to meet you, Willow. I ain't got no need to go back either. I had two weeks left to serve but was headed back to the street where I had no future. I have nothing or no one to go back to, and I would be easily signed up for another five years for breaking out.

Even if they didn't penalize me for this break, I would have no way to turn my life around on Earth. I'd be back in the can within a couple of weeks, just trying to feed myself. I like your mission here if you can use a hand."

"Oui, Shiv, I yam please to meet you also. Merci... Thanks to you for saving me in de riviere. I yam mose grateful."

Shiv nodded at his new pal, Stud, and said, "I'll beat the give-up out of you any day, brother. But, Mac, what's the plan? You seem to be the boss here."

I smiled. This guy was going to be helpful. "Still too early to have a plan baked, but Willow said it best. We need to get safe, make a home, then start planning 'gorilla' warfare, if you'll excuse the pun."

Shiv liked this. He gave a thumbs-up and started looking around. "Well, I guess we better get movin'. We gotta find someplace safe from those apes or those goddamn purple screamers. Gawd, those things are huge."

***

I nodded and stood. After a quick survey of the surroundings, we headed downstream toward the mountain's base, challenging our path. We would be at its base by nightfall if we could stay out of sight.

I led the way, and Shiv was happy with that. Willow followed, and the bald warrior slipped into line before Jean, the Stud. He was soon lost in the sway of her hips as she made her way through the tall grass before him.

Stud tried to start a conversation but was waved down by Shiv, again pointing at the sky. He didn't want any noise to tip the Giants or the purple screamers of our position. Etalon gave up the conversation, stopped to relieve himself, then quickly caught up.

We were close to the mountains now; we traveled through some trees, and the nearest mountain blocked the West-leaning sun. The screaming started again. We dove for cover under the root ball of a fallen tree.

Shiv groaned as he clapped a hand over a bleeding knee as he took a hit from his dive onto a jagged rock. While lifting his hand to assess the damage, we watched as a two-inch gash dripped blood in stringy drops from the side of his leg.

The screamers were on us. Diving raptors ripped the bark off the log above us and screamed madly at the massive root ball they couldn't shake.

We tucked in behind the massive roots where they could not quite reach. The Screamers dove in a system of well-timed dive bombings with bowling-ball-sized rocks aimed to flush their prey.

The purple raptors pounded the log in endless waves. Then, without warning, the permanent sneer of a monstrous green beak lay at our feet. Behind it, a glassy eye turned dull.

An arrow the circumference of Shiv's forearm quivered from the iridescent feathers.

A massive force lifted the root ball effortlessly and flung it to the side. Two King Kong hands swept down and corralled us before we could bolt, then lifted two captives in the air in each hand. It held us with enough pressure to ensure our capture, leaving us enough room to breathe.

Above us, several raptors screamed high in the thermal winds against the cliffs of the mountain range. As hapless captives, we were packed for several strides and dumped unceremoniously back on the river's shore. In front of us stood a striking blonde Amazon of a woman, fresh-faced and radiant. She took in our undignified plight with her arms folded and a slight smile trying to spread across her face. She wore a waist-down, shiny purple kilt but nothing on top.

"Greetings, Earthlings," she chuckled, "I'm Tiffany, and this is my giant."

She waved a stately hand at the forty-foot Sasquatch standing with a crooked grin behind us.

Jean was the only one who could speak. "Mon Dieu!" Instinctively, he covered his bare genitals with his hands. Although the rest had become accustomed to each other's nudity, we subconsciously followed suit.

One eyebrow went up on Tiffany the Amazon, and she asked, "Do any of you speak English?"

I stood. "Yes, we all do... Did I hear you claim ownership of this tower of fur?"

She broke out in a belly laugh now.

"No one owns a giant. For that matter, no one owns anything in this world. He is mine in the sense that he is my friend. She turned to the giant and made several hand gestures. Shiv seemed to recognize the American Sign Language. He later told us he had used most of his young life when he still had a deaf sister. The creature gestured back, and I was fascinated.

Shiv broke the silence. "She just introduced us as friends, and he answered that we were sure pink. Except for one", he grinned. "Mac, he called you charred." Comparing us to cooking food, under the circumstances, didn't raise much humor.

Tiffany eased the strain on everyone's mind. "Don't worry, Chuckles prefers purple chicken." She pointed at the dead bird and signed again. Chuckles retrieved the bird and his bow and quiver.

"We just escaped a human farm East of here and are trying to get as far away as we can to save the meat on our bones," I interjected, "These beasts eat human flesh."

This time, both her eyebrows rose. "You people were the guests of the tribe that hosted the humans who invented the transporter you rode in on."

"Chuckle's tribe prefers bigger game where they don't have to put out so much energy for one meal. He and his tribe live in the pass ahead, where Purple Screamers are thick.

I escaped along your path a couple of months ago, and my giant scooped me from my captors. So, you see, Chuckle's Band and the Tower tribe do not necessarily see eye to eye."

"I stay as close to the tower as safety allows because we want to break that tower so they can't fish the human gene pool anymore. Dan, Kia, and I are trying to figure it out."

My eyebrows rose now, "Dan? Kia? Did anyone else escape?"

"Not many have come through, but I know many have broken out of the cages. We assume some lived in the thorn bushes or escaped in other directions. I hope to find some of them at some point and help organize resistance,"

Her arm pointed East, "Three women, Dan, and another man live with me in the Pass Camp. I know of a couple of men that have moved on to the Coast, but I have seen a few other tracks in the river sand, so I expect, or at least hope, a few more that made it to the shores. According to Chuckles, no Giants live at the Coast."

Shiv piped up now, "Coast? Bitter waters? So, there is a coast out there? Is it treed? Is it tropical?"

"Whoa! Hang on; lots of time to answer questions. Do you mind getting out of this noisy heat and having tea with me?"

I looked up at the squealing birds. "That sounds pretty good to me, and I have news for you. I believe I have broken the tower transporter, but I feel there are more around this planet. We'll catch you up over tea."

51 Pegasi - Black Mac

Willow followed my gaze. "I second that motion."

***

Chapter 8

Introductions - Education - and Boot-camp with an Amazon

Tiffany gestured to the giant. It reverently lifted her to a basket harness on its quiver strap, and she rode like a queen on his chest. The giant scooped us again. Then, with the bow and quiver on his back and the bird hung from a hook on the quiver, its load was secure.

Shiv couldn't take his mind off Willow's breasts while squeezed tightly against her. I could tell she was amused but apprehensive of its effect on him. The hardened penitentiary inmate was blushing.

They rode in the hands of the giant, like a furry circus ride for miles. Cliffs stood high on either side, and we spent a few miles watching Chuckles wade in waist-deep river water with no flat land between the cliffs. The Purple Screamer floated behind him.

Shiv said, "I wonder if it's too late to learn how to pray."

It only took the Sasquatch twenty minutes to reach a fire in a clearing well into the pass, where he dropped us gently. Nightfall was coming, and the fire felt good. Chuckles took his leave to go wherever Giants go in the dark.

Tiffany pointed out a few thatched roofed huts tucked back into the trees at the edge of the clearing.

"We built shelters inside the forest to keep them out of sight of the Screamers. This also keeps them from under the feet of the Giants. This camp is theoretically on the West edge of the Screamer's territory. We have seen single screamers out here, so we assume they serve as scouts, and there is a nest on the cliff on the far side of the river, upstream some. So, we have no doubt if they figure out our huts, we will be in trouble."

We noticed a few people moving between huts. They waved but did not approach or call out. We waved back, and I felt there would be a time for introductions when Tiffany was satisfied that we were worth knowing.

"Where do the Giants sleep?" Willow asked.

"They can't be bothered with shelter except in the monsoons. They build rudimentary wood and thatch shelters for that but pull them down and burn them once dry. Their fur is an amazing insulator, very similar to our polar bears. It works as well in the heat as in the cold."

"Would any of you like robes or kilts? They can hold off the evening chill."

We were not accustomed to the evening chill, and everyone nodded, so she beckoned us to follow her to one of the huts. On a stick shelf were several kilts of sectioned Purple Screamer feathers, shining translucently in the dusk. Under them were shelves of full-sized tunic-style robes with hoods made of a soft chamois. Us men opted for the feathers, and Willow asked for a robe.

"OK, about my questions...." Shiv piped up while tying on his kilt.

Tiffany cut him off,

"Let me get you all up to speed. Then, if you need to ask questions, feel free."

"As you know, we all found ourselves plucked from our daily lives and woke up in cages in a rainforest. As you are either aware or suspect, we are not on Earth. I'm unsure where this is, but we are lighter here, and the days go faster than we remember. I would think that would make this rock a bit smaller than Earth. So far, so good?"

She scanned for nods, then continued.

"The Giants are brilliant. Don't let their appearance fool you. They are advanced and have an intricate tribal community. They have science that is at least as advanced as Earth and, in many ways, superior. You don't see it because they never thought building an automobile important."

"They don't waste schooling on children; they officially learn all their lives. They have specialists and generalists, and when they disagree, they agree to disagree and separate into tribes that do settle.

They have no boundaries and trade comfortably with each other. They don't get sick. According to Chuckles, they found natural cures for all ailments but old age.

They naturally live around fifteen hundred moons, which would be around one hundred and twenty-five years, and die when they feel it is time." she continued.

"As far as the Tower Giants are concerned, they farm a lesser species for food. The pass Giants have decided that we are intelligent, are more trouble than we are worth for food, and cute and entertaining, so they keep us safe."

She paused. "Any questions? ...Good."

"This has been going on for a few years in Earth time.

It started in North America, but they began to harvest Europe, Africa, and North Asia in the last few years. They keep expanding with disguised towers on Earth. The Pass Giants have given me a lot of inside information. The Tower Giants have help on Earth.

An organization feels they are cleansing Earth of undesirables, but their definition of undesirable is very subjective, and they have now been grabbing people they feel are competitors. Or simply people they disagree with."

Tiffany noticed the rapt attention she was getting. She could tell this was the first time we all got the complete picture. The beautiful warrior could also see we understood the gravity of the situation and had decided as a team the planet was beautiful. Still, we had to stop the delivery of humans to the Giants. She was pleased to see we had committed to ending this horror as she had.

"I am going to stay here and find some way to kill that tower, but I know it's not a simple job. If they built one, they can and probably have built more."

I had heard enough to begin filling in the gaps.

"Tiffany, I'd like to interject. First, I believe I had cut off the Tower Tribe's supply chain.

I have disabled their teleporter, captured a few more, and hidden them where they can't reach them. However, there are several more transporters on this planet and Earth, and we have work to do."

I had her attention. "The transporters I have hidden can't stay where they are for long, however. So, we need to bring them here and out to the coast where we can set them up for our purposes to use for positive use. We must fully understand the technology and close shop for the bad guys on Earth."

"Amazing." She pointed back to the village. "Please save the details for Dan and Kia. When they get here, we need to bring them up to speed. They both have the education and training to dig into this with you and take us forward. They should be here soon."

Tiffany nodded back to the huts, "We come from all walks of life. I agree that we need to bring together a human band with the knowledge and insight to work together and break this system. We had thought there would be no way back home if we broke it. Are you saying that may not be the case?"

I nodded.

"So far, none of us seem to have much to go back for. We think we can make a better life here, but we may have a most important use for teleportation."

"Until we master this incredible opportunity, what can we do in the meantime?" asked Willow, "How can this little band of humans make a difference?"

Tiffany smiled. "You can collect people.

I would advise you to continue downstream, about a hundred miles, to the bitter water. That's what the Giants call the ocean."

"There is a frothing ledge, where heated mineral water boils up in a shoal and mixes with the sea. The Giants have no use for the area. The Purple Screamers prefer the mountains and plains, and there don't seem to be any natural enemies for humans, at least, that we have identified yet. We had hoped to hear back from the guys that went on but haven't heard anything, so I'm sure there are dangers we don't know.

However, we explored the coast once, so we know there are swarms of Humpbacks and blue mushrooms at the coast.

There are berries in this pass, so I believe you will find ample food and shelter, and I will continue to send escapees your way."

Shiv wasn't sure he wanted to distance himself from the tall blonde. Not being much for diplomacy, he injected. "You look like you could use a good strong man with stainless steel balls around here, girl. How about I stay and keep you warm at night?"

Tiffany laughed, "If you didn't have balls, we could talk. But, I would rather Willow stay to keep me warm." She winked at Willow, who grinned and winked back.

Shiv was silent for half a beat, then murmured. "...Got any straight sisters?"

Still grinning widely at the quieter Shiv, she shook her head.

I nodded and looked at the rest of the crew. "You in?"

Each nodded in turn. It was easy to see they all felt better about living some distance from the Giants and the raptors.

Tiffany pointed West, "In the morning, I'll show you a trail that leads to the bitter water. You will have to cross the river several times and work your way over a couple of falls, but you can get to the ocean. So come meet my clan."

***

Tiffany introduced Dan, a cell phone engineer from Atlanta. Then, Randy, a Sous Chef from a five-star restaurant in New York. Ann, a seamstress from Detroit, was next, responsible for their robes and kilts. She introduced Penny, a secretary from L.A., Kia, a radio wave engineer from Dallas, and Stacey, a farmer from Idaho.

We noticed that the village all seemed to wear kilts in the daytime and tunic-styled robes in the cooler evenings.

I asked about that.

"Yes, after the initial shock of living naked, we found sandals most helpful most of the time, but kilts in the day and robes at night became the norm. Modesty had nothing to do with our decisions, just our environment." Tiffany waved her hand around the camp to indicate her comfortable tribe. After hearing the plan, Randy and Stacey asked to join the expedition West.

Shiv supposed a cook and farmer would be good additions, and everyone agreed. Ann and Penny had bonded, and Dan and Kia wanted to investigate the tower and follow up on the transporter detail. I updated them with our adventure at the tower cabin.

I agreed a couple more people in the trek would give us a better chance of building a home at the coast. Willow was happy to see another lady on the march. She felt somewhat outnumbered. Stud and Shiv were pleased with another woman and a cook added to the crew. Both of them were sad to see Willow leaning toward me.

We had a seedling of a plan that would launch with me returning to make a trip back to the berry briar to capture the hidden transporters and loot. Perhaps we would gather more escapees to join us on the coast. We needed more detail on the movements of Screamers and Giants.

Tiffany suggested she could get more detail on the habits and activities of those challenges from passive questioning of Chuckles and his tribe, but she knew better than to pitch one tribe against another. We would need to plan to be on our own for that adventure.

The following day found the troop ready for the trail. Tiffany, Dan, and Ann showed up bearing gifts. They also gave the men robes to supplement the kilts in the evenings.

Willow asked if they had a spare kilt. Ann grinned, peeled off a kilt to reveal another below, and handed it to Willow.

"I thought you might."

"Wear these toga-robes when it's cool or you are in the open. The tan color matches the dirt of the trail, so you are not quite as visible to the Screamers, but in the hot sun, you can roll them down around your belt like this."

She donned one of the robes around her torso, then rolled it down and secured it with a vine rope.

"I have seen very few insects, and the ones I have seen are the size of small birds; the weather on the coast is pretty much like Hawaii back home. Of course, it's more normal than not to be overcast on the warm mornings near the sea, but unless you are fresh out of a nunnery, half-naked is often the best way to be most of the time. Think of how Hawaiians dressed before the white man."

The group dressed. Tiffany pointed to a simple bow and quiver set for each and a paperboy-type sack made of the chamois. "Weapons and food. Take a close look at what you have; you will want to look for the same thing until you learn the larder of the coast better." She opened a pack and pulled out a dried mushroom. It was faded blue. "These are regenerative; I recommend you build your diet around them. You find them at night; they radiate a blue glow when fresh."

"Hey, are those what made it glow blue under the berry bushes?" Shiv remembered his night in the thorns.

"The same. If there is a blue glow, you can bet you are sitting on a supply of these. Take note that these may be key to our health on this planet.

We have found they help with healing and overall health when used as a staple in our diet. For example, we believe they cured Ann, who had stage four lung cancer when she arrived."

She let that sink in, then added. "We have had minimal issues with our bodies reacting to the local food. That fact flies in the face of science, but we feel the plant and animal DNA is very close to Earth, and we feel these mushrooms may be the catalyst that allows our body to adapt so well."

With no response from us, she continued.

"It's too bad, but you lose the colossal berry bushes as you drop down to the coast. There may be a few bushes between the upper and lower falls, but I have seen empty bushes there, so either they don't grow well, or something depends on them for its diet.

It is worth the trek back up to visit us because it doesn't take too many of those berries to make a load for your store. Cut in strips and dried, they make great trail food. You will see several dark purple ribbons in your bags that are dried berries. Dry the strips near your evening fires."

She dug in the bag again. "This is dried Humpback meat. They are thick in the marshlands near the coast. Excellent eating." Tiffany was waving a red-brown-tinged jerky. She pulled out what may have been a deflated yellow balloon. "This is a Humpback stomach. It is the best water bag and doubles as a cooking pot.

You witnessed it being used over the fire last night. The stomach is porous enough that water seeps through while boiling and keeps the lining from burning. Of course, you destroy it and your meal if you run out of water."

"You have lots of river water for your trek, but it will become necessary as you travel. You will also find knives we stole from the tower cabin and flint stones in each bag.

Don't lose them, they're damn hard to come by, and the only good flint stone I know of is here in this valley. One of Chuckles and his family's best trade goods. He showed me the cliffside to the East, a mile or two, where we can get our own."

"We found some amazing knives in the form of thorn buds in the berry briars," Willow added.

Shiv nodded enthusiastically. "One of the problems with traveling naked. No pockets."

This revelation brought a laugh all around.

"Hence, the paperboy bags." Tiffany laughed. "Remember to come back soon. There is your trail." She pointed at the trail paralleling the riverbank. Chuckles and a smaller giant came back into the clearing. They waived as our band headed West, just like old friends.

We all looked back for one more look at Tiffany and the Giant.

***

Chapter 9

Becoming a Tribe and Finding Freedom

Our new, expanded team stepped into the coastal rainforest and began our journey downslope and West. We made good time since the game trail along the riverbank seemed well-used, and most of the underbrush was yards above.

Four days of uneventful trekking found Shiv trying to build a relationship with Willow, but she gently changed the subject each time, and Shiv noticed she was particularly partial to me. Finally, the fourth day's evening found us huddled around a small fire. Shiv had to break the hormonal tension that was beginning to affect his demeanor.

"Hey Mac, is Willow your woman?"

I looked up from the flame under furrowed brows. "I expect you must ask Willow. We have been mates for a while but by an arranged marriage. She has only been free a few days and has had little time to adjust. What do you think, Sharon?"

I set my eyes back to the flames, but my forehead furrows stayed put, even though I struggled not to smile.

The new reality dawned on Sharon Rowlands for the first time.

depending on your view, Willow had gone from a driven ball-breaker or the ideal people manager as a casino pit boss in Oregon to a naked pet held for the amusement of a giant owner. Then she was mated with a black man she had just met, with offspring as the goal. Her job, until recently, was to have babies. But she knew she couldn't conceive.

I looked up momentarily at her shock at being addressed as Sharon and the peculiar position she was now in. "I hadn't thought about it. You're right on the money, Mac. No offense, but I have the choice for the first time in over a year, and I'm not ready to be a mate. Now that I have free will, I could just as easily pick Tiffany back at the pass. Give me time to reflect on what I want from this new world."

"Ah, I have time to prove I should get a spin." Shiv grinned.

"Probably not; I have never been attracted to bloated ego boys."

"Awe, that wasn't nice."

Everyone broke out laughing, including Shiv.

"Don't worry, Willow. I've been without for some time, and I need some booty.

So don't take it personally."

"Well, that is kind of personal." Willow was still grinning, but she arched her left eyebrow.

I noted to myself that Stacey didn't move her gaze from the fire, didn't say anything, but she scrutinized every ounce of the blustery Shiv.

She would bide her time, but I felt she could take his mind off Willow.

The following day, our trek was well on our way before the sun cleared the hills, and the wiry cook, Randy, took his turn as the point scout. When the sun was directly overhead, we began to get worried. We still followed his tracks in the riverbank's clay dirt, but he should have returned by now.

Finally, we found his return track, yards from the top of a waterfall, but it stopped abruptly. He had reached the falls, looked over the edge at the now close coast, and turned to come back and report. He had retraced his steps about twenty or thirty feet, then disappeared. All that was left was a scuffed pair of last footprints.

All eyes turned to the skies. There was nothing but a few straggly clouds dotting the blue. A bit more scanning and a lone raptor was spotted far to the Southeast, tacking in the rolling coastal winds that banked off the mountain range. Then, over the roar of the great falls, we heard a far-off screamer call.

Shiv put into words what we were all thinking. "Purple Screamer. Randy didn't even hear it coming. From now on, this is Randy's Rock." We stood on the massive rock at the top of the falls that marked Randy's most Westerly view.

I pulled the crew off the trail and into the bush, where we found the game trail working back and forth down the slope to the bottom of the falls. Once in the trees, Willow pulled me close and buried her sobs in my chest. We took the rest of the day to absorb our first tragic loss, but I was up and back on the large rock at the top of the falls before everyone stirred. Working through my thoughts, I struggled for silver linings.

At least Randy got to see the coastline.

I stood stretching on the boulders at the top of the falls. Far out to the West was a line across the bottom of the sky and over the forest.

As far as we could see, a level line reached from South to North; the horizon was in view. I heard splashing in the pool behind me, and I watched, admiring as Willow climbed out to shake her head vigorously to rid it of the excess water.

"Willow, come see this."

She bounded from one water-smoothed boulder to the next until she stood at my side. Her gaze followed where I pointed.

"Look, there's the coastline. We will be there in a couple of days."

Standing at my side, she turned and pulled herself close to me. The first time since we were acting for the Giants, she reached for me without needing help from the dangerous river or the Giants' demands. "Mac, do you understand what I meant at the fire last night?"

"Yes, yes, I do. I wish it were different because I'm finding I am attracted to you, but I fully understand. You need to make your own decisions to be happy."

She looked up into my eyes. "You know I do love you, Mac; I'm just not sure it's the right kind of love. Yesterday's loss made me think, though. There are no promises in this new land."

I nodded, unsure how else to respond.

Shiv and Stacey watched from across the stream. They had just caught up with us. Then, as we now called him, Stud followed them out of the bush and into the water.

"Shit," Shiv muttered.

Willow and I turned to see the rest of the party. Willow laughed at Shiv.

"Can't a woman take in the view with her best friend?" Shiv dove into the pool and came up near our feet, spouting a long stream of creek water from his mouth up at our feet on the rocks.

***

"Come get a look at this." I waved to the crew to join.

"May I present the coast?"

A murmur ensued as the team of travelers lined up to look at their fate.

We spent the rest of the day getting to the bottom of the raging falls. The main river coursed to a crescendo of noise, mist, and rainbows at the top of the valley of the blue mushroom.

The river widened to a shallow, wet gravel and burnt orange moss expanse. The trees could not be called evergreen because of their silver growth tips and deep blue depths. They did, however, seem very similar to the coniferous trees of our homeland.

Although deciduous trees did fill in the undergrowth, the real difference was that they grew at least twice the height of any Redwood any of us knew from Earth.

Even the leaved trees towered up to extremes that would not be possible in the winds of home. Moreover, we had yet to experience one of the monsoons promised by the Pass Giants. The tribe was planning to be ready when we would. With each experience, we were getting to know our new world.

We agreed to stop early to use a bit of daylight to set up camp, so once done, the afternoon overcast skies didn't have the chance to soak us. Our campfire was in the mouth of a cave near the bottom of the falls. The natural chimney crack drew the smoke around the rock face and out of camp.

Shiv and Stacey were a little late returning from their last foray for firewood, but they managed to stock us up for the fire in time. Amusingly, they were both a bit flushed. "We got lost." Shiv supplied a simple explanation, and we dropped the subject.

Stud had gathered water, Willow and I had built a fire, Stacy then prepared the last harvest of fresh blue mushrooms and had made a Lump Back stomach pot for boiling them along with some meat strips supplied by Tiffany. After dark, we sat down to eat and talk about our day.

I started a new topic, "Tomorrow, we will be at the coast, folks. I sure hope it's everything we've been dreaming of."

It took us a while to sleep, except for Shiv and Stacey, who slept rather well.

Again, at the bottom of the falls, we found the river spread thin and shallow as far as we could see. Dotted in the stream were countless islands where the river spread to a lively delta of soft sod, brooks, creeks, and quicksand.

Pulling Stacey from one of the oatmeal cauldrons of quicksand showed the team what signs to look for and avoid.

Finally, we crossed the delta to the North, where the land rose a few yards from the flow because it seemed safer ground, then gingerly made our way to the roaring surf we had heard for over a mile.

Our little rag-tag band found the ledge of bitter water.

The water boiled out of the ground in rolling mounds, rank of tangy sulfur. The ledge ran down the coast for over a mile. The shelf stuck out into the ocean for up to five hundred feet in places.

Shiv said he could see why the Giants didn't like it; the water stank.

I smiled. "Friends, this mineral water will be nice after a hard day." I headed to the North end of the shelf, where rising steam oozed and cooler water and sea breezes replaced it. The area was pock-marked with lava bathtubs filled with varying temperatures as you moved closer or farther from the center of the frothing ledge. On the ledge the air was fresh.

"We have the makings of a most impressive spa." I dropped my bag, robe, and kilt on the dry shore and tested each lava bathtub until I found the one I liked and settled into the water. I reached up and snapped my fingers. "Waiter, I'll have my wine now."

Willow followed suit, and the rest found nearby pot-holes. Regardless of the hint of sulfur smell that eased as we acclimatized, Shiv and Stacy found a suitable tub that fit them both and settled in, grinning at each other.

We sat in just-hot-enough water, looking at each other and smiling until we noticed an empty pothole between us.

Randy wouldn't be joining us this evening. How did that play out? We went silent, contemplating our new life in the luminescent glow of the boiling ledge. It may be beautiful, but it could also be tragic. The speedy darkness dropped around us, magnifying the luminescing blue light from the surf. This new world held a lot of stock in various hues of luminescence based on cyan blue.

I reached out, picked up a handful of beach sand and pebbles from a shallow pool near my tub, and held it up to reflect on it. On Earth, I would have observed the sparkles of Mica, commonly found in a handful of sand, but here, there was a healthy smattering of tiny clear crystals. The soft blue of the surroundings produced a faint light spectrum in the palm of my hand.

"Tribe, we are a long way from Earth." The crew looked at my outstretched hand. "I hold a handful of our new world. What should we call it?"

Willow said, "You know a lot of languages call it Terra back on Earth, but the word Earth has some roots in the word Aarde, A.A.R.D.E, or Erda."

Shiv gave a thumbs up and added, "Keep it simple. Aarde doesn't need so many letters, though. How about Ard?"

Willow responded, "I think we need some recognition of our heritage. I'll drop the e if you let me have a double a."

I laughed. "This is good negotiation. Votes for Aard?" The response was immediate.

51 Pegasi - Black Mac

Our new home was named by unanimous vote.

"Ok, tribe, let's make this our last night without a roof. What say we build our first village on the coast tomorrow for the tribe? What should we call it?"

"Bitter Waters." Stud offered.

"New Plymouth." Suggested Dan.

Willow had been thoughtful through the village name conversation. Then, when the ideas slowed down, she said. "To me, this village means freedom. Perhaps the most freedom I have ever known before or after captivity."

Ann shouted, "Freedom!"

That brought on a unanimous chorus of "Freedom!"

I smiled. "Ok, Aardians, let's build Freedom."

Stud liked that.

He was ready to get down to business. "I study at Tiffany's huts. I think we find vines and branches easy, no?"

I noticed Stud's English was improving... Perhaps Shiv's was, too.

Shiv agreed. "I 'been watchin' for vines, fronds, and poles, and we have lots of driftwood, too. I seen Tiffany had Screamer hide across her rafters, under the fronds. So, we may need to start hunting our predators." His tone deepened. "We got this."

Maybe Shiv's English would take a little longer than Jean's

***

Chapter 10

Building Freedom

As daylight unfolded, we searched for the best advantage for our new home. Over breakfast tea, we decided on a set of requirements. We needed shelter, security, a slight slope for rain runoff, and shade from the sun. Most important were buffers from the ocean winds, fuel, game, freshwater, and view.

We found a slate rock face that diverted the wind and shaded the lightly sloping, treed, and shrubbed highland. It stood above a rocky drop to the ocean, protected by a crown of large coniferous trees. These trees guarded the rocky bay below. The rocks gave way to a sand beach sparkling with diamond chips and shells.

The Northwest-facing rock cliff added warmth at sunset while shading the protective trees and shrubs through the day's heat. Part of the face shone smooth. Under examination of the rubble at its base, we had a source of slate for flagstones. This setting also welcomed gentle sea breezes through the midday, and the troop found several shallow and a few deeper caves in the base of the cliffs to store dry goods.

With work, it would provide additional shelter when the monsoons came. Freedom was officially founded.

Rolling hills with a lacework of Humpback trails through the trees led to higher ground to the North. The slope led to a plateau dotted with small, reeded lakes and winding streams.

The vista spread between the ocean and the mountains far to the East. This environment seemed to be a fine hunting ground.

To the South, the ground stepped down in layers to the wide delta, teaming with small animals and the rich ecosystem of tidal flats. The tides provided an inspiring variation in activity, with twin surges and twin ebbs driven by twin moons. This unique Aardian feature provided rich eddy pools where one surge could overlap an ebb trying to find its way back to the ocean body while another was flowing in and out through a parallel channel.

The result was more movement and fresher pools than I could remember back on Earth. Beyond the delta, the ground rose again, and I could see hills rising to hold the delta in, but no mountain range seemed to rise as it did to the North. I made a mental note. *The South Vista needed some scouting.*

Everything seemed to fall into place for our small tribe, and looking around, I saw everyone happily bustling across the scene in pursuit of their self-directed tasks. I headed for the plot I had laid out for Willow's cabin with my new load of poles.

Decades ago, an event killed off a grove of young coniferous trees at the delta's edge. That trauma resulted in a harvest of dried tree trunks the circumference of my upper arm. The dry stalks were easy to break off in sections with the proper fulcrum.

This provided dry, straight, solid poles for our building purposes. Stud and Shiv appeared to be very handy in this regard. Willow and Stacy were already directing traffic and serving as architects, along with their efforts to bring in raw materials.

Within a few days, we had five small shelters surrounding a central firepit.

Stud had perfected the art of willow branch weaving that was beginning to supply comfortable chairs, benches, and beds. Building the beds catalyzed change in our camp, living arrangements, and society. This monumental change started with a simple question. Stud finished his first bed, which he claimed as a single-width cot.

He demonstrated the strength of the cane weave and the overlay of fronds. Then, while lying on his back with his arms folded behind his head, he said. "What do you think?" I was quick to applaud his work, as was Shiv, but the ladies were silent. In moments, we noticed, so all eyes went to Willow and Stacy.

Willow finally broke the impasse. "Jean, how hard would building one twice as wide be?"

The silence became profound for a few moments as we turned to see Stacy nodding enthusiastically. Willow had to break the silence again. She swallowed hard, looked at me, and asked. "Mac, would you share my cabin with me?"

Noting she did not ask to share the bed, I got her message and, with a concerned look, replied, "These huts are not very big. Do you think we could fit two of these beds in them?"

Another moment of silence and the whole camp erupted in laughter. We laughed till tears ran down our cheeks. We now had answers to the unspoken questions that grew during our trek. The relief that came with the clearing of the subject was a new sign of freedom for the tribe.

"I need a wider one, too," Everyone looked to Stacy, and the second wave of laughter rang from the new village. Shiv turned several shades of red, but he was grinning.

Now that we had five working huts, we put three to immediate use. The revelry continued into the evening as our happy band sat around a comforting cooking fire. The village shared newly learned skills across the fire as we solidified our tribal knowledge. New artisans shared tricks and revelations from our new life and grew as a tribe.

I found this the right time to let everyone know I was about to return to where we had come. "I need to get Dan and Kia into the technology of the transporters, find out what we need for an antenna, and get a transporter back to Freedom. Then, we must help build our new world with the personalities and skills required to be sustainable, happy, and healthy."

At first, the reaction was negative, as the village saw me as a leader, and the tribe had not thought about the lead roles they could all provide. It was time for me to delegate. It was critical to plan for succession in this challenging new world. I must highlight the leadership skills of the people around me.

From Freedom, we would spread out to hunt, gather, and make room for more refugees. We also needed to raid the Giants to remove more humans from their cages.

I knew then that I must inspire more leaders to take on these challenges. So, I took the opportunity to start pointing out some of the tribe's finer skill sets.

***

I pointed at Shiv. "Shiv, you are a natural leader. I expect you to do anything I might have done, usually better. It took a sharp mind and the heart of a warrior to save us from the Giants and screamers the way you did. None of us would be here if it were not for your heroics. We are also going to need your warrior spirit in us all. Between you and Willow, we can be an armed force."

I nodded at Willow. "Willow, you are a talented archer. We have the weapons, and we all must become as good as you are to ensure we continue to thrive. We must also enhance our archery acumen to turn the tables on the Screamers. We must begin harvesting feathers, hides, meat, and talons for our use as we gain respect from the birds. We must help them understand that attacks on us are costly.

"Tiffany mentioned something about reeds for arrows, and her bow design seems perfect for our situation. However, we need to investigate other opportunities to grow and improve continuously. Your history ensures we have that built into everything we do if we train for it in our boot camp."

My attention now went to Jean. "Stud, you are proving to be a master builder. We must learn from you. We should never get as good as you because you constantly grow and improve. You have also proven to be a skilled scout. You probably know our surroundings better than anyone now."

"Stacy, along with the meat we get from the local animal population, we need plant-based food. We may find berries here, but can we find mushrooms? The celery stocks we had eaten in the cages may also be critical for our health.

What else can we find, particularly with some plant-based proteins? What can we cultivate in this rich soil, and what must we avoid? I feel you will be a critical part of our survival."

The team stuck with me through the lecture, but enough was enough. Shiv looked at me through his eyebrows. "How the hell do you think one guy, alone, will make out on that trip?" I noticed his language was growing a bit milder, at least around the ladies.

The more he associated with Willow, Stacy, and possibly the rest of us, the more I noticed him tempering his vocabulary. Willow joined in. She had just asked me to share her hut. "This is what I get when I practically propose?" She laughed, but I could tell she was only partially kidding.

"I must do this, team. We can't afford to delay because it means lives.

Probably hundreds of human lives. I'd much rather stay here. Especially in that little cabin over there," I pointed at what was now termed 'Willow's Cabin.' "But, if I get Dan and Kia set up now, I can return and focus on Freedom. "

I looked into Willow's eyes. "I will be back before the Monsoons. I do not want to face that river when that pass is a funnel for a monsoon. From what I have seen, I suspect that delta just South of us will be wider than the mouth of the Mississippi."

I reached and took Willow's face in my hands. "I don't think I have more than two weeks to make this trip, so I must travel daily. I want to be nowhere else as much as I want to be right here."

I got no more pushback, so I asked Willow to take me home.

Willow and I slept together on her brand-new bed for the first time. We had much to discuss, so we quietly shared dreams and goals for much of the night. I learned a lot about Sharon Rowlands, and that amazed me.

She had endured the well-known uphill battle for a woman in a rough and tumble world between base desires and money. Women had to be attractive enough to serve the old-boys club ideals. But they had to overcompensate with compassion and empathy for the tough persona to be deemed worthy of a leadership role.

This balance made her not quite good enough on either side of the fence because half of her peers would consider her a ball-breaker, and the other half would attribute success to her looks. She confided that escaping from the Giants was her first experience as an adult, that she felt equal to her peers. That feeling of freedom to be herself was permanently attached to the name 'Willow.' As Willow of Aard, she was now who she should be. She would never, willingly, go back to Earth.

I explained that I had to go back at times and shared my life story. Fully open, we came to a succinct understanding of our relationship. Neither owned the other. We had our paths, but we would be the highest power of friends with benefits built on respect and an ever-growing bond of love.

51 Pegasi - Black Mac

We consummated love that night as neither of us had known before.

I left before full light in the morning.

***

Chapter 11

Back to the Giant's Briars for the Cache

By the time I reached the top of the lower falls, I was sweating profusely, but I had an ambitious first day in mind, so I powered through the day's heat to the bottom of the second falls.

I was beginning to think I had bit off more than I could chew as I started climbing the rocks beside the raging falls, so when I found a mound of damp moss to settle into halfway up the climb, I had to take in the view back toward the ocean.

I noted that the sun was too close to the horizon to watch the sunset, so I looked to my left at the massive volume of water flashing by. I started to look away, but something caught my eye. A two-foot-wide ledge ran from my vantage point to a dark hole behind the falling water.

Before I knew what I was doing, I was testing the security of the moss covering the ledge and was on my way to discovering a stunning cavern behind the falls. There was a rainbow of mist at the entrance. On the far side of the falls was an opening facing Southwest. That opening allowed for full sunshine from a dry vista to the sunset. I decided this would be my camp for the night and quickly packed some dry moss into a hollow to sleep on in the cool shade.

By daylight I was scampering up the remainder of the fall's climb with renewed energy and drive from a powerful snack of dried Humpback, dried berry, and a small slab of dried mushroom... and a few handfuls of waterfall to wash it all down. I reflected on Randy's rock and headed up the trail toward Tiffany and Company. Let's see if I can make four days happen in three.

I quickly powered up the well-used trail and had no interruption from screaming eagles, although I tuned in for their calls. This lack of Screamer made me curious about their seasons. I would imagine they had mating seasons.

I imagined seasons where there might be egg maintenance, molting, and different prey seasons. It would be worth studying them to understand their weaknesses and strengths better. I found lots of time to think on the trail, but I was careful not to forget my surroundings.

I had no idea what could step onto my path, and the unknown produced the most fear. Two and a half days from the falls, I hollered at the camp as I saw my first hut.

Ann and Penny rewarded my call as they trotted out to welcome me.

"Mac! Welcome! Man, you're looking good. This world is good for you. Me too." Ann did a little pirouette to show off, and I had to admit the shameless flirting and gregarious welcome was a ray of sunshine on this severe planet. Ann had toned up some since we were here last, and I could tell she was loving life.

Penny laughed and said, "Annie, you have no shame."

We were joined cautiously by another couple of people I had not met, who came from a hut to see what the noise was about.

Penny saw them first and was eager to introduce them. "Mac, this is Doctor Fletcher. We call him Dr. Tim; and Sirih. Chuckles brought them to camp a few days after you guys left."

I shook the doctor's hand, "Hi, Doctor, I'm Mac. It's great to meet you."

I reached for Sirih's hand, but she nodded, staying slightly behind Ann, and said, "Glad to meet you, Mac." I noticed she had trouble making eye contact, so I didn't push it.

"Nice to meet you, Sirih."

Ann grabbed my elbow. "Come have some tea, Mac. Tiffany, Dan, and Kia will be back shortly. They figured they would be back by the middle of the day. They are scoping out a new trail with Chuckles. Tell us about the trip to the coast and how everyone is doing at Bitter Waters."

She led us all to a small fire amongst some rocks behind the Westernmost hut, where an old cast iron kettle was simmering. She produced a set of cups: tin, ancient ceramics, and a couple of glass mugs with handles. I recognized them from the tower cabin.

"Ah, I see someone has been to the tower."

Penny was quick to respond. "Dan and Kia have been there twice. They've brought back many treasures. I think they are planning another trip. That's why this trail tryout today."

51 Pegasi - Black Mac

Ann waved at a circle of rocks, log sections, and stumps and said, "Make yourself at home. We like to do our visiting back here in the trees. You never know who is watching," as she pointed to the skies. She also pointed at a small cave entrance against the foot of the mountain. That configuration protected the camp against the river.

"We've set that cave up for storage but have used it as sanctuary a few times when the screamers have swung in. They know we are here now and occasionally visit to keep us on our toes."

I nodded as Sirih helped her pour the tea.

"So, where is this trail the team is exploring?" I asked anyone who would answer.

Penny lit up as she pointed at the cliff across the river. "It's on the cliff on the other side of the river."

I looked across at the sheer face, and the reality of this new trail came into focus.

"Yikes! A cliff-side trail in the open, in Screamer territory."

Ann saw my shock. "You're right, Mac. Most of it is bare and exposed, but you will understand better when the crew returns and explains." Then, on cue, a whistle came from the East side of the camp, and the trail committee stepped into view. It took them a moment to recognize they had a visitor, but in moments, excited chatter surrounded me.

Ann poured another round of local tea, and they pressed for details of the team. First, they wanted to know the details of the trek to the coast.

Then, the name we had settled on for the planet and the new village name.

The Pass tribe was excited about the Aard name and were happy to be called Aardians. The crew, however, was saddened to hear that Randy did not make the trek past the falls, and it confirmed that living on this planet was as dangerous as it was beautiful.

***

Now, done with my story, it was time for Tiffany and Dan to bring me up to date with their adventures.

Tiffany started with hardball. "Mac, could you use more citizens in Freedom?"

"Of course, that has been the plan all along. Our plan's always been to transport escapees West as they came through the pass."

"Mac, we need to move to Freedom with you. With Chuckle's help, we have been to the tower cabin, and the Giants and their human partners know we have been there now. The only problem is that we need to go on a major recruiting drive to get troops to fight this war now that they know about us.

They know the Pass Giants are protecting us, and the place is heating up. So, we will have to move operations to your camp on the coast if that's OK."

I smiled. I couldn't imagine having Tiffany and her crew around as much of a chore. However, I was very interested in their trips to the cabin, how they got back and forth, and the opportunities and threats of the new trail.

"Folks, please fill me in on the results of your trips to the cabin and the new trail. Can we get one last big expedition back to pick up the cache we hid in the berry warren?" Dan and Kia filled me in on what they found. Humans were back in the cabin again, and they had seen new, updated equipment, monitors, and a fresh stock of diamonds.

But they stayed back once they saw how much traffic the place was getting and a new, incessant hum from the tower.

Kia had been to the lab on Earth.

"Mac, one transporter box is calibrated to and from the lab. When it seemed we would lose access to this stuff again, I followed your example and tried it out. I figured out how to set the landing time and set it for 2:00 A.M. PST on Earth and got a great look through the lab.

I scored some more technical data, but most were web URLs as they no longer keep much paper. Of course, we don't have much access to Earth's internet here, but if we can build an Earth base, we can learn much more."

"We can do that. After this trip, I plan on visiting my brother and father to set that up if they have not already. As I see it, our priorities are to get you all safely to the coast. Next, we must ensure we have a safe route to and from the tower Giants. Then we must perfect our transporters.

Finally, we must sabotage the bad guys in a way that kills their supply chain." I could tell Kia was thrilled with my priorities, but Dan was eager to start, too.

I looked at Tiffany. "Let's hear about this trail."

"Chuckles is trying to set us up to survive when they move South. He showed us a narrow path that starts from the boulders at the top of the falls."

"We call that Randy's Rock." Sorry, I just realized you three had not heard we lost Randy." I repeated a shorter version of his loss but continued, "I know where you mean the trail starts."

The news hit the tribe hard, so it took them a few minutes to ask questions. We finally cleared the air enough to get back on track, and Tiffany continued her story. "The trail stays close to the riverbed.

Sometimes in gravel beds and shallows until it reaches this camp."

Staying in the trees, she led us to the riverbank and pointed at the waterline across the river, just East of where we stood. It was hard to see in the bright light of day. A thin line angled up the sheer cliff until it was about forty feet below a rough screamer nest we had observed before.

There didn't seem to be any activity at the nest now. But we could easily see droppings down the side of the cliff and over the trail we were contemplating. The path began to come down the canyon face from that point, and about sixty feet from the river, it came back down to within ten to twenty feet, where it disappeared around a bend in the river.

"We have just come back from there." Dan brought the conversation back to the camp. "Most of the trail is near the water. The ledge seems to have been carved by the high-water mark during the flood stage. The path will always be only as good as the last flood left it.

The Screamers have been quiet for a week, so today, we went to the grasslands and back in one easy day."

"Well, I am going to do the same thing tomorrow. Does anyone want to help me bring the stash from the berry bushes?"

"You are reading our mind, Mac," Tiffany smiled. "We planned to send someone off to get you to make this trip before the Monsoons. But then, just like that, you're here and ready to go."

The day was getting short, so Dan, Tia, and I started planning our trip to the warren while Tiffany spent quality time with the rest of her band, They were packing packs for the journey West.

After the last Pass Tribe dinner of Humpback, mushroom, Aardian celery, and dried berries, the camp settled into sleep and rested as much as possible.

Early morning trekking was becoming a habit as we headed for Randy's Rock. Excitement charged the trekkers. None of this was easy, but every crew member looked forward, not backward. They all had reasons of their own to take this next step, and each felt driven toward a common goal of a new, healthy, happy life.

***

Chapter 12

Be One with the Wall and the Tribe Grows

Dan, Kia, and I were on the new Northbank river trail by the fourth day. I struggled with backtracking that far, but we all agreed we needed to know the route.

This sketchy highway is critical for the future. We must have it well-mapped and understood. Despite several forays into knee-deep water, we made good time and soon returned to a point where we could look across at the old camp.

At this point, we cached our bows, quivers, tools, and bags as we wouldn't want to carry them across the cliff faces and through our mission to carry the cache back. We could re-negotiate our load once we returned.

Kia stopped and looked closely at the clay wall rising above us. At the bottom were soft pillars of fine clay that ended with the water. While standing in the shallows, she reached for a handful of the powder, dipped it in water, and applied it from head to toe, down the front of her torso, arms, and legs. "This will keep the worst of the sun from my skin. Fortunately, it will also make me the color of the cliff."

"Kia, you are a genius." Dan quickly mimicked her methods, and I followed suit.

We were patting clay on each other's backs one moment, and moments later, we looked like the clay wall. We still hadn't heard screamers, but as we started up the bare cliffside, we were critically aware and listening for any hint of distant screams.

As we climbed the two-to-four-foot ledge toward the nest above us, the sun baked us mercilessly against the clay-colored wall. Thankfully, the layer of clay provided better protection than we expected.

We rose on the trail to the highest point under the nest, and the stench was hard to bear even after it had not been active. Directly under the nest was a shallow indent. It could not be called a cave, but deep enough that the three of us could fit in, hidden from scouting eyes from overhead. We did know, however, that screamer eyes over the river would see activity there with no problem.

Dan pointed at the guano on the trail with a low moan. Covered in the mess but easily identifiable was a human femur. I softly kicked it off the path, and we heard it splash below. We didn't need that reminder on the trail.

Before returning to the ledge, I looked at Dan and Kia. "Folks, if a screamer attacks us, I'm following that femur. Our only hope will be the water."

Dan said, "That fall would probably kill us."

I smiled slightly, "Ever see Butch Cassidy and the Sundance Kid?"

They both laughed.

"You wouldn't like the view from that nest."

With that, following Dan, we were back in motion, working our way down the cliff to a broader, more comfortable ledge a dozen feet above the river, and around the next bend, the mountains fell away, and we were in the grasslands West of the tower. It was still silent. Too silent, and I wasn't comfortable with it.

I remember Tiffany saying that Chuckles had felt the tower Giants had killed many of the Screamers, but he also mentioned the new nest, so some had to be still nearby. We were now back in Tower Giant's territory, and I wasn't fond of the memories of my last event with them.

"What do you think about hanging out till dark to let the moons lead us back to the berries? We can follow the river if we stay with the right tributary."

We packed very light, knowing we would need room in our packs to bring our loot back, but we still had Humpback jerky and dried mushrooms. We ate, drank a little water from the river, then bathed to remove the clay. Unfortunately, we would not fit in with the stream flora, and our trip upstream would be more challenging than it had been coming down last time.

We welcomed the first moon as we sat in the night. Kia said, "I call them Alpha and Beta. Just a little Greek to assign them first and second."

"That makes perfect sense. I haven't considered this before, but are we sure this is Alpha? Perhaps they have different orbit speeds."

Dan chuckled. "I thought of that too, and I've been watching them since I've been here. We are a little North of the equator, and Beta follows Alpha closely on its orbital path.

At one point, they may have been the same piece of space junk but broke in two and became twins."

I thought about that. "I know the moon we grew up with doesn't stick to the equator but hangs out within a couple of degrees, so it hangs out in the Western and Eastern latitudes equal time each month."

Dan nodded. I think these two follow the same basic rules. We get a double bump in tides and other lunar events. Maybe even lunacy."

With that, he laughed, and we did, too. Beta got the joke, too, as the second moon peaked over the dark rainforest to the East.

Kia added. "I think we have much to learn from these celestial ladies, but the first lesson is to get our butt in gear when Beta shows up near the tower." Again, we chuckled but took the hint and started power-wading the shallows with the rippling silver chevrons streaming from our legs.

We passed several tributaries, but the much smaller stream we followed now wandered to some degree toward the Northwest side of the berry thicket. We could now make the warren out as a black lake in the silver moonlight. We could now also hear a hum. We could see the darkened cabin as we came closer, but our goal was to stay with the stream. We must keep our tracks in the water and try to be as invisible as possible.

Soon enough, we came to the dead tree. Staying in the creek, we observed the ford between the tree and tower and saw a well-worn path. Interestingly, the path still carried fresh evidence of Humpbacks on top of a troubling sign of shoes or boots. The cabin was now getting a lot of attention from Earthlings.

We kept right on moving.

***

Dark traveling paid off, and daylight was breaking as we reached the entrance to the warren. None too soon, we slipped into the security, comfort, and shade of our cool sanctuary. About forty feet into the warren, along the creek, I stepped out of a Humpback watering hole into the dark passageway I was looking for.

I had an old sandal hidden behind a berry stock as wide as the trunk of my body. This landmark was my sign. I pointed down the dark passage to the West and said, "This way."

A hundred feet West, I stopped again at another fork that headed North. Behind a rock, I lifted the mate to the first sandal. "We're here."

We stepped down the new path a few steps and turned sharply East into my cache.

"Okay, team. Let's rest as this is the only place nearby where we can be comfortable enough to sleep during the day. We need to work again tonight."

We made a few hammocks by twisting the chamois tarp in three through the thicket, and as soon as we allowed our bodies to ease, we all surprisingly got a good quality nap.

Later in the afternoon, we ate again, wandered off to take bio breaks, and then rallied again at the cache.

"Team, do you fancy visiting our old friends at the cages?"

Dan and Kia both lit up. "I was hoping you were thinking like that," Kia grinned.

Dan asked, "Do you have any rope in here?" pointing at the cache. "We used vines from this thicket when Tiffany helped us escape, but rope would be much easier to work with."

"I do." I fished it out, and we headed East, leaving a trail like the sandals to get us back to the cache from the giant's camp. The sun was setting. An ordinarily dark forest got darker as we peeked from the brambles at the metal cages.

We noted an occupied cage hanging close to the forest floor. It had a fastened doorway. The first cage I had seen with a door. They were far enough above us; we couldn't see how many were in the cage, but we could hear them talking. Some seemed to me English speaking and some Spanish. Another cell was on the ground, with the roof off, and another hanging high in the trees, but it seemed silent. I picked up a sign on the occupied cage that translated roughly to "Transport."

"These people are about to be moved," I whispered to my team.

"Damn rights, they are!" whispered back Kia.

I was beginning to see her passion.

We waited until we were sure the camp was clear of Giants, then I called out softly to the hushed people in the cage.

"Please stay silent... por favor quedante en silencio."

There was a quick scuffle to the side of the cage facing us, and a half dozen faces peered down in the blue glow growing around us to see Dan working to tie dry thorns sideways to the rope and Kia scrambling up the horizontal doorway bars on the grounded cage. I pressed my finger to my lips, and the audience got it.

Kia had now scrambled up their cage doorway and pulled herself onto their roof. I followed her example to the top of the topless cage and turned to look at Dan's progress. Done, he flipped the loose end of the rope to me. I captured it and repeated it to Kia. She fastened the rope to the ring on the top that suspended the cage.

She then worked her way back down the rope ladder to stand with me on the top of the open cell and worked her way to a latch. She lifted, pulled the loop off the hook, and pulled down, and the latch separated, and a large gasp fell out of the captives as the corner of their prison dropped a few feet. After that, Kia slipped the rope ladder into the captives and helped them climb up to us.

We helped them one at a time to climb out and scale down the doorway to the ground, where they ran over to the coaxing Dan. We didn't have to do anymore, but Kia scrambled back up to save our rope. When she returned to the edge, I helped her swing her legs over, step on the top of the sagging cage walls, and back down to me. We climbed down the way we came up and joined Dan and our new band in the thicket.

To the glow of the berry thicket night lights, we made our way back to the cache.

We fed the escapees Humpback jerky, fresh berries, and fresh mushrooms. When everyone settled, I asked how many spoke English. Three replied with "No Ingles."

"De donde eres?"

"Columbia y Ecuador"

"Gracias. Traduciremos al ingles pero sera util. por favor aprenda."

My rough Spanish would take some polish, but I received nods of understanding.

"Si, sabemos un poco. Nostotros mejoraremos." Their spokesman suggested they knew some English.

I decided to start introductions in Spanish to finish the hard part first, then open up to the English speakers to get everyone on the same page.

So first, I introduced Dan and Kia to the Spanish speakers. Dan knew some Spanish, so he helped fill in the blanks, and Kia helped explain to the English speakers what we were doing, who we were, and where we were going.

We kept our voices soft to ensure we didn't bring extra attention to our growing band of human immigrants.

We got to know Jesus Ramirez, who escaped servitude to a Columbian drug cartel by joining a migration to the United States. However, things went wrong.

He dodged a hail of gunfire as he broke into Panama to wake up in the cage. He thought they killed him and wondered what hell he had landed in.

Next was Maritza Almedia, who had lost all her family in faction fighting. She survived by running into the jungle and going to the city. She was struggling to feed herself in Quito, in the Pichincha province of Equator. She fell asleep behind a restaurant and woke naked, in a cage.

Julio Escobar was a judge who came from Santo Domingo. The current political climate did not favor him, and he fled the country to save his life. His wife would not go with him as she was used to the good life and was willing to compromise to stay home.

He was on a small plane headed for an international airport when the lights went out, and he woke naked with the rest in a tropical rainforest cage.

Kia introduced us to a Canadian from a little community called Maple Ridge, outside Vancouver in British Columbia, who had been turned out by her family for her sexual orientation. Vera Nemechek had started experimenting with drugs to fight her overwhelming depression.

Her last memory of Earth was a hard park bench in Stanley Park in Lower Vancouver. She didn't look very healthy, was shivering from fear, and jumped at any sound.

Next for us to meet was Hilda Schultz, a German from Basel, Switzerland. She grew up on the German side of the border but went to a university in Switzerland's oldest school town, Basel. Part of her ecological program in school included a series of classes in English, so Hilda understood and spoke it well. However, her family was angry that she had no use for her old hometown.

Frankly, her partying during Carnival and Fasching was getting out of hand. Somehow, she thought she was being punished and panicked like Vera.

Lastly, we met Lawrence Hempler, a lawyer on the fast track to becoming a politician in Washington, D.C. He was getting to know all the right people but perhaps some of the wrong people. He felt he was the target of a political hit.

Of all the new citizens, Larry probably had the most to learn.

A steep education was at hand, and we had to make some critical choices before we loaded up and headed West. In two languages, we spent extra time explaining the nudity, the life-and-death world of Giants and Purple Screamers, transportation, and the realities of life on another planet.

We explained that anyone not entirely in would be left behind.

However, but those who stepped up to build our tribe would never be alone unless they wanted to be. They all had free choice, but an unforgiving world would force them to live or die by those choices.

***

Chapter 13

A New Path with no Tracks

The litmus test was the load at the cache. Everyone would need to contribute, and we would hurry to the coast. We heard the expected calamity and roar of the Giants to the East when dawn broke but were surprised that the noise and activity seemed to head South.

For some reason, the Giants appeared to change to focus away from us.

We asked the new citizens to cut strips from the berries and mushrooms and store them in their packs. They would want them later when we could not stop to cook. Kia volunteered to prep them for the trip. She fed them enough for challenging travel.

She explained living barefoot, bio-breaks in the wild, and things they had never thought of that would become natural by the time we reached Freedom on the coast.

Dan and I quietly explored the known exits from the war

-ren while staying well hidden.

51 Pegasi - Black Mac

We listened for distant screams to hear the familiar grunts of the Fur Giants and the rumble of heavy footsteps.

All was eerily silent. We explored the far West exit that the Screamers had thrashed during a well-remembered melee when we first tried to escape the tower Giants. I was amazed to find all new green growth as the briar patch repaired itself, but I was getting used to the speed of this planet.

The environment was so quiet that we ventured out a short distance into the tall grass to see if there would be any re-action. We did find fresh giant tracks, at first parallel with the thicket, coming from the East, but they turned at this point and headed for the sentinel tree and the tower. We expected Giants, at least during the day.

Dan looked worried as he asked, "Do you think we should take this short route out toward the tower, Mac, or should we stick with the stream exit back near the cache?"

I thought for a minute, then replied, "Dan, I've been thinking, and I'd like you to check my logic and give me your thoughts. First, these Giants are intelligent. I feel they are going to try to outsmart us. We can see they also have human help.

Humans can go where we go.

It didn't make sense for them to stomp off to the South when they found the empty cages. By now, they know we are settling in the West."

He nodded but continued to listen without comment, so I continued. "Dan, I think that was a red herring to make us feel safe to leave either from here or the creek. That's why they checked this exit already and headed for the tower.

They are looking for our tracks to ensure we haven't already headed out. You can bet they have already checked the creek by the cabin for any sign of us."

Dan nodded and asked, "So you think they will be waiting for us around the tower or following the creek?"

"Yes, I do. What do you say we explore the warren tunnels to the South and find an exit that provides a more direct route across the plains to the mountains? That puts us far from our known pathway and cuts the distance to the mountains.

The downside is that we are out in the open. Very little brush or trees away from the creek leaves us open to Screamers should the creek shrubs grow thin. However, we have the moons to guide us through the grasslands, Screamers don't appear to hunt at night, and Giants need to be in our proximity to see us in the tall grass."

Dan got the whole picture now, "I agree, Mac. That sounds like the most plausible plan, but I realize it is not foolproof.

The Giants will find our tracks at some point and know where we are going." I nodded.

"Yes, I have no doubt we have a probability of seeing Sasquatch before we hit safety. Maybe they will even follow into the tight canyon flowing into the Canyon Pass. We can either set up housekeeping in the warren, giving them time to plan our removal after the monsoon."

I paused. "Or we use the element of surprise to get a head-start. The Giants will also expect us to follow the river's South shore when we get to the pass, as we did last time, but we will have the North side trail this time."

Dan nodded. "Yes, I like your plan. Let's find that Southern exit, then go back to tell the rest of our plan to see how they buy in."

"Agreed."

We stepped back into the briars and tracked for Southern trails. It wasn't hard to find one. Within a short distance, they all lit up as the Southern sun shone directly into their openings. This extra lighting is when we were surprised by a revelation.

A small stream flowed West, just inside the boundary of the briars. It left the briars to the South from where we stood and angled off to the right and the all-important West.

We may have found another tributary of the massive river that took us to our freedom. We marked our tunnel entrance and returned to the escapees and Kia. We told our story, and the only questions came from the lawyer. I guess that was his job, and old habits die hard.

Larry said, "What guarantee do we have that the Giants don't have that creek staked as well?

"There are no guarantees," Dan was blunt.

"Well, I think we will be safer taking the known route. We know what to expect there and have a better chance to make it across the plains in the dark." Larry was beginning to get his back up.

We didn't have time for litigation, so I explained the options, "No problem, Larry. You've heard our reasoning, and Dan and I are going the Southern route.

Everyone is welcome, but they are also welcome to follow you along the Northern path. We are all about choice here. But, with choice comes consequences.

Remember, however, that we do not have time to wait for anyone. Monsoons are about to hit the pass at any time, and once they hit, the river and falls are impossible to traverse. We have told you the story of the Northern Ledge, the falls, and the hazards. We wish you luck and a safe journey."

I strapped on my pack, which included three transporters wrapped in an old pair of jeans, and started for the tunnel corner that marked the turn South. Everyone followed, including Larry, and he was silent. Kia followed me, then the new citizens, and Dan brought up the rear. By the time we were at the briar exit, the sun was on the horizon. The sloping sunshine made it challenging to see out over the vista.

The Spanish speakers worked hard to use as much English as possible. The English speakers were also trying just as hard to include Spanish words where they could. The result was a bit painful. At least, I had a smattering of Spanish through my old business, and Dan could speak some.

Surprisingly, Larry had a good grasp of Spanish due to his legal practice and desire to communicate in politics. He was proving to be useful as we staged for moonlight. Perhaps he would take to Aard.

***

I turned back to the escapees. "We call this the river of freedom, "El río de Libertad," It may be small now, but in the end, it is mighty and means life to us."

The troop understood three basic rules before we stepped into the stream and headed out. First and foremost, silence.

No one would communicate with sound unless critical, and then it would be in whispers at close proximity. Secondly, no one steps out of the water.

Then, we were to leave no evidence, including broken branches or twigs. Also critical was to stay as low as possible to ensure we kept movement below the underbrush surrounding the stream.

The grass height averaged about five feet, so in the creek, we were out of sight, and in the grass, we could stay hidden if we had to by ducking down. The first forty feet provided berry thicket cover as the briar patch was happily growing along the stream.

Beyond that, low brush, shrubs, and a few trees stood above the grasslands and folded in on the creek. We were underway, and the only issue was the soft feet and bodies of the new immigrants. By now, Kia, Dan, and I had ground-toughened feet, but we all remembered our first trek out from the cages. In the open, it was easy to see as Alpha and Beta were sailing in all their glory, and they lit up the amazed faces of our new tribe members.

The reality of this new world was beginning to sink in, and Kia, Dan, and I relished the awe reflected on the faces of the new Aardians. I felt better as they began to understand what our lives had become.

Vera and Hilda were probably the most frightened as they were the most removed from nature in their lives back on Earth.

However, our Hispanics also showed silent amazement at their new world. Julio and Maritza appeared to be the most happily engaged, and I could tell that Julio had a few lessons in people skills, law, and community for Larry when things settled. I felt he had more English acumen than he was admitting to.

The young ladies and Jesus were doing surprisingly well treading on the stream pebbles and sand, but Julio and Larry struggled most with tender feet. Luckily, we were traveling with the Pegasi-warmed water. As we made our way past small tributaries, deeper pools appeared at corners in the creek. Our waterway did, indeed, track more to the West. As I began to feel happy about our progress, I heard a sharp "Shh!" from behind me and ducked. Dan motioned everyone down.

Once settled in the same pool, I raised my head with Dan and Kia to see a herd of flash-lights bobbing back and forth to our North and Northeast. I glanced at Dan and Kia. I whispered, "Those are humans out looking for us. Judging from their position to the berry warren behind us, I suspect they are just West of the cabin, searching along the creek we would be in right now, on the original path."

I looked at our huddled migrants and whispered, "Ahora solo nadamos – now we just swim."

Even with the packs we had strapped to our backs, I got an almost unanimous nod, and we started. Surprisingly, we seemed to make at least the same speed, probably better, even though we needed to wait for Larry occasionally. We did this for an Earth hour, stopped, and peeked up. This strategy worked as the lights were still in sight but much farther to the East.

We checked again in what seemed the same amount of time. We could see no lights, but we could now see the horizon. It loomed, lighter, over the Eastern rainforest, making the darker briar mass stand out against the grasslands behind us.

The mountain range to the West seemed closer, and the river moved us much faster. I scanned the Western horizon from North to South and saw no large, moving black lumps. We hoped that meant no hairy Giants waiting at the gates to freedom. I directed the tribe to the North bank of our stream.

We would want to exit at this point before the river was too big to cross easily. I remembered our last trip West and our struggle to get out of the current. We finally reached the point where the canyon wall rose from the grasslands, and we had to leave our liquid sanctuary. Before we stepped out, I let the team know what to expect next.

"Team, we are moving to our most exposed stage of this trip. Here are the facts you need to know." I pointed to the ledge rising from the grass to a point where it disappeared around the canyon wall a few feet ahead. At the base of the clay cliff were the powdery pillars left from wind and water erosion, marking the shoreline between the cliff and the water.

"We will cake clay mud over our bodies to become the color of the wall. We want to disappear against the clay cliff. We will be exposed for a few miles and on a narrow ledge as we move West. It is wide enough to be safe, but we cannot go around each other.

We have two major enemies we need to be ready for. The Giants may come splashing downstream looking for us, or the screaming raptors may want to pick us off from the air.

Neither fate is acceptable. In each case, the solution is to drop your pack, dive into the water, and swim downstream as hard as possible. Spend as much time as you can underwater."

I stopped a moment to let that sink in, and Julio made the sign of the cross and translated for the Spanish speakers.

Larry took the opportunity. "Why didn't we take the South shore? It has a low bank and a cover of trees and shrubs.

I was expecting him, so I pointed downstream. "Just around that bend, the canyon walls rise on the South side, too.

There are no usable ledges there, and we escaped on the South side the last time, so the Giants will be looking for our tracks to come out on that side. We had friendly Giants that helped us last time, and they are no longer here."

"If the Giants are waiting on the South side, won't they be able to see us on the ledge?"

"Yes, if they think this small ledge is a path for us, but they don't know that yet, and our mud baths, our stealth, and our silence will hopefully keep them from seeing us as their focus is on the river and lower riverbank."

Larry had more to say. "You said we may have to jump in and swim. I can't swim."

"I'm sorry to hear that, Larry. I hope this isn't where you have to learn, but if it is, your people here will try to help you until we get to a place to pull you out."

"Any more questions?"

Larry was silent, so we stripped off our packs and rubbed them and each other with clay mud.

This activity was bizarre for the new immigrants. But they felt the gravity of the situation, so they pushed modesty aside.

***

Chapter 14

Giants and Screamers in the Canyon

Brief moments later, we were making good time, single file, along the ledge that rose ten or twenty feet from the water.

However, travel slowed as we moved higher, and Dan, Kia, and I watched the canyon precipice as much as we watched the trail. So far, so good. I shouldn't have thought that. Vera started to shake and moan. Kia reached her first, softly turned her head toward the cliff, and held her hand gently over Vera's mouth. Vera nodded and kept moving but moaning softly against Kia's hand.

We were nearing the nest above us, and I pointed up and raised a finger to my lips. Vera was silent and watched the inner edge of the trail as she felt her way along. It was hard to get her moving again when we came to the indent under the nest, but when we started to move, she gingerly stepped back onto the ledge.

We were now sixty feet above the river, and looking down, it felt like miles. However, the path slope was downward, so the fear subsided slightly, and the pace picked up.

A massive roar battered the cliff sides from one to the other, and the water erupted behind us with four raging Giants rushing downstream in water to their waists.

The Giants were waving and roaring at us. They had a half mile to reach us, and we were safely out of their reach, but the band of new citizens froze in fear. I pulled Maritza after me, and Kia pushed Vera and pulled Hilda into action. It wasn't hard to convince them to flee.

Larry was still frozen, though, and Dan could not get him to move. Julio increased his speed to catch up, and Jesus reached back to grab Larry, but when he tried to shake Jesus off, Larry fell, pack and all. He screamed as he fell toward the water, then was silent once he hit. Jesus looked up at me silently, dropped his pack over the edge, and jumped in.

As this happened, Hell opened above us, and two Purple Screamers leaped from their nest and attacked the flailing Giants. They didn't even know we were there, scrambling down the ledge. Their enemy was the Giants, who were out of their element in the water.

The war raged behind us as we struggled down the cliff to water level and into the protective forest to the West of the clay cliffs. We didn't even have time to notice the deserted pass camp on the other side of the river.

We kept pushing downstream as fast as we could until the sound of the rushing water drowned out the screams and roars behind us. Then, finally, we found a quiet opening with mossy-covered rocks inviting us to rest. Dan, Kia, and I pulled the shaken survivors up the bank to a peaceful and tranquil sanctuary. We all needed to rest and recuperate.

I looked at Kia as she lifted her head from between her knees. "Those raptors were nesting. I'll bet they were on eggs and thought the Giants were attacking their nest."

She nodded.

Hilda surprised us with, "Nesting eagles can rely on their crop for some time while hatching eggs, but they need to eat every few days. Sometimes, they trade off or hunt for each other in the cold when the female sits longer. They do like their privacy, though."

Hilda was going to be a force on Aard.

Her out-of-the-blue comment so soon after an overload of adrenalin said a lot about her character.

My wind had returned, so I got up to scout the shore for signs of Larry and Jesus. I didn't have to say what I was doing; Dan was also searching. We saw or heard nothing.

"Let's stay here tonight, Mac. I think we are safe now that the sun is low in the sky, but I'd rather head back for our cached weapons in the morning before we drive for the falls in the daylight if that works for you."

I laughed. I had forgotten our gear cached near the cliff. "Agreed, Dan, let's stay close to the river for any noise or signs of the guys, but let's eat and rest. It will only take the three of us an hour or so to go and get our gear."

We didn't hear anything through the evening, but as we all washed the clay from our bodies, Julio asked what we thought the chances were that Larry and Jesus survived.

Everyone listened as I said, "I'm hopeful, but nature is as blunt as it is beautiful. The canyon walls come close together and force the river into a powerful and deep channel at that point, so the water is deep enough to protect them from the bottom.

They do not have to worry about the cold water shock, but the river is mighty through the canyon and would move them quickly downstream. One way or another, I feel they are downstream from us, and I hope to find them tomorrow."

I gave them an honest appraisal and left room for hope. Julio made the sign of the cross again and knelt in the soft moss to say a silent prayer.

"We have a couple of days to get to the falls, and we will all be on the lookout for the guys. At this point, I don't think it will be a bad thing to call out occasionally, make some trail noise, but keep listening for any calling from our friends."

The new Aardian immigrants agreed, and we captured as much rest as possible for tomorrow's trek.

The morning sun rose at our back on the trail. All our trekkers were searching the shallows part of the time. Everyone was looking under cutbanks and overhanging trees and limbs. Some of us checked the upper banks on each shore for any sign of life.

We headed back downstream for Randy's Rock and the Falls. The only movement or noise besides us was the plentiful Humpbacks that kept us fed. I noticed that now that we had fresh Humpback, selective diet was coming into play. Hilda and Vera accepted only mushroom and berry jerky instead of meat.

51 Pegasi - Black Mac

We were going to have to find some plant-based protein.

***

The troop made good time as we were all anxious to catch a sound or the flash of an arm or leg around every bend. Everyone was stretching their limits to cover as much ground as they could.

We were all tired and deflated with all the hope and nervous energy poured into the day. Everyone was quiet when we ran out of light and had to camp for the night. The talk was quiet, still hopeful, but the camp seemed subdued as we made camp, ate, and settled in.

We talked about the weather. It was changing. Behind us to the East, hot air still poured through the canyon on our backs during the day. However, we felt the wind shift to our faces this evening, and a cooler breeze was coming from the West. It was not cold, but it was refreshing. We felt a cleansing in the air, and our lungs seemed to inflate better with richer oxygen.

Julio asked me what to expect in our new coastal home in halting and broken English. "What is our nuevo hogar en Libertad, Senior Mac?"

I described the village the tribe had built and the setting we built in, but I warned them again that we had yet to experience a monsoon that would be on us very soon. I described the shelter we had and the clothing we had acquired. Although everyone grew accustomed to being partly naked now, the thought of clothing took over the conversation.

I was beginning to see how much clothing meant to humans.

I began to rethink my theory that given the opportunity to drop society's illogical need to cover certain body parts, they would happily be naked on top if the environment permitted. Still, something deeper made us feel better if we covered our genitals.

I had noticed the love for the coveted kilts and robes but hadn't considered the reasons beyond the elements. The end of the monsoon season might tell me more about the human condition on Aard.

With the image of their new home, the curiosity, some trepidation for the rainy season ahead, and the deep concern for two of our own, the camp broke into light murmurs as people began to nod off and tuck into sleep.

With Kia's leadership, the ladies found comfort in a puppy pile, and I noted a bond beginning between Hilda and Maritza, but Vera was beginning to warm up to her new family as well. In addition, I could tell Kia was taking a personal interest in her health. Finally, the camp fell silent, and most found some sleep.

As the new day broke, I searched the riverbank ahead for tracks with no luck.

I had a fresh Humpback cleaned and ready for the spit over our little cooking fire. While thinking of cooking, I caught the glint of steel peeking out from under a root in the water. I had walked right by it on the way downstream, but from this angle, it caught my eye. Excited, I dropped my bow, quiver, and Humpback and jumped into the water.

Up to my waist in the river, I fished my find out from under the root. The cup was held tightly by a leg of denim jeans.

I held the pack made of a pair of pants and rope that Larry had been carrying. It took me a few minutes to tug it back against the current to break it free, but I managed to get it to the bank. 'No sign of Larry, but his pack was surprisingly complete.

By the time I returned, Kia had water boiling in an actual steel kettle we had brought back from the cache. The camp exploded around me as they saw me enter with the pack. The excitement died when Larry was not with me, but we were all still hopeful of what we would find downstream.

The rest of the day was uneventful, but the team was happy to hear we would reach our major milestone sometime the next day. Randy's Rock and the falls were near. We noticed around the camp that night that the flow of fresh air from the West was constant now.

The days were cooler, and the nights were even fresher. We even sported goosebumps in the middle of the night. The tribe began wearing some of the clothing we had used as packs during the evening.

Halfway through the next day, Dan, leading us down the Humpback trail, stopped and held up his hand. Then, as we pulled up around him, he said, "Anyone smell what I smell?"

Everyone put their noses in the air.

"Smoke?" Vera's eyes were open.

"Yes, you are right. That is wood smoke." Kia was happy.

Dan grinned. "Let's hope it's a campfire." He called out, but nothing came back from the muted forest.

The breeze changed, and we couldn't smell it now, but the tribe was excited, and the pace picked up as we hurried toward Randy's Rock.

Late in the afternoon, we were there. We had smelled the smoke for only a short time, then it was gone, but the hope was still strong. We pulled up on the rock, but sadly, no one was there.

The river at the top of the falls spread wide with myriad small streams winding around huge, volcanic boulders.

This diffraction enabled us to hop across the river from one rock to another.

Randy's Rock was a gigantic obstacle for the river, embedded deep in the river floor at the top of the falls. We were so focused on getting to the rock and finding the source of the smoke that we had not been as vigilant as we should have been.

I headed back to the trail to look for tracks. I saw nothing on the shore we had just left. Dan and Kia followed my example while the new band members stood on Randy's Rock, looking far off to the West at the horizon line between the sky and a thin strip of ocean.

***

Chapter 15

Magic Moss and Back in Freedom

"Hola amigos, ¿Qué te contuvo? ... What kept you?"

We snapped our attention to the South shore, then high on the mountainside above the falls. Jesus was waving happily, and Larry stood slightly unsteadily at his side.

"Better late than never," I called back.

I had to hurry to catch up as the immigrants all bolted for the far shore to meet our waylaid amigos. It took some time for them to get down from the hillside through the underbrush, moss, and rubble. It became evident that Larry struggled, and we soon noted that his left arm was in a sling.

Jesus called again, "Nosotros temenos que ir despacio, por favor espera... we have to go slow. Please wait"

Julio translated for the English speakers, and we waited in the moss on the South bank for the descending desperados.

Finally, when they got close enough, Dan helped them down to the river shore. So, we were all together again, a little banged up, but together.

We decided to camp right there. Jesus said they had been looking for food and found berries up the hill but had nothing else to eat over the last three days. This revelation reminded us that we hadn't eaten today.

A new priority ensured we started a fire on the embers of the one they had built and warmed up some food for all. Larry showed great pain, and his shoulder looked to be the issue. Both men had bruises and scrapes, but the shoulder was the only issue that needed attention.

The afternoon was getting late, so considering Larry's arm, we decided climbing down around the falls would take all our focus, and daylight would be most helpful. As we cleared up from the meal, we looked closer at Larry's arm. His fall had knocked it out of place to hang painfully more to the front of the joint.

"Disculpame, por favor... Excuse me, please." Without translating, Maritza gently took over. She looked the injury over carefully and softly traced the outline of Larry's shoulder with her fingers, then removed the moss from the valley floor till she found a flat stone. She left the moss intact around it and gently eased Larry to a sitting, then a laying position.

She placed his left shoulder blade over the flat rock.

Larry was gray and sweating from the pain, but aside from jealously guarding any movement or handling of his arm, he followed her physical direction. Once he was flat on his back, she straddled him in a most compromising way that took a lot of focus off his arm. Maritza watched the stress and confusion in the poor man's frightened gaze.

She cooed gently as she gently massaged his chest, ribs, and clavicle, creating a mesmerizing and hypnotic scenario.

Maritsa's unique approach had us all glued to the scene. As she was doing this, Maritsa straightened her arms slowly. It seemed she was trying to stay as far away from his body as possible. I started to see where this was going. At precisely that moment, she launched all her weight down on Larry's unsuspecting shoulder, driving it back into its socket.

Larry jumped with eyes wide and mouth gaped in a silent scream. The unsuspecting patient went instantly from fear to painless relief. Maritza winked, rolled off, and went to the fire to get a cup of tea.

None of us knew what to do until laughter broke out. The relief and release of the last few days flowed over us in peals of belly laughs, chortles, and glee. Larry looked at Julio. "Could you ask Maritza if it would be okay to hug her?"

Julio laughed. "Ju asks her. Say, Puedo abrazarte"

It took him a couple of tries, but he did get it out, and Maritza laughed and accepted.

We could all climb down the waterfall rocks tomorrow and make a beeline for the coast. Tonight, a happy, bonding tribe spent time getting to know each other better. The chatter was comforting as people who used to focus on themselves began thinking about community, friendships, family, and possibly even more.

You couldn't call it pecking order because the group concentrated on each other's strengths instead of weaknesses.

They did not focus on traits that they could use in the future to feather their own nest. I found this fascinating and was determined to see how survival bonds distinctly different people. I still worried about Laurence, though. After the hug, he slipped back into his loner style and did not speak unless spoken to. He seemed to have to force his distance.

We felt the dampness in the air more pronounced tonight; for the first time on this adventure, we saw clouds on the horizon.

Kia mentioned we were probably feeling the effects of the mist from the falls that roared over the cliff less than a hundred feet from us. She had a good point. I would expect the mist would be causing much of what we felt, but a change was coming. We must waste no time. I suggested as much to the tribe.

I vowed to pay more attention to Kia's thought leadership. She was quiet but she put a lot into the statements she made. We would all be wiser to listen to her advice.

Tomorrow, we need to clear both sets of falls. Perhaps even meet the Freedomites. We settled in for what may be the last evening on the trail, and the excitement at being this close to our goal was too much for most of the team but Jesus and Larry were first to doze off, and much later than they should, the rest of us new Aardians faded off to sleep.

***

We awoke to a marine layer of low clouds and gusts of foggy wind. The winds were warmer than they had been but steadier. Dan and Kia understood my anxious look at the horizon, as did our friends from Columbia and Ecuador. They understood Earth's Pacific weather.

This weather would be much like they had grown up with. I didn't have to work too hard to convince anyone we needed to move quickly.

The climb down the top falls was slow but uneventful, and as I passed the ledge I had found behind the falls, I glanced. But I did not point the cave out as I didn't want to distract the climbers scrambling down from rock to rock. I didn't want to slow our progress. There would be time to explore later.

By the time Larry and Julio were firmly off the falls decent, the wind was gusting and now carried some rain. I urged the tribe to gather speed now that we were on the ground as we had another set of falls to descend from, and I dreaded the thought of trying it in the dark. I also dreaded climbing down in the wind and heavy rain. The trekkers took to the challenge, but it was still late afternoon when we arrived at our last big obstacle.

The next set of falls was much smaller than the last, but it was still challenging. And now rain and wind magnified the challenge in the waning light. The cloud cover shortened our day considerably. Worried, I couldn't imagine tonight's crew camping in these elements.

Dan started over the edge first. The new folks followed him over the lip, and Kia and I followed. Kia backed down over the top rock, carefully making her way to the next ledge, and I started to do the same as I saw her reaching her destination.

An escalating hiss from the darkened undergrowth to my upper left made my head snap around. I saw nothing at first, but the hair on the back of my neck stood up. Quickly, I turned to jump down off the first boulder.

As my head spun to see where I was going, I caught a flash of neon green. Then, I felt a slash across my right shoulder.

The blow ripped my backpack off and spun me in an ungraceful arc to land backward next to Kia. The momentum caused me to tumble back off the ledge she was standing on. Then, it propelled me off again to land flat on the massive rock below. My backpack and the three transporters fared better than I did.

They hung up on a shrub that hooked the surviving pant leg and swung tenuously in the wind beside Kia. In a matter of moments, Kia and Maritza hovered over me. At the same time, Jesus pressed upward to address what had attacked us.

By the time I understood my surroundings and got my wind back, Maritza was packing my wound with moss and wrapping my shoulder in a shredded shirt from the tower cabin. Kia retrieved my pack, and Dan set himself below me with an arrow fitted in his bow and aiming above Jesus. We saw nothing else, and the scene above was quiet.

The New Aardians helped me the rest of the way down the falls, and we set a brisk pace for the highlands to the North and Freedom.

Our pace picked up as lightning started. The rocky streambed didn't seem like a good place to be. Once we got out of the river bed, I knew we were close, so I stopped momentarily in the darkness to attempt Tiffany's famous Tarzan yodel.

We could hardly see each other in the driving rain, but we jumped with joy when the yodel returned in a much more controlled version.

I called out that we were on high land but in the dark.

There were no moons, no stars, and heavy rain. This combination was probably the first time I had seen complete darkness on Aard. Moments later, approaching shouts brought a hint of light as pitch torches began to appear through the brush.

Shiv, Willow, and Tiffany led a band of happy Freedomites to our rescue. Then, another wild slash of lightning lit up the incoming rescuers, and they saw us. Within minutes, we were drying out around a communal fire. The clan had built a welcoming fire in the protective mouth of a cave. The rock face above the village provided a buffer for the driving wind.

Ann was the first to notice my bandaged arm and called Dr. Fletcher to check me out. In a few moments, he assessed Maritza's packing. The good doctor complimented her on the compressed moss that had stemmed the flow. He examined the packed wound and noted the reduced inflammation of the fresh laceration.

As he had become known, Dr. Tim explained that our local orange moss has similar properties to Liverwort on Earth. He added that it provided a medicinal compound comparable to THC but without the high.

He had made it a habit to educate the village as he administered treatments in case anything should happen to him. "Moss filters and retains water and does the same for our blood." He explained that humans had packed wounds for centuries, but during World War 1, when cotton balls were scarce, medics used moss in this manner with great success.

"It was much more absorbent than cotton and provided an effective antiseptic." He explained as he inspected the wound and replaced the packing as he found it.

"Let's change it in a couple of days or if you feel more pain, swelling, or get a fever."

"Thanks, Doctor, I'll take over now," Willow interjected and led me to our cabin.

Shiv, Tiffany, and Stud took over the immediate care and sleeping arrangements for the new immigrants and, for the first night, assigned the ladies one cabin and the men another. Of course, as soon as they found dry beds, no one minded that arraignment. There was much excitement over the new immigrants.

I expected they all had adrenalin to wear off. Understanding this, I felt the festivities could last much longer, so I was happy to be tucked away in a cozy cabin.

I was back with my Willow, and she was pleased to have me back in the fold, and we had private time to catch up.

I was content as I listened to the rattle of the pelting rain on the Westward shutters as the winds buffeted against the rock face and spun the rain in constantly changing directions.

I was happy and safe in a warm cocoon with my favorite person. I soon slept dreamlessly and genuinely rested for the first time since I came to Aard.

***

Chapter 16

Monsoons

Everything in our life was wet. With the constant driving rain, flashing lightning, and roaring thunder, no nook or cranny was safe from dampness. If not from rain, then from the mist and fog that permeated our world.

As a village, we were learning new coping methods, innovating, and expanding. We were all clothed now, dropping the freedom we had known for several months in favor of warmth and comfort. We were becoming citizens of our new world.

Innovation was vital in this time of need, but the tribe had not been idle in my absence. Stacy and Shiv had been most productive in building on what we had.

Stacy brought berry seeds to plant in rich delta loam. The tribe also planted on the plateau to our north. That highland environment featured lakes and small streams flowing from the foothills of the mountains to the East.

Before the monsoon, the new berries were all doing well.

Stacy and Shiv had found trees rich in gummy sap and had found a way to capture and contain the liquid.

The process looked much like the maple syrup collection on Earth. They had transferred the sap in smaller containers to an eight-foot hollow stump while it was in its most liquid form in the heat of the summer.

The team had protected it with a thatched roof. They bored a small hole and plugged it near the bottom, allowing for easy dipping in dried moss and frond-covered sticks to provide torches.

Ann had been hoping Penny would provide more sewing to help clothe the Aardians, but Penny had other ideas. Still, she made significant progress with the materials she had and invented something most helpful during the monsoons.

She found they had a plentiful supply of Humpback stomachs to heat water over open fires. However, they failed after several uses. The supply was handy for cooking and carrying water almost daily. Unfortunately, the stretched stomachs grew much larger with use and lost the porous properties suited to use with fire.

They were, however, excellent ponchos once the team modified them with arm slits and a collar with seams to prevent ripping. The new ponchos covered the upper torso and provided a louvered layer over the purple kilts. The Screamer feathers were also water resistant due to the waxy features of the massive feathers.

Penny had become the storekeeper and kept an excellent clothing inventory tucked into one of the rock-face caves.

Her efforts came in very handy with the introduction of the needs of the New Aardians. Stud had evolved into a fantastic scout. He and Tiffany had explored both North and South.

Among their finds were promising hills to the southeast. Another exciting find was the robust plateau to the north. The highlands sported teaming wildlife and vistas in the mountains and over the cliffs to the sea.

Of note geographically were the chimney holes found at the top of the cliffs. They suspected a series of caves below but had not had the opportunity to explore the coastline before the monsoons hit. They had also crossed the delta to see massive dunes and grasslands to the south, which went as far as they could see to the East, suggesting another ecosystem to explore.

I was excited to see the ad-hoc partnerships forming as needed and then reforming in another direction to build on another skill set. Stud and Tiffany had become explorers.

Tiffany, Shiv, and Willow became boot camp and weapons trainers. At this point, they were the best archers and armorers who understood the local resources for their weapons.

Stacy and Dr. Tim studied the local vegetation and wildlife to identify, assess, and ascertain safety for consumption and medical applications as much as possible. They had already identified several new foods and medicines that could support the tribe. In addition, we had another source of meat from a flightless bird in the delta.

This bird looked like a giant Snipe, about the size of a turkey. It sported a long needle-like beak for harvesting mollusks like clams and mussels that were larger than we were used to. This shore life had also found its way into our diet.

Stacy had found a shrub with hanging pods that supplied hard legumes the size of hazelnuts.

These legumes tasted more like peanuts but cooked up like pinto beans when soaked for a day. Dr. Tim reckoned they would be a great source of protein. These introductions inspired Penny to a new calling. Aard had forged a driven provider from a camp gossip. I wonder how many new levels she will find in her growth.

She brought a natural need for order and neatness, so she offered a hand in storing fresh foods and medicines. This skill set developed into a full-time job as she built our stores in the rock-face caves and had the answer when anyone wanted an item.

She also set up a seed bank with the seeds, nuts, and grains Stacy had gathered. Penny also started to get good with her arrows.

I couldn't wait to see how the New Aardians we brought back with us would fit in and contribute to these partnerships. The priorities for the next month would be to keep as dry as possible, stay out of the way of flooding, and education. We had much to learn about the seasons in this tropical setting and what we could prepare for and harvest at these times.

***

The next couple of weeks saw the village of Freedom settle into a society. We designated the original cabins by gender and adjusted as people gravitated toward each other in terms of their interests or attractions.

Maritza began spending more time with Ann as she studied the local fibers. She also spent time with Dr. Tim building medical resources for the Aardians.

The South American started pounding woody roots and plant stocks to learn their fiber signatures and found some with longer, hemp-like strings from the legume plants. She experimented with stripping the willow-type branches and supplied a harvest of the inner bark to Dr. Tim. He proved the pain-relieving properties of drinking tea from the dried product.

Maritsa moved in with Ann but still spent much time with the good doctor. Both were about ten years her senior, but the three often consulted over research.

Hilda began hanging out with Stacy because of her interest in the ecology around them. The two had long chats about sustainability and innovative ways of ensuring that humans positively influenced the environment they lived in.

Hilda rigged a composting toilet with a simple outhouse constructed over a steep bank that allowed the waste to mix with other compostable waste and peat from the delta. With some effort, the resulting mixture was rotated and combined in the open air to become inoffensive.

Given time to mature naturally, fertilized dirt for Stacy's planting starts became a hit. The rain helped clear the air nicely at this time of year, and after the first surge, the lightning and thunder rolled away, leaving only the pounding rain.

The Fraulein was also excited about the planting and harvesting of their efforts. Shiv was more than accommodating, with Hilda spending so much time in their cabin. Hilda found collaborating with Stacy easy, but Stacy ensured she understood that Shiv was off the market.

Hilda was also drawn to Stud, though. She was well-versed in French, and he understood German and Swiss well.

As a result, they often fell entirely off-topic, chatting, laughing, and reminiscing about Europe. They talked about similar backgrounds and places they knew. Their conversations were often hilarious international tours through at least three or four languages.

She began going on short explorations in the rain with Stud and Tiffany, whom she looked up to in more ways than one since both were tall.

At first, Jesus also related well to Tiffany and Stud but was much more in tune with Shiv. They had a language barrier to work through, but both had experienced gang life, prison, drugs, and death, and both wanted to make amends and become positive influences in their community. Both quickly became champions for Aard and the Freedomites.

Shiv was impressed with the story of Jesus diving into certain death to attempt to save Larry. He also enjoyed having a "brother" he could collaborate with. Shiv paid particular interest in teaching him archery, using the Atlatl, an old Earth weapon used by indigenous peoples, and competency with a spear.

They were practically the same age and height, but Shiv had put on more muscle over the years. Jesus made it clear he wanted to bulk up, and Shiv was happy to have a workout buddy. Kia had taken up a hut when she arrived at Freedom, but Sirih approached her to see if she could join the discussions.

She asked to be included in the training for the transporters. Sirih explained her technical background to Kia on the trek to freedom. Excited, Kia was more than happy with someone technical to talk with. Their conversation went well enough that Kia invited Sirih to move in.

Kia's hut became the venue for the discussions over the transporters, and a small table and four stools took one end of the cabin, with the two transporters finding a home on a shelf on the end wall.

The documentation took center stage on the table, and Kia, Dan, Sirih, and I began working out the antenna requirements for our first installation. I did notice, however, that when she was relaxing, she often sought out Vera for quiet chats. I expected she was trying to include and engage the shy Canadian.

Lawrence was trying. 'Larry' seemingly had an epiphany about the importance of community in this world. However, he struggled to understand the thoughtless sacrifice of a Hispanic man who was an ex-gang member and had willingly risked his life to save him.

Larry's life... which he had apparently dedicated to vilifying everyone who came from south of the United States border, was in a twilight zone in his head, and he opted to stay in the cabin with the Hispanic men. It seemed he had lost all anchors to his thought process and back story.

If anyone would push the button to return to his old life, Larry may be the one. Larry seemed to be at a crossroads where the rose-colored glasses were removed.

Julio had no passionate drive to change or build a world but was more than happy to help where he could and had a world of knowledge to share if requested. He saw Larry as his first opportunity to help. I think Julio was taking the role of a missionary. He naturally became an ear to listen to and a wise voice for advice.

Vera saw no reason to move. She still had Hilda, who was near her age and could speak English. The Canadian was slow to come out of her shell but was at least curious now.

Hilda was good company, and now that Maritza had moved out, she felt she had a chance to bond. People had moved on from her all her life, and she was sure it would happen again. I was happy to see Kia taking an interest in diversifying her experience.

I suspected Hilda would be focusing more on Stud soon. Hilda was happy for the company, too. Still, she had no intention of remaining single long and was not interested in a sexual relationship with Vera or any woman. Instead, she had her goals and was refining them.These pairings saw two each in the original his and hers huts, and that would probably be a good mix through Monsoon season, at least.

***

Chapter 17

Village Retrospective

The rains were easing now after twenty-seven days. There were cloudy days, but today, the sun broke through.

The tribe was exploring farther, but the delta was a massive, angry river that pushed silty, brown water and broken trees far out to sea over the bitter waters.

My shoulder healed, and the time had come to set up our local transporter landing. I called the tribe for an afternoon gathering on our first sunny, warm day at the community fire. Everyone was happy to come together in our first full tribe meeting since introducing the New Aardians.

Once everyone had a cup of tea, I complimented the village for powering through our first monsoon season. "You are all looking healthy and, for the most part, happy, tribe. This meeting is our first all-hands-on-deck gathering. We need to do this regularly to keep communication and inclusion strong. I'm most interested in your thoughts on our progress so far."

I noted that I had full attention. It seemed the tribe was ready.

"Knowing how some of us tend to speak up more than others, I'd like to call a name and drag out a comment or two to make sure everyone speaks, then have open social time for everyone to talk to everyone as they wish. Vera, since you are beside me, I'd like to start with you."

I hoped her fragile confidence could handle being asked first, versus the anxiety build-up as she waited for her turn. As I expected, this was hard for Vera to answer. Finally, she uttered, "Hi, I'm Vera, and I'm good." She looked at Hilda, next to her, to defer all eyes on her. However, I was ready for her response and asked her an open-ended question. "You're looking and sounding much stronger, Vera. But I have a question for you. Who has been the biggest help in getting you to this point?"

She wasn't expecting that challenge but momentarily looked me in the eye. "You've been my biggest help, Mac. You got me here and brought me into this family.' She then turned toward Hilda. "But Hilda has been my biggest mentor because she has helped me adjust every day.

I could not do this without her constantly answering my questions, teaching me how to live here, and holding me when I cry." She looked down, and Hilda reached out to hold her while Vera's shoulders shook in silent sobs.

I noticed that Kia took particular interest in Vera's reaction and stood looking for a moment like she wanted to go to her but changed her mind when she saw her tuck into Hilda.

"Vera, I know how hard all of this has been for you, but I see you living, growing, and learning, and I thank Hilda for her dedication to your happiness and health. I expect you will notice others reaching out if you can be open to that."

At this comment, she looked across at Kia and smiled weakly. It was time to take the spotlight off her, so I went to Hilda next.

"Hilda, thank you for stepping up for Vera and the tribe. What is the biggest surprise you have seen since being on this planet?"

Hilda looked up, and her answer was simple. "Me."

I smiled. "That's deep, but could you expand on that, please?"

She looked at Vera's head tucked into her shoulder and said, "I was a spoiled little schoolgirl on Earth. From the moment I came here, people needed me. So, I needed to be much more than I thought I was. For the first time, I saw purpose and stepped up to it. From when I strapped a pack on in the berry bush to working through life in a downpour, I recognized my potential for the first time. "

She looked around at the tribe before continuing. "It's good to know I'm a badass. Hanging out with Stacy has made me see I am much stronger in a team than by myself, and Stud has been showing me all the ways I can grow as we discover new corners of this world together."

She smiled up at Jean, who was smiling back at her. I noticed he wasn't the only one watching intently. Everyone was. It became apparent how much this community needed this chat, and I could see everyone was deep in thought. Stud was next.

"Jean, you have been through a lot with Willow, Shiv, and I, then with Tiffany and the tribe, blending in with us.

You have proven to be a self-starter of the first magnitude, and Freedomites owe you a lot. What is the most important thing you have found about this world that we all need to know?"

The man known as Stud was silent for a moment, then, in his engaging accent, he said, "This world, she is magnifique. She is both dangereux et beau... beautiful. She is both demanding mistress et Mere... Mother. She feed us, and if we do not pay attention, she feed us to da rest. Aard demand respect, et she respond avec amour."

Everyone knew what he meant by respect. Aard had a way of teaching that quickly.

Next to Stud was Stacy, leaning against Shiv's chest with his arm draped over her shoulder. I smiled at that image.

"Stacy, what has the monsoon taught you?"

She was quick to respond. "Don't plant anything in the rich dirt of the delta if you want to keep it."

A chuckle went up around the camp as she explained. "All the berry plants coming up so strong in that rich soil are sprouting on another continent now." The chuckles grew louder as her notorious humor delivered another bump in her legacy.

Shiv broke in, "We need to remember that, tribe. That river doesn't give a shit what is in its way, and when the water goes through, nothing in that channel will be the same."

I smiled. "OK, Shiv, your turn. What advice do you have for the tribe?"

Everyone laughed.

"Oops, sorry." Shiv's face went bright red, but he continued. "We need to be damn sure we know the lay of the land when we build anything. We did a pretty good job of scouting out the site for this camp, but it may not be the safest either."

He pointed toward the mouth of the roaring river, whose anger we could hear in the background. We could see the roiling, brown water surging past the camp from our vantage point. He made a great point. "Unfortunately, we may be too close."

The top of the river was only six or eight feet below the low spots in our village.

"Well put, Shiv. We may need to re-evaluate."

Tiffany was next to Shiv.

"Tiffany, what should our priority be at this point?"

She took a moment to think this through before responding.

"We need people who want to be here. We need people who want a second chance and want to contribute to who we become. As we have all seen, it won't be easy, but our lives mean so much more here. Some arrived because someone decided we were no longer useful on Earth. Most of us found our calling here.

We need to take the decision away from whoever is making it back on Earth and enable folks who have hit the end of their rope to find a new rope here."

Tiffany made a considerable impression on the tribe. I was probably the most affected by her statements.

I had been thinking along those lines, but the more I tried my theories, the more I learned what I needed to know. I couldn't help but wonder if it was a specific person or culture she envisioned that we needed. I decided she may be hoping for a one-on-one conversation, but I was wary of my assumptions.

***

Dan had been in conversation with Tiffany and Shiv before this impromptu roundtable, so I called on him next. I decided to take him out of his comfort zone.

"Dan, what amenities are you missing on Aard? What would be your priority to help in our day-to-day lives?"

He grinned, "You mean other than phones, right?"

That got a laugh.

"Personal hygiene, Mac. I bet that wasn't what you expected. But honestly, our ancient ancestors took care of their teeth better than much of our modern history. We started on this planet eating raw meat, as the Giants do, but we all have shown we prefer to cook our meals.

This fact means we need to invent or import things like toothpaste. Eventually, we acclimate to our environment. We accept the smell of sweat, but some ladies tell me they have been missing some personal hygiene products."

Everyone was surprised by his choice of topic, but the Freedomites rumbled into a full camp discussion on the subject. I let it continue because it hit a nerve and felt like a learning opportunity. I had to smile when the din died, and several sets of eyes looked to see what I thought of the runaway train.

Finally, when it was apparent that I was enjoying the open conversation, a self-conscious Dan said, "Who's next?" He looked directly at Ann, who had been ramping up on his topic.

"I'm one of the ladies who has been talking to Dan. He is pretty intuitive, and somehow, he manages to smell good all the time." Ann's humor broke the tension, but Dan had made a considerable impact.

Ann continued. "Hand tools, Mac. I could use steel needles, tacks, and tack hammers. Any hammers, for that matter. Nails, screws, how about a yarn shop, cotton, and a whole hardware store?" This string got her more laughter, but she brought up a topic everyone related to. "We simply took for granted all those luxuries of centuries of innovation on Earth, which became apparent without them." Ann got a robust ovation.

Maritza was a constant with Ann now, so I called the resident nurse to the floor.

"Maritza, how is the cross-training between Spanish and English speakers going?"

Her ready smile wasengaged. Maritza's acquisition into the village got her quick acceptance as she stepped up to make a difference. This gained speed as Ann and Dr. Tim encouraged her to engage. She was probably the most proactive of the New Aardians to blend in and often led.

"Señor Mac, I understand very well now. Ann knows Spanish too, and she teach muy bien. I teach, too. Anyone, verdad? ... Doctor Tim?"

Dr. Tim took that as his segway. "...Tienes razon, Maritza."

His slow, Southern drawl and a brief search for the right words stretched his intro, but he followed up with, "Mac, I think, like Tiffany, we need to grow our village. But I'd like to take her lead in a little deeper.

We need skilled immigrants to fill holes in our knowledge and skill sets. We will constantly teach each other, but we need more medical backgrounds and perhaps tradespeople who know more about architecture and infrastructure.

With our transporters, I doubt we will ever need mass transportation like we were used to on Earth, but we need skills and knowledge beneficial to the village life we are leading."

Wow, Dr. Tim made some significant points. I saw the light of realization come on around the fire as brightly as he lit the candles in my mind.

He interrupted my thoughts. "Mac, could I have one more moment with the village, please?"

"Certainly, please continue."

"Folks, I want to tell you what I have found about the properties of the blue mushrooms we have been enjoying on this planet. I suspect compounds in this mushroom, much like the Reishi mushroom on Earth, which acts as a potent immunomodulator. It appears to build up our immune systems and helps with sleep, lung, heart, and respiratory health.

But even more, it seems to fight off ailments that humans have dealt with for centuries without cures or reasonable treatments. I think we can beat cancer and many other illnesses that attack us similarly."

"They are, however, potent birth control. So, to create the first native human Aardians, you must go off the blue mushrooms through fertilization and gestation. Mac, I would like tools from Earth to help with my research if possible."

There was a muffled response from around the fire.

"Dr, that is incredible. I have no idea how you figured that out, but I see the need to get you more tools. I can tell the crowd will want to talk with you about the possibilities. Wow!"

There was a chuckle from the crowd, and all eyes returned to me.

I turned to Jesus, who was standing with Julio.

"Jesus, what do you think of our weapons?"

He turned to Julio and asked, "Que son weapons?"

Julio answered, "Armas."

"Oh, dierto, armas."

We understood without translation.

Jesus looked at Shiv first, then at me, "Si.., uh, yes, we have good... but we need puntas de metal... uh metal...tips." We need... steel cuchillas...blades... knives."

He looked back at Shiv, Tiffany, and Stud in turn. "Nosotros necesitamous una major defensa. We need defense. Better."

Jesus received a solid round of nods around the camp, including from me.

I looked at the seated Laurence between him and Julio.

"Larry, what do you think?" I left the topic wide open.

"I want to go home."

"I get that, Larry. I'll get you on the first bus."

"It's Laurence."

"Got that, Laurence. Of course. I should have your ticket within a couple of weeks."

He nodded and filled his tin teacup from the fire.

***

Chapter 18

Preparing to Off-World a Threat -
Goodbye Larry

I made a marked point with my primer for Julio. "Julio, how can we best design rules of law and politics in this new society?"

Laurence's eyes opened wide, but I had directed the question to the judge.

Julio did not have to think long. "Menos es mas, ... *less is more.*"

"I agree, Julio. Let's avoid making rules until we must, only when the people have discussed and decided."

Kia, Sirih, and Dan had moved through the discussion to talk to Willow at my right.

"Kia, you, Dan, and Sirih have been busy over the last week or so studying the documentation for the transporter antennas. Do you have any epiphanies to share with the tribe?"

"I do. We have discovered in the bad guy's notes we found in the cabin that certain trees have highly conductive heartwood. You can think of it as carrying a lightning rod to protect against lightning. Overuse is what happened to the large dead tree near the tower.

It was their first proof of concept when trying to move away from the massive tower.

However, it was not the best example of an antenna tree. The tree they found best was an Aceraceae-type tree, similar to palm trees on Earth, with no branches until the top.

Although a dead tree works well, a live one works even better, as the green heartwood appears more conducive.

Keep in mind that this is only on intragalactic or Intersolar-system transportation. Transporting around, locally on Aard or Earth, doesn't require an antenna. On Earth, the grounding rod of a building will work just fine."

"Amazing! Sirih, anything to add?"

"Yes. We know where all their landing antennae are, or at least a map of them. They are hundreds and even thousands of miles apart. Seven working systems are still operating.

Three are in the other hemisphere, and one is a few hundred miles North of here. There is one station due East, about a thousand miles on our legs; one is Southeast, on the equator, about eight hundred miles away.

The last one is on an island due West of here, probably no more than a hundred miles from your camp on the coast. I have star maps for each location.

The island, they call Island of the Bleeding Flower, is the site of their diamond mine. It is critical to their transporters and of course, the wealth of the humans who have contracted with the native giants. We must remove their access.

Sirih just made the island important to our quest.

Maybe, most importantly, the Giants don't have the technology. It is human-built. But, on the other hand, it is human, so if we can disrupt the human supply chain, the Giants must eat purple chicken. We have our work cut out for us."

I was thrilled that this challenge had pulled Sirih from her shell.

"Sirih, you have exceeded our wildest dreams in how quickly you have taken to the technology team and learned so much about this science. We are so lucky to have you."

I wanted to change the subject for now, as I had suspicions about Larry's future ambitions. I didn't like to discuss this technology too much around him. I was nervous we may have said too much, so I turned to Willow and deflected the topic.

I smiled at the winsome woman at my side. "Willow, In the Aardian history books, how would you like your legacy to read to our ancestors?"

She chuckled.

"Hmm," The tribe went silent momentarily as she gathered her thoughts. Then, she looked slowly around the fire at the expectant faces. "I'd like people to know that I made a positive difference. A positive difference for the people I have met here. The people back on Earth may never know this world and society existed and both planets' ecosystems. They may never know, but Aard affects them directly.

We have a second chance as a species, and I want to help make that difference healthy, happy, and humble."

I smiled into her eyes and said, "You've already aced that goal, Willow. You are the template we all need right now."

I looked back at the little village of Freedomites and waved my arm around the camp.

"Folks, what an amazing village this has already become. I suggest we spend some great quality time around the fire tonight.

Continue getting to know our neighbors, and continue asking questions until we fit like family. We all need to know what we all know, you know?"

Even the moons showed through the clouds for some time to see what the laughter was about. The relief from watching the last of the monsoon move on was palpable. It was time to celebrate, plan, and prepare for our next steps.

After an hour or two, people drifted off to their huts. When Willow and I turned in, Shiv and Jesus were drawing maps in the dirt with a stick. On the other side of the fire, Dan, Kia, and Sirih were in an animated conversation over the core of a small broken tree trunk, and Stud watched as Hilda was braiding Vera's hair while they all watched and listened in on the transporter team.

***

The weather turned hot quickly, and the river to our South gave back the delta. However, the delta was now vastly different. Most of it was barren rock and sandbars. The soaking tubs had been swept clean but for soft sand bottoms in most of them, and a small, sandy island had formed a hundred yards from the shore.

The transporter team was excited.

They found a tree that they felt was an ideal antenna about a day and a half North of our camp. We planned a trip to try it out in a couple of days. I also had a long chat with Lawrence.

He came to me the day after the village meeting to discuss his trip back to Earth. He caught up to me while Stacy showed me where her berry starts in the delta had been wiped out but assured me her gardens in other spots had survived the rains and were now thriving in the heat.

Lawrence asked me to walk with him, to which I happily obliged. I wanted to get a better read on his disposition and goals. When we were alone on the shoreline, he opened up.

"Mac, I don't want you to think I'm ungrateful for saving me from the Giants and getting me out of harm's way... although there were a few minutes where I didn't think you'd succeed."

"I fully understand, Lawrence. I also understand that this life is not for everybody. Most folks here had no reason to return, but you had a career to build."

He nodded. "Thanks for understanding. It's not that I don't see the possibilities here, but I have worked hard for some of the better things in life. At home, I have a wonderful house in Maryland, even though my ex-wife got the best one. I have a couple of brand-new cars and a real chance at a U.S. Senate position in the next election. At least, I think I do. I have a close set of friends that look out for each other."

"I understand, Laurence, but I have to ask. You know the criteria that got most of the folks you have met on Aard into giant cages.

Do you know why someone like you, with so much going for them, would be in this particular supply chain?"

"I didn't know initially, but I have had time to think about it. Three possibilities come to mind, two of them being ex-wives. The third is probably the most likely. I am a strong conservative, and the Liberals hate me. I think they have some devious connections that the American Public needs to know about, and I'm almost positive they know somebody who could and would do this."

"I see, so your best theory is political."

He didn't have a response, so I offered, "However, I would suggest you keep your mind open when you return.

The group that seems responsible is global and biased against those struggling in society. From what I have learned from you, your profile doesn't seem to fit."

He thought for a moment, then replied. "I could be relatively safe from human enemies if I stayed here, but I want my life back. I want to find out who did this to me. So, I have to go back."

"Okay, the transporter team and I are headed to a site North of here in the morning to see if we can set up a transporter. Then we will test it, and if it works, I'll come to get you. In the meantime, you have adapted well to the clothes and shoes we borrowed from the tower cabin. I think the first transport goes to Seattle. Do you have anyone or any resources in Seattle that can get you back to the East Coast?"

"Yes, I have a sister in Kirkland, just across the lake from Seattle. She can get me back home."

"Okay, get some rest, and hopefully, we will have you on your way in a couple of days."

He smiled, shook my hand, and left to prepare. I headed back to the camp to find the transporter team. I found them huddled over our precious store of transportation documentation in the ladies' hut.

"Hi, team. Are we ready for the morning?"

"We're ready right now, Mac. All we need are the coordinates you want us to use." I gave them the coordinates for the King County Metro Parking Garage, directly behind the Greyhound bus station at 503, South Royal Brougham Way in Seattle.

Once he reached his sister, Laurence could get transportation from there in several forms. I suggested we store the documents in a new location tonight. The team found an exceptionally safe place and a spot Laurence would not find, should he be looking for them.

I listened to my inner voice. *The bad feeling about Laurence was getting stronger. He'd seen enough diamonds in the beach sand to buy several more houses and cars.*

He heard Sirih talk about the diamond mine on the island of the Bleeding flower.

He also saw what we used for fuel in the transporters. He didn't hear the details, but he is smart.

Dan suggested Shiv or Stud may be a safe but unexpected spot for tonight. We all agreed, so Dan folded the papers into a purple kilt and headed for Shiv and Tracy's hut.

He left the folders under Sirih's mattress fronds with a bit of frond edge inside the top folder.

Near the end of the day, the team lounged around the fire. They left the hut unoccupied, and when we all turned in, we'd asked Sirih to check for the placement of the frond edge. We planned to compare notes on the trail tomorrow. Expectedly, no one saw Laurence that afternoon, and the hut was out of sight from the community fire.

Sunrise found the transporter team and me almost halfway to the new landing site. Willow joined us and brought Stud, who had first located the place. Stud brought Jesus, who was happy to see more territory. Shiv stayed back to watch the camp and one unhappy camper.

Sirih reported that there were signs of a search in her hut, and though the folders were very close to the same positions, the piece of frond was missing. A little more searching found it on the floor, slightly under her bed.

I explained my concerns to the team on the path North. I was worried we may not see the last of Mr. Hempler with this transport.

We all agreed he may have seen an opportunity. I let them in on my thoughts behind turning him loose in a public place on the West Coast when his primary resources were on the East Coast.

I didn't want him to find his way back to a transporter button to Aard, but I felt he may have learned enough to find one or possibly to find people who knew what he was talking about back on Earth.

The trip to the specific amtenna tree on the plateau was smooth, and we set up camp on a slight knoll beside a beautiful reflective pond with a silver shoreline.

Across the pond, Dan pointed at a small grassy hill with a palm tree near the top.

***

The landing pole was perfect. With a small tool kit found at the cabin tower, we connected it easily. Dan pulled out a chisel, a hand brace, and an auger bit. With the help of a home-made wooden mallet, he neatly placed the button in the pole at about the 5' mark. He then set the configuration machinery in the base of the antenna in the back.

He configured the electronic hardware for a 4:00 AM PST Earth Time landing. Then, he connected it to a cylindrical diamond core for fuel and finally attached the ground to the hardware.

I applied the configuration to the box I carried in my paperboy sack, for a way back home. Now, I had the coordinates if Dad and Tony had set up, but if not, I had my portable transporter to get me home.

The landing pole was ready for its first outbound traffic within an hour. Since I had the most experience traveling back and forth, I stepped up for the first trip. I changed into a rough pair of jeans, sandals, and a shirt, ready to push the little stainless-steel button.

"Keep the home fires burning, folks. Here is the scenario. I will walk a couple blocks South in the SoDo district, where my father has an old packing house.

As you know, he and my brother are also setting up landings, and I will get their update on an official Seattle landing."I paused for questions, but there were none.

"But if they have yet to set them, I will use the rig I'm carrying to build a return button site. If I'm not back by tonight, please head South to get Laurence.

He will blow a gasket if we don't get him back on concrete." I kissed Willow, stepped to the pole, and pushed the button.

Planning for an early morning at the bus barn tunnel was a good idea because the few early bus drivers and homeless wanderers didn't look twice when I stepped out of the shadows.

I hiked East to 6th and headed South.

In less than ten minutes, I had found my father's old packing house, and the door key code was as he promised. I tapped in the numbers, stepped in, and locked the door behind me. Up a flight of stairs, I found the office he had designated and the cupboard with a cell phone plugged in. The phone lit up to use as promised, and the address book had two entries. My father and brother. I called my father.

There was no answer, but I left a voicemail with an update. I called the next number, and my brother answered on the second ring.

"Tommy!" The delight in his voice was welcome and uplifting.

"Tony, it's awesome to connect. I'm at the packing house. Where are you?"

"Your timing is awesome. I'm just outside. Perfect. I have some equipment I need a hand with. Let me in, will ya?"

I hurried down the stairs and unlatched the front door with the phone still talking in my hand. Upon opening the door, I saw an old Chevy pickup backed up to a loading bay to my left. Tony saw me and barked at me on the cell phone. "Hey, run over to the bay door and push the door button, please."

I closed the connection on the device and trotted over to the bay door he was backed against and pushed the button, and the door motor hummed behind the noise of the hardware rising. Tony was waiting with a hand cart stacked with small wooden boxes.

"I recognize those." I smiled at my brother while reaching for a hug. "You've been busy."

He laughed as he wheeled the boxes into the facility and pushed the door button to close. "We made a quick visit to the transporter guy's lab a couple of days ago. Dad is installing one in an ice cave on Aard at this moment. We've got a sweet little vacation cabin set up in the Artic region of our awesome new planet and want an official bus stop."

As the door latched against the floor, Tony parked his electronics and waved me to follow. "Cm'ere," and we trotted up the stairs I had just come down. He took me to an abandoned food processing oven beside a large dumbwaiter elevator and an electrical closet behind the open room. There was a simple button on the wall in the closet.

He brought me out, again, into the spacious oven room and showed me a small cupboard with an open box holding a chess board and game pieces.

He lifted the game, and under the box was a hidden floor that led to a small compartment and transporter configuration box.

"Set it where you want it on your landing, and your bus stop is built."

I noticed he had connected the transporter to a solid steel bar that rose through the ceiling.

"Let me take a moment." I leaned over the box to set the coordinates for our new landing pole on Aard. I adjusted the scope to include only the biological payload, which was the default. While I configured the transporter, Tony set up the chess board, and we sat in the natural sunlight streaming in the high windows.

We launched a friendly game as we caught up and compared notes. It turns out Tony and Dad had made a couple of trips to the transporter lab.

They had grabbed several more transporters and, possibly more importantly, a horde of electronic parts for the machines that allowed for repairs and reverse engineering necessary to grow our knowledge of the technology and the ability to expand and improve on it in the future.

"We have learned how to ship freight, Tommy. We built a hardware store at the Fantail Glacier."

"That's great timing, brother. I've got a shopping list."

He laughed. "Well, I'm going to teach you how to fish rather than give you a fish." After the game I handily won, he led me downstairs and unlocked a windowless office.

He opened a locked cabinet and produced a folder full of paper.

"Brother, you can study this here; we have a few copies of this folder, or you can take it back to Aard to share with your team. This data will show you how to calibrate for freight. In the meantime, you may want to drop by the Glacier with your shopping list, but you can do much better right from the packing house. We can start your collection if you like, but I want to suggest a rule for your shopping list."

"I'm all ears."

"No plastic. You can configure it in the calibrations."

"Wow, thanks. You have been busy. That can be a golden rule on freight to Aard." I'll recalibrate before I go home so I can pack the folder. We have some studying to do, to catch up."

"Well, Tommy, I need to store these boxes, do a few chores, and get back to the Glacier. Pops is going to be needing my company soon.

If you ever need the key to the pickup, it's in the locked room desk drawer, and a spare key is on the high ledge over the fireplace oven."

"Got it, Bro! Give him my love. I've got to get back to get one of our crew transported back to Earth. I will drop him at the bus station up the street, but he has family that he feels will pick him up and get him back to the East Coast.

I'm a little worried about him because I think he may be planning to get rich off of transporting technology, and I'm afraid he will look up the bad guys. He may be a problem for us in the future.

Keep an eye and ear out for a guy called Laurence Hempler."

"That could be an issue, Tommy. I'll keep my eye out.

When do you think he'll be in the neighborhood?"

"I'm going to see if the team has him ready when I get back, but I will set the transport to drop him near the bus barn about noon tomorrow. If you happen to be in the neighborhood, he will be the poorly dressed politician, looking for a comb and a suit."

He laughed, "If I'm nearby, I'll try to help him along."

"Stay safe, Bro."

"You too." He said as he left in the pickup for his next chore, I locked the doors behind him, reset the configuration to include my paperwork, and pushed the button in the closet.

A crowd greeted me at the landing. Laurence Hempler was front and center. He had a beard now, where he had been clean-shaven before visiting Aard. He looked a little unkempt. His clothes didn't fit as well as they could; he wore no socks, and the monsoon season had washed away his Aardian tan.

Ironically, he would not be out of place on the streets of Seattle.

I handed my folder to Kia and asked Laurence if he was ready.

"I'm forever grateful for the effort you have put in to get me back to Earth." Laurence looked like he meant it. His notice-able relief made him credible.

"Good luck, Laurence. I have no doubt you will return to your home and life, but I want to remind you again that you got here because of someone's choice, so please be wary of your surroundings and the people you deal with."

He nodded his head. "Trust me, Mac. I have laid awake nights since I have been here, thinking those thoughts. I will be careful."

I pointed at the button on the pole. "Laurence, I tried it out. You will land disoriented in a crowd, but most people around you will have seen stranger things. It won't take you but a few moments to get your bearings, and the folks at the Greyhound station will probably help you make a call if you let them know your sister is in Kirkland."

"Thank you, Mac, and call me Larry. I have a plan and can get to my sister." He looked around the Freedomites, "Thank you all. Thank you, especially Jesus. You saved my life when you could have stayed safe yourself. Thank you, Maritza, for the best medical treatment I have ever experienced. I won't forget you all and hope you all stay happy and healthy."

He pushed the button and was gone. I thought back to the medical assistance he received from Maritsa.

Sometimes, an event like that could change a man. Larry seemed to be on a mission to get back. *I sure hope I never see you again, Larry.*

I looked around the team, "Transport team, please get to know the section on transporting freight. Note the statement about plastics. We need to go shopping. I had a great conversation with my brother, who has established a base in the Northern pole region of this planet.

He has had the time needed to study this technology. He has also set the transporter lab folks back substantially. Unfortunately, they will be madder at us than ever. I'm sure they think we are their only headache."

I stepped over to the pole. "Team, I need to go back for a few minutes longer, but I'll be right back."

Before anyone could object, I was peering out from behind a bus in time to see a disheveled lawyer heading up the eastern sidewalk on Fourth Avenue. As he was about to stride out of sight, I noticed an older, blue Chevy pickup turn a left blinker on and wait for traffic to let it in.

I sat down on a park bench in a mini park to watch the exit and observed a homeless guy on the other end of the bench. He was opening a can of spinach that sported a pull-tab opener and shook a mouthful of the contents into his mouth. Looking sideways over his rice sack suitcase to assess the man on the other end of his seat, he hesitated. Slowly, he extended the can toward me in an offer to share his meager meal.

It hit me. I realized my full beard and mismatched clothes made him assume I lived on these streets, too. Something made me feel I needed to accept his offer, so I slurred my words in a soft thank you and took a mouthful of his spinach. It wasn't half bad.

"Hi, Popeye, thank you for th' muscle mush. That hits th' spot. They call me Black Mac."

"Uhh... Paul's the name, but Popeye works. So why do they call you Black Mac? You got a camp?"

"Not roun' here, brother.

There's a guy over on North Third called Red Mac." I drew my statement out.

He nodded. "Ya, me neither. I'm alone. Going to try to find cover for the night. See ya around, Black Mac."

"Will do, Popeye. Gon' find me a lil' anti-freeze. See ya."

He headed off toward First Avenue, and I headed for the packing house. From the locked office, I found a stack of notebooks with cellophane open and a few notebooks missing. I found a box of pencils and some power bars in the desk drawer, so I grabbed a power bar and a handful of writing sticks to complement the pair of notebooks I borrowed. I adjusted the calibration and pushed the button.

A few moments later, I returned to the landing with my stationery.

***

Chapter 19

The Blow Hole and a Shopping List

"Folks, I feel like I should have jet lag, but does anyone object to getting back to Freedom? We have a shopping list to build."

The reaction was all thumbs up, and we headed South. We were well into the last phase of the day, so we camped upon the crest of a line of cliffs overlooking a small pond. As our evening meal was warming over a fire, Stud called us over to the Western side of the trail. It was now too dark to explore, but he had us be as still and quiet as possible.

"Elle respire... she breathes." He pointed Westward and held his hand behind his ear.

We all followed suit and heard what he was talking about, one by one. Finally, we agreed. It sounded like Aard was breathing. The breathing was very measured but had a deep, hollow sound that suggested it came from something far more significant than an animal.

"We had better not go looking for the owner of those lungs in the dark," Shiv broke the pensive mood and made us chuckle.

"Agreed. Let's get some rest and reset for the morning.

I hope it's a benevolent breath, but we can take turns standing watch through the night to be ready if it's not." No one argued, and we ate and revisited our day around a small fire, then got what sleep we could in turns.

Jesus woke me with a gentle tap on my shoulder as the light broke and pointed toward the trail. Stud and Shiv were standing expectantly and waved me over. They were trying to be quiet to let those sleeping sleep. But as I looked around, everyone was awake and focused on the team on the trail.

We all followed the scouts to a hole in the ground. It wasn't much bigger than a Humpback, but it was breathing. We watched as the grass around the edge flowed inward and outward on inhale and exhale like an old man's mustache as he snored.

We investigated the hole for a few moments but decided it would take a much deeper exploration when we had the time to spend on the discovery it warranted.

We resumed our trek to camp and shared our adventure stories with the rest of the Aardians by nightfall. Everyone wanted to know about Larry.

I found that interesting because I was sure he wasn't thinking about them. At least individually. I took the thought as a sign that the right people were building this village.

Although the breathing hole in the ground garnered much attention, it fell quickly on the priority list as there was so much to do.

The river was receding, day by day, and the scouts were anxious to see what changes we would be dealing with. The village looked forward to using the bathing tubs on the bitter water's hot springs shore.

The Freedomites were also busy with the notebooks I produced to build the list of essentials they felt we should import. I was fascinated to see the items each villager deemed most missed and desired.

For example, although personal hygiene items were high on the list, no one asked for soaps, perfumes, or makeup. On the other hand, tools from sewing needles to spades were popular. Blades of many kinds, ropes, cords, and strings rose high on the list.

No one felt the need for weapons beyond arrows and spears, although they discussed arms in detail. I thought tarps and waterproof clothing might make a list and was ready to reinforce the rule about plastic.

However, once Ann mentioned the purple screamer hides, the canvas remained on the list. Hide, meat, sinew, feathers, and bone from flying raptors meant we must count more on our local supplies and expand our hunting skills to Purple Screamers.

The only related items that made the list were cotton or wool-type blankets. Those, like clothing, were listed as temporary while the Aardians invented and produced their own. The citizens were beginning to see the difference in what they thought was significant compared to what they had valued on Earth.

This exercise became surprisingly introspective for everyone as they realized how much their values, needs, and personalities had changed through this adventure. The epiphany became a popular topic of conversation around the fire.

An awakening grew as they all compared notes and learned from and about each other. It amazed me to see the beginning of a unique society built from the collaboration between people from vastly different backgrounds, cultures, and upbringings.

As this shopping list grew, the teleporter team was busy working out the freight settings for the transporters. The calibrations added a new layer of complexity to the calculations due to different elements in the same session.

They were happy with what they were learning. Dan, Kia, and Sirih found the science fascinating. Willow, Tiffany, and Shiv were now busy designing boot camp training for new immigrants.

There was a lot to learn when immigrating to a new world. Beginning with survival and the importance of a tight bond with your tribe, the impact of early lessons was critical. These lessons naturally expanded to care for the planet from lessons learned on Earth.

The village already boasted some great archers, with a few more showing promise. Surprisingly, there was rapid progress from Vera.

She proved to have a natural ability, and her passion for the skills associated with archery was an inspiration for the others around her. Best of all, she found purpose.

51 Pegasi - Black Mac

My mind was in Seattle. First, I needed to check in with my brother. Then I must talk to a homeless man about a button.

It was time for a deep conversation with a man who would share his spinach with a stranger on a park bench. If a human in that situation could think about someone else's needs, they would make a good citizen if offered a second chance. I had to try my theory with some empirical testing.

***

When the day was winding down, and Willow and I were returning to our hut, I brought up my plans with the Free-domites, which had become my universe's center.

"I see a pattern here, Mac. I see I'm going to be a grass widow a lot. Either that, or I need to trek with you to get one-on-one time."

I looked at the concern in her eyes and answered first with my arms. "Yes, Sweet Lady, I've been thinking the same thing. Let's discuss this because I need your thoughts on our future together, with the operative word being together."

Her eyes were moist as she looked up at me and said, "I don't know yet what I want this to become, but one thing I am sure of is I want to spend as much time as possible within your reach. I want to spend the rest of my life with you. This place is as dangerous as it is beautiful, and we never know what each day will bring or which day will be our last."

She was saying what I thought every day. "Sharon, when we broke out of the cage and escaped to the coast, the vision in my mind was you and I. We would live quietly.

We would know comfort and safety for the rest of our lives. Now, living through what we have, learning and understanding the bigger picture, we know the horrible reality of the Giant's supply chain of humans. We will be fighting for more than just us for a long time."

She looked down at her feet. "I know. I'm scared more of losing you than anything now that I have found you. I'm scared of living in this world without you. I don't think I could. You have taken the lead in this world, and in doing so, you take huge chances for our people.

My life is like I am married to a soldier who keeps going off to war."

I reached out and tipped her chin up to look into her eyes. "Willow, let me help you understand how I think this may roll out if I can make the difference I'm hoping for.

Tiffany made a great point in our last village retrospect. We need more people. We need more people to be leaders. You have taken a natural leadership role in the village and the boot camp. Tiffany and Shiv have taken leadership roles in safety and defense and are joining you in bringing that leadership to the boot camp."

She nodded as I continued. "Stud and Jesus have taken leadership in scouting roles and are joined by Shiv and Tiffany to share the load. We have a transporter team of scientists and technologists leading in that area.

We have trades beginning to form around our clothing, tools, farming, and even medicine. I see a point where I can retire to a helper role as younger, stronger, and smarter people join us to take the lead."

Willow nodded. "Yes, I'm no spring chicken either. I'm catching up to you."

This made us both chuckle and broke the mood.

With a better frame of mind, I added, "In my mind, we need a lead recruiter to bring people with skills to Aard gentler than the Giants are doing and in a way that will survive after we break their transporter network. We also need the tools and personal items the village has requested. Then, when I have completed those tasks, I feel I can settle in and farm, fish, gather, and grow old with you.

I can magine relaxing in the hot-springs tubs with you every night before we turn in."

She smiled big. "It's a deal, my man. Until then, I will work hard on the boot camp and village."

Darkness was falling, and the daylight coming in through the open window shutters had waned. The moons had risen, and the soft, silver glow was painting my lover in a satin sheen I could not resist.

I closed the shutters, laid my lady on her stomach on our bed, and started rubbing her scalp under her flowing hair. My hands and lips took me on a sensual journey across her skin. They massaged every muscle on both sides of her body, from her head down to her slender feet, until I gently pulled each toe to soft moans.

My lover insisted on repaying the favor, and an hour later, we rolled together to tend to each other's deepest needs. We slept dreamlessly while the sun warmed the hut.

Refreshed, revived, and deeper in love, we rose in the morning to step out into our day.

It may have been obvious how our night had gone, but as we walked hand in hand to Bitter Waters to check out the latest status on the hot tubs, we were greeted with warm 'good mornings' and knowing smiles.

The tubs, refreshed by fresh river water more than usual, were cooler, but the water was clear, and we noticed that Shiv and Stacy had the idea first. We had a great chat with Shiv and Stacy. Soon, other villagers followed our lead.

Stacy had been one of the crew that had taken the notebooks to start the shopping list, so I asked her if they had finished it.

"Julio took the lead on compiling the notes, Mac. I think he is finished for now, but whenever we thought we were done, someone would have another idea."

"Thanks, Stacy. I'll go check with him."

Willow and I walked back to the village and found Julio.

He responded to my query by handing me one of the notebooks, "Si, I made di call... anoche..., *to make final. I think we make new* lista otro dia."

"Yes," I agreed. "There will be more lists."

I prepared for my trip, grabbed the notebook, dressed the part, and headed for the landing.

***

Chapter 20

Chapter 20 - Retail Therapy and Popeye Paul

I had worked up a good sweat when I reached the landing. It reminded me the weather had been cooling down when I was last in Seattle.

I estimated mid-October, so I configured landing in late October, hoping Popeye had not moved on. I had a bit of work to finish first, but when done, I would head for the food bank in the morning for my best chance to catch up with him.

I pushed the button on the pole and soon stepped into my father's processing plant. My first task was to use the cell phone and make a few calls.

"Mac's Logistics and Supply, how can I direct your call, please?"

"Lisa Mortensen, please."

"Who can I say is calling?"

"Mac."

"Mac, who, please. Can I get a last name?"

"The full name is Tom MacAdams.

Lisa knows me as Mac."

"Oh...Oh! Mac. Of course, sorry. I'll get her on the line."

"No problem..." fell on dead air.

A moment later, an excited voice called. "Mac!" as though Lisa was trying to shout at me from Arizona.

"How's my favorite Office Manager? I'm calling you from rainy Seattle today."

"I don't know. I'll have to ask him. I'm the VP of Acquisitions and Expansion at ML&S now."

"Why doesn't that surprise me?"

"It's so good to hear from you, Mac. I was worried the last time I saw you, but I should know better. You've got the world on a string."

Still laughing, I said, "Can I talk some business?"

"Right to the point, huh? Of course. How can I be of assistance?"

I embellished it a bit. "Lisa, I'm setting up an offshore rehab for struggling folks. I need to order hardware and equipment for gardening, hunting, fishing, and personal gear. Maybe a little bit of first aid and medical supplies, too. Are you able to help with my shopping list?"

"Of course. We normally do all this on the web or by email form. What works for you?"

I had to think for a moment. "I have a handwritten notebook... I probably need to find a fax to start with. Will that work?"

"Yes, let me text you a fax number, my email address, and a link to the form to fill out on the website for the future, which also provides a download option to save the form for email or ordering by text. Oh… and my personal cell number to get me direct anytime."

"Wow, technology is blowing right past me. All of this on text messages now?"

"Yep."

"Okay, Lisa, you've given me my tasks. If you can watch for it, I'll get the order in one way or another, and I'll give you my card details and delivery address. Thank you so much. Oh… one more important thing. No plastic, please."

"What? Many medical supplies involve plastic, like syringes, pill bottles, elastic bandages…."

"We probably need to think about a century back for some of this stuff, Lisa, but that rule is solid."

"Okay, you do like to challenge me, don't you."

"If anyone can do this, you can. You're the best. But if any of the items can't be organic, we can live without them. I thank you from the bottom of my heart for all you do for me."

"Anytime, Mac. There is a place on the form for all that info. By the way, we are opening an office in the port of Everett. We should be open just in time to take the Thanksgiving weekend off."

"That's fantastic, and that may be very handy for me. Will there be anyone I know in that office?"

"Only me. My new role has me opening that office for our new trade route with the Pacific East and Canada.

I don't know if you knew this about me, but I grew up in Bellingham before the folks moved to Tucson."

"I didn't know, but I'm glad to hear it. I may be poking my nose into Puget Sound occasionally. I need to get busy on this order, but in your notes, please keep me posted on where you will be and when that will be."

"I will, Mac. So good to talk, and you owe me dinner soon."

"Of course. Off to my chores, and I will see you soon. Thank you again, my friend."

As soon as I hung up, I called Tony. He was quick to answer.

"Hi, Bro. How've you been?"

"Mac! I was hoping to catch up with you soon. I'm at Pike Place Market having a bite but headed for the plant in a few minutes."

"Excellent. I'm at the plant and preparing to do some shopping. It seems it's all done online now. Any idea where I can get to a computer and the internet to fill out an email form?"

"Directly across from you, on the open second floor is another row of offices off the catwalk. The middle one takes the same key code as the front door and the office with the phones. We have a couple of computers on a desk there, and you can log in to the machine with the same code. We have our own email server.

Your email address is your full name, first and last, separated by a dot and pegasi-d.com".

"Brilliant! Thank you."

"Saw you coming."

"Okay, found some tea.

Will have it heated when you get here."

"On my way in 10." He hung up.

My phone pinged, and I opened it to see a text message from Lisa with all the needed details.

In about fifteen minutes, I heard the old blue Chevy pull up to the door, and a few moments later, we hugged it out, grabbed our tea, and headed around the catwalk to the office on the far side of the building. Tony pointed at the keypad on the door. I entered the code and opened the door. We pulled two chairs up to the desk and sat down.

I logged in to the laptop he had indicated on the desk.

Tony said, "Can I see your phone, please?"

I opened it up, and it showed me an email icon on the face. "Your email is here on this computer," he pointed at the lighted screen. "And this icon is your text messages."

My hovering brother said, "Where is this order form?"

I opened the text message app. There, the only two messages were a test from Tony and a message from Lisa.

He clicked on Lisa's message and plinked his cursor on a link. It popped up the website form in a browser.

"Okay. Let's open up your email on the computer."

I found the email icon at the bottom, logged in to my account, and Lisa's message was in an email, including a link to click. It produced the same form.

"Now, where is your shopping list?"

I showed him the notebook.

"Ha, I knew it." He laughed. "Old tech to new tech."

He moved over to a multi-function printer and scanned the note pages to my email.

"Now you have new tech to new tech. These documents in your email are in PDF format, letting you copy and paste them from one screen to another."

Within a half hour, we filled out Lisa's form with the computer text version of each line of my notebook. We had filled in the address to ship it to the packing house and applied the credit card information I had saved from Tony the night we met in Northern Canada. A new email message on the laptop stated we had placed the order and provided a confirmation number.

"Brother, I'll transport it to you when that gets shipped here. Just have someone keep an eye on your port."

"I can't thank you enough, Tony. These supplies will make a huge difference to some great people."

He nodded, "Think nothing of it, brother. He took a long sip of his cooling tea. "About the dude you kicked loose on your last visit...."

***

He had my attention.

"He knew his way around. I followed him up 4th to Yesler, over to Smith Tower, and up 2nd to Cherry. He went into a law office there. I hung out for half an hour with a new Starbucks coffee, and he never returned. I suspect he knew someone there well enough to get a lawyer's attention away from their case-load. After that, I don't think he had trouble returning to his life."

"Thanks, Bro. I assumed as much. I hope he heads East, gets back on his political path, and forgets about us. I'm not sure how you scrape off an experience like Aard and go on with your life, though. Most people would have trouble getting any-one to believe this story, but I think Larry saw an opportunity. I suppose we will see."

Tony had some chores and his shopping errands pend-ing, so I prepared the plant for a scenario I hoped would hap-pen and headed uptown to see if I could find Popeye. When I talked to Tony about him last time, he had done some stalking for me and had produced a stack of old news articles on him. It was an awful domestic story that painted him in the worst light, and the retraction that followed was one sentence in ital-ics at the bottom of the reprinted story. This guy needed a fresh start if anyone did.

It was the middle of the day now, the clouds were threat-ening, and it was chilly.

I figured I'd start where I last saw him and headed for the park bench where he had shared his can of spinach with me. He wasn't there, so I started spiraling out, a block at a time.

I saw plenty of homeless people and many who looked much like him. They were all looking for shelter since it seemed ready to snow, or at worst, freezing rain, one of those cold, winter-type rains where you wished for snow.

I finally found Popeye on a park bench at Westlake Center. He was looking worse for wear, but he had found an old Mariner's baseball hat. The hat, added to his fully matted beard and Frayed overcoat, hid most of his face, so he was hard to identify. I sat on the other side of the dirty rice sack, representing his worldly belongings.

"Hey, fren'. Any chance you could spare a sip?"

Popeye looked up at me momentarily and said, "Sorry man, got none." Then he recognized me.

"Black Mac, is that you? Where have you been?"

"Yup, 'ts me. Jus' back from holidays somewheh' walm"

He chuckled quietly as he looked me over.

"Hey, Mac, looks like snow. Think we can find a place to get out of the elements? I bet you've got some great stories."

I nodded, stood, and started for the packing house. Paul hesitated momentarily, then grabbed his sack and quickstepped to catch up.

"I gots a place, Popeye."

I led him to the packing plant in silence and taught him how to break in using an unlatched window at the top of a lower-level service door. I had placed an old steel desk inside the entrance to hop down on once inside. I wasn't ready to give him the code to the door locks.

Instead, I had shut the main power switch off and staged the oven room to look like the place was deserted. I made a fire in the oven and sat Popeye down for a chat. I pulled down the chess board Tony had carved on Aard to ease into the conversation.

"It look lak you don' drink, Popeye."

"Nah, I have enough trouble without booze or drugs."

I figured it was time to get him thinking. I addressed him in plain, educated English for a while as we played to let him know there was more to this visit than he was expecting. Then, after a few games and small talk, I got down to business.

I stood, picked up an old copy of the Seattle Times on the hearth, and dropped it on his lap, where he sat near the fire.

I had it opened to the business section, where the headline titled 'Paul Sutler Shocker' detailed his story from years ago.

I said, "Popeye, read the last line in italics. I understand what has happened to you and your girl."

Tears displaced the look of shock. He threw the paper into the fire.

"Popeye, you've got game. Let me ask you something."

It took a moment for him to respond as a rainbow of emotions swept across his weathered face. Then, with a touch of anger, he finally responded. "Shoot."

"If I could show you a place where you could build your life over, would you build it differently?"

He thought about this for a moment.

"You bet your ass I would. Far too late, I learned that the reason I should have been successful was for my family. The life my little girl must live now is my only real regret.

All the rest of us got what we deserve or at least will in the end."

He moved a pawn and looked me in the eye.

"What's the best thing you could do for your daughter now?"

I admired his perseverance in this challenging topic. Most people would have raged out by now or at least shut down. But, defiant, he stuck to his ground and kept talking.

I suspect it had been a long time since he spoke about this subject and even longer since he had someone willing to listen.

"Well, I have had lots of time to think on that, and I suspect the best I can do for her is stay as far from her as possible. Any connection with me from now on would just deepen the pain she has to live with."

"You ready to move to another environment to start over?"

"I would go in a heartbeat if I had the means."

"C'mere"

I stood and pulled a candle from the steel cupboard. I lit it with a sliver from the fire and motioned for him to follow. Night had fallen. No light streamed in through the high windows.

The light of the fire and the candle were the only means to see.

In the next room, I opened the steel door on a breaker panel closet and pointed at a small button by itself near the bottom. There was no marking, and the button was a simple, stainless steel, half-inch diameter cylinder.

"When you're ready to start over, just push this."

I headed back to the fire, so he followed. After sitting down, I pointed at the chess board, "Your turn."

He tried to get me to explain more, but I kept my attention on the games and told him he needed to trust me to learn more, and I hooked a thumb over my shoulder at the closet door. Popeye finally wore out and asked if he could go to sleep. I nodded and was surprised at how quickly he was out. Throughout several games, he told me his story, and I learned that an intelligent and thoughtful man was under the frayed exterior.

I also learned that he rarely drank. Occasionally, a beer was a luxury, and there wasn't much room for indulgence. Since he had no social life, social drinking stopped, and he had no use for it otherwise.

Popeye also summarized the destruction in his life that had brought him here. Although he had tried to numb the pain for a month or two at the beginning, he couldn't stomach much and couldn't bring himself to slide into the drug culture around him on the street.

The worn man had watched the drugs and alcohol peel off the lives he met in his new reality.

It hurt him to see lives that used to mean something to their families and friends slide out of touch and succumb to the pain and greed from those that supplied the numbing agents.

He mentioned that he was running out of stamina and was losing hope, but he would rather die by his own choices than at the hand of one of the neighborhood pushers.

I watched the exhausted man sleep for a spell as the fire died, then slipped into the closet and pushed the button. I set up camp at the landing because I didn't expect him to take long to follow.

***

Chapter 21

Popeye Warms Up

Awareness began to seep in as the poke to his ribs became increasingly uncomfortable.

"Hey, Popeye, wake up,"

"Stop it, man. I'm awake, dammit."

Paul Sutler began opening his eyes to the bright white heat around him but slammed them closed again against the glare of a hot midday sun. Slowly he worked them open to slits and soon after could focus on the chuckling black man in a red tunic sitting above him on a small hillock.

"Welcome, Popeye, to my home." I had removed any hint of street slang during our chess games in the warehouse.

He looked around now in confusion. The grass was glorious, but he struggled to identify any flora around him, and I watched as he put his head back down and studied the grass at his elbow. Then, finally, realization dawned as he noticed the low grass blades were different, having three edges instead of two.

"Mac, where are we? How did I get here?"

51 Pegasi - Black Mac

"You pushed the button, my friend. Look above you."

He looked and noted that he was lying at the foot of what looked to be a tree trunk or utility pole with no branches. Gray in color, rough in texture as tree bark would be, but for a smooth patch and one small stainless button.

"If you ever want to go back, remember this place."

Popeye looked up at me, grinning, until he noticed for the first time that I was holding a white tunic and some laced sandals, and he glanced down to find he was naked.

I chuckled at this surprise, and his head snapped back to look at me in time to collect the tossed garment around his ears. Standing quickly, he slipped it on like a tee shirt, then sat again to lace on the sandals.

I had supplied him a robe like I wore and a pair of home-made greek sandels that were most helpful when arriving on Aard.

While doing this, he saw his dirty, old Seattle Mariners ball cap on the ground.

He reached, picked it up, and put it on. *The bill of the cap should help him with the sun.*

I had tweaked the transporter to include it. I hoped it would save a piece of his identity if he needed it. I felt he would be self concious about his appearance. I broke out in a belly laugh that left me choking and gasping.

In indignation, he planted his fists on his hips and glared at me, but I only laughed harder and pointed at the pond near him.

"Look at your reflection, Popeye." I pointed at the small silver-edged pond with inviting, deep, dark-green water a few paces from where he fumed. It seemed, in a moment, he agreed. The image was indeed funny, and through a couple of self-conscious snorts, he began laughing too.

A Greek Mariner was chuckling back at him from his reflection.

"I thought you might need the hat for a spell, but the nasty clothes had to stay behind."

"Are we in Greece? Can I swim in this pool? I need a bath."

"You have come a bit farther than that, my friend. Welcome to the 4th planet in the solar system, 51 Pegasi-d.

The closest Humans have been able to come to see this place is a radio signal from what they call 51 Pegasi b, a large, hot, gassy planet near the local sun smiling down on you. We like to call this place Aard, nothing fancy like Xanadu or something you can't wrap your tongue around."

"Wow."

He knelt to examine the tri-blade grass and gazed across the pond at the silver-blue tint of the shrubs and trees. I grinned as he began to understand and threw him a lump of homemade soap Stacey had made. A few minutes later, I saw a much cleaner version of Popeye, now back in his robe, looking more like Jesus with his long hair and beard flowing down over his tunic.

"Am I in some science fiction dream here?"

"Yep, but from now on, it is your life, and it is, by far, more real than your last one because you will deal with nature more directly here. Technology is isolated. You will live here a few Earth centuries back, without electronic media. No TV or radio. So, to gain information, you need to communicate directly or read simple handwritten notes."

"Technology is here, no doubt, but we try to limit it to necessity, hoping to avoid the damage to the environment we were fighting back on Earth."

He blinked a couple of times while this was settling into his grey matter.

"Am I being punked? Is Ashton Kutcher going to walk out with the cameras?"

I laughed out loud.

"No, all of this will feel natural in a few days."

Popeye's head was spinning now. "So, this is a utopia?"

"No, Popeye. This world is far from paradise. There are things here that want to eat you. However, once you get to know your environment and the amazing people already here, I think you will feel at home, perhaps more than ever. You can be the judge."

I stood up, still smiling, and as I did, my hands were full of equipment.

"Popeye, turn around and look at that button. Press it now or come here and take these. Your decision. You have some heavy boot camp to go through if you stay."

He turned to look at the insignificant little button, then turned back to me.

"My name is Paul Sutler."

"Ok, Popeye Paul," I handed him a long bow, quiver, and a hide shoulder bag; "Take a few minutes to dust off if you like. Once you are freshed up, let's get on with your training. Remember this little pool for later. Here is an old-fashioned safety razor, scissors, and our local soap that works very well as shaving cream.

The shoulder bag has a handy little wax-lined pocket inside for your soap. Experience tells me you may prefer to shave in this tropical heat.

If you decide to accept the role I am going to challenge you with, this will be your bathtub. That little creek upstream will be your clean water source.

I'll explain all this as we head for Freedom, why it is essential, and why I think you are the best choice for the job. I esplained the village we were headed for was called Freedom."

After his shave and bath, I headed for a grove of white-trunked trees with glistening silver leaves quivering around heavy, hanging fruit or nuts. He followed.

I swung my arm with my pointing finger outstretched. "All of this will be your home when you are ready. You will be the keeper of the Landing." We stopped for a moment to take in the view.

Paul followed my gaze from the dark hills far off to my left, the silver-leaved grove we had left behind, and small trees and open grassland to my right.

They seemed to end on the Western horizon, but there was just enough shrubbery and trees to keep us guessing what was beyond. Shortly, we entered a grove of bigger trees.

My forehead beaded with sweat in the heat. Luckily, a refreshing breeze met us in the shade of the trail as we entered the grove.

"Mac, tell me if my senses are working right. The high sun is slightly in front of us, so it seems it is close to midday, and we are headed South. Hills to the East and shrubs to the West. How close am I?"

I grinned over my shoulder but kept moving. "You're getting it. We're rotating the same way Earth does. We are in the Norhtern hemisphere but much closer to the equator than Seattle."

***

The recruit stepped up his pace to keep up.

Checking on him occasionally, I was impressed at how much attention he paid to his surroundings.

"Mac, Is Aard's mineral makeup similar to Earth?"

"The same Popeye. Cut from the same cloth. The only difference I've learned from reading what some folks have written about this place is that some of Earth's precious metals and gems are commonplace here, and Iron is rarer. You'll see it occasionally, but the soil has much greener and grayer oxidation than orange rust."

He went silent and focused on his surroundings again. From the look on his face and the spring in his step, I figured

Paul Sutler would love Aard.

As he followed, I began his education.

"How many arrows have you got in that quiver, Popeye?"

A quick count came to eight. "I have eight, Mac."

"Pull one out and have a good look at it. Tell me what you notice about it."

He studied the arrow for a few moments.

"Well, the feathers are stiff and thicker than any feather I have seen."

"Those are called flights, and they are split feather sections from the breast of a Purple Screamer. You will get to know those birds well since they are potentially a main source of food, leather, lacing, decoration, and danger."

I let that last word sink in for a minute and then continued.

"There are three major things to know about that bird. First, they are Aard's premier bird on the food chain. The perfect raptor. Picture a cross between the reptilian raptors of Earth's distant past and an eagle with a twenty-foot wingspan. Secondly, they are almost as smart as you. Smarter than some humans, to be sure.

They hunt in packs and are very social, like wolves, but have progressed to even laying traps for prey. Thirdly, and most importantly, they consider us prey as much as we consider them prey. Probably more."

I looked back at him as I watched him grasp my meaning.

"What else about the arrow?"

"The shaft is very straight but has joints like Bamboo."

At this, I led Popeye off the trail, through a small grove with no underbrush, to a wall of woody grass growing at least twelve feet high against a hidden pond.

"Pull out a stock of grass. Popeye."

He tried every way he could think of, and I could see how powerful his arms were, but no bulging veins in his forehead or arms could get a single stalk to let loose of the Aardian soil.

"Now, grab the stock below a joint about a foot from the ground with one hand. Then, above the joint with the other. Bend the stock between them."

With a quick twist, a crisp crack, he held the grass stock in his hand.

"Look closely at the stock. "

He tipped the stock to the horizontal and recognized his arrow. It was like half-inch bamboo stock but for the walnut brown color and the smooth, tight-grained texture, which seemed almost metal.

"From the bottom, break off a piece, four sections long."

A quick twist, and he had his sized arrow shaft.

I handed him a bone-handled knife with a sparkling blade edge.

"That is arrow grass. Get yourself five more of those stocks. Each has two frond blades and a seed pod.

Save a half dozen of these grass blades, all the seed pods, and shafts in your quiver pocket, then let's get back on the trail."

The process didn't take more than ten minutes. When done, Popeye looked at me for what was next. I handed him a belt and scabbard for the knife.

"Strap it on Popeye."

He nodded his thanks and cinched the belt around his toga.

"You may notice the things I point out have simple names. We find no use in giving everything a Latin, Greek, or localized name... Ok, we call that a toga, and you are on Aard," as I grinned and pointed at his clothing. "Saves a lot of effort in translation. Let's return to the landing trail and put in some miles."

"Landing trail?"

"Landing trail.

The trail goes to and from the landing pole that brought you to Aard. Our next stop on the trail is the Base Camp at Freedom, where your training will help develop you into an Aardian."

"Mac, why don't you build the landing at the village?"

"Until we are confident that we won't have bad guys popping in for a visit, we want to keep our landing away from the people to give a cushion against attack."

"Attack?"

There are some dangers you will learn about.

I mentioned the Purple Screamers, but just like Earth, we need to be attentive in the wilderness. Here on Aard, it's all wilderness.

You'll get all the details in boot camp, so don't worry too much about it right now.

You are safer than you were on the streets of Seattle for now."

He absorbed that detail as we stepped out of the cooling shade of the silver-leaved grove and continued our journey toward the base camp.

A long distance toward the Eastern hills, I saw soaring specks in the sky and heard far-off screams. Popeye noticed my gaze, and I nodded as he turned his unasked question to me. Paul Sutler had heard his first Purple Screamers.

The years on the street had toughened his feet and built up his legs, so he didn't hinder me much as we silently ate up the distance. Miles dropped behind us as the sun sunk over our back trail.

The air became cooler, and wildlife noises seeped into his awareness. I noticed his head was now on a swivel. The education on Screamers and now alien noises in the bush were getting to him.

"Getting hungry, Popeye?"

"Well, now that you mention it, the Friendship Center eggs are long gone."

"Ok, we are making good time, so we'll take a few minutes to eat and still be at camp before dark."

51 Pegasi - Black Mac

I stepped off the trail and followed a faint, smaller path through low shrubbery.

Soon, the track broke into a small opening with a lake reaching out through the woods. It was time for some practice.

***

Chapter 22

Culinary School and Bootcamp

"Get an arrow cocked, Popeye."

He followed my instructions, not knowing what to expect.

"Stay where you are. In a moment, you are going to see several Humpbacks. Kill one, but don't kill me."

I leaned over the water and smacked the surface several times quickly. Suddenly, the brush came alive with activity. An army of homely reptiles the color and texture of frogs scrambled around us. He let loose three arrows before he pinned one to a rotted stump.

I was chuckling but slapped his back as I bent to slit the throat of the unfortunate creature. I flipped him a flint from my small pack and said, "Build us a little fire. Use some of this dry grass and deadwood twigs and branches."

He went to work while I cleaned and skinned the animal. I built a simple spit from green willow, collected the seedpods from him, and tucked them into the empty carcass. I laid the Humpback on a stump.

I used a few green willow twigs to 'sew' the cavity up and set the humpback to cook on the spit. We talked about the experiance while it cooked, then pulled it off the fire when done and laid it out on the stup. The cavity splayed open to present "peas," the size of a quarter.

The delicate little legume had popped out of the pods to present a great side dish to the tender meat.

"Don't eat the pods. They're very bitter and will leave you with heaves. They work like syrup of ipecac and a laxative at the same time. The seeds are an amazing combination of plant protein and fiber."

We ate a flavorful meal within an hour of stopping and were soon back on the trail.

"Popeye, that was a simple trail meal, but when we get you settled, you will learn how to build a feast from the local farmers market we call home."

"I am looking forward to it, Mac." He grinned and patted his stomach.

"We have a couple hours of daylight left, Popeye; let's make tracks."

Hours didn't mean anything after we had been on Aard for a time because the day moved quicker here, but for someone new to the world, I felt it was easiest to set a measurement they were used to. However long it was, it seemed fitting when we saw firelight flicker ahead through the quickly growing night.

I watched as Paul Sutler's eyes lit up. We stepped into an active camp with several permanent shelters and three times as many hide tents. The clearing was a hub of activity.

Everyone seemed to be on a mission, but everyone, to a soul, waved and grinned as they greeted Popeye and me into the camp.

"Welcome, Popeye."

Startled, He turned to the voice and stuttered a polite reply to a sinewy and somewhat scholarly-looking woman. She wore a purple-feather skirt tied at the waist with a woven cord and was naked from the waist up. I could not help but notice his appreciation of her perfect "coffee au lait" skin, sporting a satin glow of enticing sweat.

"I'm Willow. I run the training camp."

"Uh... Hello Willow, it seems I am at a disadvantage. As you seem to know, I'm Paul... or Popeye, and I suppose I am a new charge for your boot camp."

"You are indeed. Check into the tent directly behind that building with the porch. It'll be your home for a week or so." Willow smiled and moved her attention to me. "Mac, I've a briefing for you anytime you're ready."

I grinned, winked, and hugged Willow. "I'll be back at Red Star over Purple Screamer. If you watch that tallest snow-covered peak to the East, you will see a rather bright red star appear over it. That's 51 Pegasi B. That'll be about an hour from now. Meet me on the porch over there, and we'll impose ourselves on the lovely Willow's hospitality."

I nibbled her ear quickly and walked off through the camp. Willow nodded at Popeye with a smile, turned on a bare heel, and headed for her house.

A couple of days later, Popeye Paul told me about the emotions that washed over him the first time he had a few minutes alone on Aard. When Willow had turned him loose that first afternoon, he headed for the designated tent with nothing better to do.

In the tent, Paul stowed his kit and weapons. He took advantage of a small canvas cot that took up one side of his assigned space, and he lay flat for lack of anything better to do.

He told me how he immediately felt relief from the tenseness he hadn't realized was pulling at his neck and back muscles. Surprised by this, he contemplated his day. He told me he didn't suppose he had ever had a more important day since his daughter was born. He told me how his tears welled up against his will as the broken past came into full view.

The image of the drama forced upon his daughter threatened to take over. *I noted how much his daughter's shattered life meant to him.*

Finally, he said, he got up and stepped back into the twilight night. Although cooler, the tropical heat was still a warm embrace. While still in awe, he met Alpha and was introduced to Beta soon after.

He recounted how he noticed Willow as she stood on her porch across the dirt common surrounding her hut, in friendly conversation with a man sporting expressive hands and a French accent. Willow noticed him and called him over with a wave.

He told me how Willow introduced him to Stud, explained the tendency for everyone to earn a nickname.

She explained Stud's, hers, and a few others' Aardian names while waiting for me. The tradition seemed to stem from the need for the victoms to identify themselves differently as explorers and survivors on a positive note.

They were chuckling as I stepped back into the village under the first peek of the red star.

Willow noticed me first. "Damn, that's a fine sight."

We all chuckled at the comely woman as she dropped her eyes and followed with a wink.

Popeye looked around and noted that all dressed the same: a tunic folded down to the waist. Around us, the traffic was quiet now, but for a few tending chores. Again, most dressed the same, but some wore simple loincloths. No one batted an eye, and I smiled as I saw an epiphany settle over the newest immigrant.

I joined the crew on the porch, settling in beside Willow with a quick kiss on her cheek.

"Well, Popeye, Whad'ya think?"

"Amazing Mac, what's next?"

***

"Well, I guess it's time you got a history lesson. Let me see. How about we start with how Willow, Stud, Shiv, and I found this place?

"Willow was known as Sharon Rowlands in Oregon a lifetime ago. Etalon, or Stud, used to be Jean Belanger from Besancon, France. We met as prisoners of the Sasquatch giants."

Popeye's eyes widened, and the group around me chuckled at his shock.

"I was leaving my office in Tucson when my life changed, and I woke up in a cage in a tropical jungle.

There was no food, water, or clothes, just humidity, heat, and rain. Sharon was working out in her apartment when the same thing happened. Jean was riding a bicycle through his town when it happened to him."

"The only thing we had in common," I continued, "was that we had all just turned a corner in our lives. I had just re-read the news on the loss of my wife and her friend in a car accident.

Willow had just had an issue with an employee at work in a town far from family, and Jean had found his girlfriend in bed with a stranger. None of us had anyone close, but we had people who wanted us gone."

I let that sink in as he reached for the water skin, drank deep, and passed it around.

"One of the giants picked up my cage and packed me to a meeting place where he stacked my cage on top of Jean's and across from Sharon. These beings are huge. I suppose they average about thirty to forty feet tall. They look like our Cro-Magnon ancestors, except they have fur, so they resemble more of a King Kong or a giant Sasquatch.

The big difference is that they have intelligence equal to or better than ours. In addition, they have very advanced technology. Some of that technology is from Earth, however. They have human partners."

51 Pegasi - Black Mac

Popeye looked stunned.

"Are you keeping up with this, Popeye?"

All he could do was nod.

"That is probably enough for now.

We'll let you get some rest, and tomorrow, Willow and Stud will introduce you to Shiv, and you will get a lot more of the story. It is much more colorful when described by Shiv. And most importantly, you will learn how to live and thrive in this world.

Then, we will discuss the landing assignment to see if you are still game for it. We need to get someone on their way up there in a day or two. We have freight coming."

I looked around at the faces on the porch. "Team, Willow needs my attention for a debrief. I think we'll turn in."

Willow blushed but stood up first to go in.

Stud said, "C'mon, Popeye, you probably cannot sleep. Let us look around the camp until you get tired."

Popeye jumped up. I could tell by his broad smile, Stud was right. Our newest citizen was not ready to return to the thoughts that chased him from his tent earlier.

I went inside and focused on the beautiful woman, learning a new kind of patience as she built a relationship with me. I knew now just how much I loved this golden woman. It turned out the debrief needed no dialogue.

When Willow and I joined the onboarding of Popeye in the morning, Pegasi was rising.

Stud had just started his first lesson, and Popeye would be the chef serving breakfast this morning. The recruit had met several citizens by now, but they had all moved on with their chores. Stud set up the classroom by the river and started teaching school.

He had supplied Popeye with a freshly harvested Humpback.

With the knife I gave him yesterday and with some close direction, he applied careful focus while he cleaned and skinned the animal. Then, with the patience and expertise of a butcher, Popeye worked through his lesson.

First, with Stud directing, he pulled the stomach from the Humpback and rinsed it in the river near the stump he was working on. Next, Stud taught him how to harvest a willow-type switch from the water edge and cut off a foot of the thick end.

Popeye-Paul then pulled the rest of the switch into a circle the size of a standard cooking pot.

Then he bound it with a length of fresh, pliable silver vine that grew in abundance up the trunks of the local trees. He now stretched the elastic mouth of the stomach over the hoop. Popeye was proving to be a quick study.

The stomach mouth folded neatly around the loop and gripped it tight. Stud then took a moment to illustrate the technique. Then the student poked the short stick through fresh horizontal knife slits near the top beneath the loop. He then tied more of the pliable vine to both ends of the shaft, wrapping both inside and outside the stomach. Popeye now had a handy water basket, which he promptly filled with water from the river.

He then handed it to Stud, who hung it on two protruding branch stumps beside the stump they had cleaned the Humpback on.

Stud pointed at the fire pit and the spit.

"Use your flint and the back of your knife to build a fire, Popeye."

The tinder and small twigs were already in a pile near the pit. There was also enough wood for the breakfast fire stacked within reach. The two had been busy preparing for the lesson.

"Make a note of the spit that holds a green limb about two feet above the top of the fire, Popeye."

I could tell he was absorbing every detail. This man had survived in a cut-throat business environment where detail was critical. As a result, his focus was well-honed. Popeye's guide hung the new animal stomach basket with a half-gallon of water over the fire and told him to throw in the seedpods they had collected. He did as instructed and watched in awe as the heated stomach beaded with water that steamed off to be replaced with new beads.

Popeye added the Humpback to the spit, and as the water heated, the seed pods swelled to burst forth with a row of pea-style seeds that grew to the size of a quarter.

"Don't eat the pods. They're poisonous. The seeds, however, are better than good for you."

Popeye grinned wide. "I already got that lesson from

Mac. It's great that I can cook them in water and the carcass. This stomach pot is freaking amazing."

We all chuckled at his exuberance as the lesson sunk in. Stud threw in a half dozen strips of mushroom jerky and another half dozen of the berry jerky. He gave Popeye the lowdown on the mushroom's unique nightlight and contraceptive properties and the massive advantage of preserving berries the size of basketballs.

After a hearty breakfast, Willow took over, and Paul Sutler became a hunter and defender. His history in the gym helped prepare his stamina, strength, balance, and hand-eye coordination, so it wasn't long before he was competent with the long bow and fire-hardened and tipped arrows. Of course, like all of us, the more we used a tool, the better we got, but he had the mechanics and theory down on the first day.

***

Chapter 23

Landing Camp and the First Freight Shipment

Shiv and Tiffany returned to camp before Popeye finished his archery lessons, so they became an avid audience. When Willow finished the lesson, she provided introductions, and we began planning our trip to the landing to set up camp.

Late in the afternoon, we discussed who we needed on this trip. Shiv, Tiffany, and Stud were the premier hut or cabin builders and probably the best suited to help Popeye set up camp.

Dan, Kia, and Sirih were all fascinated with the freight opportunities of the transporter, but Dan and Sirih were busy building a store for this inventory in a cave in the rock face. The race was on to organize storage for the incoming freight.

They decided Kia would make the trip to the landing with Popeye and stay long enough to establish a routine with the cargo. She would look for issues and opportunities and keep Popeye company for a few days as he acclimated to the role.

Kia was trying to come out of her shell more and be social, so she thought this might be an excellent opportunity to reach out and make a friend.

51 Pegasi - Black Mac

As a tribe, we assured Popeye that he never had to be alone. Someone would always be at the camp with him, and he would only be alone when he wanted to be.

This was all the assurance he needed, and he made it clear that this challenge was what he wanted. The landing would be bustling for a few days, and the traffic up and down the landing path to Freedom would be steady.

Stud decided to stay a few days to get Popeye started on woven willow future and general building skills. When Hilda heard that Stud would remain to help Popeye settle in for a few days, she asked to go too.

Hilda wanted to learn from Stud and was also curious to get to know Popeye. This request raised an eyebrow for me, and I grinned as it raised an eyebrow from Stud, too. Even though the age difference between Hilda and Popeye was more significant than with Stud, the comment introduced a new dynamic to the village.

After some soul-searching, Willow decided to join me in a transport to Seattle. She had been missign me and wanted to spend time with me and meet my family.

We would be working with Tony to make the transfer. Then, with the team assembled, we could start planning for the new camp and the ramifications of bringing the hardware, materials, and personal items needed by the villagers.

We finally settled in for a good night's sleep and headed for the landing between dawn and sunrise. Before the sun of Pegasi started working on us, an hour of cooler travel was a good start.

51 Pegasi - Black Mac

Through the gaps in the tree cover from time to time, we could see the tiny dots of soaring Screamers far off to the East over the plateau. We heard their distant screams.

I wondered what kept them from sailing out to the coast. They could be here within an hour if they were so motivated.

Someday, I will find the answer to that question because it may be the difference between life and death.

What felt like a couple of hours later, we were among taller trees. The trail that had begun as a Humpback path through hundreds of meandering trails around small lakes, ponds, and streams began to look like a regular human trail. The track showed footprints etched in sandal treads and bare feet.

The Freedom-to-Landing highway signaled humans lived here. The air was a bit cooler among the lakes and streams, and we appreciated the shade of the trees that lined our trail.

The chatter on the trail was cheerful, and friendships grew. Bonds were started and enhanced. Adventures like this were excellent vehicles for the society we were building. The trip seemed quicker than usual, and we soon broke into the landing. The scene featured the shining pool to the side of the little hillock that supported our landing pole. The place seemed serene and welcoming.

I encouraged Popeye to pick the spot for his first hut and was impressed with how he pulled Stud, Tiffany, and Shiv into a huddle to discuss the options. They chose a site down the trail far enough to be hidden among the small trees, best for shelter, shade, and building materials.

The site overlooked the other side of the pond near a massive volcanic rock and a few taller trees.

It would not be seen from the pole unless you knew it was there. Yet, one could easily monitor the landing pole from the hut commons. Once they had a consensus, they began staking out the hut in a natural clearing.

Kia and I began working on the incoming configuration settings at the base of the pole. Willow and Hilda initiated hunting and foraging for a meal. As the day began to cool down, the hut was well underway, we had eaten a great meal, and the landing configuration was complete.

We broke for the day and finished up over the next few days. We sat around the cooking fire, comparing notes and discussing the future of the landing camp and the next few days retrieving and transporting our goods back to Freedom. The talk was exciting, and the future felt positive from the vibe in the camp.

"Mac, I have a question for you." Popeye already loved the landing.

"Shoot, Popeye."

"When I landed at the Landing Pole, I asked why Freedom wasn't built here. You explained the reasons some, but said you would expand on it during Boot Camp. Is now a good time?"

"Good reminder, Popeye. Thanks. You are right. There is more to the decision to keep the landing seperate. Well, there are a few reasons, but I'll give you the bigger ones. Freedom was the first spot we came to as a tribe that seemed perfect to build a camp.

The river, hot spring tubs, protective rock wall with storage caves, local game, abundant mushrooms, and ping-pong seed pods were all strong selling points."Popeye nodded, so I continued.

"The site for the landing came second, but we needed to build it far enough away from the camp to provide a warning if the giants or their human partners found it. We also required the prime transporter location to have a suitable antenna tree, some height, and a bit more open sky for a solid signal.

You see, the keeper of the landing will also be our light-house keeper and will send a quick message to Freedom should there be trouble, news, or freight."

I leaned toward Paul to make sure I had his undivided attention. "The lighthouse keeper will also be our primary re-cruiter and immigration agent. You see, we will be counting on you to make some critical decisions on who comes to live with us, and there will be an uptick in immigration."

Popeye went silent and reflected in the fire. However, I knew he was good with his thoughts as he was smiling.

***

The builders were fully engaged in finishing the Landing Cabin by the time Willow and I left for Seattle. A handy concave on the face of the bolder struck Stud as a perfect backing for the campfire. The heat would radiate on a chilly day but offer a buffer from the wind during a small fire for cooking. The camp was looking better all the time.

I told the crew it was time for Willow and I to step off planet to see about our freight plan.

After a few hugs and nodds, we stepped out of the hub of activity. I pushed the button first, and then, with some hesitation, Willow transported. She joined me on the catwalk outside the locked office. In a moment, we were on the phone with Tony. As he answered, I heard the ringing footsteps of someone on the catwalk, and Dad walked onto the open second floor.

"Hi, Tommy. I was expecting you, and Dad is in town."

I looked back from my grinning father and answered Tony. "He just walked into the office. I want you both to meet Willow."

"Okay, cool. I'll be there in a few. Tell Dad to entertain you till I get there. Hey... you've got a shipment inside the far loading bay."

Dad heard both sides of the conversation and said, "I'd dance ya a wee jig, but I left me kilt at home. Eht's grand ta meecha"

We all laughed as he reached for Willow's hand, lissed it, and said, "C'mere. Take a look."

I disconnected the call as we went to see a load of supplies.

The shippment was neatly stacked on wooden pallets and wrapped in linen sheets, cotton blankets, and oilskin canvas instead of plastic wrap. Another advantage was that the shippers had everything neatly tucked in for transport. The downside is that we couldn't see the contents.

"Here, I can smell your wires burning." Dad handed me a bill of lading with a complete list of the supplies and which pallet they were stacked on.

The pallets were identified by printed washcloths lightly stitched to the canvas with content lists printed the same way on hand and dish towels. Lisa was brilliant.

The door swung open, and Tony stepped in. Before he did anything, he simply walked over to Willow and gave her a bear hug. He stepped back, grabbed her shoulders, looked deep into her eyes, and said, "Thank you for fixing my li'l brother. He was kinda broken for quite a while. Looking at him now, I see a man changing the world... a couple of worlds. He wouldn't be half as super if he hadn't met you."

"It's getting kind of deep in here, bro...."

Everyone laughed, and Willow said, "It works both ways, Tony.

Mac has made my life worthwhile for the first time I can remember. What we have been through together has made every minute count. That's why I'm here. I want as much of his time as I can get."

Tony smiled. "Well, if he doesn't treat you like a queen every day, I want you to tell me."

"Okay, you guys, that's enough. Let's talk about how we get this freight to Aard." I pointed at the pallets.

Dad was waiting his turn. "Okay, son. I've done this a half-dozen times to stock the glacier cabin, so I've found the way around a few gotchas. There are three parts to this journey. The first is kinda tough. You must source it all and corral it into a neat bundle. The third part is tough but simple. Finally, you unpack it and distribute it to where it's gonna live."

Willow said, "You missed the second part."

Dad grinned and pointed to a small steel button on the bay wall, "You push that."

As our eyes focused on the simple button, he said, "It's all configured for your landing. We've been there; it's a sweet spot."

"That's it?" Willow was shocked. Frankly, I was amazed, too.

"Okay," Tony pulled out a tape measure. He measured from the wall to the closest pallet, then the overall pack's length, width, and height.

"This will take up a patch of your little landing 15 feet by 12 feet.

It will stand 7 feet tall and be seven and a half feet from the pole. You don't want to stand within seventeen feet from the pole and seven and a half feet to either side."

Willow's eyes got big. "I need to go back and ensure the landing is clear."

"One of us does, yes. What about the last one to push the button to go back? What are we going to land on?" I was asking the obvious, but we needed to be precise.

Tony winked. "I got you covered. I reconfigured the closet transporter to drop you behind the pole. We have twin configurations on both ends. One marked human and one marked freight in the config settings. I tried it out a couple of days ago."

Dad said, "Let's move some freight."

"Okay, let's get the supplies on Aard because we have people standing by to begin the work.

I need to discuss some recruiting. Are you guys busy, or can we come back and chat for a bit?"

Tony nodded. "No worries, Mac, I'll start some tea so we can sit and chat. Then, if one of you goes back from the closet, sets things up, and comes back, you can watch the transfer from this side."

'Okay, but someone must confirm that it's all good on the other end. So, one of us needs to experience the other side, then return and give the thumbs up."

Willow started looking around, "Which closet? I'll stay on Aard, confirm it works as we hope, and return when it's over."

I led her to the closet, and she pushed the button and was gone. As my turn came, I turned to Dad and Tony and said, I'll be right back. I pushed the closet button.

By the time I arrived, Willow had already cleared Kia and Hilda sitting on the Knoll. She explained the transport and set expectations before I stepped from behind the pole.

I noted that the entire team was gathering now and was excited to see the results.

When all was clear, I waved, pushed the pole button, and stepped out of the closet. I leaned over the catwalk railing and said, "All clear. Fire up the rockets."

Dad pushed the button, and the freight left with a hiss.

The hiss continued after it was gone, then I noticed the hissing was coming from a tea kettle in the office.

Tony almost lost it, watching my expression as under-standing sunk in. So far, the transfer was anti-climactic. Willow was taking a bit long, so I headed back for the closet, sick to my stomach. As I stepped to the closet door, she appeared.

"Sorry, I just had to see them open the first pallet. It's Christmas back there. They are in party mode, yelling, holding treasures over their heads, and calling each other to come see what they have found. It's all good, though. I told them I was coming back to collect Mac, but I'm not sure anyone even noticed. So, let's have some tea. I want to hear what the MacAdams clan plans next, but I also want to get back home."

That was the first time it hit me between the eyes: just how much Willow considered Aard home.

I understand now her reluctance to push the transporter button and come to Earth. But she only did this for me. I had to reflect on that moment because t I realized that was exactly how I felt. The difference is that I knew I had a lot of work yet to do on Earth before I could comfortably 'retire' to Aard.

***

Chapter 24

Professor MacAdams and Jewels

As much as we wanted to get back to the celebration, Dad had a revelation about time and travel to share as we gathered in the office with a pot of tea.

"Son, Tony and I have been spending some quality time at that lab at night, and we found connections to other places the organization uses. They have some smart cookies working on time and distance travel.

It turns out they have much more ability than anyone imagined. Still, the biggest secret they have discovered is a technology that can enhance a person's mental ability to learn to do anything they want by adjusting the time and distance related to the learning event."

I began to see my father in a different light. As kids, we didn't have the benefit of getting to know him so well, as he was always gone. But I knew he was knowledgeable and involved in things he could not discuss. "I had assumed their technology was deep and wide, but you're hinting at things that will change human life to something we never imagined, not too far in the future."

He nodded and continued.

"There is a lab in Colorado that can educate you in 20 minutes.

How would you like to be a doctor? They started by pushing sentient intelligence from a person to a machine. Scientists to robots, so now they had a machine whose biggest fear was having someone turn off its switch. Science made a huge effort around the artificial intelligence world to code safeguards to protect humanity, but they did little to protect the sentient robot or intelligent machine."

The ramifications of that reality made me shiver. "A machine with emotions...."

"Tommy, I want to illustrate this process in a way that will benefit you and your people in the future. This process involves the teleportation science we have been learning, combined with Machine to Human learning, or M2H as it's called." He stepped into a metal closet with a chair and a headset with a visor, earphones, and a microphone hanging on a hook.

"Okay, so what do you want a degree in?"

"A degree? Uh... My bachelor's is in macroeconomics, so can we expand on that?"

"Okay, have a chair."

I sat down, put on the headset and visor, and in a moment, I watched a dizzying movie on extreme fast forward. Scenes, faces, sounds, smells, and tastes flowed through my brain like the Rio de la Libertad. The family around me watched as I jerked and twitched as my body tried to follow the events in my brain.

I didn't call out or appear to be scared, so they watched, chatted quietly, and drank tea. It must have felt like hours for those watching, but it felt like moments to a fully engaged brain.

Tony timed the process on his watch, and my lessons concluded at the sixteen-minute, twenty-three-second mark.

Dad unhooked me and asked, "How do you feel?"

"Well, I feel like I have sea legs, getting off a boat, but that is calming down."

Tony laughed. "Feel any smarter?"

We all grinned, but I thought briefly before responding. "Yyyes... If I take a moment to think about what I know about macroeconomics, I know much more about global economics than before. I know details about global marketing plans, politics, economics, cultures, and leadership styles across all those elements. This technology may be helpful, even in our little village."

Dad had moved over to the laptop on the desk, opened a browser, and typed in an address. "Come here and log in."

I knew the username and password to log in to the University of Phoenix student portal. In the portal, under my academic plan, I found the complete history of my Master's and Doctorate programs. In addition, I found the links to my records and downloaded the electronic versions of my diplomas, certifications, and transcripts. Not bad; 4.0 GPAs.

"I feel like I did these things."

Dad responded, "You did. You paid for the tuition up front and worked through every lesson.

51 Pegasi - Black Mac

You communicated with the instructors, professors, and student peers, and learned the stuff. It's all real; you were there. You went back in time, spent the time, and earned the knowledge. You were then brought back here, to the future…"

"Back to the future." I chuckled.

Dad got serious. "Son, this is a double-edged sword. You can go back and do things to change the future. However, some things will devastate the future for untold people around you, for instance, if you were to try to adjust for the death of a loved one… or yourself.

On the other hand, if you change the past to avoid a death, the future will change.

You probably won't even meet that person again; if you did, their whole perception of you would be different because of their altered past. You must understand you can not interfere with death once it has happened."

I was left in shock as I absorbed the meaning.

It was Tony's turn to school me. "Now, I'd like to talk to you about a struggling young lady in Oklahoma. You may want to spend a few minutes in the other direction, looking at the bright side. You can use the same technology to go back a few years and help this young lady decide what to do with her career. At the moment, she's drowning in the wrong advice."

Willow said, "Wait a minute. I want to go home. I have work to do. This is Mac's calling."

I laughed. She had a point, and Tony had a point.

"Okay," Tony said. "Just remember, time is relative to your own plane.

So, Willow, you could go back to Aard and back to your world, and Mac could join you tomorrow. And, with no connection to a couple of months, he experiences in Stillwater, Oklahoma. I don't know how long this might take, but Mac would have to accept a teaching position at Oklahoma State University. They are desperate for an Economics professor with the credentials and personality of Professor MacAdams."

He looked at me through his bushy Scottish brows, "Where a young lady is about to go down the drain if she doesn't see a better choice."

"Wow, that's a compelling sales job, boys."

"Are you okay to put in that time, Mac?" I was surprised to see how important this appeared to be to Tony and now, Dad.

"Mac, just stay safe and hurry home. I'm going to get back to the gang at Freedom. I'll let them know you'll be back soon." Willow was on board but headed home.

I stood and pulled her up for a hug. "I'll be back as soon as I can."

Willow reached up, kissed me, and headed for the transporter. "Be careful of those college girls." She blew me another kiss and stepped into the closet.

"Okay, where do I sign up?"

Tony sat me back on the education chair. "Just before you head out to your new job, you need to know this young lady has an issue.

She has a few symptoms you may recognize as you get to know her. She has a growing brain tumor.

To date, her only clues have been regular headaches that are getting more frequent. She notices some hearing loss in her left ear and intermittent dizziness. I'll tell you one day how I know, but for now, you'll have to take my word for it. She needs the blue mushrooms."

***

I started my new job the last week in August. By the beginning of the first semester, I had my curriculum, classroom, student list, and a little apartment to hide out when I wasn't working. I also had a steakhouse owned by Tony and Dad's friend, who took care of my dinners.

I found Julie on my student roster and learned the details of her education. Stellar high school marks landed her a full ride at OSU. Her immediate goal was to start in business and then transfer to a Vet program. The notes on her background said she had lost her father early and was on the outs with her mother. She had no siblings, so Julie was alone in the college town.

A couple of teachers had added notes to her student profile suggesting she may not be connecting with the right crowds to facilitate study and schoolwork best. A counselor had reached out, but she brushed them off.

By the middle of September, it was clear Julie would need help or miss her opportunity. She was dozing off in class, struggling to understand assignments, missing turn-in times, and not reaching out. The students filed out for lunch on a quiet Monday,

I walked to the back of the class and woke her up.

"Miss Phillips, I know my seminars can be rather dry and boring, but I'm afraid you will need some of my information to pass."

"I'm sorry, Sir, I'm just so beat. I need my evening job to get through school, but it means I don't get much sleep. I need to find a new job that will ease up my days and let me get some rest."

"I'm glad to hear you understand the issue, Julie. Unfortunately, your marks have been sliding. Is there anything I can do to help?"

"No, Sir, I think I'll be alright now."

"Julie, I want you to feel free to talk to me if you are having trouble. I can help."

I tried to keep from adding pressure but wanted her to understand I would be a safe place to vent if needed. Before I gave her options, I wanted to be sure this was not the path she wanted at this point in life.

"Yes, Sir, I sure will."

Things seemed to improve for a couple of weeks. She was on time and catching up, and I saw she could knock out good grades. It didn't last, however; by the month's end, she was right back where she had been.

During this time frame, while dining at the steakhouse, I discovered what was keeping her awake through the night. I turned my placemat over to read the local business ads, and there was Julie in the middle of an advertisement.

The ad was for the Blue Diamond Strip joint. It made me wonder how my brother got to know about her.

Just before my morning lecture, I finished the last couple of assignment scores and found by her grades, she was lost again. When she walked in, I asked if she would stop by my office after the lecture. She was scared, but she knew why we needed to talk.

She knocked on my office door.

"Come on in, Miss Philips."

She sat quietly in a chair across my desk and waited for me to finish typing on my laptop.

I typed for a couple of minutes more, then slid the machine back on the desk, closed it, and directed my attention to the scared girl on the other side of his desk.

"Do you mind if I call you Julie?"

"No, Sir, that would be fine."

"Julie, I want to see your big picture. I want to see what you want to do with your life and how you plan to get there. I would like very much for you to open up to me."

I smiled softly, and Julie melted. She no longer had reason to hold anything back.

"Dr. MacAdams, I am in trouble. My dad worked hard on the ranch to get me into college. I wanted to be a veterinarian to be valuable on the ranch. My father died a few years ago, and my mother sold the ranch. I no longer have a reason to get my degree, and I get massive headaches while trying to study."

"I'm sorry to hear that, Julie. From where I sit, it looks like your future has changed considerably."

"I have no future. I have no reason to my life now. I work, come to school, and sleep when I can. My life is not my own."

"Where do you work, Julie? How are you living?"

She dropped her head, and her eyes overflowed. "Sir, I'm a stripper over on East 6th."

I could tell she could hardly believe she had dropped the bomb, but it was out on the desk.

I smiled gently. "Julie, my favorite aunt, raised seven kids by dancing against a pole. She did what was necessary to get her kids into university. She paid for the start of all their careers, then retired to be a wonderful grandmother to their families."

Julie looked up with amazement.

I smiled.

"Julie, what would you like to do with your life if you could start over?"

"Sir, I would make it simple. Just make a living and live outdoors as much as I could. I love animals of all kinds and would love a chance to help them. I don't care where anymore, or even how, but it sure as hell wouldn't be in a city. I know my headaches would stop if I dropped the stress."

"Have you seen a doctor about your headaches?"

"No insurance. I just need rest."

"Julie, do you trust me enough to visit me tomorrow after school? I have something to show you that may solve your problems and give you a new goal.

I will supply dinner, but don't worry; this will not be a date. I only want to show you some possibilities that fit you better."

"Well, Sir, I have trusted far less scrupulous people with my life, so I would be happy to."

"Okay, be ready after school tomorrow, and you can ride with me."

***

True to my word, I was packed up and had locked the economics computer lab when she found me after school. Julie was surprised to see I drove an old Ford pickup with no bells and whistles. The back of her straw cowboy hat didn't have to bend against a headrest. She usually had to take it off in a vehicle. She commented as much as she latched on the lap belt.

"Well, Julie, I don't need much. I carry more cargo than people and am satisfied with the basics. You'll probably notice that side of the bench seat is hardly even broken in."

Looking down at the seat around her, she had to agree. The vinyl cover still had a waxy sheen, and the cushion provided no clue of wear.

"Where are we going?"

"A friend owns a quaint little steakhouse out on East 6th. Are you old enough to eat in a bar?"

"Well, I have been twenty for a couple of months now, so I suppose to keep your reputation, it had better be a restaurant."

"No problem, Freddie's has sections. We will have a better talking atmosphere in the restaurant section. I was aiming for it for other reasons as well."

We pulled up to the restaurant with neon reminders that they served the best prime rib in the country and had a fully qualified lounge for non-smokers. The cooks and wait-staff knew me and shocked Julie with their familiarity.

"Hi'a, Mac, what's cookin'?" The head chef was peering through the server window and waving at me.

"I 'spect I should be asking you that, Rudy. How's Penny?"

"All good, Prof. Prime Rib is spectacular tonight."

"Sounds like my usual tonight, but let's see what Jewels would like from the menu first."

Julie snapped her eyes toward me as the waitress tugged my elbow.

"This way, Mac, your table's waiting." Her smile was genuine. These folks seemed to love me, and Julie was noticing.

"How did you know about that stage name?"

A touch of fear rose in her throat as she imagined her professor watching her show from the back of the audience.

"No worries, Jewels, I am not a dancer stocker.

The name fits, but if it bothers you, I'll return to Julie or Miss Philips if you prefer."

"No, Sir, I was just surprised you had heard it."

"Well, Jewels, since we are friends now, please call me Mac like the rest of my friends do."

We sat, and the waitress dropped off menus and took our beverage orders. Julie took off her hat and set it upside down on the seat to her right.

"I know what I want, so you take a look and pick what you like. Don't worry about the cost. I have a great discount at this place."

Julie looked over the menu and flipped it closed.

"Do you mind if I get a coffee and a flat steak salad?"

"Not at all. That's one of my favorites."

The waitress dropped by to fill the coffee cups and take the orders. When she left, I showed her the laminated place-mats on the table and flipped hers over. Julie recognized the show bill for one of the clubs on East 6th.

Her jaw dropped.

"That's the poster for the review. That's me!"

"Yep, you see, you are more famous than you think."

"Gawd!"

"Jewels, I'm going to offer you a chance to start all over a world away from here. Are you interested?"

"That depends." She looked suspiciously at the middle-aged black man across from her.

Well, come with me for a moment. I stood and headed down the hall toward the restrooms. She stood but hesitated when she saw my direction.

I stopped short of the restrooms and opened a door with a sign that said, "Employees Only."

She followed as I flicked on the light switch. I opened the steel door on a breaker panel and pointed at a small button by itself near the bottom. There was no marking, and the button was a simple steel, half-inch diameter cylinder.

"Jewels, when you are ready to move to a whole new world, live mostly outdoors, work with a wide variety of animals and happy people, and be productive in a much simpler life, come to this panel. When you're ready, push that."

I headed back to the table, so she followed.

We just had time to sit down when our meals arrived.

"Eat well, Jewels."

"What will that button do? Where do you want me to go? What will happen?"

"Jewels, the button will take you to a whole different life. There will be no lights and sirens, no drama. You will just be transported. It's new science. You have never heard of the place. You can come back anytime, but people you know here will find you missing.

There will be no trace. If you return, I will move the button to protect the world you have seen.

But I'll make sure you can try again if you want to. No strings or closed doors. You will always have your free will."

I knew this was a big pill to swallow, but I could see she wanted to believe.

"Like any big change, it will take a leap of faith, but you will own your life on the other side of that button. You will make your own decisions and make new friends that accept you for you, as you will be expected to do with them. The key here is that you will live a much simpler life close to nature. It will not always be easy, but it will be organic and natural.

They ate in near silence.

"It sounds like Peter Pan. Can I get to the button if I decide to go?"

I laughed. "It does, kind of. I assure you, it is very real. Yep, you will find the room unlocked when you come back."

I dropped her at her boarding house before ten and drove off to the tune of a loose tailpipe.

I left Julie to contemplate the conversation we had had. This was a wild introduction, but I followed Tony and Dad's hunch that she would take the leap.

She had no reason to stay here. Her degree was hollow, her father was gone, her mother had moved on, and her job was in a downward spiral.

The next day in class, there was a substitute teacher. Professor MacAdams was suddenly off on a family issue. It took only two days to work up her courage, but she pulled on her straw hat and returned to the steak house.

As she entered, the staff greeted her as a friend. "Hi Jewels, would you like the usual?"

"Hi, just a coffee, please. I don't think I will stay long." She drank half her coffee while building up her nerve, left two dollars by her cup, and got up.

Then, hesitantly, she opened the Employee Only door while watching for witnesses and found the metal panel. There was the button, alone and ominous, at her eye level. She felt ridiculous and scared, but she pushed the button.

***

Chapter 25

Aardian Immigration Begins at the Landing

I landed in the 'education closet' and stepped out to join Dad and Tony in their office. They looked up expectantly.

"She'll be at the landing soon, so I will head back to Aard to prepare for her arrival. Tony, you said you would explain about her later. Is it 'later' enough?"

This is where Dad took over. "Son, you had a half-sister. When Tony's mother left the family, she was with child. I wasn't aware until many years later. That child was named Sandra, and she eventually married a rancher in Oklahoma.

They had a daughter before she became restless and strayed. I don't know if that was my restless blood or her mother's, but when her husband got sick, she stuck it out just long enough to capture the nest egg from the ranch. Sandra liquidated it and left. Having Julie made her realize she wasn't cut out to be a mother or to stay in one place. Spending almost twenty years on the ranch was all she could do. We're not sure where she is now."

He stopped for a moment to reflect, then continued. "Julie's father was a tall cowboy named Samuel Phillips.

His brother, Richard, or Ricky, owns a string of steak houses throughout the Midwest.

He hadn't stayed close to Sam because of issues with Sandra.

When we found out about the family, Tony reached out to Ricky, and Ricky was happy to connect."

Dad's forehead furrowed now, "Ricky's wife, Sheila, is a doctor who kept her maiden name. She was Julie's doctor but never let on that they were related. Ricky told us Sam died of a malignant brain tumor.

She said his symptoms were much the same as Julie's. Sheila had done a CAT scan that confirmed as much, but Julie had stopped coming in or communicating when Julie's mother sold the ranch. She had ignored the urgent request to come in for a consultation after the results. Her address had changed, with no forwarding address or phone number.

When Tony connected and updated them on Julie, they were shocked to see what Julie's life had become and were happy to help us pull her out of that environment. Ricky's office was in the Stillwater restaurant, so he took a hands-on approach to helping his niece.

Once Tony was satisfied. Ricky and Sheila were open enough to the fantastic story they were about to hear, he explained.

At first, Ricky was skeptical, but Sheila was fascinated to hear about the possibilities for medicine. She convinced Ricky to take a spin on the transporter Tony set up.

They both took a quick trip to Seattle to meet with me, visit Pikes Place Market, and return within a few hours.

Tony had to promise to set Ricky up with a Seafood connection in Seattle. By the time the in-laws were ready to transport home, they had a plan to save Julie."

I sat there in shock as all this news sank in. I now knew why the folks at the steak house were so friendly and helpful. But I also knew there was no time to waste.

"Why didn't you tell me before I headed for Oklahoma?"

"Sorry, Tommy, I should have, but I didn't want that extra pressure on you. We just rammed you through your doctorate, coerced you into taking a leave of absence from Willow, and sent you off to save a young lady. I hope we left you with a little break in the drama while you were doing a most important task." Dad had a hopeful smile as he explained.

Jewels needed blue mushrooms and Aard as soon as possible.

"I get it. Hindsight being easy, I imagine you are right. I might have been in a bigger hurry and maybe would have applied too much pressure. It's more important now to hurry up and get her to Aard."

I repeated. "I've got to get back to Aard and prepare for Jewels."

My family agreed, so with a couple of bear hugs, I was on my way to the transporter closet.

***

I opened my eyes to dark surroundings.

I was on the landing knoll, but this was my first landing in the dark, so it was a new experience. There was a faint blue glow from under the grasses and shrubbery around the pond, and the beauty of the reflection across the pond struck me.

On the other side of the pond, I saw the campfire flicker reflected on the concave rock face behind it and the silhouettes of people around the fire. Then, across the fire, I saw the rosy glow of my beautiful Willow.

The Aardian blue nightlight produced by the amazingly useful spoor guided me to the trail, and I worked my way around the pond to the landing camp. The moons had not yet risen, so the beauty of Aard starlight at night was almost overwhelming in this state. I missed my home and my mate.

"We need a bell on that pole," I spoke as I entered the light of the fire.

Willow jumped up and ran around the team to jump into my arms.

"I missed you so much. I'm so happy you're home." She wrapped herself tightly around me.

"How long have I been gone?" I was a bit worried by the statement.

"All day!" she bellowed.

With that, everyone laughed. Shiv, Hilda, Tiffany, and Willow stayed with Popeye while the rest of the team hauled a load of goods back to Freedom. More of the group had planned to be back in the morning, and the whole gang was assigned packs to haul the remaining goods back to the village.

All but for the supplies that would stay at the Landing Camp for Popeye and team.

"Well, crew, I feel our landing immigrant will be arriving soon, so we need at least Popeye to be here for a few days. Can we cover his load back to Freedom?"

Tiffany said, "That is wonderful news. We need to grow our villages into a strong society. I'm so excited to see our transportation begin to work under our terms. If you can cover Popeye's load, we have it figured."

"It's a deal. Are you good with hanging out alone for a few days as we take care of the supplies, Popeye?"

"You mean, hang out in paradise with nothing to do but explore and write my book? It'll be tough, but I'll take one for the team."

His description of chores brought a round of laughter.

"I'm kinda serious, though. I took possession of a bundle of notebooks, a pack of number 2 pencils, and a couple of pencil sharpeners from the supplies. I've started an immigration journal to log the people who come and go. I've already got a section on offloading Larry."

The laughter continued.

"I have a feeling we may not have seen the last of Larry. I hope I'm wrong, but he appeared to be a skillful opportunist, and I think he saw a lot of opportunity here."

Tiffany agreed. "We now have a map of the known transporters on Aard. At least those in control of the giants and their human minions.

We need to import some warriors to help us neutralize their abilities." She pointed across at Shiv, who nodded. "Shiv and I have started planning for a new raid on the Tower Giant's cages."

I was impressed. "Well, it's obvious this team doesn't let any moss grow on them unless, of course, they are using it for bandages. Popeye, the immigration journal, is a great idea, and written word books are even better. We need to record our progress, people, science, everything, and everyone as we build our society."

Hilda grinned from her spot near the fire. "I can't wait to meet some of those warriors."

I chuckled. "Well, I've had a couple of tips that have led to our incoming shippment. I plan to go visit someone soon, that my father and brother have suggested, but perhaps Tiffany, we should sit down and build a conscious list of people we know on Earth.

People who would fit the criteria of our new society, in the warrior or protector mindset, and do some active recruiting. We could start by building a list of people we know that may fit the model."

Shiv had been quietly listening in deep thought, but he now found a spot to share his thoughts. "Bullshit! We need randomness of the people we have saved from the cages, and I've also got to say, they fuckin' need us more than pissing away our efforts on hand-picked offerings we select from Earth.

I think that to get the variety we need, we are far more fucking useful as a new society, finding people deep in shit. People who need us, not people we need."

I wasn't used to this much depth in Shiv's comments, but he spoke volumes with that input that defined what we were trying to do on Aard. Every one of us could have gone home, but at our core, we wanted to save people from the dead ends we had all experienced, and, of course, we wanted to keep them from the fate they fell into with the giants as well.

Shiv looked directly at me while the rest of the camp went silent.

I smiled wide. "Shiv, it's about time you showed us how deep your brain goes. That was brilliant. Popeye, you may want to take notes because Shiv just laid out our charter. You may want to edit our official records, but maybe not. Shiv has a way of laying down facts."

The mood broke, and even Shiv laughed.

I continued. "I see cases for both approaches, but Shiv is on the money. Before focusing too much on cherry-picking, we must help as many people as possible escape those cages.

The bad guys are cherry pickers. We also need to remember cases we become aware of where a human goes down the drain without a second chance. Every human deserves a chance at life and happiness."

I looked at Tiffany, "Now tell us about the plan you two are hatching for your rescue mission."

I noted as I changed the subject, that Tiffany held no grudge. She reached over and hugged Shiv. Nothing was said, but they were a team.

***

I sat on a stump by the fire as Willow handed me a cup of tea. Tiffany and Shiv spent an hour as the moons came up, describing their plan to hit the briar patch cages and split into two groups on the escape.

One group would bring the escapees home to Freedom, while the other would head for a Northern transporter about three hundred miles North of the tower. The team coming back plans on traveling primarily at night for safety. They had decided that Tiffany, Shiv, and Dan would head North to find and disrupt the nearest transporter. Jesus and Stud would shepherd the escapees back to Freedom.

"You realize you are taking all our warriors and scouts on this trip, right?"

"Tiffany answered with fire in her voice. "Who do you think the best archer is in camp?"

All eyes went to Willow.

"Who do you think is the second-best archer in camp?"

All eyes went to a shadow sitting behind Ann. The shadow noticed the attention and visibly shrunk. I said, "Penny, have you been holding out?"

Willow was nodding. "Penny has practiced more than anyone in camp, and it shows. She has been practicing with arrows longer than her, and she can drive them deep into a tree at 50 feet."

"Ok, I get it. We all live here and need to be warriors and scouts. I will sit this out then and stay in the camp until you return. Please come back, all of you."

I said, "If you can, please capture any transporters you find; we can use them to build landings near the bad guys in the future to keep us from the threats of travel and get us to those far-away transporters."

After planning, we settled in for some sleep before our trek tomorrow.

Two days later, Popeye stepped into camp with Jewels. Already acclimated with her tunic at half-mast under a straw cowboy hat, Jewels looked comfortable. He introduced Jewels to Willow, and I welcomed her to camp with a hug.

"Welcome home to Freedom, Jewels. What do you think so far?"

"Professor MacAdams, I am home. I can already tell this is where I need to be. I can't wait to meet everyone and learn how to be Aardian. My last job made the transsition easier and Paul has been a perfect introduction to Aard."

Popeye handed me his journal. "Here you go, 'Professor Mac.' Please read up on the new immigrant." I laughed at his dig, and so did Willow.

"I'll bring her back later for immunizations and hazing." He winked, and they were off to meet the camp.

Willow and I sat on the porch of our hut and read Popeye's notes.

***

Chapter 26

Cure for Cancer and Bootcamp at the Landing

I looked at Willow. "Did you see how often he said she would fit in just fine?"

We laughed.

Willow observed. "I think Popeye is going to be our historian, and he seems to be a bit infatuated with our new citizen."

"Well, we will see how this plays out. There is a significant age gap, and Jewels will meet several people closer to her age. She is young, but she seems to have an older soul. She has had to mature quickly. I'm not too concerned, but we must get Popeye some company at the landing."

I caught Willow's gaze.

"I have other concerns, too, Willow, so I need your help to keep me from bias. I didn't know this before, but Jewels is my niece. It turns out her mother is Tony's full sister, so she is my half-sister. I don't think it's time for that announcement, but I must ensure I stay objective and treat her like everyone else. To complicate matters, she has an inherited medical condition."

"Well, boot camp starts tomorrow. Is it ok to continue?"

"Absolutely. Please focus on the stuff she needs from you. I'd like Popeye to do most of her boot camp at the landing. I need to spend some time with them both tomorrow before deciding. One thing she needs is to get on to a diet of blue mushrooms, and with the connection she is making with Popeye, it may be helpful for them to bond in a way that means more to them in the future."

Willow looked at me with wide eyes, "Cancer?"

I nodded. "A malignant brain tumor. Would you please check her feelings about returning to the landing to finish her Bootcamp and ensure she understands it's her choice? We must assure her she can return to Freedom anytime."

This time, she nodded. I hugged Willow closely. "Tonight, my priority is you. I don't care if we even leave the hut... unless a trip to the tubs is in order, but I want you next to me. Tomorrow, I will spend quality time with Tiffany, Shiv, Jesus, and the team.

I want to see where I can help with their plans. Then I need to accompany Popeye back to the landing and head back to see Tony and Dad about one more immigrant they want me to assess. Would you like to come?

"Mac, two things mean the world to me: you and the health and happiness of the village of Freedom. I don't care if I ever push that button again. My life is here, so I want to live, and someday I will die on Aard.

I know you have a bigger calling.

You need to communicate with Earth to keep us safe and the door open for our growth and health. I will always be here when you come back. I will always need you to come back."

I pulled her closer and kissed her deeply.

One thing led to another, and we burned off a lot of stress. Later, in the overheated darkness of the hut, I suggested a stroll to the luminous spa at the bitter water's tubs.

Willow did not need convincing, and we walked hand in hand to the rocky shelf to find several of the tubs occupied. One of the bigger ones was hosting Popeye and Jewels. The constant crash of the waves made it impossible to hear what they were saying, but their pleasant animation spoke volumes.

I smiled as Willow, and I sunk into another tub and let the warm and cool water cycling waves swirling past us draw all our cares from us, if only for an hour.

In the morning, Popeye delivered Jewels to Willow, and I found time to sit in with the warriors and scouts. The team was packed and prepared but had waited to talk with me before heading out as a courtesy. They hoped to ensure I could plan locally while this critical team was out of the village. We all understood some of them, or all of them, may not make it back to Freedom. It was a fact we lived with in this world.

Popeye joined the talks when I did, so once we finalized the planning, Popeye and I went for a walk to discuss Jewels and the landing.

I opened the conversation. "Popeye, you, and Jewels have hit it off very well. By the way, I loved your journal.

The history of Aard and Freedom will sound like a novel you can't put down."

He chuckled about the journal but became serious about Jewels. "Yes, I'm amazed, Mac. She is so young, but she is in tune. She is mature and wise beyond her age. Given all that, I was hesitant, but she admitted she wanted to know me better. Mac, she asked if she could come back and learn from me at the landing."

"You're stealing my thunder. I wanted your take on that very topic. If you both want that, I'd like you to take over her education, but I have something you need to know about her."

"Uh oh."

"Popeye, she has a cancerous brain tumor. Now, listen carefully. Dr. Tim has evidence that the blue mushrooms will probably cure that cancer. Jewels doesn't know she has this yet but may recognize the signs she has been struggling with. She has headaches, dizziness, and hearing loss on her left side.

The mushrooms start working immediately as their medicines hit the bloodstream very quickly. She will feel some of the effects within minutes with fresh mushrooms."

When I think back, we all felt immediately better when eating these blue miracle workers.

Popeye was gobsmacked. For a moment, he had nothing to say.

"Do you understand?"

He swallowed and nodded. "Mac, how long does she have, to get to the mushrooms?"

"I have no idea, but you gave her a bit of dried mushroom already, didn't you?"

"Yes, but I didn't get a reaction from her."

"The medicinal properties of the dried fungus are much weaker, but in a steady diet, they would work. There is a good stock of mushrooms near the landing, so you can work fresh mushrooms into Jewel's diet.

We've all gotten healthier from our diets here, particularly with those mushrooms.

At least we know she doesn't have any objections to mushrooms. I'll make a dish that makes them a new favorite. I want to take care of her, Mac. You should hear her sing... and the poetry she can write is way beyond her years. There is no task she won't take on, and she makes me feel good with everything she says and does. Mac, she is a special human."

"Understood, Popeye. I want everything above board. She is very young, you have a great age gap, and sometimes that is hard to get around, so you will both have challenges if you decide to do this."

"I've got it, Mac. We will certainly fail if we don't try."

"Agreed. Let's see what Jewels and Willow are up to and how the training is going. Please don't say anything about the tumor until you two are alone, preferably after a meal of fresh mushrooms, as she should feel the difference in a few minutes."

We went to find Willow and Jewels. We found them at Willow's hut and they looked like old friends.

***

I brought up the opportunity for Jewels to move to the landing with Popeye; the look she gave Paul was answer enough. She was emphatic that she could build a wonderful life learning how to help Popeye in the immigration office for Aard and the village of Freedom.

I hoped this case of love at first sight, would turn out to be a winner. I felt the motivation was right from both sides.

In the morning, the freedom force headed East, and the landing party, with me in tow, headed North. The walk along the plateau was uneventful, with a lesson on local flora and fauna at every turn, but for Jewels' question about the far-off screams to the East. Popeye filled her in about Purple Screamers.

I was surprised at the reaction to Popeye's no-frills description of the dangerous but beautiful raptors. She drilled him for details, and the theme of her assessment was technical and scientific. Jewels sounded like a biologist who had studied raptors all her life.

Both Popeye and I had to admit we simply didn't know the answer to many of her questions. I remember an early conversation with Jewels when she told me she always wanted to be a vet. *I felt many more avenues of study were open to her in Aard.*

I decided to test the waters to see if her interest in animals could take a specific direction on Aard. "Jewels," I asked, "Now that you have experienced your first taste of Aard, have you been inspired to follow any of your dreams from your life on Earth?"

"It's funny you should ask, Prof..., Mac. I'm especially looking forward to two things in this fascinating new environment. First, I want to know everything about every animal I meet, and I want to bring music and the arts to Aard. I know you expected me to mention the animals, but I also dream of the human expression of the fine arts. I'm particularly interested in music and what it can mean for the people of this world."

Suddenly, Jewels doubled over in agony, clutching her head. She dropped to her knees and silently struggled with the pain, squeezing her eyelids closed against the tropical sun. Tears ran down her cheeks as she asked Popeye to help her get to the shade.

We helped her to a trickling creek a few yards off the path and sat her in the shade of a mossy volcanic bolder. She slumped against the stone and apologized.

"I'm sorry, guys. Sometimes, when I get excited about something, I get these massive headaches. I'll be ok in a few minutes.

I'll have it for the rest of the day, but a little time in the quiet shade will tame it enough to handle till I can sleep it off."

"Don't worry, Jewels. I think I have something that will help." Popeye headed for the North slope of a dark hillside a few hundred feet East. I knew what he was after, so I made Jewels as comfortable as I could with a moss pillow to lean on. Moments later, he was back with a powder blue orb. He cut it into half-inch slices and pressed a piece between two strips of dried berries.

"Eat this Jewels. I think it will help."

"I don't know if I can keep food down right now, but I'll try anything."

We both ate as well, to show her it was a safe and natural food on Aard. She managed to eat what Popeye gave her but had to work to finish it all and settle her stomach. While she was dealing with her stomach, we diverted her attention by pointing out some of the features of her environment. Within a few minutes, her headache subsided and disappeared.

"Guys, I must always keep a supply of that stuff near me."

Popeye looked at me, "Jewels, you will learn to love that mushroom. I have some great recipes."

We got to the landing with plenty of daylight. I knew Jewels was in good hands, and I had no doubt she would have those headaches behind her when I returned to Aard. I said my goodbyes at the landing cabin and stepped around the pond to the transporter pole.

Looking back over the pond, at the landing couple, I hit the button for Seattle while the new couple settled in. Popeye and Jewels still had time to build an evening meal. Popeye later told me he dove into his evening journal to document the process. He started with the trail to the ponds I showed him when he arrived.

***

Chapter 27

Adelphi and a Veterinarian

Sitting in my father's office again so soon after the last adventure was a novel feeling. I was getting the story of the young woman in Greece who he insisted was a natural for our community.

I was also getting closer to the enigma that was our father. Some of his history was beginning to fall together. Tony was at the glacier on Aard, but Dad had stayed back for this conversation, so I knew how much it meant to him.

"Son, I was on the run from some bad guys after a meeting in Belarus. I made it down through Ukraine, Romania, and Bulgaria and thought I had slipped out of the noose when I reached a little town called Mount Rodopi in the Northeast panhandle of Greece. I was in a little hotel and was to meet a boat at the mouth of the Lissos River that would take me to a ship waiting near Athens.

A friendly waiter brought me a mug of hot water and a tea bag. Fifteen minutes later, my throat was closed, and I was dying.

A young woman, happening by, saw what was happening, smelled my tea, rubbed a bitter salve on my tongue, and fifteen minutes after that, I was sitting up and talking with her."

I was speechless hearing this story from my father.

I began to understand why he didn't share details on why he was gone so much or where he was, but I knew better than to pry. He kept his family a secret from his work as much as he kept his job a secret from us. "I'm not even going to ask."

He continued. "Adelphi took me on foot to a hidden root cellar, fed me, and called a relative to deliver me to my boat in the morning. By the end of the next day, I was in safe company."

"Wow, Dad, how can I help?"

"Tommy, she was only fifteen at that time. I learned that from her uncle, who got me to safety. She was already living alone on the mountain, selling eggs and herbs. She gave me a mailing address that would take letters to her. I sent her a letter expressing my gratitude and an offer to help if she ever needed it."

A few weeks ago, I got a letter from her, postmarked last September. I don't know how it took so long to get to me, but I can send you back to a time we may be able to help her.

I don't know what that is, but she speaks perfect English with an American accent, a hobby her uncle told me about. I feel bad guys will be watching for me there, so I may be a target if I go myself. Will you help?"

"Sure, Dad, but I have to ask. Tony is around you much more than I am nowadays. So why does he not go?"

There was a short pause, and he said, "Because he looks like me."

I laughed out loud till my eyes misted up. "The black kid gets the short straw!"

He was worried about my reaction, but I slapped his back, and he laughed too.

"The black kid simply has the edge."

I laughed again.

"Son, even though you have the edge, I hesitated to include you because it could be dangerous if they make the connection, but I also know the mission you are on and feel it all works."

Dad set me up with a transporter to configure, and a few minutes later, I was sitting up in the backyard of an old Mediterranean villa high on a Grecian hill. Above me was a thin trail with bare footprints in the dirt. It led up the slope to a little stone hut built centuries ago. I strode up the hill through a small flock of chickens and knocked on a narrow green door.

There was no answer, so I sat on a small stool and leaned against the wall. I was dozing in the shade when I heard a woman's angry voice, "Τι κάνεις εδώ?"

I jumped up and said, "Adelphi?"

She was silent for a moment. "You are American?" She spoke in a perfect mid-American accent.

"I am Tom MacAdams. My father, Evan, sent me. People call me Mac or Black Mac."

I tried to connect the dots to my color difference from my father.

"Evan? MacAdams? Her mood changed immediately. She never questioned my color; she just asked me in for tea.

She heated the water and asked, "You can take me from Mount Rodopi?"

"Yes, Adelphi. Where do you want to go?"

"Anywhere I can take my books, my herbs, my seeds, and myself that has good dirt, water, moss, and people who need healthcare."

"Adelphi, we have a place like that, with more for you to work with, but did my father tell you where that is?"

"He said another world, but he said he would send you to explain."

Over tea, I explained Aard and the village of Freedom. She didn't bat an eye. I explained transporting in lay terms, and she simply nodded.

"When do you want to move, Adelphi?

"I want to move now, but I cannot. I have to deal with my dying father and my aged mother. I'm not sure how long. Maybe a week, maybe a year, but I fear if I stay too long, I will die before I can come."

"Do you have a private spot where I can install a small machine that can allow you to leave when you want?"

"You can do that? Yes! In my root cellar."

She stepped out of the stone cottage and hurried around behind the building. I followed. Another small door led into the hillside. She turned an old key in the lock, stepped in, opened a matchbox, and lit a candle. I had configured the transporter to our landing pole on Aard and installed the button facing up on a plank shelf above eye level.

"Adelphi, when you want to leave, push that button." I made a motion to push down with my finger.

"We will have to make another calibration when we know how much and what materials are involved. You said books, herbs, and seeds.

I can't guarantee the seeds because this is another planet, but the dried herbs and books will be no problem if they are gathered here in this room, and we know how big the bundle is. Just push the button and come to tell us when you are ready, and one of our folks will come back here, recalibrate, and your goods will come to our world."

Adelphi was thrilled. She hugged me quickly, then embarrassed, she backed up.

"Sorry."

"No problem. I will go now. You come when you are ready."

I turned and pushed the button.

***

I briefly visited Popeye and Jewels to tell them they would visit Greece at some point and noticed they were still in honeymoon mode.

Jewels had a question for me, however.

"Professor, I have an embarrassing question for you."

I found it interesting; she addressed me by the title she met me with.

"Of course. Shoot."

"I just want to update you on my health and ask a question about my education. First, Paul explained the brain tumor and why I was brought here. Thank you for your part. I also want to let you know Dr. Tim has given me a clean bill of health."

I was about to explain that there was more to why we brought her to Aard, but she continued.

"Secondly, I think I may have dropped out too soon. I think I'm going to need my veterinarian skills here. Learning about animals from Earth and transferring to critters on Aard will be weird, but I think we may need to domesticate animals at some point. They will need care. Any advice on what I should do?"

I smiled. There would be lots of time to give Jewels the full family details of her immigration. "I'm just about to drop in on my dad with a report on my last trip. So come along, and I'll answer your question. Can you spare her for an hour, Popeye?"

They were both dumbfounded, but Popeye nodded. "I have some chores to do."

Jewels nodded at me, so I headed for the button. As I entered my father's office, she arrived in the breaker closet and followed me tentatively through the door.

Dad looked up from the laptop he was working on and said, "Hi, Son, how was Greece? Hello Jewels."

I motioned a chair for Jewels and pulled one up for myself.

"I'll fill you in in a few, Dad, but first, you know the story on Jewels. It seems we pulled her out of school a little too soon. Now that she is healthy, we're wondering if she can take a crash course like I did?"

"Fancy that, he turned his laptop around and showed us the veterinary program at Washington State University. "Would you consider the fast program at WSU," He asked."

"Uhh, how long does the fast program take?"

"Do you have twenty minutes?"

"Y-yes."

"Have a seat in the classroom. "Dad pointed to the closet where I had earned my Master's and Doctorate." I stood and invited her in. Dad came around his desk, hooked the headset and visor on Jewels, then said. "Relax and have fun."

The program started, and I returned to the desk with my father and filled him in on Adelphi. "I'm not sure how long it will take to get her affairs in order with her parent's health and age, but she can come at any time to get help with her books and herbs. Not sure about her seeds. Any advice?"

"No seeds between worlds. The machinery will neutralize them on transport."

He explained his logic.

"I'm sure it would be easy enough to adjust and grow seeds on another planet, but we are still unsure how ethical transplanting humans is. We wouldn't have done it this way if the bad guys hadn't already broken that seal."

He thought about it for a minute. "I would bet seeds will be allowed within a few years because this technology is going to bust open across the world, and those who want us on other planets will have the imagination of everyone."

"That soon?"

"That soon. The space race is on. The US, China, Russia, Britain, France, India, Canada, and even some smaller countries are innovating extraordinary daily expansion."

We heated a pot of tea and discussed the uses for the education transporter, Jewel, Adelphi, and the future. I could have talked it through all evening, but Jewels was back.

"How long was I gone?"

"Fourteen minutes and twelve seconds." Dad pointed at a stopwatch on his desk. "How do you feel?"

"Smart." She smiled.

"I know how to neuter a dog, identify bird flu, assess a horse's Navicular bone, pull a breached calf, and get the silkiest hair on my head by using horse shampoo. I'm already thinking of ways to apply these skills to Humpbacks, but I have many animals to meet before I know just how much I will do."

Dad nodded and then pointed at me. "By the way, your brother is now a Doctor of Physics. He is studying transportation concepts with newer variations of radio signals.

I think he's also beginning to identify some loose cannons associated with the Giants."

"Thank you, Pops. We'll get back to Aard now.

Popeye will be beside himself if we are gone any longer."

Dad came out from behind the big old steel desk and hugged us both. He took Jewel by the shoulders and said, "Lass, your father would be so happy to know you are healthy and happy now."

"I'm not sure you know this yet, but if not, you may want to sit down. We're related."

Jewels did sit down.

"I'm your grandpa. Although estranged, your mother's mother was once my wife.

I don't think you knew her much, but she was much like your mother. Your father was the best thing that ever happened to your mom; he was like another son to me. Sam was a mighty fine gentleman, and I owed him my life, so I'm happy I could help his little girl. Live a massive life happily for him." He teared up a bit, but he used his bushy eyebrows to hide his eyes as much as possible.

"Wow!" Jewels grinned. She looked at me. "Uncle Mac?"

I beamed. I hadn't thought how good that tile would feel.

Jewels stood and hugged him again. "I'm looking forward to growing our relationship, 'Grampa,'" she grinned. "We must get back, but I want to come back and get all the stories."

He also owed me another story, but we left him to his thoughts.

51 Pegasi - Black Mac

We landed near the pole, one after the other. Popeye was pacing. His smile lit up the landing when he saw Jewels arrive in all her spender.

"Mac, while you two were away, I got a quick visit from Adelphi. She will be ready to immigrate in a couple of days. Jewels and I need to drop in on her and help her launch. She has a library to bring, and I have the coordinates for her root cellar."

"That's excellent news, Popeye, and Jewels has a boat-load of news for you too."

The day was getting late, so I faked that I wanted to get halfway home before camping for the night, borrowed some jerky, and moseyed on down to the string of ponds where I taught Popeye to hunt and set up camp in the blue glow. I figured they needed their space.

***

Chapter 28

Preparing to Hunt the Hunters
– Stud Comes Back

I had to return to camp to cover for Freedom being shorthanded. I was on the trail early, and as the sun came up over the peaks in the East, I noticed specks soaring on the winds and could hear the far-off haunting screams. Walking by myself, I had time to think.

I wondered how much distance we would need to cover to reach those mountains. I also wondered how much cover there would be as we tried to get close, and I wondered what those raptors were hunting. Perhaps it was time for us to go hunting. I scouted the plateau as much as I could from the trail.

My feet were on autopilot while I considered the terrain, the evergreen cover, and the degree of difficulty traveling to the mountains and back with cargo could create. It seemed to me the distance would be about the same as the top of the upper falls in the pass, but it wouldn't be as rugged as the riverbank.

I noted that the landscape rose slightly most of the way to the base of the foothills. This revelation inspired me to climb a tree to see over the tops of the light forest, and I confirmed a slight slope all the way.

That meant it would be downhill while carrying a load on the way back.

The double-edged sword was the heavy forest near the hills would be challenging. However, the good thing would be the cover it would provide a scrambling group of humans as they escaped with food, hide, and feathers.

By the time I got back to Freedom, I had a full head of ideas to serve the villagers. The camp was quiet. Many of our most gregarious residents were still away on missions. The rest of the village was concerned as they knew our missing brothers and sisters were in grave danger, in service to each of them.

An Aardian week went by as I sat with the camp around the fire in the evenings, building plans A and B for our next steps. We could not afford to sit back and wait for our warriors; we had to continue to build our strengths.

Plan A would be put into play if we did not see any of our warriors within two days. Willow and Penny worked on archery skills with the rest of the band, and even Julio became a marksman. I hoped he never needed to kill.

Hilda was practicing with the longer arrows with Penny, her strength an advantage.

She had decided she wanted to bring home a Screamer.

I suspected her goal was to surprise and impress Stud. The Frenchman had been getting a lot more of her attention lately, and I knew she was one of the more worried citizens as she quietly prayed for his safe return.

Ann, Dr. Tim, Stacy, and Maritza all felt they were more useful in support roles.

I also noted that Kia had taken a more significant interest in Vera. In return, Vera was happiest when she was near Kia.

This turn of events has been a positive change for Vera. She was now often smiling and helpful around the camp.

Vera had built muscle and, at 5'8", was becoming one of the more substantial contributors in the camp. It seemed Kia was finding a lot of comfort in her companionship. I asked if anyone was interested in the first hunt to the Screamer Mountains and found I had an avid group that wanted the challenge. Willow, Penny, Hilda, Vera, and I began planning for the hunt.

We started by discussing the change of plans we could count on depending on who made it back in time. This version would be our plan B, and we would adjust according to who we had to join us. Then, around to plan A, I shared all my observations on the plateau on the way back to freedom with the primary team to attack the task.

We pulled up some of the longer arrows for specific testing and training on frond bundles, tightly bound and hanging high in the trees. We were happy to learn that Penny and Vera could bury arrows in these bundles without fail, even suspended high in the trees. When lowered and assessed, their tips were almost through the bundles.

I did not miss the fact that Vera would not eat meat when she arrived. This modification of her character was a significant change, and it answered one of the many questions I pondered on the effects of this life on the human condition. She had started tentatively nibbling Humpback jerky on the trail and found it satisfying.

With no one saying, 'I told you so,' she continued experimenting with meat and found life this close to nature made it easier to see her place in the food chain.

Now, she was one of our most accomplished hunters.

I did notice, however, that she built a revered relationship with her prey and began discussing their health and well-being with Jewels. I found this character's journey a fascinating evolution of a personality in a natural ecological environment.

My arrows buried just past halfway. Willow and Hilda could bury their tips almost to the halfway point, more than enough for a kill at 50 feet. We also experimented with targets on the bundles to perfect kill shots, and we experimented with different tips. The best tip was the rock-hard and razor-sharp tips of a Humpback tail that were perfectly barbed for self-defense.

Smaller tips would go deeper, but these tips provided the hunter the best chance not to become the hunted. We packed the paper-boy sacks with knives and food but planned to travel light as this would be an overnight trip in and an overnight trip back.

We decided the twin moons would be our guide up the plateau. We would keep a quiet camp until the late afternoon to prepare, then action in the hour before dark. We wanted the darkness to close the conflict and allow our escape into the moonlit trees. Perhaps, some help from the neon mushrooms. By now, we understood the Screamers were daylight hunters.

Penny, Vera, and Hilda decided to do a dry run this afternoon to plot trails and work out details.

They expected to find challenges like creeks to ford, windfall obstacles in the trees, and perhaps animals they were not expecting. They packed light, but I noticed they took a few long arrows... Just in case.

"We'll camp up there tonight till it's dark, then work our way back to experience what we may need to do much faster next time." Penny was excited. This adventure was her first real opportunity to lead and show what she could do.

I fought my biases and held my tongue; it was clear we were all concerned. I was determined that my leadership was organic and focused on building new leaders to carry on long past my time. This was one of those opportunities.

"I know you three will be careful, and I wish we were all going, but we should have a big team here when the warriors return in case they need help. I'm having enough trouble sending five of us out on the actual hunt when so many are already out on missions."

"Please be careful and come back for the posse." I finished.

They promised they would and headed for the plateau. As they left, there was no fanfare. It was not a celebratory march. Instead, the hunters were demure, making last-minute checks, helping each other with their packs, and full of resolve. They knew what they were about to challenge and were all okay with it.

I thought about Hilda, the spoiled college ecologist planning to hunt.

I was curious to see how living much closer to the land would hone her drive for sustainability. I felt she was expanding her horizons with life in Freedom.

I marveled at Penny, the tiny camp gossip I met at the Pass Camp, who was now a formidable archer. She didn't brag or embellish anymore because she knew her worth. Penny was naturally the leader of this small band, not because she had asked to lead.

I was also in awe of the suicidal kid who had just stepped out of her troubled teens. Vera now had defined and powerful muscle mass and a new confidence the once shy Canadian had never known.

Her pale skin was now tan, textured with life, vibrant and glowing, with no hint of shame. Aard had given them each the life they had been looking for.

***

When night fell, a much smaller community gathered around the village fire. When Willow and I joined, dinner was ready, and Julio held court with funny stories about his hometown. He grew up in a small village before moving to Santa Domingo, so he told stories of his childhood in a life not too different from Freedom, or as he called it, Libertad.

Julio told the camp about the town bully, a strutting Bantam rooster. He was the butt of the joke as the rooster constantly made him find new ways home. His stories led to several shared hometown stories around the camp, and I was inspired by how these stories bonded this sprinkling of humanity into a cohesive family.

As in any family, there was some bickering at times, but it was easy to see an outside force would find an iron-clad unity that would make the citizens of Freedom-Libertad a much bigger entity than its parts.

My reverie was interrupted by a Tarzan call from the darkness to the Southeast. This had become our standard call signal as someone came back to camp. We now knew this was one of ours.

"Bonjour Liberte! Dr Tim s'il vous plait...please." Stud was back.

Dr. Tim was near the storeroom cave and pulled out two pitch torches. He handed one to Maritza, and as they approached the fire, Stud arrived with a bald young woman and a young man.

They were exhausted, hungry, and all three needed medical attention.

There was blood running down the left side of Stud's head. It seemed the worst wound, but Stud pointed at the young man while Dr. Tim examined him.

"I yam good. Check Oli-var. He has de broken arm."

"Tengo esto... I get dis." Maritza waved Dr. Tim off as she took control of Oliver.

Willow was already guiding the young woman to the fire. She had a smaller gash across her right knee and a scrape down her ribs on that side, so Willow sat her down as Ann showed up with the medical kit. Stacy brought a pail of water and a few of the camp's new washcloths.

Willow and Stacy cleaned her wounds and packed some moss under some of our new gauze and tape. Meanwhile, Oliver's right wrist was blue and swollen, but with gentle tension from Maritza, his face showed relief.

Dr. Tim looked across from wiping down Stud to see the progress and nodded. We watched the stress and pain leave Oliver's face as Stacy helped Maritza splint, wrap, and sling his right arm with his hand at heart level.

His complexion went from skimmed milk to a healthier homogenized color.

Stud was a bit more trouble. He had a slash running from the top of his head down the left side to the bottom of his ear. The end of the wound culminated with his ear lobe missing.

Dr. Tim reassured him. "It's all surface stuff, Jean.

I can fix this, but I need to cauterize the bleeding from your ear first."

Julio was holding the pitch torch the doctor had carried, and Dr. Tim motioned for him to bring it closer. The Dr. had Stud's ear pinched so tightly it had stopped bleeding, but he had to keep the pressure on. Then, with Oliver settled in and accepting a cup of tea from Ann, Maritza joined Dr. Tim.

"Maritza, can I have a tongue depressor from the kit, please?"

"Si," she handed the doctor the flat stick.

He took a small swab of the burning pitch off the torch and blew the flame out. He then applied the bubbling pitch to the wound.

But unfortunately, he also applied it to his own fingers that were holding the wound closed and protecting the ear canal. Both men visibly cringed for a moment but made no sound.

"Please, pass me tweezers."

Maritza handed him the tool, and the doctor used it to peel the pitch away from his fingers to separate him from his patient.

"Okay, Jean, that was the hard part. Your scalp isn't bleeding so bad. I will irrigate it, numb it with some of our new topical anesthetics, and sew it up."

"You sure da hard part, ez ohffer?" Stud grinned weakly, but it was obvious he knew he was in good hands.

"I also need to give you a bit of a haircut, Jean."

"Datz okay, Doc. Maybee a shave too?"

The laugh was good for the tension. We all wanted details, but the shave and the sutures were more important.

Ann prepped the old-fashioned steel razor and passed it and warm water to Maritza, who took the job on like a pro. First, she shaved down each side of the laceration, just enough to give the doctor room to work. From here, it was quick work. Stud was sewed up like a major league fastball in a few minutes.

We all settled in to get the story, but first, Stud wanted to know where everyone was.

"We are missing some jeunes dames... young ladies. Where is Hilda?

I found it interesting that Jean had asked about Hilda by name. I also mentally noted how Ann stayed in the background but was always ready to help Dr. Tim and Maritza. Things came together in my mind now as I watched Ann watching Dr. Tim and him smiling back at her in a knowing way. *There was much more to that story.*

I raised an eyebrow as my attention went back to Stud's query. "She's scouting for a hunt with Penny and Vera.

You can have their story once we have yours."

***

Chapter 29

Oliver the Princess and Purple Turkey

We brought out food and tea for a complete meal as we cleaned up the M.A.S.H. Once we had Stud and our new citizens comfortable and mostly fed, we asked for the debrief. He sat down and told his story.

"We did not have trouble getting to le berry patch. We enter grass in dark and go back up de riviere like we came home last time. We go by Tower Creek, and Tiffany, Dan, et Shiv go in cabine, and we go to berries." Stud paused for a moment.

"We do not see them again. Hoping they are here." That statement made us all pause. "Jesus et Moi, we go to cages, and they are still in same spot. Four people in my old cage. Broken bar only fixed with rope to next bars. At night, we 'shh' captives. I climb up tree to cut rope wit bud knife. We show them how to come down on willow tree."

Stud was getting more animated with his story now. His hands were expressing as much of the story as his voice. "In the berries, Jesus and I talk about the best way out, and I say we go tonight, on the Southwest ruisseau...uh, courant d'eau... uh, creek. Jesus say he try new way.

He think a wide valley go out to sea below bitter water. I say he garcon fau...crazy boy, but he say we have two times better chance to get someone home."

He shrugged and said, "So I say oui, but I go now. Who comes wit me? First, we give escapee's choice. Boys want to go wit Jesus. Girl wants to come wit me. I say ok, and start to go and Oliv-ar, he say I come too. I say Oui and leave wit two."

"So, I suppose that is the last you saw of Jesus and his crew?" I knew the answer but also knew everyone else wanted to ask.

"Oui, we have easy time going at night with two moons and no chase. But it change when we get to pass cliffs. Giants find us and make big noise. Now Screamers come too. I tell my new friends we swim all the way in the pass, and water takes us fast. We have to go underwater and swim sideways, sometimes in dusty water. Now Giants splash around us, and Screamers dive in water too, but they fight."

He smiled and pointed at his charges. "They swim like Olympians."

For the first time, our newest recruits smiled.

"Giants give up by old pass camp, but Screamers try to get us all da way to Randy's Rock. Water is not deep above the falls, so we in danger. We all try to climb ovar de edge at same time, but they dive on us. Princess fall, and Oliv-ar try to grab her and fall, too. I fight Screamer with stick, and he try to grab ma tete"

"Your what?"

"Ma tete... my head."

"Ahh, now it makes sense. It looks like it almost did grab your tete."

This comment brought some smiles and schoolboy giggles to the English speakers, but Stud initially didn't get it.

"We go very fast between falls. I bleed too much, and everyone hurt."

"Jean-Etalon-Stud, you did a magnificent job saving these folks, and we are most grateful you got them to Freedom. It's probably time for some introductions. Princess and Oliver, this is only a small part of our village.

They will mingle with you so you get to know them well. We would like to know about you so we can help you become part of the team in a way that works best for you. We want you to be happy here, so knowing you will help us reach that goal. Princess, can we start with you?"

She stood and walked closer to the fire. There was a slight chill in the night air with an onshore breeze, and we all felt it. "I have stage four pancreatic cancer. My parents are high-class snobs in L.A. and had disowned me years ago. Who else would name their daughter Princess? My Greenpeace passion didn't fit with their big oil money."

She sat down closer to the fire, and I couldn't help but notice the gaunt tightness of every shiny surface of her body as she relayed her story. Hearing what she had said, Ann was already wrapping her in a robe.

"My boyfriend rolled up in his dreads and tie-dies and split when he found out I had to fight for my life.

It turned out he wasn't worth a shit when it came to a fight. I was loaded with chemo and sleeping, hooked to a dozen machines when I was grabbed. I couldn't believe how much better I felt in the cage. So, I was a little reluctant to leave it."

She looked around the camp, then at Stud. "And then this big Frenchman took me on the Jumanji adventure.

I kept looking for the film crew." This got a belly laugh from the camp.

"Are you OK?" I was stunned.

"I have never felt better. I think I'm going to love spending my last days here."

"Princess, it may take you a little while to believe me. I think you will be cured of your cancer in a very short time. I suspect you will like that about this place, but you might not like the fact that most of us are omnivores in this world, and we are going hunting tomorrow to help feed and clothe the camp."

She looked up slowly and caught my eye. "I understand by the teeth in my head that I was born an omnivore and have made peace with the human condition long ago. I'd rather not but have nothing against eating meat if I have to and if it is responsibly harvested, but I've been made to understand that my time is short for so long now that I will need proof before I start dancing."

"I understand, but you now have time to see that proof. The mushrooms you ate tonight and some you may have been fed in captivity are the key to your recovery, and I'll let Dr. Tim fill you in.

How about you, Oliver?"

"Story's the same, Mate. I was cryin' like a little girl in me back garden in Leeds. I had just buried me Mum down at the Beckett Street Cemetery and had run fresh out of relatives. Mum was all I had. I was a shopkeeper in her specialty tea shop. Never knew me dad."

I noted Oliver was probably in his late twenties. He continued his story.

"I was at the funeral.

There were some people I didn't know there, which was strange. I wondered what they were doing there; it was just the mortuary crew and me... and them. Mum was a very private woman. I headed for the closest stranger but blacked out and woke in a hot, soggy pen in a tree with me new mates."

"Well, Oliver, you have many new mates now, and we are honored you two did the Jumanji adventure to get to our little village, Freedom. Willow is planning to set Princess up with some of the ladies for tonight, and tomorrow, we can sort out where they should bunk as we get to know more about them. Stud plans to take Oliver. He can stay with him till he chooses his hut."

Everyone seemed satisfied, so I helped Willow settle Princess in, and we retired for the night.

***

A cacophony of epic proportions ushered in the morning. The hunters were back, and they had cargo. The whole village was soon welcoming three women and their packs. They waved happily as they saw me running toward them. Penny set the tone with her hands up in a "slow down" gesture.

"Are you alright?" My face reflected what they were expecting; the village was in shock, and they were trying to ease the calm in time for explanations.

"We are ok, Mac. This wasn't at all what we had planned, but we escaped and have a lot to share. We have meat, feathers, and all the rest that comes with a Screamer, but we obtained it in self-defense."

"What happened?" I asked the question simultaneously with several others in the camp.

"Getting to the foothills was easy at night. The moons were more than ample to see our way, and the plateau was loaded with mushrooms.

When we got to the foothills, we found holes in the ground that led underground at a slight angle, and the openings all seemed to open facing away from the mountains." We were all glued to Penny's explanation now.

"We felt that the holes would make great cover for us in the day, so we entered one to see if it would be big enough or safe for our hunters. Vera took the lead in the hole, and we had to bend to walk in, but we could move on foot. We stayed in sight of the opening, and the hole opened into a bigger chamber. It looked perfect for a hunting party to stage and to wait for darkness for our trip home."

"Did you find danger in de hole?" Stud was now front and center.

"I'm getting to that. That's what got us in trouble. An animal charged out of the darkness at us, and Vera shot it.

We instinctively dove out of the hole, and another of the creatures came out squealing. That was when the Purple Screamers saw us.

I shot the other animal, and we dove back into the hole as a flock... or maybe a pack of screamers hit the opening of the hole." Penny's eyes were wide as she recounted the scene.

Hilda took over. "The screamers took the animal we killed on the outside and raged at the opening all day. Mac, it looked like they could almost climb in with us as their heads and shoulders wedged into the hole. They would back out and try to reach us with their talons, but they could not get their bodies in with us."

Penny chimed in again. "Even with the screams, we realized we were safe for the moment, so we investigated the animal in the hole with us. We concluded it was an herbivore by its teeth, so we harvested what we could from it and stuffed it in our packs."

Vera said, "Then we had to settle down and wait out the raging screamers. I'm still shaking from the volume and sheer rage. Penny told us to get comfortable until the sun went down. Later in the afternoon, it got quiet, and the screamers left no trace of the dead animal.

We thought they might have gotten tired of us, but when we poked our heads out, we found one waiting, and he charged the hole, just missing my arm." She showed a scrape down the outside of her left arm. I couldn't believe something that big could move that fast."

"I'd say that wasn't quite a miss." Ann pointed at the dried blood along her arm. She went for water.

Penny said, "We settled back in then but peeked out to see our guard from time to time. As the sun went down, I suggested we get the beast to rage at us again. As it did, we would all be ready with long arrows. It was like shooting purple turkeys in a barrel. Any of our shots could have killed it, but we got lucky because it backed out of the hole to die.

We could still be working our way out past that beast. Luckily, as big as those birds are, they are built to fly, so they are much smaller when you take their feathers off."

Hilda said, "We had to leave most of the feathers and some of the meat in the hole, but we could go back and get it tonight."

Willow was back with the water, and Dr. Tim patched Vera's scrape while plans were in play to process the bounty the hunters had brought home.

There was no doubt about the skills that were developing in the camp and no doubt in anyone's mind how the characters of the rag-tag immigrants had evolved into something much greater in each of their lives as they grew together in a strange, beautiful, and unforgiving land.

Maritza and Hilda took particular interest in the creature cleaned and quartered to fit in all three packs. Maritza said it reminded her of a Capybara from the mountains near her home back on Earth. The amount of meat did not easily fit in the bags, so this creature seemed to be a good food source.

Vera had hung two front quarters together and slung them over her shoulders. Hilda and Penny had packed the rest, with slabs of screamer breast and a rolled hide over Hilda's shoulders. Penny also had a full load of wing tip feathers.

The processing, storytelling, and planning took us well into the afternoon. When all was done, Hilda talked Stud into going back with her for the rest of the load, and I was happy. Smaller scouting teams felt a lot better to me. I was starting to feel we had the camp covered again, but I was still worried about our missing trekkers.

The events of the last couple of days made me think about my adventures. I was happy to see new leaders stepping up to build this life. I wanted to spend more time with Willow.

***

Chapter 30

The First Mayor of Freedom

Stud and Hilda made short work of the trip back to retrieve the last of the hunt, and the camp quickly processed the load. They named the new animal Aardvark, meaning Earth Pig in South Africa.

However, it appeared closely related to a rodent with overly developed incisors and small canines. The spade-like claws for digging won the animal its new name.

Hilda began to spend much more time with Stud as they explored outward in an ever-expanding spiral to discover the good and bad of our home. I was amazed to see another age gap relationship grow. I didn't know what to think of this theme, but I was sure human nature would sort it out.

They had set out South of Bitter Waters this morning, hoping to find some evidence of Jesus and his escapees. It had been two days since Stud had delivered his charges, so depending on how far off the path they had to go, he felt they should show up soon.

By late afternoon, they had returned with lots to say about the grassy plains South of us.

The prairie rolled off as far as the eyes could see in waves of tall grass.

They planned to visit Popeye and Jewels tomorrow, then strike out North of the landing to look for evidence of a Northern pass through the mountains.

"Belanger and Shultz," I joked. "The Aardian version of Lewis and Clark."

Neither of them knew who that was until I explained. Then, Hilda remembered something about it from her studies. She had read about Sacajawea's son, Baptiste, spending time in Prussia somewhere in her history books. I suggested they remind Popeye that we would look forward to his books as we start writing our history. By daylight, they were already on the trail to the landing.

At the same time, Princess and Oliver had started boot camp. Willow and Penny introduced archery, and Stacy stepped in to discuss the local vegetation foods, medicines, fiber, and the associated harvesting. Within a half hour, Oliver wanted to sit out the hunting and archery training. "Guys, this just isn't me. We would all die if you had to count on me to hunt ferocious animals or kill beasts.

I can help the village better by inventing teas and snacks that serve our needs and comforts." He was adamant as he studied the vegetation around him. "I can expand and enhance our food sciences."

Both Princess and Stacy were fascinated with his idea. From where I sat discussing village issues with Julio, the discourse caught my attention. There would be several in the camp that would want to join Oliver in his quest.

Even some villagers eating meat just for its protein value would easily sway to a more vegetarian diet as variety increases.

On the other hand, Princess was offering her feedback on the training and was much more focused on defense.

"I want to learn how to protect the village. I want to learn how to protect Aard. We trashed Earth, and I want to be a warrior for our people and planet. I like Oliver's take, but I'm not fool enough to think we can passively protect our people and planet."

She quickly glanced at Oliver. "Sorry, that was a bad choice of words. I think you know we need to defend ourselves and suggest others will be better on the front line."

Princess was bringing passion to the planet. We would be hearing much more from this sparkplug.

Oliver smiled and gave a thumbs-up.

As she recognized her returning strength, it was apparent that she would be a ferocious advocate for the planet and its fauna. "The only way I will take a life is in self-defense. I want to be the best at self-defense."

Willow said, "Okay, you come with me. You are starting with Archery, Spears, and Atlatl. Penny and I will show you how to use technique over strength. Knowledge will beat strength and size every time."

Stacy waggled her finger at Oliver. "You come with me."

I turned back to my conversation with Julio.

While all the adventures had been flaring around him, he had become the anchor of the village. He offered a Spanish grace before every meal, and everyone respected it. People gravitated to him or Willow for advice on camp life and more to Julio lately.

Willow had been referring people to Julio for answers. The community's makeup had been gelling around him, and once a week, the evening fire had become a council meeting around the de facto Mayor of Libertad.

The purpose of my chat was to point that out. "Julio, have you noticed that people come to you for answers about our storage of food, clothing, supplies, and weapons?"

At first, he was defensive. "I don' try to take autoridad, Senior Mac... I jus' try to help."

"Julio, a true leader does not ask to lead. They do things, and people follow." I waved my arm around the waking camp. "The people of Freedom, or Libertad, have come to you because they know you care."

He looked around for a moment. "I do care." He turned over something he had been working on. In extraordinary detail, it read Freedom – Libertad, on a village sign he was carving. It was inspiring to see language and culture pulled together in the tribe.

"Exactly, that is why I want to introduce you at the fire chat tonight as the first Mayor of Freedom, or Alcalde de la Libertad. Can you build another sign with those titles on them?"

He took another moment as he teared up. "Si."

I stood up. "Gracias, Alcalde. Hasta luego."

About midday, I checked in with Willow, Penny, and Princess.

"How's it going?"

"She's a natural, Mac." She pointed at a target full of arrows fifty paces away, a frond bundle with a long spear pinning it to the ground and another bundle a few strides past with a shorter atlatl spear in its belly.

"Penny will work with her for a few days, maybe even longer, as I think a friendly rivalry may grow.

They are the same age, both determined to be over-achievers on Aard. One a hunter and one a defender. This should be good."

"Are you free to go for a walk now? I'd like to take a short trek South for the afternoon to see if I can see any sign of Jesus and company."

"Yes, let me grab my bow and quiver."

"Good. I was about to grab mine and a medical kit."

We headed for the medical store from our hut and found Maritza sorting and arranging.

"Buenas tardes, Maritza. We are going South for the afternoon to see if we can find Jesus. Do we have a small medical kit we can take?"

"Si, I take. I come."

"Excelente, let's go."

***

We made short work of the river delta and were soon surveying the tall grasslands below the river mouth. To our East was a long bank of forest rising to the mountains that drained the land through the Río a la Libertad, and we curled around slightly to the Southeast to a thin, jagged ridgeline on the horizon far to the East.

A vast prairie with no end was South of the wall of forested mountains. Directly South, we could follow a thirty-foot sand bank sloping down to the ocean shore.

"Perhaps the border between the mountains and the plains might be our best bet since I expect Jesus to use only landmarks he can see on his way West. Ideas?"

Maritza said, "Where Jesus grow up, there is no grass field like dis. I tink he want mountain and tree like where he live."

Willow added, "From the edge of the mountain, we can get a view over the grass to see farther. It may be easier to walk along the border between the two and step up the hill to get a look from time to time."

"Settled." We turned East along the edge of the grass and, at the first opportunity, climbed the hill for a vantage. At each viewpoint, I tried the Tarzan yell. We won no response until mid-afternoon when we decided to return to camp before dark. While discussing the decision, Willow held up her hand for silence. We heard distant screamers, but the angry sounds appeared to get closer as we listened.

With a nod to my fellow trekkers, I went silent and climbed the hill farther into cover.

We found a short rock face, maybe 20 feet tall, with a thickly wooded crest and a few deadfalls hanging over the edge. The fallen trees provided some protection in the open space below, but I felt it wasn't enough to protect from Screamers.

I headed up one of the hanging logs, and Maritza and Willow followed on hands and feet. We were soon in the thick cover, with bows ready as the screaming got louder.

A screamer soared into the opening below, but with a flip of its tailfeathers and a shoulder twist, it zigged upward and circled back out of sight. Jesus burst into the landing with two young men in tow. They dove under the hanging logs.

A second raptor hit the log directly above them with a slashing beak, then grabbed at the log end and hauled it high in the air before dropping it to smash down.

The men had darted under a second choice, but the Screamer screamed a different pitch in agony as it swung back over the grasslands, an arrow protruding from its breast.

The second screamer was back but distracted by its struggling mate. It again howled in pain and rage as another arrow found the flesh of its formidable upper wing.

"Quick, up the logs. It's safer up here." I called down to them.

The startled prey looked up to follow my voice, and I didn't need to repeat.

A third purple raptor thundered down on the logs as the last foot disappeared into the thick forest.

As it raged at the logs, it took two arrows and died.

It fell into the clearing. The two wounded birds did not return, but we heard them screaming off in the grass, just out of sight to the East. Then, finally, one stopped vocalizing, and we listened as the last, screaming its rage farther to the East until it, too, went silent.

We all hugged Jesus and welcomed his escapees.

"Pete, Mutt, dis is Senior Mac, Senorita Willow, and Senorita Maritza. Dey jus save us. We gonna be okay now."

"Hello, guys. Let's get you back to camp. Is anyone hurt?" Willow was already assessing for injuries.

"No, we're good. A couple of scrapes and bruises, but we're okay." Pete looked thankful, and Mutt just nodded.

Okay, It's quiet. I think it's safe to leave and return to camp. It worries me that those screamers have come so close to Libertad. We're only about an hour away."

I noticed I was still thinking in hours, but I wondered if they were now Aardian cycles of time my brain connected to.

Our knives and paperboy sacks become very handy. We took what we could carry from the dead Screamer. Finally, Jesus packed a section of the rolled hide on his shoulders. In short order, we were back across the delta to Freedom.

Jesus was welcomed home as the conquering hero, and Mutt and Pete were the newest celebrities in the camp. Dr. Tim and his crew tended to the scrapes and bruises, and we sat for the evening meal. Soothing tea was distributed to all, just as Stud, Hilda, Shiv, Tiffany, Popeye, Jewels, and Dan strode into camp.

51 Pegasi - Black Mac

Dinner turned into a celebration. I noticed like usual, natural conversations seemed to radiate from around Julio, who held unofficial court through the evening meals. He asked for introductions.

I started with a request for an introduction from Pete, a farm implement salesman from Omaha. I asked him why his name was so normal since we had folks with characters like Mac, Popeye, Shiv, Willow, and Stud. His brow furrowed as he replied.

"I like Pete."

I noted he was short-winded for a salesman but questioned no further. Instead, I changed the subject. "Well, Pete, how did you get here?"

"Same as you. I found out my wife had picked up with the local sheriff, an' I din't have a home to go back to. I jus came from a come ta Jesus meetin' wit the sheriff and m'wife where they tol me I had twenty-four hours to disappear, or they would help me. So I was walkin' in the rain with nowhere to walk to when I woke up from sleepin' with no clothes, with Mutt, Oliver, n Princess."

"Sorry, Man, didn't mean to pry."

"Don' worry about it. I ain't over it yet, so I don' talk 'bout it much, but I read your story in the cage, an' I ain't looked back."

I left it at that and directed my questions to Mutt. I could tell why he got the name, so I didn't ask. Mutt was one of the hairiest men I had ever met, with a shock of white hair mixed with black, over and including his left eyebrow.

But he seemed to have a pleasant disposition.

"How about you, Mutt? What brought you here."

"Same thing, I guess. I never had any friends until I came here. Jesus was the first one who ever cared whether I lived or died. I never knew my father; my mother died when I was ten. I was a long-haul truck driver, so I didn't have to deal with communities much. But, since I got out of that cage, I have lived more than I lived in my thirty-four years in Alaska."

"Jesus, we are going to want the full story of your Southern escape trip, but this is the first time we have had all of us together, so I have one announcement. Then I will turn you all loose to get to know each other."

I moved over to where Julio was sitting and rested my hand on his shoulder.

"Julio, are you ready to show the village your project?"

He grinned from ear to ear as he pulled up his carving and presented it to the crowd.

"Folks, I want to welcome you all... again..., to the village of Freedom – Libertad". I announced.

"I also want to introduce our first mayor. So please pay your respects this evening to the Mayor of Freedom. The honorable, Mayor Julio Escobar, Su Honorable Alcalde Julio Escobar!"

The village roared to life, and the party went on for hours. I felt confident there would be more to learn at the next council meeting.

***

Chapter 31

Hitchhiker Reparation

Jewels came trotting into camp mid-morning and found Willow and me working on a new hut for the expanding village.

"Mac, Adelphi arrived but had to go back for her dress. She explained that it was far more than a cover. She said she would be back at the same time tomorrow, but we're not sure how that will translate to Aardian time."

"I see. That does add a twist, doesn't it."

"Mac, she requested you be there when she comes back."

"Was she frightened?"

"No... more like determined. Adelphi was surprised to land naked, and she was surprised she wasn't already in the village. She went back before we could get to the bottom of her concern. I'm sure she will be back because her books are here."

Willow said, "Go ahead, Mac. There is nothing like an old friend to meet you at the airport." That got a laugh. I went to pack and headed up the landing trail with Jewels.

We made good time, spurred on by the growing enigma that was Adelphi. Popeye was happy to see us come into camp. He had made good use of the time waiting for everyone to return. First, he found that part of Adelphi's freight was a small, two-wheeled wooden cart. The team had loaded it with books. Popeye made a platform from dry wood and rope.

Then, with his coveted hammer and the nails from the last freight haul, he attached a pair of runners to the bottom to protect the binding and joints. He piled the rest of Adelphi's now Aardian belongings on the small sliding platform. He now had a plan to protect her cart from the weight and help the citizens to transport Adelphi's life work to Freedom.

Popeye stacked the freight neatly out of the way. Finally, we were ready for Adelphi... I hoped. Popeye had also built a spare room and prepped a bed on the West end of the hut, so after an evening at the fire, I was the first to enjoy the happy couple's guest room. I figured he had the first two-room hut on the planet.

The morning was warm, then quickly became hot. We stayed near the landing pole but followed the shade as the sun made its Southern arc. Still early, our conversation was interrupted by the telltale hiss of the transporter.

Adelphi was back, clutching her dress, but with her was a man we had yet to meet. The man was holding her from behind, and she woke screaming. I jumped on the naked man and flipped him off of her as he began to come to. Adelphi scrambled up the hill to Jewels and pulled her dress over her body in a fluid rush.

"Ποια η κόλαση!"

The man was stunned. Adelphi translated, "He just said, what the hell."

"Does he know any English?"

She shook her head, "I don't think so."

"You're going to have to translate for us, Adelphi. What is he doing here?" Popeye had captured and knocked him to the ground again as I spun him down the hill. He kept him pinned to the ground with an arm twisted behind him while she explained.

"That is the street vendor I gave my chickens to. He figured he'd come early to see if he could scavenge anything else. He was in the root cellar when I arrived without clothes. He had a lantern. He was startled at first when he saw me, then became friendly. As I attempted to put on my dress, he attacked me. Luckily, he pushed me against the wall with the button."

"What a creep." Jewels snarled from the knoll.

The stranger raged into the tri-edged grass folded around his face. It probably wasn't too comfortable, but Popeye didn't care. He pushed harder.

"Jewels, arm yourself, please. We're going to let him go. Adelphi, do not tell him about the button. If you do, your bridge back to Earth must be destroyed. Popeye, are you good to let him go? I have you covered, and so does Jewels. There is nowhere he can go and nothing he can do. He likely will spend some time just figuring out where he is. We will head for the camp, and he will follow for lack of anything else he can do. The village and Adelphi can help decide what to do with him."

Popeye pulled his knife and nodded. "Jewels, please lead the way."

He kidney punched the crud under his elbows and stepped away from him as the hapless naked Mediterranean stood, bent in pain.

The Creep was still gathering his wits when he realized he was naked.

I followed the women down the trail, and Popeye covered us from behind. He was shocked to see us leaving his sorry ass standing on the landing. We were hardly out of sight when he started wailing and raced after us. Popeye was ready.

Creep grabbed his shoulder to swing him around, and the immigration officer let him have it. Leveraging the shoulder yank to swing with the arrow in his grip. The sorry specimen hadn't noticed what Popeye had ready in his hand. The arrow whipped him across the face, knocking him off his feet. He stood slowly, leering at all of us with fear and hatred from under his lowered brows. An angry welt grew across his left cheek.

Popeye flexed the arrow still in his hand and pointed the tip at him. He got the message and lifted his hands in submission. We all turned our backs and walked away, hauling Adelphi's books.

Creep followed at 30 paces. We stopped to eat dried Humpback about halfway to camp, and I tossed a piece to him. He caught it, nodded, and ate it. We stood and continued soon after. By the time we got to camp, our path was well-lit by the twin moons. Walking into camp, we raised a ruckus as Willow and Stud came running to meet us.

Willow was ecstatic. "Adelphi! You made it. Wonderful. She smothered her in hugs and kisses. Although excited to meet her, Stud stood back a bit.

He pointed. "Who is dat?"

"Stud, Willow, meet Creep. He just tried to rape Adelphi back on Earth."

All now turned to look at the stranger, and he visibly shrunk.

I took the Greek to an empty canvas tent used by folks waiting for huts. I pointed, and he nodded and entered without comment. I headed back to the little group. Ann took him a bowl of soup from the camp caldron, but Dr. Tim went with her and carried a spear.

"Thanks, Popeye, good job. You, too, Jewels, you did the right thing. The last thing we need is for this guy to understand how he got here and where here is. Let's step over to Willow's cabin. We have a lot to go over. Stud, will you please drag Shiv, Tiffany, and Julio in? We are going to need their input."

Stud ran off to find Shiv. We headed for Willow's porch.

"Tomorrow is going to be very interesting. This man's fate depends on what we want as a society and the opinion of the woman he attacked." Willow seemed resigned.

Everyone showed up in a few moments, and when all knew the objective, Julio asked to spend a few moments alone with Adelphi. So they went for a short walk, and when they returned, Adelphi addressed the team while Julio nodded.

"Tomorrow, Murus will need an interpreter.

I am the only one who can serve that role, but I will translate all we say and ask him to answer with nods and shakes of his head. You will all see that he understands. Julio will ensure everything is fair." It was decided.

***

At daylight, Julio called court on Willow's porch. Stud went to retrieve "Creep" from the tent. He found him sitting quietly outside the door flap, patiently waiting for his directions.

The tribunal was waiting as they stepped into the foot-worn courtyard in front of Willow's hut.

I turned to Adelphi, who had spent the night in Tiffany's hut. "First things first. Adelphi, what do you think would be suitable reform for Creep?"

"Please let me speak with him a moment, and I will answer."

I nodded and pointed at the outcast in the shadows near the end of the hut. Then, with complete confidence, her robe tied at her waist, Adelphi walked within inches of the Creep and looked into his eyes. It wasn't for several breaths till she addressed him in Greek.

She addressed him again while she pointed at the dirt, then lifted her arms to flex her biceps. She then untied a small pouch from her belt. He carefully dropped his eyes to the ground and said nothing. From the pouch, she poured a small sampling of emerald powder into the palm of her hand and offered it to Creep.

He hesitated, nodded, then licked the powder from her hand in one quick motion. I looked around the citizens to see their reactions. It was the first time I had seen Tiffany, her mouth agape in awe.

It took a moment, then his eyes widened, and Creep ran retching into the brush. The crowd could hear him losing his dinner and his bowels. Then he ran for the ocean. Adelphi padded back to the awed group at Willow's porch.

"Julio, Mac, when that man returns, his name will be Marus. He will put every effort into learning English and demand that you work him hard so he can again build up a proud Greek honor. He will no longer be a threat, and I forgive him."

No mention was made of the ritual we had just witnessed or the result we heard retching in the brush.

We all released a collective breath, and attention moved like a shadow back to me.

I motioned for Popeye to come over.

"Popeye, we have more recruits in our village. They seem even to be hitchhiking in. You and Jewels need to grow the landing and begin training. We must build more shelters at the Landing and a base camp there. Please enlist any help you need. I think you may get more company soon."

I now had an audience.

"Freedom is an amazing start, but we can't all be in one spot if we get trouble from the East or from Earth. Shiv, Tiffany, and Dan brought us a lot more opportunity, equipment, and knowledge.

However, they have pissed some powerful people and giants off, and of course, Penny and team have pissed off some Purple Screamers."

Penny appeared as Marus was running off, and she was pleased to hear her name come up with praise in the conversation. Even if it was backhanded.

"Tiffany, you have been planning a raid on the new human farm you found at the North Tower. You have plotted a path back through a Northern pass and a plot to break people out of their cages. We know they have been gathering again, and we must spring everyone we can. We probably need to decide who should go with you, but we have a couple of other big initiatives we need to launch."

I turned my attention to Dan, who had come in with Tiffany and Adelphi. "Dan, you told us last night about how important the island is, off the coast. Your last visit to the lab has shown the island holds a mine with solid veins of diamond, and this is where the human traffickers are getting the kinetic fuel for the transporters.

They guard their location configuration for that mine much better than the other landings. Adelphi has shown interest in some of the plant life of an island. We must get to the island and disrupt their access while securing all the necessary fuel."

Next came Shiv.

"Shiv, you found an explosive at the new camp. I'm not even asking how you knew what to look for. You mentioned the legs of the Tower at the berry briar, but if we knock it down, they will likely move.

We will need to find them again, so we may need to think a couple of chess moves ahead."

"Jesus found the new path along the Southern edge of this mountain range, but screamers followed him and his escapees much closer to Bitter Waters. I think the ocean isn't an issue with them. Maybe just the minerals in the hot springs. Giants and Screamers seem to have an advanced sense of smell. The sulpher must bothe them much more than us."

Adelphi was standing next to Tiffany. "Adelphi, does Marus have experience with the sea?"

"Everyone from Southern Greece has the sea in their blood. I will find out how much when he returns."

"Are you sure he will return?" It was good to break the tension as we needed laughter to go with the gravity of our world and the real dangers we had to face. On Cue, Marus returned to camp, still dripping from a freshening in the sea.

Ann handed a toga to Adelphi, who passed it to the contrite Greek. He looked around and wrapped it around himself.

Adelphi spoke to him quietly, intently, but with no malice in their native language.

While answering, Marus nodded eagerly and pointed both thumbs back at his chest. Then, in English, he said, "Sailor." After that, they talked a bit more; Adelphi said, "he comes from a shipbuilding family in Bakalis."

"Do I have any volunteers to become Freedom's first sailors?"

Stud quickly volunteered. "I want to see this island.

I come from the mountains, but I go to my uncle in Marseille in summer.

We sail to Ajaccio summer home many time with only wind... and small motor when we need."

Hilda said bluntly, "I want to go with Stud. I want to see how much damage mining does to a tropical island. If we can save the island from marauding machinery, I want to make it happen."

Adelphi agreed that Hilda should go. "Because we have been working on the features and opportunities of the local fauna together. If she would go, I have some experiments for her to run and some samples to gather from an island habitat."

Kia had her hand up while Stud and Hilda were talking. "We need to shut down that transporter. I can move the box and reset for our visits to the island. Anyone else trying to land there will find the transport doesn't work.

The only sport I ever took time for in California as a kid was sailing. I loved the sound of the water hissing by and never got seasick. Dan got to go on the last transporter adventure, so this one is mine."

I admired how she had built her confidence since our last trip to plunder the tower cabin to save some citizens.

"Adelphi, do we have Marus' agreement to go on this trip? He must know we must go far out to sea in a raft he needs to help design. If he's up for it, Stud can lead this expedition, Marus can Capitan and navigate, Hilda is onboard for payload and environmental control, and Kai can be the mission scientist. I think we have help building with some of the new citizens."

Adelphi got solid confirmation from Marus, then asked Hilda if she could talk to her more about exploring some herbal specimens for food or medicine. Hilda was happy to learn from her and was excited to do more scientific study.

I turned to Shiv. "Could you help Stud, Marus, and Kai build our first ocean-going vessel?" Shiv smiled. "We had better start building that raft in the morning. We have about a month and a half until the Monsoon season returns. Those storms could roll in at any time after that, and we'll want those four off the water by then."

***

Chapter 32

Aardian Mariners

Now I turned to Pete. "You have been working on a fishing net. How is that going?"

"Great Mac, the thin vines from th' pass 'er perfect for this here net. We've a couple uh trial runs, an' Mutt has the perfec' weights on th' bottom, and Oli, he's gathered floating balls that seem like dead sea-life, ex-o-skel'ton balloons. Just like Jap'nese glass floats, but lighter. We've pulled out a few local fish, but they seem mostly am-phib-ious. They fins're stubby, and we have seen'em crawling on the beach. No tellin' what we'll find."

"OK, you three seem to be perfecting that harvest. I'll bet you can design some great drying racks, and we can start finding out what's good and what isn't."

I looked over the crew. "Princess, Stacy, Hilda, you now have Adelphi, who has a fantastic organic food and medicine background. With some advice from Dr. Tim and a unique viewpoint from Maritza, I think you have an opportunity to expand and improve our food and medicinal sources.

We have a growing supply of food choices, and the fishermen here will supply another, but this is a new world. I'm sure there are some species we want to know better before we get too intimate with them."

The new team gathered to get to know each other in their perspective roles. I could tell they were game for the challenge.

"We also need to build some new huts. Tiffany, since you designed the first Aardian huts, would you agree to lead that effort?"

She nodded slightly. Tiffany threw an arm over Adelphi's shoulder. "Would you like to help us? We need shelter for the whole camp that will keep us high and dry for two months of warm, steamy rain. We'll need the fish tested, dried, salted, buried, or hung out of the way of the wild-life, and we need camp tools and comforts."

Adelphi's response was warm and natural. I grinned and looked back at Willow. Dusk was beginning to settle in.

"As soon as we get our mariners launched, Willow and I are going on a little journey of our own. We ought to be back within a week. This camp is full of great leaders with more skill sets added constantly." I suggest we all hit our beds and get a good start at these tasks in the morning."

I turned and waved over my head as I urged Willow toward our hut. But I noticed more pairing off as the camp broke for the night. I noticed Tiffany and Adelphi in deep conversation as they ambled off, arm in arm. I noted the tender look between Popeye and Jewels as she smiled and led him off to their tent. Stud and Hilda were deep in conversation.

As I pulled the door curtain, I saw Ann and Julio sipping tea with Dr. Tim at the fire.

Even more noteworthy, an intense conversation had struck up across the fire between Dan and Oliver.

The next morning came early, and everyone got to work. Jewels and Popeye loaded up with tools and prepared for the Landing. Tiffany and Adelphi had recruited Jesus, Ann, Dan, Oliver, and Sirih to their building team and were busy gathering thatch, poles, vine, and newly acquired hardware.

Stud and Shiv had rustled a handful of axes, hammers, lag bolts, and other assorted ship-building tools from the freight delivery a few weeks ago, and the air rang this morning with the sounds of construction. Shiv and Kia cut dry poles for the hull, and Marus laced in the poles for the raft. Stud used his engineering skills and Marus' experience to guide materials into a seaworthy cabin, mast, and tiller for the 20 by-12-foot raft design. Seeing this craft laid out in 20-foot parallel posts, Marus called Adelphi over and pointed at the craft. He spoke a few words in Greek, and she nodded her head. Next, Adelphi approached Shiv and Stud and repeated the conversation in English.

"Marus just pointed out a major flaw in your design. You have no keel. Your sail and rudder will be useless without it."

Shiv nodded and pointed at a pair of Purple Screamer Sternums leaning against a tree near the riverbank. The bone and cartilage were drying in a thick coating of yellow wax-like paste.

"Those are going between these two center logs. She'll tack like a champ."

"What about putting an organic instrument into the sea? Won't it attract predators?"

"Come here."

Shiv led her to a stand of coniferous trees framing the rest of the continent from the surging surf. He plucked a large, shelled insect next to a congealed sap stream near the bottom of the tree. The stream was thick with these shells.

He folded the hard shell backward with practiced fingers, exposing the soft underside, and shelled the creature with his thumbs. It looked much like a boiled shrimp. A smooth underside opened to the world and popped out with a bit more squeeze. He pulled the white meat from the shell and shared it with her.

"Recognize one of our delicacies?"

He plopped his half in his mouth and chewed with relish.

"Yes," She ate her half.

"See that sap stream? That's a pure high-grade shell mixed with tree sap, much like pine tar on Earth. It tightens up to a shiny ball if you drop a bit in the salt water." He pointed at a steaming hollow rock in a lava pocket fire pit. The liquid version of the hardened sap stream was softly bubbling in it.

"Shellac?"

"Yep. The sap is a magnet for these critters."

"We could use some varnish to cover it, but for this trip, our whole ship will be covered in it for strength, waterproofing, and just plain good looks."

Adelphi smiled. "Handy bugs."

He grinned; she nodded and turned to look at Marus. He was already smiling and nodding.

An hour later, the twin keel was in place while the raft was propped at an angle to accommodate the protrusion.

Stud had a small cabin taking shape in the center, with a mast poking through. Aft of this cabin was a smaller cabin with a hole in the floor. They were now set for "bio breaks."

The fishermen's vines were also working here, along with ligament from Purple Screamers. Ann and Penny had learned how to tan screamer hide and keep the feathers attached. This created a most magnificent sail.

***

No one left for their daily tasks until the raft was complete. Instead, everyone wanted to witness the launch. Even Popeye and Jewels stayed back to help where they could until the shiny golden coating was fully applied. We weren't disappointed.

It took only two and a half days, with the help of many of us, to finish the vessel, so we found ourselves in the unique position of being scared witless for our friends and overcome with pride as our naval history started on the seas of Aard. Finally, with preparations completed in the late afternoon, the decision was ready. An afternoon launch would be just as effective as a morning launch.

Without much discussion or ceremony, we launched the raft. Marus caught a stiff offshore wind with the purple feathered sail, and Stud held the rudder fast while our Aard Mariners sailed away.

Then, all too soon, they disappeared over the Western horizon.

Looking around the landlocked crew, I didn't see a quorum of optimism. We were all scared and feared never seeing these brave sailors again. No one said anything because they didn't want to voice the event's gravity.

The following day, we all leaned into our tasks. The new huts were under construction, and Willow and I accompanied Popeye and Jewels to the Landing.

Willow had convinced me it was time to visit my father and brother at the glacier. Her theory is we had separate visions of how to take advantage of humanity's second chance, and we should continue to compare notes and collaborate to keep from building rabbit-hole bias. Willow continued to impress me with just how deep she was. With quick goodbyes at the Landing, we hit the button of the recalibrated transporter in turn and zapped North.

Willow woke in a massive cave with a transparent ceiling, softly sporting a pink tinge. She stood and stepped toward a gigantic, curved wall swooping down from the spectacular cover. I appeared where she had lain and rolled over with a light moan.

"Never get tired of that trip."

I chuckled and stood up. Popeye had set the box to allow our clothes and tools. Good thing, it was damn cold here, and we both wrapped our tunics close.

"So, what do you think of the cathedral of Ice, Sugar? Wanna get married?"

Willow spun wide-eyed toward me and laughed. "What, and ruin everything?"

We both looked into each other's eyes for a moment, then laughed, then marveled at the hollow echoes rolling back and forth across us.

"Come on, Darlin', look at what I have to show you."

We walked toward the lighter end of the cave and were out into weak sunshine within minutes. It was then that Willow could grasp the fan-tailed glacier that spanned as far as she could see. It soared in an arc in both directions.

She followed me out into a tundra bog, "Be mindful to test your footing as you learned from your chosen man." I smiled at her over my shoulder. I watched her face as she thought about that term of endearment for a bit as she worked her way through the hummocks and swales created by the constant runoff.

"Mac, more than I had ever done in my life, I feel 'my man' is the natural term to use for you. Three facts are clear as I ponder. First, my trust in you is absolute. Secondly, I know that you feel the same about me. And third, I will one day die near you. Wherever that may be." She was right. Neither of us would be without the other again as long as we both lived.

I was full of feels, but I couldn't think about death and dying right now, so I needed to change the subject. "Look."

I had stopped, turned, and pointed back to where we had come from. We had walked out from under a massive glacier tail that fanned out in perfect geometric form, like the tail of a dove.

The ice was tinted pink, just as glaciers on Earth were tinted blue-green. We could never have imagined this scene without seeing it.

"I just needed you to see this. This image was what made Dad and Tony build their Aardian home here. I felt it was worth the chilly excursion to see. So now we go back under the ice cube."

I led her back under the fantail glacier and much deeper into the bowels of the frozen cave than she wanted to be. She had to walk past the button to get to this frozen pink hell, but reluctantly, she followed deeper. We stopped when we ran out of cave and found another transporter button. This one was red. I held her hand and pushed it.

We woke sitting on a soft sofa in a warm cabin with a fresh brewed coffee aroma streaming past us and a fire burning merrily in a stone fireplace.

A pair of black powder rifles were hanging crossed over the hearth, and a bright white animal skin rug covered the rough-hewn wooden floor. Almost all of the floor, and it was a vast room.

"Biscuits?" We turned to see a jovial lumberjack, complete with a plaid shirt over long gray Long-Johns, arriving with a plate of steaming soda biscuits and a coffee pot.

"Tony, you old wood butcher." I jumped up and hugged my brother, and Willow took her turn.

Willow sat back down. She looked back and forth. "I'll never get used to your Ying and Yang tones, but the more I see you two together, the more I get it."

51 Pegasi - Black Mac

We were all laughing now.

"Brothers from a different mother." Tony laughed as he pointed at Mac.

"How is Dad?"

"Same old Dad. He drops in occasionally, but his home is the universe. Hard to keep him in one spot long enough to feed him."

"Where were you when I was here last time? I missed you."

"I was huntin' or bein' hunted, depending on who's tellin' the tale."

"Well, it seems you won. You're still here."

"Yep."

"What were you hunting?"

"You're walkin' on her."

Mac and Willow looked down. The rug. "What is it... was it?" Willow kneeled to caress the silken fur."

"Let's just say they make some damn big pussy cats on Aard."

"A cat?" Willow was stunned.

"Yep. 'Bout the size of a rhino on Earth."

"W...wow, what did you do wi...?"

"Don' worry Miz Willow. I used it all. She's one good grub stake in the winter. Fur don't come any warmer.

This one gave me catgut that's stronger, longer, and more flexible than any rope you can imagine." He grinned amiably, knowing the background of Willow's questions. "Well, you folks got way more on your mind than kitty cats. So to what do I own the visit?"

I was silent for a moment. Then I looked seriously at my brother. "It's going to be a wet monsoon season, big brother. As you know, we've started importing supplies.

We can survive as we are, but to truly be happy, humans must be able to create, at least, tools and weapons to live off the land."

Tony was getting the idea.

"Willow made a great point that we should learn from each other to offer the best sustainability to the community and the planet at the same time. Never going to need gunpowder, though."

Willow glanced at the crossed rifles on the fireplace, and both Tony and I noticed.

"You figure its time, do ya? Well, don't let your coffee get cold. Don't worry Miz Willow, those are only for show. My kitty cat came down using an atlatl spear.

***

Chapter 33

The Mourning Rains

We compared notes on tools, utilities, and gadgets that could make life easier for humans on Aard without affecting the longevity of life on the planet. We noted that diamonds, although products of carbon, pressure, and heat, leave only powdered carbon when their kinetic energy is released. The planet had an abundance of gems.

We all agreed that we could live without crude oil or resulting fuels and products like plastic. The planet had plenty of hydrocarbons, but to date, none of the locals had found a need for it.

Steel razors, scissors, and mechanical hair clippers would be fine, as many of the men found the beards stifling in the humid heat. The women had also requested ways to trim their hair. Our last freight load delivered several items that were popular throughout the camp.

Tony gave us a tour of his cabin and the items he and my father found necessary or coveted in their experience. Most of our tastes were similar. He and Dad had imported things like dinnerware, pots and pans, utensils, and cutlery.

In addition, they had built a store of organic rope, twines, strings, needles, and thread for sewing clothing, upholstery, and hide covers.

They had found a lot of local plant and animal-based supplies that provided them with soaps, creams, lotions, and salves that would be most interesting to our village as we worked out the pros and cons of the resources around us. Adelphi, Tracy, Dr. Tim, Hilda, and the rest of the tribe had produced experience-based discoveries, innovations, and inventions that we could also deliver to Tony and Dad.

We had a great visit, but we needed to be on our way as we wanted to swing by the tower cabin to check for refugees on the way home. We didn't know what to expect. Willow and I packed our packs in the morning. Tony then calibrated a launch to send us to the cabin.

We discussed the best landing spot and agreed we would less laikely to be spotted if we landed in the cabin. I had the coordinates from my adventures there. He set it for the middle of the night to give us the best chance of avoiding bad guys. So, with hugs, we were off.

The cabin was much different than the last visit. There was no dust, and the electronics were gone, but the place looked more like a field office. On the desk was a rack of file folders; the top had a title written in Sharpy marker. "Howard Thom – Coastal Flush."

Inside, we found a plan to surprise us during the last of the monsoon to attack. First, Thom would personally lead a small party that would hit us. He wrote that, with surprise, they would probably clean us out.

They would follow up with reinforcements if needed. He had a plan and was confident two smart people and a few Giants could be done in a couple of days.

The notes mentioned Lawrence as Guide, so my concerns were on point. They would know a lot about our camp. There were two new buildings nearby. They seemed to be barracks, and there were dim lights in a couple of the windows. They were occupied.

Willow looked at me with open fear in her eyes. "Mac, we have to get back."

The gravity of the handwritten notes hit me hard, too. This attack was happening too fast. We had to return before the monsoon because we needed to prepare Freedom.

"Ready?"

Determination replaced Willow's fear as she nodded. Freedom meant everything to her; I could see it written in her eyes. She reached for the door.

Everything was bathed in a dull orange glow from outside, and we noticed the berry briar to the East was burning. As far as we could see, the fire had been started at the cages, and someone was pushing it West. We could see the flames still consuming the brambles in the distance. We had to leave now. The door was locked with a standard locking knob from Earth but no deadbolt. We flipped it to lock and softly closed the door behind us. There was no evidence we were ever there.

We still had shoes from our trip to the glacier, and boot tracks were thick around the cabin.

51 Pegasi - Black Mac

We made our way to the creek in the moonlight and orange glow and waded downstream wearing the shoes. There would be no tell-tail barefoot tracks. By the time the moons went down and dawn began to break back East, we were at the clay cliffs.

"Sweetheart, are you ready to strip down and step into a layer of camouflage clay?"

"These wet clothes are cumbersome, Mac. Clay seems like a nice change. It is far more humid now that we are back at the Pass."

"Yes, it seems worse than usual.

The air is completely still, even in the morning. We need to get home because the monsoons are about to hit."

We threw our clothing and shoes into the river. *Possibly, they would come in handy for someone near the falls.* We were clayed and moving along the cliff ledge in moments, with only our packs for weight.

Stealthily, I followed Willow as we passed through the stench beneath the Screamer nest within a couple of hours. We could hear activity above but made no sounds until we were nearly back down to river level. The river was low this time of year, so travel was easier than usual.

The next day allowed us to travel unhindered all the way to the lip of the top falls. We used a quiet day on the trail, but dusk was coming.

Sadness enveloped us as we reached Randy's Rock and remembered our first loss of life on Aard. The milestone reminded us to stay in the shadows and watch the skies.

51 Pegasi - Black Mac

From the viewpoint on top of Randy's rock, we revisited the conversation we had while trying to decide whether to be a couple or not. I looked down into Willow's upturned eyes and said, "I love you, Sharon."

Willow pulled herself to my chest and said, "Mac, the happiest I have ever been has been in your arms.

I love you too." We spent a long moment holding each other in a silent embrace and listening to each other breathe while looking out toward the sea.

I pointed to the West, where we should have seen the ocean on the horizon. Instead, there was only a black wall. The night was quickly falling, and it was beginning to be a night we had never seen in this world. As usual, the light faded from the sky quickly, even more so because of the wooded canyon walls.

***

Behind us to the East, the sky glowed green as soon as the daylight was gone. The moons had yet to rise, but a shimmering glow filtered the stars. I pointed up.

"We need shelter, Willow; something is happening we have never seen. The monsoons are about to hit. I expect that wall of darkness over the ocean is our fate for the next few months, but the Northern lights effect behind us makes me think we are on the front line of a war of nature."

She looked at me with resolve. "What are we going to do?"

"I discovered a shallow cave on the face of the cliff the falls go over. Remember the climb down here when we first came West?

Roger Haller 326

We didn't need it then, but a ledge ran back to a small cave under the falls. It's just about 20 feet over the edge. If we cannot get to the bottom of the falls and to a safe spot, we may need to use it. We can find that shelter.

We need to ride out this collision of weather. Tomorrow with some light, before the river gets out of control, we can dash for the lower falls.I can feel it, the quiet before the storm."

The sweat glistened in a smooth sheen on our bodies as we contemplated climbing over the edge in the dark. The night grew brighter as Alpha neared the horizon.

We might have enough light. Indeed, between the moonlight and the growing glow of the Northern lights effect, we picked a path over the edge and began our descent. I watched Willow above me, between new handgrips and footholds. *God, how I love that woman.* She made no complaints. She just did what was necessary.

Suddenly, moonlight faded, and thunder rumbled. Flashes in the distance and pouring rain told me we were out of time. We had made it to the ledge and began the horizontal journey along the ledge toward the cascading water. I felt Willow's hand on my shoulder as I stepped to the side to give her my old position, and I felt relieved knowing she had made it onto the ledge.

We had to use both hands for a time, but her reassuring touch would return in moments.

I reached the mist from the falls and entered the blackness behind in a few more steps. Then, still another couple of steps, I realized Willow's hand was missing, so I reached back to guide my frightened soulmate to the shelter.

51 Pegasi - Black Mac

The world around us exploded in cascading lightning and earth-shaking thunder. I was momentarily blind and deaf. My world smelled of burnt rock, and all my hair stood on end. I franticly reached for Willow but found only heavy driving rain.

With my ears ringing and my eyes useless, my feet shuffled back along the ridge, feeling for my mate, but there was only lightning and thunder pounding my senses. Searching with my hands and feet, I found nothing, including the ledge. There was nothing where the shelf had been.

I stood clutching the maddening wall and screamed for Willow over and over until my voice broke.

The rain now hit so hard that I thought the river had changed course. I worked my way back into the evil void, where I sat on the rock floor while my brain tried to tell my heart the truth. I cried all night, wrestling with the what-ifs, guilt, and torturous images of what may have happened to my reason to live.

The crashing and flashing eased before dawn, but the rain didn't. As soon as I could see my surroundings, I returned to the lip of the ledge. I had to find Willow.

What I found was devastating. Two feet away from the waterfall, the ledge was no longer there. Instead, a long black scar seared down the cliff, disappearing in the mist below. The cascading rain and rising fog blocked my view of the valley floor.

Several yards of the ledge were gone, and the rock face was smooth. I would not be going out the way I came in.

I tried calling Willow again.

But as much as I prayed for an answer, I knew there would be none.

The only thing I could do now was find a way out of this cave and try to find my Willow. With my hands, in total darkness, I explored the cave, which was shallow but had no exits. I followed the edge to the other side, but it was just a wall of moss-covered rock.

The cave roof was high and showed no promise.

Back on the rock wall, there was no purchase above or below this small balcony. The only exit was down.

I had never seen rain that brutal or such a perfect prison, and I had never felt so utterly empty and alone. The color of life lay somewhere below that mist.

I understood there was no option.

I peeled off my pack with bow and quiver and flipped them as far over the burnt rock face as I could so as not to drop them on Willow, then I went back into the hole in the wall.

My only option was easy now. I was okay with any outcome since I felt I had nothing to lose. I crouched in the back of the cave like a sprinter, then impaled the torrent in a dive through the cascade.

***

Our village pulled through. I had told Shiv and Tiffany that we had planned to come back through the tower cabin to see what we could do. We were overdue.

Shiv and Tiffany bolted for the falls when they saw the weather hit the canyon.

They knew we would be scrambling back against the on-slaught.

Later, they made no bones about letting me know that waiting for me to return from my missions was always unnerving. But this time, Willow was on the trek, and this tempest hell turned the odds against us. I got the whole story when I could think in a straight line again.

It was hard going, and they didn't like the possibility that they would be right up against a Rainbow Lizard before they knew it was there, but there was no question in either of their minds that this mission was critical. Although it took them twice as long in this rain, they reached the bottom falls before night and climbed into their favorite old lizard tree to wedge in and rest through the night. They told me they clung to each other for body heat and safety.

Worry kept them confined to small talk. Each one being afraid to voice anything more. It was a long night, and although morning brought little comfort, it also brought no lizards. They carefully climbed the falls and headed upstream.

The well-worn path along the river seemed the best route, seeing they needed as much warning of trouble as they could. They noted the river was higher than usual by now, and as the storm worked its way inland, they realized this would be a poor place to spend any time.

Shiv excused himself and stepped away to relieve himself while Tiffany moved slowly up the trail, scanning the forest, paths, and water for any signs.

Shiv almost jumped into the river when Tiffany screamed his name.

He came running with his spear positioned, but when he arrived, he found her bent to a task at the river. She was pulling me out of the water.

"What..."

"Give me a hand! Hurry! It's Mac."

They told me I was unconscious but breathing. The fall had dislocated a shoulder, broken my nose, and broken an arm between my left elbow and bicep.

Tiffany pulled her plastered hair off her face and leaned her ear into my mouth.

"He's breathing."

She looked up at the wide-eyed Shiv. "Hold him steady.

I will pull his shoulder back into place, then set and splint his arm. This injury is too common at the falls."

Unknown to me, but with deft confidence, she stretched and rotated my arm back into place while Shiv held me still. She put gentle traction on my left arm.

"Get me sticks for splints and rip strips off my tunic to bind them."

Shiv supplied the splints but tore strips from his own tunic instead. Tiffany nodded her thanks as they applied the sticks and bound my arm.

"Shiv, Make us a shelter and a fire, will you? First, we need to warm him up. I'm going to apply my body heat to him. His core is cold, so we are dealing with hypothermia as well as his injuries."

She opened her robe, pulled me into her embrace, and lay on her side in the middle of the trail while

Shiv built a quick lean-to and produced flint, fluff, and dry twigs from a Humpback stomach. He broke semi-dry branches off dead trees and landlocked driftwood stacks.

Within an hour and a half, Shiv had a moss-roofed shelter with a smoke hole and a warming fire. He was pulling evergreen boughs into the sides of the shelter to build a floor out of the mud and runoff.

Warming, I woke up, looked around, and sobbed like a child.

My friends heard, "Willow...Willow...Willow..." Then, as I was able to say more, "Fell... Lightning... Upper falls."

***

Shiv grabbed his weapons and ran up the path.

It took him two more hours to get to the upper falls, but the mist at the bottom was so thick that he had to take one step at a time to approach the base. The river was rising now, but it was still in its bed. He had to find Willow quickly.

Shiv's adrenalin was pumping so hard that his world turned to slow motion. He readied his spear in the launcher, and his eyes darted around his space. He had as good an image as he could get. My friend couldn't afford to make a mistake.

As he approached the roar of the falls, he heard growling and roaring of something far more ominous than the crashing water, and he realized his worst fears. He would have to deal with at least one Rainbow Lizard in the mist.

Silently, he crept closer until he could see the muted images of two giant lizards sparring. They were already bloody and wounded, and neither was backing down.

Either he could dispatch one of them with a very well-aimed spear, then deal with the other from a safe perch in a tree, or he could let one dispatch the other, then finish the victor.

Since they were so intent on each other's destruction, he felt the latter would be the best option, and he didn't have to wait long.

The battle ensued with a savage rendering he had never imagined. They both lost front legs and suffered bloody gashes during the fight, but neither let up until the smaller one finally managed to gain access to the neck of the larger one.

Suddenly, the thrashing stopped.

It seemed they both understood the outcome and surrendered to it. The larger lizard slumped and rolled onto its back, and the smaller began chewing. It shredded the exposed neck and was gorging as Shiv's spear drove deep into its side, just behind the mangled front leg. It died without moving.

Shiv waited a moment to ensure no more lizards, then stepped past the carnage to find Willow half buried in burnt rock. She was missing a hand.

When he had removed enough rock from her to pull her free, he knew she was long since dead. Her body was lifeless and cold. The event had broken many of her bones.

It became apparent that wasn't her cause of death, though. She had taken a direct hit from lightning.

Her left side was blackened from shoulder to heel.

Willow had felt nothing. She died before she knew she was in trouble.

Shiv's eyes welled up as he slung his weapons over his shoulder and gathered her in his arms. The big ex-con cried all the way back to the camp where Tiffany and I were hoping beyond hope.

We cried until our eyes were sore and dry, but I was already dry. I shook with silent sobs all night as Tiffany loaned me her heat, and the feeling returned to my extremities. The rain let up to a drizzle by morning, and Tiffany helped Shiv return to the cliff base to collect what they could of our packs and weapons. I stayed, rocking Willow and trying to will life back into her broken body.

Finally, the broken friends returned with their precious cargo to the Lower Falls.

The descent at the lower falls was a challenge. With the help of a screamer hide and rope, Tiffany and Shiv managed to lower me first. They then gently lowered Willow to my one good arm. Once we were all down, the trail for Bitter Waters was miserable in the growing rain.

The wind was a problem, and we were fighting for each step by the time we reached camp. Willow's promise to warn Freedom drove us on. Just before the light left us, we made it to camp and were welcomed by an exuberant crowd who fell quiet when they saw Willow.

No one pressed for details, but Adelphi, Ann, and Maritza took Willow from Shiv and carried her into her hut.

Adelphi dismissed all but me.

"Mac, I'm going to prepare Willow for her journey. You can stay if you want, but you may rather not see what I do."

"I trust you. Just please let me know when you finish. I want to bury her at the Landing."

"I will."

I was physically stronger now, but my voice shook when I talked. I stepped back onto the little porch where I had shared so many soft nights with Sharon Rowlands. I paid particular attention to her cane chair and bench on the porch. That chair had been her throne, and the bench her court.

"Friends, we must leave Freedom while the rain is heavy. Howard Thom and the Tower Giants are planning an attack on our village. I know of three choices, but I am open to ideas. We can go South to build a new community in the valley below us or go North of the Landing.

The third option is for some of us to go South and some North.

This might give us a better chance at survival when the giants come looking for us, and they are coming. I expect them to arrive before the rains have finished because they want to catch us while still huddled from the elements. Talk it over amongst yourselves. We will decide once we have laid Willow to rest."

"In the meantime, we must make Freedom look like a failed settlement. Remove all evidence of our stay here that makes our departure recent.

The torrents pouring over us now will do a lot for that work, but don't leave any new evidence. When safe, I would like to see Freedom rise again one day."

Adelphi came out and nodded toward the hut. As I stepped back into our home to mourn, she went into the village to update them on Willow, and the tribe planned a trip to the Landing in the morning.

***

Chapter 34

Willows Cathedral and the Breathing World

The morning saw a somber funeral procession up to the plateau and off to the Landing. Willow rode in a beautiful livery of purple feathers over green thatch with a woven roof to keep the steady, steaming rain from her cart. With the help of Shiv and Jesus, Adelphi modified her cart to become a hearse.

Six poll bearers managed the two long handles on each end and the grasp handles on both sides. Willow's loving Aardian family had me walk directly behind her. Following me was her cane chair and bench, carried lovingly by her friends.

It was late in the day when we arrived at the Landing, and an excited Landing team became as devastated as the rest of us at the news. As if on cue, the rain stopped, and gusty breezes tore holes in the clouds throughout the day. We spent the late afternoon and evening digging a grave on the slight slope between the Landing pole and the calming little pond.

Adelphi convinced us to bury Willow beneath the light of the twin moons. I felt she was right. Willow would love that, so we wasted no effort as we all did our part to lay a legend to her rest. Julio gave an amazing eulogy and service.

We all cried together as we closed her grave and covered it with sod we had previously removed to start the process.

Our Willow was home. We laid a slate path toward the pond from her plot and placed the bench and chair with a prime view of the pond.

We sat around the fire stone at the main landing cabin late into the night, telling our favorite stories about Sharon Rowlands, who had become the heart of Freedom and the core of our village. Her legacy would carry on as we planned her monument for the next day.

Popeye and Jewels heard our plans to move, and the topic excited Popeye more than I expected.

"Black Mac, I have another option. I'd like to show you all once our monument is complete." I smiled for the first time since my last embrace with Willow as I noted Popeye had used my Seattle street name for the first time on Aard.

"Just tell me when you are ready to see something fantastic."

"Paul, I could use something fantastic. What have you got up your sleeve?"

With Jewels watching carefully, Popeye asked if I felt up for a stroll. I think he could tell I could only take so much gathering after the loss of Willow, so he thought a bit of good news and a quiet distraction would be welcomed. He was right. As we strolled around the pond to Willow's grave, Popeye and Jewels gave me a high-level summary.

"Mac, do you remember the breathing hole near the trail below?"

The memory of that strange discovery came back. "Yes... I do."

"We have solved the riddle of the breathing holes, and they led us to amazing caverns overlooking the sea. We'll show you what we have found as soon as we finish the monument in the morning."

I didn't sleep much but rested. Finishing the monument was a quick task when the filtered sun came up. I told Popeye I was ready to see their discovery.

He and Jewels led me down a new trail to the west.

"Mac, we have made some progress since we last talked, and I need to show you something. I have planned to dismantle the transporter pole and button at the Landing, and we can move it when ready if you approve. Under the circumstances, that move will remove attention to Willow's new resting spot until it's safe again."

My left eyebrow lifted at the news, but I said nothing.

"Mac, Jewels, and I have been doing a lot of exploring, and the breathing hole is one of many. They may also be our salvation when dealing with the giants and Thom."

The trail dropped down a rocky washout, and we began to hear a rhythmic rumble as we descended.

Jewels pointed back up the hill. "I was up on the bank there when I heard this rumble and came down to explore."

We came to the source of the rumble, and Jewels pointed down a sunlit hole about four feet from side to side.

I waited for the exhalation part of the roar and threw a handful of dirt into the slanted hole. It shot skyward in a jet of forced air.

I pulled a long stock of grass and held it over the void to continue the experiment. It fluttered skyward momentarily, then relaxed and bent into the hole with the same force. I let it go, and it shot out of sight as though into a massive vacuum cleaner.

"Hmmm."

Popeye waved his arm in an arc back the way we had come. "Mac, this hole is a diagonal chimney for a series of caves below, to the west, which open to the sea. They emerge less than a mile from here.

There are several blow holes between here and the coast, mainly within the dense trees, but they all act alike. Although, some carry streams from the plateau. Most have several smaller holes feeding light and airflow to the tunnels and chambers below. We have scrambled through the tops of a few with adequate daylight and constant ventilation."

Popeye pointed westward. "Want to see the new Landing and home site?"

I nodded but said, "Let's bring the rest. They need to know this."

"Most of them do, Mac, and were waiting for your reaction before any detailed investigation or action. Of course, we didn't know trouble was coming so soon."

I saw a problem with the whole village waiting for my approval.

In my current state, it was apparent we needed more leaders. I had to work harder at offloading authority.

We returned to the Landing and gathered the village for the 'quiet walk.' Somehow, I felt like Willow was responsible for this find.

I recalled her terror in the cabin when she learned we would be under attack. Popeye showed the posse what they had shown me, and he and Jewels led the way to the bluffs overlooking the sea. The clouds were still high and broken, but we knew it was temporary.

***

Forest surrounded most of the trail but opened to clear vistas at the bluffs. The gusts grew much stronger as we took in the view and worked our way down a steep incline on winding animal trails between short, weather-worn trees and battered but rope-strong shrubbery, much like the Scottish Broom that infested the roadsides back on Earth.

We couldn't pull it from its tenuous perch, and it had the strength of sage brush branches. We used it to steady our descent to the crashing surf below.

At the bottom, Jewels stepped out onto a narrow strip of pebble beach and turned South along the shore, and we all followed in single file. Ahead was a massive rock wall blocking our path. She stopped at the sheer cliff and looked back at us.

"To all observers, this would seem the end of the trail, but look at this Proff. Follow me and stay within three feet of the wall."

In turn, we stepped into the water and waded around the bluff. The water never reached my knees, and with everyone following, we rounded the bluff and stepped into a towering crevice in the wall. The cleft rose 50 feet above us but was never more than 12 feet at its widest. Inside, the passage became narrower, allowing for a path from the water that allowed one person at a time, and the waterway beyond dropped off.

"Mac, welcome to Willow's Cathedral caves. We are entering a cavern that breathes. In and out."

Popeye pointed at a series of rock channels sloped down into the sea. They had holes worn in their sides where you could see daylight above water and churning seawater driven in and out of the channels as the double tides pushed waves in and out. The canals worked like bellows as the air sucked in on ebb and drove up the chimneys as the water rushed in.

The channels continued on assorted slopes upward and disappeared in the darkness. A few showed dim daylight higher in the portal. I imagined these channels opening in the forest above.

"Let's show him the new Landing, Paul." Jewels showed her excitement.

He seemed pleased that Jewels used his given name as he nodded, turned, and led us into the side cavern. It was huge. A small fire burned near another natural chimney, and the smoke lifted straight up to disappear into a small opening at least a hundred feet overhead. Off to the side, it didn't seem as affected by the in and out movement of the pushed air.

Driftwood packed into the back of the cave. It nestled in a few full-sized logs, now dry and stripped of bark.

Signs that water was considerably lower than it had been at one time.

Sandstone steps had been carved to a higher set of chambers near the back of the cave. Highlighting the back of one smooth-walled cavern was a sturdy driftwood log that stood upright in a green, oxidized rock tube. A natural copper seam rose, possibly to or near the surface.

Willow? How did you do that?

"I haven't tested it yet, Mac, but I think this may be a natural site for our transporter."

"Look what else I found, Paul," Jewels led us out the back of the upper cave, into the windy channel, and up a series of boulders. A much larger cavern stretched to the North, with clean floors and a solid ceiling just a few feet over our heads. It was almost like walking into a rock castle with hand-hewn walls.

The edges were rounded, but the floor and ceiling were flat and parallel. The walls were as smooth as glazed pottery. Light streamed into the chamber from three small openings in the thick rock overhead and lit rooms to the West. On investigation, small gaps of three to four feet across opened in several spots to bare-walled cliffs over the ocean.

We were in a fortress with human-sized portals and decidedly livable quarters. A few small streams were flowing through a corner of the chamber, and they dropped, feathering over the edge of the entrance and out through channels they had carved to spray down the outside of the cliffs, except for one which flowed into the breathing cavern to trickle down to join the waterway in the entry.

"We can get in and out through the ceiling as well.

Look at the steps I built in the corner." We climbed easily out into a deeply filtered forest above. Our cave ceiling was a robust 12 feet deep, and the shelter of the forest was perfect.

Popeye looked back up through the sun ports and noted that the day was getting long.

"Let's get back to camp, folks. What do you think, Mac?"

I looked around slowly.

"Jewels and Popeye, you have outdone yourselves.

Willow's Cathedral seems to be a timely gift for a traumatized village." I dropped my head with no concern for my overflowing eyes, and the village wept with me in gratitude.

Although Popeye and Jewels were our newest heroes, Willow certainly had something to do with this.

By nightfall, we had all our people back to the top side Landing and were preparing for our move. Unfortunately, the rain and wind started, and water, battering winds, and mud challenged our move.

Within a week, however, we were living in the shelter. The accommodation was rudimentary at first, but within the next few days, Willow's Cathedral developed creature comforts. The village had atepped terraces, raised beds, cupboards and shelving, larders, and storage pits.

It had well-placed fire-pits, lookouts and private rooms, commons, and bathing shallows. The tide worked like the wind. It flushed the shelter's waterway entrance on the bottom floor and had several egress ports.

The site featured easy access to food and water and, perhaps most importantly, protection from anything bigger than a human. We were also a fortress against humans, should they find us. All access focused on small portals that could be protected easily from many angles.

Within a few days, there was no record but for well-worn trails and empty huts at Freedom and the old Landing. The monsoon raged on, and we spent the time filling our larder, upgrading our armory of weapons, and preparing to be invisible for as long as it took. We also watched every day, from the bluffs, for a purple-sailed vessel from the West.

***

Chapter 35

Mariner's Return on the Storm

While the storm raged, I asked for a couple of volunteers to come with me to do our daily check of the shores. Today I planned to check the tubs at Bitter Waters for our overdue sailors.

With the entire tribe living at Willows Cathedral now and Dan and Sirih having set up a working pole in the caverns, Popeye and Jewels were happy to break their routine. Pete, Mutt, Tiffany, Princess, and Adelphi were keen to come too.

Shiv and Jesus were hunting but had mentioned a fallen tree upstream from the delta that could take them to the South side. I had a feeling they were already looking for the raft. Dr. Tim and Maritza were building an infirmary in a tranquil corner of our cathedral caves, and Julio was working with Ann and Penny to make our new storerooms.

We covered our togas in Screamer oiled chamois and headed down from the plateau. The tribe spread out at the bottom of the plateau trail, with one set of searchers starting from the North and the other heading for Bitter Waters to work backward.

If we didn't join ranks within an hour, we would turn up the speed to get to the other team since they would need a hand.

We hit the shoreline below our old Freedom camp and headed South to the bathtub rocks. With all eyes on the crashing shore, our attention focused on the sight we had been craving for weeks. Finally, Tiffany whooped and pointed. We all ran to see what she was pointing at through the sheets of rain. The bright white breastbone from a Screamer stood tall on the bathtub rocks. It looked like a sundial over top of the battered raft.

"It's upside down!" Tiffany took off at a sprint.

Although we couldn't keep pace with her, we tried. We first saw Stud weakly pulling at the stiffened rope around his middle as we approached. He was alive, sitting up-shore from the teetering raft with his back to us. As we reached him, he looked up and smiled through tears.

"We made it.»

"You sure did, buddy." I clapped a hand over his shoulder and took over, releasing him from the tether. Tiffany ducked under the beached raft. The broken cabins were holding the deck in the air. There, she found Hilda breathing but unconscious. She untied her and lifted her gently in her arms. When Stud saw her come out from under the raft, his tears turned to sobs of relief. "Hilda! Marus is in the cabin under the deck. Hilda has an important cargo for Adelphi and Dr. Tim." He had his report front of mind.

He pointed at the deck. Pete, Tiffany, and Princess dove for the cabin, but I still couldn't do much with my arm in a sling, but I could comfort and support Hilda.

They pulled out sacks of goods, a large wooden crate, and Marus. He seemed lifeless, and his left leg and arm were severely burned, but Oli listened to his chest.

"He breathes!"

I looked at Stud. "Kia?"

Stud's tears welled, and he shook his head. Adelphi was already administering aid to Hilda, whom she wrapped in her robe. She looked up at me and said, "She just needs to warm." And she headed for Marus. It wasn't lost on anyone that Marus had been forgiven.

Jewels, Popeye, Vera, and Mutt joined us on the run and split up to help those administering to the wounded mariners. Jewels pulled Hilda to her chest and wrapped her robe and oil-skin over the cold sailor. Hilda began to wake up as she warmed in the care of Jewels and Popeye. She immediately called for Jean. He stumbled over, weeping to see her awake. She looked up with concern and said, "Make sure Adelphi gets the plant blood from the Island of the Bleeding Flower."

He hugged her tightly. "Le famille..., she have it."

When Vera heard Kia didn't return, she dropped to her knees in silent sobs. It dawned on me how deep their relationship had been. I reached down with my good arm, pulled her up, and wept with her. She had to be hurting as deeply as I was.

Adelphi said. "Marus is going to need more help. We need a litter to carry him to shelter and Dr. Tim."

Princess stood up and gave Adelphi her robe in the pouring rain. "I'll run ahead and get Dr. Tim and Maritza to prepare." She was off at a run before anyone could counter.

Mutt took over, comforting Vera, and tucked her under his arm as they headed back.

On the way up the trail, I walked with Stud and let him know what happened to Willow. "Take care of Hilda, my friend." We wept in the rain for much of the trail back to Willow's Cathedral. Dr. Tim and Maritza were, indeed, ready for Marus. His burns were bad enough, but he was also in arrhythmia.

Dr. Tim had a dose of Digoxin prepared for him, which was strangely very close to the treatment Adelphi had given him as "punishment" when Marus first arrived. This time, it was what he needed to save his life.

His ordeal was not over yet; Dr. Tim had to become a burn specialist and transplant a few patches of skin. This would take some pain medicine, but Adelphi insisted on a non-narcotic substitute she had created. Marus would take it easy for a while, but he would survive what Willow could not.

By the time the rescue party had prepped the patients and headed up the hill, Shiv and Jesus had returned. Stud asked for help bringing the cargo from the raft. Although they had some small game, hunting in the downpour had not been fruitful, so it was easy to lend a hand.

We spent the next few days lost in stories of Willow, Kia, their larger-than-life legacies, and a pair of impossible journeys. The village spent the first day planning our next actions; as I insisted, we needed to spread out to ensure we survived. Our biggest challenge was from Earth.

We had left Freedom looking very deserted. We left the shipwreck at the hot spring tubs, and the delta would be a challenging environment to find clues to our direction.

We removed the landing huts and scrubbed the fire pit to the point that the boulder was, again, just a boulder in the woods.

Willow's grave was now invisible, the pole was gone, and her monument, chair, and bench now lived in her cathedral until we were safe enough to move them back. The path to the plateau was now just an animal path.

Shiv and Stacy decided they would move South and pulled together a team to cross the fallen log bridge and explore the area Shiv and Stud had found to the South of the grasslands. Vera asked if she could join. She needed a change of scenery and a new lease on life. Sirih had been paying close attention and asked if she could bring a transporter and join them. They readily agreed, and I was happy to see we could be transporter-connected.

"Mutt, Pete, Oliver? Do any of you want to come along? I'm feeling outnumbered here." Shiv was looking a little concerned.

Pete stood up. Shiv had been a constant mentor to him and Mutt. "I'd like to come along and help with the ladies." The laughter echoed across Willow's Cathedral.

Tiffany's plan had settled on a nomadic tribe, proactively using guerilla warfare against the giants and their supply chain. She felt they could be the couriers that kept the tribes connected. Adelphi wanted to go anywhere Tiffany went, and Jesus and Princess liked that idea, too. The distribution was taking shape.

***

51 Pegasi - Black Mac

I needed to find some solitude once my arm healed, but the weather was breaking, and I didn't want to leave the village before I knew they could handle the impending attack from Thom and the giants. I didn't know if the giants would come out to Bitter Waters, but I expected we would be enough pain to warrant a visit, and Thom would be incensed.

Popeye and Jewels had discovered we could access the shoreline South of the cathedral cliffs with a short swim around a pillar.

Shiv and his team took their leave after hugs all around,.

Tiffany and Adelphi decided to try to get one more soak in the tubs before heading out. So, they stepped into the water, swam around the point, and headed for the delta in the shallow water along the beach to hide their tracks.

I wasn't ready to swim yet, but I found a perch on the top of the cliffs where I could see the entire shoreline to the distant delta and hot spring tubs with a set of powerful binoculars the freight shipment had delivered for Willow.

I watched as Shiv's team set off with purpose and Tiffany and Adelphi as they frolicked in the surf.

Something was off. I soon realised there was a massive ebb tide. The ladies were suddenly standing yards from the water edge on a long, curved lava shelf that hosted the soaking tubs the village had grown so fond of.

Adelphi and Tiffany were startled as the ebb turned, and Adelphi's far-off scream of warning came as a vast wave swallowed breaker after breaker in a hungry charge at the shore. Tiffany was next, and there was no time for escape.

Tiffany dove downward, off the edge of the ledge, as the wave rolled over to smash the shore and blast Adelphi up the beach into the delta. She was lifted like a sea bird as water that could not fold back into the sea rushed inland. She crashed into the trees at least fifty feet from the shore and eight feet from the ground.

Tiffany bobbed up hundreds of feet from the shore and swam with all her might at the receding beach while watching sister waves bear down on her from the ocean. She caught one near the crest and rode it swiftly landward until she fell off the back of the wave and slid down the trough.

She caught the next wave farther down the wall and rode it to shore like a dolphin.

The ebb was overpowering now, and the ebb deposited her back in the sea with acres of broken tree trunks, branches, and dozens of panicked and squirming small animals.

She screamed, "Adelphi! Adelphi! Where are you?" The delayed sound of her panic reached me on the cliff head. Mutt and Stud had just joined me and bolted for the bottom of the landing trail. There was no time to cover their tracks, but I and the rest of the tribe could handle that from our end.

I watched as new strength welled up in Tiffany. Suddenly, her predicament meant nothing. Adelphi was gone; muddy water and debris were swirling where she had last seen her.

Although she was now North of the tubs, Tiffany duplicated her last success and powered her way through the mud and onto land.

With terror, her head swiveled to see behind her in the ocean and ahead of the broken trees.

There was no flash of the bright purple kilt nor the soft olive skin she could not imagine living without. There was no sign of Adelphi.

She stopped momentarily to listen but abruptly charged back into the rubble and mud. She dove into her quest, charging inland over the path of destruction. The Amazonian beauty was bedraggled, bruised, and bleeding from several cuts. Her naked body flashed in her efforts to rake tree limbs back and yank away landed seaweed and silver-feathered evergreen boughs.

I could still hear her calls from my perch. "Adelphi! Answer me! Please let me know where you are. Please hear me!"

Her pleading went unanswered for over an hour before she found her lover tucked under a log with sand pushed up around her like a dune. They were on the back edge of the delta, where the flooding was over.

Tiffany clawed the sand from Adelphi and gently pulled her from her tomb. She was still breathing. Tiffany pulled her close now and cried. She cried for long minutes. Partly with relief because Adelphi lived, partially because the surge had so beaten her woman, and because Tiffany now knew her armor was gone. She cared far more than she wanted to, which was out of her control.

I watched as she rocked her Adelphi and stroked her hair while talking to her. I couldn't hear what she said, but I saw her start as Adelphi began to respond. Tiffany managed to free her from the sand and mud.

I watched the Greek's soulmate gaze down at her as she moved her extremities, one after the other.

I started to scream for them to watch out but caught myself before any noise came out. With adrenalin blasting,

Adelphi looked up and saw the danger first. She didn't have the energy to scream or jump as a bent tree whipped over them, and the net fell over the women.

Tiffany jumped up and was neatly swept off her feet by the lower edge of a hoop, and the pair were swept into the air to be folded together by an enormous butterfly net.

Two furry giants stepped out of the thick trees that gated the river's source to the delta.

The giants were ecstatic as they lifted the struggling women high in the air for display. I could hear them. Their grunts and chirps were excited. The Tsunami had played their hand perfectly.

A human voice joined them. I couldn't hear the words, but I knew the source. Tiffany and Adelphi stared down at Howard Thom.

They were here.

***

Chapter 36

War

I cursed quietly as I watched that bloated scum poke the flesh of the dangling captives as he taunted them from below.

He laughed happily and signed to the Giant that held the net. I noted a half dozen of the giants in the delta now. A few minutes later, they deposited the women into one of the cages they had experienced on the East side of the pass. The beasts unfolded the walls, floor, and roof, latched them together, and dropped the net into the open top. They then hung them high in a tree but not high enough to escape the reach of the dregs of Earth.

Night was falling, so the bad guys built a fire on the broken beach, but it would do me no good in my windy perch. Ann showed up with a blanket and told me the whole tribe was active in a rescue plan. Only Marus, barely awake now, and I would be left at the cathedral through the night. A chill still leached into the air at night, but Tiffany and Adelphi suffered silently while cuddling in a spoon to keep warm.

At this point, there were three giants left in the group of captors and two humans.

The giants had been in a sign conversation with Thom, and the remaining Giants moved back from the humans to a spot away from the sulfur of the hot springs. The other man, dressed in camouflage, had started a fire. Once it lit up the scene, he joined Thom. He wore his hat low and his collar high, but I was not curious long.

Tiffany pointed at him and hissed. "Laurence!" I could read what she was saying in the growing firelight. Without hearing, by reading her rage and her lips as they turned into a sneer, I knew.

I owned that mistake. I turned him loose when my gut warned me his life should have taken a different path. My philosophy had tied my hands, but it did not ease my regret.

The men made small talk, but most of the conversation was in American Sign Language. We watched carefully. I wasn't sure if Laurence had ever heard that Tiffany used hand signs to communicate with the Pass Giants. From the signing I could see at the fire, Thom was convinced the village had traveled South.

Since Laurence had shown him the deserted village, they agreed. He had seen Shiv and crew's tracks at the log bridge. Because he had the women, he felt the rest weren't far. Howard was sure they still had the element of surprise. He didn't know I had brought back their plans weeks ago.

I could only hope Tiffany was capturing their conversation and would find a way to use it against them. However, we knew the men would interrogate them about the survivors in the morning. The discussion with Lawrence showed Howard was confident the women were easy to get the information from.

The binoculars were getting hard to hold to my face, and my eye sockets were strained from the pressure, but I couldn't put them down.

Thank you, Chuckles. You didn't tell anyone about your chats with the Pass Tribe.

The campfire died, and Thom and his grifter goon pulled sleeping bags from their packs. The remaining giants curled up together like puppies. Forty-foot puppies. The sight was almost touching until you remembered that they farmed humans for food.

Tiffany twisted her head to look at Adelphi's face. She wasn't smiling. They changed positions to warm their other sides. There was nothing to say. The women held each other and went silent.

It wasn't more than an hour. Alpha and Beta were shining on the scene, so there was a lot of light. The women started. They must have heard something. It had to be something they weren't expecting.

I could see the women scanning the forest. There it was. A hand waving from a downed tree trunk. I could make out the pale flag of fingers through my field glasses. I caught a quick glimpse of a face. Stud. The women could see him over the log. There beside him was the unmistakable grin of Mutt.

Thom stirred below and sat up to look around. Stud and Mutt disappeared behind the log. Thom stood and walked toward the water-polished tree trunk, tentatively stepping around debris. He stopped, listened, looked around, and continued, looking back at the sleeping camp after a few steps.

The wary leader listened for a moment, then stepped up to the log and relieved himself. Once done, he quickly returned to his sleeping bag and pulled it around him.

Tiffany and Adelphi didn't see the guys again through the night and managed to get some sleep. Their day had been horrendous, so nature took over and made them rest.

I must have nodded off, too, because the next thing I knew, Oliver was tapping my shoulder and pointing at the scene at the delta.

A banging on their cage rudely awakened everyone. The glee in Thom's eyes as he invaded their peace was evident.

He raged at them while alternating, shaking his finger and banging the cage. I could sense his hatred from here.

The women moved to the front of the cage. Obvious in their disgust, they glared down on the man who would be their judge and marketer. In unison, they spat at him.

He jumped to the side and laughed. The giants were awake and watching, so he signed as he raged through his snarl.

"Scum of the earth. It's time to tell me where your friends are. We know several more cockroaches are trying to live in this world. You are going back to cages where you belong... of course until you go into the cooking pot."

Thom laughed again. His glee was evident. "Did you notice only two of us cleaning up this mess? You and your friends are the failed genes of the human race, and it doesn't take more than one or two smart men to capture and eliminate you."

He waited a moment, then signed to the giant with the speckled coat and pointed at Adelphi.

The Giant set the cage on the ground, the lid snapped off, and two fingers and a thumb plucked Adelphi. Tiffany's efforts to stop the abduction were ineffective. Adelphi screamed as it lifted her through the air and placed her in front of Thom while pinching her long hair between finger and thumb.

She tried to bolt, but Laurence grabbed her and threw her to the ground. He straddled her and held her hands out from her body, pinned to the ground.

She stopped struggling and glared at Thom.

He turned to Tiffany, still in the cage, with the roof back on.

"Now, Dyke. This game is going to work like this. I'm not fond of long negotiations, so I will cut to the chase. You are going to tell me where the rat's nest is. We're going to go there and hang you two as bait, then sweep up all the livestock and take them back to their barn. Is that clear?"

"Screw you, traitors."

Tiffany's reply was short and direct.

"I wasn't finished telling you the rules." He pulled garden shears from a holster on his belt as he spoke. "You see, every time you give me an answer, I don't like, your fembitch loses a digit." He handed the shears to Laurence, who cut Adelphi's left little finger from her hand in one swift motion. The women screamed in unison, and Tiffany said. "They went to the valley above the plains South of us. Let me help her!"

Thom looked at the blood flowing from Adelphi's hand and nodded. He signed the giant standing over the cage, and Tiffany was deposited beside Adelphi.

She knocked Laurence's hand aside and squeezed the stump of Adelphi's finger until the blood stopped flowing. Adelphi watched in shock.

Lawrence and Howard laughed at the efforts. "Got that idea from a movie. Didn't know it would work so quickly."

They laughed harder, Thom still, with a tight grip on Tiffany.

A long, deadly hiss and a thock broke the short silence. Laurence rolled off Adelphi with the point of an arrow sticking out of his chest. The shot was perfect.

The dark brown Giant suddenly roared and swiped at an arrow in his neck. A few grunts and the camp broke with giant apes crashing their escape through the brush toward the South and Thom heading after them. An arrow appeared, vibrating in a sapling that saved the fleeing psychopath.

***

Our whole tribe ran for the delta, with me following as best I could. Marus was on his own for a while.

Tiffany had gathered up Adelphi, and they ran for the lower falls. Moments later, Stud joined them. They came together before they got to the base of the falls. They had concentrated on getting some distance between themselves and the giants.

The scouts thought the pass might be the best chance to get cover yet lead the posse away from the village. But they stopped to breathe as they saw us coming. We had tracks all around us now, but we were ready to make a stand.

Between gasps, Tiffany addressed Stud.

"Where's Mutt?"

He answered in the same manner. "This is his plan. He showed himself to the giants. Mutt leads them to the South but back up the trail Jesus had used to get them home. I don't know that he has any more plan than that."

Tiffany lowered her head, handed something to Jewels, grabbed my bow and quiver, and ran. Stud kept pace, and Popeye was about to go.

I asked him to stay. "I don't think the giants are finished with us. From my vantage up in Freedom, I saw one of the giants and Thom turn and head for the falls. They think we are ahead of them. We need some firepower here."

Popeye and Jewels set arrows on their strings, and we moved into the forest to the North of the river and wound carefully up the shore toward the lower falls. By now, Jewels had attended to Adelphi, and she now had a tightly wrapped stub but was still determined to get revenge, even though she had no weapons. Following as I could,

I witnessed the tribe cautiously clearing the lower falls and following easy tracks toward the upper ones. Popeye and Jewels helped me scale the Falls climb. The path was clear, but we were wary of Rainbow Lizards. With adrenaline driving, we didn't have long to go.

The Giants had stopped against the rock face near the pile of rubble where Willow had been found. Thom was nearing the top of the falls. The giant turned back to attack us but didn't get far. The giant stopped short with an arrow through its neck. Another shaft followed quickly, and then another in the center of its back.

The giant stumbled to its knees and tried to get back up with one foot but fell over. It was still breathing, but blood was bubbling up through its mouth, and the end came soon after.

Thom broke over the top of the falls and looked back at the dying giant. As he stared in shock, he took an arrow in his left arm. Thom turned and disappeared.

All eyes went up the falls, and there standing, each with another arrow strung, were Princess and Penny.

They looked back again, where Thom had disappeared, and calmly, Penny said, "Climb the trail to the left of the falls if you want to help, but some of you had better take care of Adelphi. We've got this. He's now wearing two arrows, and it's time to feed the Rainbow Lizards.

Popeye slung his bow over his shoulder and climbed the falls. The rest of us returned to Dr. Tim to get Adelphi the needed attention.

To the South, Mutt's flight ended on the hill above the plains. He remembered the bluff where we fought off the Screamers. When the giants arrived, Mutt had sequestered himself in the tight cover above the bluff. The giants could smell him and were searching the small landing.

The speckled giant found Mutt and was ripping saplings off the top of the bluff to get to him. Just as the giant reached for him, Mutt let his arrow fly, and it found its mark deep into the creature's right eye socket. The tower of fur fell backward, and the three other giants raged over his body to get to Mutt, who had backed farther into the small trees.

As they started to rip at his cover again, two of them received hard-driving arrows to their backs. Tiffany and Stud buried them deep. Stud recognized the golden-tipped giant he met in his first few days on Aard. The Giants turned their attention to the pair at the bottom of the landing but took two more arrows from the front and didn't reach the archers below before succumbing to their wounds.

The last Sasquatch took Mutt's final arrow in its ribs but turned and raged away to the East before Tiffany and Stud could re-string. As they helped Mutt down from the bluff, they heard a roar at the bottom of the hill and saw the giant stumbling back into view. It was dying with still more arrows lodged in its chest. Shiv came trotting after it and stood poised with another as it died.

The warriors gathered with hugs at the bottom of the hill. "The tsunami flushed us into the grasslands as we were headed South on the beach. We're all okay, but we knew we must return to Freedom." He turned and whistled, and his camp came trotting into view.

An hour later, Dr. Tim was tending to Adelphi's wound in Willow's Cathedral. She had asked Ann to fetch her dress. Jewels offered the severed finger, but the doctor sadly shook his head. Adelphi took the finger from Jewels, looked at it for a moment, and threw it out the opening into the ocean.

She then received her dress from Ann, reached into a pocket, and pulled out a small paper envelope. She poured the contents into her mouth and smiled.

Adelphi laid back on the doctor's platform and present-ed her hand to the doctor. "I know what is involved. You must take the knuckle to get enough skin to cover the wound. I will be asleep in a moment, so please take your time and make it pretty." Her eyes were heavy as she looked around the room and said, "Gonna take a nap now." Her eyes closed, and she smiled softly.

We all filed out and let the doctor work. He kept Maritza to help; she was already cleaning the wound and had prepared surgery tools and bandaging.

As we stepped into the main room, to our great relief, Tiffany, Stud, and Shiv's tribe came in with a somewhat bat-tered Mutt. Come to think of it. We were all rather battered.

I told Tiffany we could not save the finger and let her know what Adelphi did with it. It was time to rest and wait for Dr. Tim to finish and for Adelphi to wake. We needed to see Popeye, Penny, and Princess return, but I felt my wait was over. I needed to be alone to decide what to do with my life without Willow.

I addressed the tribe and told them so.

"Family, we have been through much in a very short time. Stud, you, and Hilda have been at the core of much of it. You now have Hilda at your side. Tiffany, you now have a soulmate in Adelphi. You complete and complement each other. Jewels, you have Pop... Paul. Shiv and Stacy have made a great team.

You are all coming together with bonds that will last as long as you live."

"I will stay till the ladies bring Popeye back, but then I am going to Earth for a while to learn what I should live my life for again. I assure you, if Willow lays by the pond at the old landing, I will always be back. Willow is my home, just as you all are, but I don't know how long I need.

Tiffany stepped forward and hugged me. She didn't say anything, but I felt the love. She turned to Stud. "Hey, Jean, you want to help me bring Popeye and the girls home?

He grinned, and they loaded up and left.

Jewels said, "I guess we can rebuild the landing and memorial again. I smiled.

"Yes, when I come back, it will be my home."

**

Chapter 37

Kelsey and Sylvia

I have been on Earth for over a month now. Looking back, I spent the first two months in blind grief over the loss of Willow. Now, I was on a mission.

My mind had strayed to the events that led me to find Popeye. I had compared my grief over Margo with the grief I felt for the loss of Willow. I guess I had been feeling the loss of Margo for some time as we drifted apart. I always assumed we would bond again as we retired, but the news of her friend in the accident suggested that would not have happened.

Both losses were devastating, but the difference was me. The difference was the life I was living when it happened. I was numb the first time with the shock of a safe and comfortable life turning over. With Willow, we lived a lot closer to life and death. Life meant more. It wasn't about the people. It was about my conditioning.

I had told the story about Willow's death to Dad and Tony, and I saw they were devastated. I think they had learned to love her in the short time they knew her. My epiphany and Willow put me back to work.

Now, my concern was the life left with the unfortunate circumstances of Popeye's story. Most importantly, the little girl that carried the lion's share of that burden through lack of communication.

Having learned the time manipulations on the transporter, I recalibrated. I was currently wandering the streets of Seattle, 18 years in the future. I knew I could do nothing constructive with the past, but I could help in the future. Things hadn't changed much in the industrial section below the old Mariner's stadium. In fact, Dad's food processing plant I used to migrate Popeye was unchanged. Some parts of the neighborhood had spruced up, but rezoning for the new tunnel extension kept most of the neighborhood in limbo.

I strolled up to the pretty young prostitute on the corner and observed that she hadn't been chewed up by the trade yet. She still had an innocent look so sought after and commercial on the street.

"How much for an all-nighter, Darlin'?"

She didn't hesitate.

"Two hundred bucks for straight up, three for kinky or old guys. Three for you."

"Hey, hey. Fair 'nough li'l girl. You old enough for this?"

That pissed her off.

"Forget it, geezer."

"Don't take offense, Darlin', just saying you look fresh. We gotta pay your pimp first?"

"I'm a self-manager. 'Don't need an agent.

You got a place?"

I hooked my thumb over my shoulder. "Right over there, Missy, my mansion awaits."

Kelsey waved at a girl watching from across the street, pointed at the old processing plant, motioned at her watch, and painted a full circle in the air. The girl nodded, and she turned to nod at me.

I led her to the same door below the window I had helped Popeye crawl through but punched the key code in the lock instead. "Welcome."

Kelsey followed me up a set of open steel stairs to a warm room with an open processing oven that hosted a sputtering fire that was thinking of going out. I quickly stoked the fire with old pallet wood while pointing at a stool-sized wire spool. "Have a chair, Missy."

Kelsey looked around. "Where's the bed? You have a bed, don't you? Do you have a bathroom?"

I smiled and pointed at a bedroll tucked against a wall. "The bathroom is under the stairs you came up, but there are no lights. If you need it, you should see it first in the light. The only light is from the windows up there." I pointed at the second-floor windows with heavy dust filtering the late spring dusk.

Kelsey demanded a preview, a little worried at the chance this guy had no money. I readily obliged by pulling a roll of Benjamin's from my jacket, fluttering the edges, and replacing them. Satisfied, she took advantage of the light and descended to the old staff bathroom to freshen up.

As she returned up the stairs, I noted the determined stride, the set tension in her jaw, and the dull but steady observations of her gaze.

"Waddidya want? Straight up, kink, dirty talk?"

I smiled sadly. Survival was ugly sometimes.

"Christ! Are you one of those goody-goody girl saviors? Are you in the Salvation Army or something? Are you a screwed-up reporter? Are you a cop? Maybe you had better pay me now for my counseling services."

I couldn't help it. I had to chuckle softly. I held out my hand in a stop motion and shook my head. I pulled out three hundred dollars and laid it in her hand. "All night, right?"

Kelsey settled a bit, "Yes, I can now counsel you all night."

I grinned. "Yes, that is exactly what I need. I need your views on that newspaper article in my paper stack by the fire." I stood and passed her the front page of the business section of the out-of-print newspaper I was talking about.

The paper was fifteen years old. She would have been four. The story was about the fall of a mighty businessman accused of molesting his daughter. The story was about Popeye.

The hardened young woman looked at me with her eyebrows furrowed. "What the hell are you up to? That's a bald-faced lie." She threw the paper at the fire. It fluttered to the floor between us. "Who the hell are you, and what do you want?"

"I'm a good friend of your dad's, Kelsey."

I know the whole story, and I helped him start his life over when he knew staying around you would mess you up even more."

"He didn't have to bugger off. He could have stayed and fought it in the courts." Kelsey's voice rose as she grew angrier.

"Kelsey, in those times, the courts were not the problem. As you can see, he was judged by the media, and his life as he knew it was over. Unfortunately, an accusation like that paints the accused with ink that an acquittal in the courts can't erase."

She was tearing up now. "Damn, you! I had buried all this, and you've dug it back up again."

"I'm sorry. Darlin', I am here to tell you your father has created a new life a long way from here and that life is available to you, too. You can have a fresh start away from all this."

Kelsey was weeping now. "That son of a bitch that married my mother was the real molester. My mother wouldn't believe me. I told them both what they could do to each other when I turned sixteen and haven't been back since." She looked up through her tears. "Where's my dad?"

"He's far from here, Kelsey, but I can take you there. You must be ready for some huge changes, though; it is completely different from anything you have seen or heard about."

"Do I fly there?"

She hadn't bolted yet. I assumed the $300 kept her in it till now, but she was surely interested.

"Come here." I stood and walked into the electrical room just off the main room.

Kelsey followed with a completely different set of emotions than she could remember. A thin whisp of hope crept into her life. I could tell the spark had ignited. I showed her the small stainless-steel button her father had used so long ago, yet so recently.

"When you are ready, you will push that button. Think of Star Trek.

That button will transport you to somewhere far from here, and you will see your father again."

"Are you shittin' me? 'You have a Star Trek button in this building? 'You think I'm a fool? You are nuts, aren't you?"

I lowered my voice to bring the mood back, "Kelsey, this isn't based on magic; it is science, but it sounds like science fiction. I know that. I could never describe this trip to you in a way that would make sense, so you will need to take a leap of faith. I know what has happened to you since bad people dragged your dad out of your life.

He doesn't know it all yet, but I can offer you one if you want a second chance. Once you are ready, you and he can build a relationship again if you both want it. No strings." I watched her eyes as her brain tried to adjust to what she heard.

"If you push the button, you will end up standing beside another button, just like it, and you will meet a very sweet young lady your age who will explain more. But you can push that button anytime and be back here without strings attached. I will go now, using that button, and if and when you are ready, you just come back in here and push this button. I'll take care of the rest."

I looked at the stunned expression on the troubled young woman. 'Yes, I think she's ready.' I handed her a Post-it note with the key code. "This is the code to the door lock. Kelsey, I'm going to disappear now. It'll freak you out some, but remember what I said. The choice is yours, but your future awaits here at this button. What do you have to go back for?"

Kelsey looked at the bundle of bills in her hand, then back at me. I pushed the button.

Later, Kelsey told me she stood motionless for some time, then returned to the fire. Instinctively, she knew I was gone, and I spoke the truth. She had watched me provide evidence and trust; my story was too real.

She walked out of the building and across the street to her friend, who was shivering on the corner. "Let me buy you some supper, Sylvie." They walked a few blocks to a sports bar and ate.

They ate with little conversation but day-to-day life, but as she paid the tab, she caught her friend's attention. "Sylvie, I'm leaving. I'm returning to Straights-Ville, so don't worry if I'm gone.

Sylvie smiled with arched eyebrows. "Sugar Daddy?"

"You might say that, Doll."

"That's all good, Honey. One day soon, I will too."

Kelsey thought for a moment. "Sylvie, are you ready to blow this popsicle stand with me?"

Sylvie grinned, "You got a spare seat in your pumpkin coach, Cinderella."

"As a matter of fact, I think I do..."

"Kels..., I spent three years turning trucker tricks from a ranchland truck stop, and I thought moving to Seattle would be the big time. It turned out to be a downgrade. I am out of options, so Baby, I'm in."

The women walked back across the street and into the old processing plant. The key code worked. So did the button.

***

The heat was back in more ways than one. The weather was hot outside, and the giants had returned with a vengeance after losing six of their tribe to the feral humans. They also lost the two most important connections to their supply chain of easy protein.

They trampled Freedom; the grasslands had been burned to flush humans out, and that made Shiv and his tribe come back to Willow's Cathedral. This offensive had gone for an entire lunar cycle, but hunting underground humans was like hunting moles.

They could smell them from time to time, so they knew they were near but could never find their warren. When they burned the grasslands, they found evidence they had been there but found no remains.

They had searched the plateau as far as the mountains to the East. The Giants found the area rife with Screamers and even found a few human tracks but didn't think we would settle so close to their predators. They had burned out the berries near their tower camp, so the escapees had nowhere to hide.

But then they weren't getting the supplies they were getting before, so it didn't matter.

The effort was not fruitful, so the Giants began to lose interest, and the stench of the sulfur waters was a good incentive to leave this small group to their misadventures. They were small and weak, so they probably couldn't survive long. At least, that is how I hoped they had been thinking as they left.

After discussing quietly, Shiv and Popeye called a village meeting in the main hall. They brought up my wish that we would spread out, and now that the heat was off, they decided it was time to try again. Shiv's tribe was heading back South as new grass sprouted stronger than ever after the fire.

This time, however, Sirih and Vera decided to stay at Willow's Cathedral. They wanted to help Julio rebuild Freedom. Instead, Pete convinced Mutt to join them, so this time, Stacy would be the only female in the tribe.

Tiffany, Adelphi, and Jesus were off to the North to free humans. The doctor and Maritza liked their setup in the Cathedral, and a much healthier Marus wanted to share time in both places.

When he mentioned that, it became apparent that the residents of Freedom and the Landing would be relatively liquid as the tribe would come and go now that there was so much history in both places.

I walked into the back of the meeting." Prepping for the fan-out, are you?" Everyone turned and swarmed. I was happy to be somewhere for the first time since Willow's loss. The conversation almost became festive as the community came together around me.

"Folks, I know I've been gone for a long time now, but in my mind, I was back here every day. You've fixed the place up nicely." I waved my arm around the giant center hall.

"If you will excuse me for just a few minutes longer, I have a task I would like to talk over with Popeye and Jewels. Be right back."

I gestured to Popeye and Jewels, "Come with me for a minute, please." I led the Landing team to the cave with the Landing pole.

"Jewels, I would like you to manage the Landing pole with a female helper for the next few days. I'm expecting an impressionable young lady who will need a female leader to start her Aardian journey. Popeye, I'd like your help on something else for a spell, if that is ok."

Jewels nodded, suggested she stay at the pole, and would ask Ann to help. "Jewels, she could show up anytime, so please stay close. Please call on Ann and whomever you two want to help so you can spell each other off as needed... oh, I have a hunch there may be two of them, and they will need robes at first." Popeye and I headed back toward the main hall.

"Paul, we'll need to ensure Shiv and Tiffany have transporters and someone who can always configure them. This fact and the loss of Kia may make this a requirement for your recruiting plan as you grow your immigration process. Let's bring it up with the village leaders."

So far, Popeye was nodding to my requests and suggestions. I sure hope he keeps nodding as he understands who the new immigrant is.

"I'm going to challenge you with this next immigrant or two, but I'd like to spend a little time on details with you first."

"Thanks for the mystery, Mac. I'd call you on this one, but I trust you, so I'm willing to hear you out." I smiled at my friend and tried to read the exact level of sarcasm in his voice, but noted with relief that Paul trusted me to make the right decisions. We neared the excited tribe, and tea and snacks were served.

It turned out Oliver found his calling. Adelphi's introduction of grassland flour and Humpback eggs had considerably impacted the tribe's diet, and Oliver and Stacy were great collaborators.

I called Ann over. "Ann, would you be so kind as to take a couple of robes for mid-sized women to Jewels in the Landing cavern, please? You may want to get some help to set up a watch in that room for a few hours or maybe a day or two. Perhaps some tea and snacks for now.

I'll drop in, in a bit to give you and Jewels a briefing."

She looked sideways at Popeye but said. "Of course," and hurried off.

"Shiv, could you hang on a couple of days? We have a recruit or two coming in, and I think they will want to go South with you."

I turned to the tribe in general, "In the meantime, let's all plan for this split to stay in tune, serve each other, and stay healthy."

"Tiffany, any changes to your plans now that we know the berry warren and the grasslands burned?

Especially since we feel we have disrupted the supply chain."

"Plans have been reversed, Mac. Instead of the tower, we need to hit the Northern Giants we discovered on our last trip. We have to be sure the supply chain is damaged. We think their organization was big enough that there will be far more captives.

We also feel the rainforest runs much farther South, so if we extract some folks from the Northern camp, we will need to keep vigilant. We, then, must head right down past the giants at the tower camp in the jungle. We should be able to move South of the grasslands to the wooded area Shiv found farther to the South, head West through the forest, and up the beach to Shiv or on up to Freedom."

The crowd moved back in to listen and contribute. We were back up to speed, and after a month of feeling sorry for myself, Willow had pulled me back to put me to work.

"Popeye, we must return the memorial and cane chairs back near Willow. Is anyone into helping us set it up and clean it up? I may even build the hut back... Kinda like it there."

Popeye stepped away to recruit.

With everyone planning and visiting, I walked back to the Landing pole to explain Kelsey to our new female landing party. I then set Shiv and Stacy up in an adjoining cavern to wait for the recruits. Shiv understood why Kelsey was so essential, the ramifications for Popeye, and my action plan. His team was ready to head South as soon as he gave the word.

51 Pegasi - Black Mac

Popeye, Stud, and I headed for Willow's Landing with Adelphi's little cart. This time, it carried the pieces for her memorial instead of my inspiration.

***

Chapter 38

It's Complicated

"Fuuuuuck!!!"

Kelsey Sutler had landed.

"Ahhhh!"

There was Sylvia Kettering, now on Aard as well.

Jewels had decorated the landing room with Screamer feathers, a few benches with soft Screamer hides folded over to give them cushion, and streamers of sunlight flowed in from the Western openings over the sea. She sat quietly on the nearest bench to the frightened young ladies, holding a pair of robes. Ann sat quietly with her. Both welcoming women wore Screamer kilts but were bare on top.

Still with silent screams in their eyes, both freshly landed girls caught sight of a striking woman their age and a pleasant-looking black woman smiling softly at them. Jewels held out the robes. Both girls looked down at their naked bodies, jumped up, and grabbed the robes.

"Th... thank you," muttered Sylvia, but Kelsey had yet to find her vocals after her rather verbal entrance.

Jewels started in a soothing voice. "I'm Julie, or as most call me, Jewels." She nodded at Ann.

"This is my great friend and mentor, Ann."

Now robed, Sylvia nodded at Kelsey and said," This is Kelsey, and I'm Sylvia. We call each other Kels and Syl.

"Where the fuck are we?" Kelsey found her tongue again.

As gently as she began, Jewels said, "You are in Willow's Cathedral, our village home for the moment, but we are near Freedom, a little village we abandoned while we were in danger. The danger appears to have ebbed, so we are now beginning to spread out into a few tribes. One tribe will stay here, one will go South, and one will be nomadic. You are on the planet Aard, in the Pegasi solar system. You have crossed time and space to get here."

"The fuck! Let us go!" Kelsey was still combative.

"You are free to go."

Silvia reached out to hold her friend by the shoulder. "Just a minute, Kels. This doesn't look that bad. Let's look around."

"No, I wanna go home. Now!"

Jewels pointed at the button on the back wall. "Kelsey, all you need to do is push that button, and you will be back where you came from."

The scared young woman jumped up and ran to the button, expecting to be tackled. She stopped for a moment to look back and pushed the button. She was gone.

"Shit. Let me go get her." Sylvia went back to the button. "Don't go away. I'll be right back."

Stacy poked her head in, hearing the drama from the next room.

"Anyone want a cup of tea? This transport could take a little acclimation time."

Jewels and Ann nodded. "Yes, they may or may not be ready, but just in case, could you make a big pot, please? The ladies may need a sip of calming tea when they get back.

The ladies were back before the tea was ready.

This time, they weren't in such a hurry to put the robes on that lay in a pile where they dropped during the transport back, but they had many questions.

Once they got a deeper picture of what Aard was about, Kelsey's questions became quieter but more personal.

"Where is my dad?"

Jewels was ready. "He's on an errand up at the old landing with Mac. Kelsey, we wanted to discuss your preferences before we let him know you are here."

"He doesn't know I'm here?"

"Not yet. We wanted to know if and how you want to meet him. He still imagines you as a five-year-old. It will be a massive shock to see you grown up. We know he is desperate to find out how you are doing and if you are ok. He talks about you all the time. Kelsey, are you ready to meet him after all this time?"

She started to cry. "The bastard left me in hell. He left me with that monster that married my mother. She was no better. He should have saved me. I prayed for years for him to break the door down and steal me away."

"Kelsey, the law would have locked him away and put you back in your situation. Society... the media... would have made it worse. I know that is hard to believe after the life you've lived, but through his friend Mac, he has broken the door down and stolen you away. You are here."

Stacey came in with the tea and passed tin cups around.

Jewels patted the bench beside her, and so did Ann on her bench. They slid to opposite ends to let Kelsey and Sylvia sit close together. The girls accepted the tea and sat down.

Jewels touched Kelsey's shoulder softly and said, "Here's what I propose. Shiv and Stacy are taking a few people South, a couple of days of travel from here, to start a new community in the foothills. The new village will be close enough to visit often but far enough to survive if something should happen to this village.

While you get used to life on Aard, I suggest Shiv, Stacy, and their crew can teach you what you need to know and ensure you are happy, safe, and healthy. When ready, you can meet your dad on any terms you want. I know he would want that with all his heart."

Kelsey looked intrigued at the young woman who was selling her the idea. "You sure seem to know a lot about him."

It was Jewel's turn to mist up. It took her a minute to respond. "Kelsey, the truth is, I love your dad... Very much. So does the whole village, but not like I do. He is among the strongest, wisest, and most humble men I have ever known.

I think a lot of that comes from the pain and guilt he has lived with over what has happened to you."

Now, everyone was tearing up. Ann felt it was an excellent time to break the mood. "Ladies, is it time to meet Shiv, the leader who will take the troop South to build a new village?"

"Wait!" Kelsey's eyes were wide. "You're going to bring a guy in here with all our tits hanging out?"

Ann, Stacey, and Jewels couldn't help but laugh. Jewels explained. "Ladies, get equal rights here. If the men can get rid of a shirt in the heat, so can we. You can wear full robes, rolled down on top, kilts like us, or lose it all, and no one cares here. Until you figure out what is right for you, I'd recommend the robes at half-mast for the adventurous and the full robe for the shy until you are ready for your style."

The girls looked at each other. Sylvie said, "Half-mast." Kelsey nodded, and they slipped the robes on while Jewels and Ann showed them how to belt. Stacy went to get Shiv.

***

Once the new immigrants were happily embedded in Shiv's crew, Jewels joined Popeye and me as we worked on the Willow Memorial Landing, and Stud and Hilda headed back to see Shiv and Stacy off with their recruits.

I was content to work with my hands for now. I found a particularly flexible willow-like tree for furniture I had designed in my head. Willow canes and blue-tinted vines supplemented with arrow reeds for poker straight rungs. With a smattering of hand tools imported from Freedom, I had everything I needed to build our memorial at the landing.

It was time for me to talk with Popeye about his daughter.

I had planted two new willow chairs in the tri-blade grass by the pond and waved Paul over from his chores. Jewels noted the exchange, and suspecting what would transpire, she waved at us and made herself busy in the camp across the pond.

Paul settled into the new chair and nodded his approval. "Time for our talk, Mac? I've been trying to be patient. I have no clue why you're so secretive about the last two immigrants, and I can't get it out of Jewels, so I'm sure hoping you're ready to come clean."

I smiled, but Paul noted that it was a guarded smile. "Well, Popeye, this will be the deepest conversation we have ever had. First, I want you to know how much you mean to me, Aard, and our village."

I looked out over the still pond at his loyal lady. "One of the ladies that arrived on the last train was your daughter." I didn't wait for him to respond. "I'll explain, but she is grown up now, and you two will have to build a brand-new relationship once you have cleaned out the debris from the last one."

Now I shut up and let Paul have the floor. It got quiet and stayed quiet for some time.

Paul turned to look at the pond and Jewels working on the other side. He saw the first willow chair I had attempted and noted that it had a broken leg. A flashback to Willow's death and her missing hand struck his memory and clogged his logic.

All this news and reflection together overburdened his thoughts. A lot had happened since he arrived on Aard, but it was magnified a hundred-fold by what his imagination pictured his little Kelsey going through since he last saw her. His eyes misted over and stung till they dripped.

"How can she be grown up? She's got to be four or five years old now... Wh... Who's looking after her? I should be there with her."

"Popeye, I can't recruit anyone not old enough to make their own decisions to come here. I had to go far enough into the future to ensure she could come here of her own educated, free will. Your daughter, on Aard, is twenty. I spent some time getting to know her while I was off mourning. Willow came to me and made me see I needed to look at the pain you were both going through... and try to do something about it."

"Where is she?"

"She and her friend Sylvia have gone with Shiv and his band. They will be safe there, able to acclimate and get used to Aard while being coached by some great folks."

Paul saw red.

"Shiv is going to be all over her. She's... in her... twenties, not covered up... I've got to get her out of there."

"See, that's the biggest reason I couldn't keep her here. Shiv has Stacey, and Stacy has Shiv. You need to accept that your daughter is now an adult, a tough one, I might add, and will be making her own choices. You can no longer protect or shelter her; she owns those privileges."

Paul was quiet again. I let the silence stand.

I saw Jewels peek around the shelter and waved her over. I stood, and Paul watched but didn't speak.

Jewels sat where I had been, and I turned to go. Over my shoulder, I addressed the couple.

"Folks, I'm off to get us a Humpback. Let this sink in and toss it around a bit, and we can take up the conversation after supper. Jewels, maybe you'd like to fill Popeye in on some insights you learned from your time with Kels. I'll be back soon."

Paul wasn't ready for this insight; Jewels didn't have the opportunity to tell him what Kelsey's life had become. He held up his hand to stop the conversation, and Jewels let it stop there.

I would try to explain more when he could take more in.

As promised, I brought supper, and the camp was quiet but for meal preparation. We ate in silence, but no one was very hungry. We cleaned up after supper and sat on benches outside the shelter. Paul and Jewels shared one, and I sat across from them. I figured I'd try again. This was a discussion we had to have.

"Popeye, Kels will need to get the full story of what happened back in Seattle. When I first talked with her, she blamed you for deserting her. You can imagine what her mother and stepfather might have said. That damage has created a huge rift you will both have to climb over."

As I spoke, I watched my friend for signs. I could see the struggle but couldn't tell how it would go until he looked up at me with rage.

"You shouldn't have brought her here, Mac. She was better off without me. We both have to go through hell again as we sort this out. Why the hell did you bring her here?" Paul shouted the last sentence. His emotions were overflowing, making him jump to his feet to deliver.

Instinctively, Jewels and I jumped up with our hands extended, intending to calm him.

Paul stepped forward to where his nose was inches from mine. "What the fuck were you thinking?" His face was red now, and the veins on his neck extended. Jewel's hands were on his left elbow, and I instinctively raised my open hands higher. Paul struck. His right fist broke my nose, and I pitched backward over the bench I had been sitting on. Jewels yelped and put all her weight into pulling Paul around.

"No, what are you doing?"

Wordlessly, Paul shrugged her off and stalked into the night toward the landing pond.

Jewels was torn between running after him and helping me back to my feet. I waved her off, so she ran to catch up to her struggling man. I righted the bench, sat back down, and rolled my head backward while pinching my nose to stop it from bleeding down my bare chest.

***

Chapter 39

A Broken Nose and the Rolling Hills

They were gone long enough now that I was beginning to worry. Just as I stood to start searching, I heard the rustle and subdued voices of the Landing pair coming back along the faint blue trail to the new cabin.

The fact that they were using soft voices encouraged me. As they came into view, Popeye was leading with Jewels holding his elbow lightly to let him know she was there.

"I'm so sorry, Mac. I haven't been that out of control for years. You did the right thing for both of us."

He looked at Jewels, "... For all of us.... It's hard, but Kelsey and I must face each other before we can heal and grow. Jewels can't get the best of me until I address my past."

"Paul, it's behind us. The second broken nose is easier than the first. I knew this would be a huge shock for you, and it would reopen wounds for both of you that would take work to heal. If I get a dented nose in the process, I feel like I'm part of the family, and if I share in the pain, I will also share in the success that will follow."

They looked at me with gratitude.

"Mac, Jewels told me what Kels and her friend were doing to survive. That was my worst fear, but I've thought about it, and she has survived. As you said, she is strong. My fears took over, and I owe Shiv an apology, too. He'd do anything to protect her... even if she wasn't my daughter. I feel much better knowing she is here than the alternative in Seattle."

He held his hand out for me to shake, but I ignored it and hugged him instead. He hugged back, but we both turned to sniffling behind us and found Jewels smiling through her tears. Of course, we pulled her into the hug.

"I'm going to catch up to Shiv and his new tribe tomorrow, Popeye. I owe it to the girls to be present at the launch of this adventure, and I want to see where they decide to build."

I pointed at my pack by the new little hut. "I'm taking them one of our transporters and setting it for Willows Cathedral. I'll be back soon to report. I'll leave early tomorrow and catch up with them at Freedom. Shiv planned to show the recruits our first village and explain why we pulled it down. They must know about the dark side of this planet sooner than later."

Emotion was still very high in the little camp, so no one replied, but Popeye and Jewels both nodded through tears. In the morning, Popeye and Jewels saw me off. I looked fondly at the hugging couple and felt it was the best time to remind them of our relationship.

"Folks, I want you to remember we are family. With Jewels being my niece, you being my nephew... in law, Kelsey being my grand niece, our generations are merging."

I let that simmer for a moment while they took in the depth, then I added. "Actually, your half-step-uncle. Tony is your full-blooded uncle. My neice and my grand neice are the same age."

Jewels laughed through happy ears. "This is going to be awesome! Kels and I are going to have great fun with this. I felt the beginning of a bond when I told her about my relationship to her dad and I know it's going to grow."

We laughed as she added, "Anything else to tell us, Uncle Mac?"

Through the laughter, I said, "Isn't that enough?" I cupped her tear-stained face in my hands and kissed her forehead. I then reached for Popeye's hand and shook it slowly. "Take care of our girl, my friend."

I strapped on the pack and headed down the path to Freedom. "See you soon, family." I had much to think about, and the quiet path would allow some raw reflection. I was clearer-minded than I had been since Willow died, and now, instead of a flood of tears every time her image came to my mind, I felt a resolve to carry on, wrapped in her smile.

I caught up with Shiv's troop at the tubs as they were setting up camp in old Freedom to prepare for an early start South in the morning. Shiv, Stacey, Mutt, and Pete set the new immigrants up with packs; everyone had the load they would carry to the new home. The new tribe was festive.

Kelsey and Sylvia already felt at home, and their stage whispers to each other as they acclimated were funny but telling.

Kelsey and Sylvia were excited. Both had quickly traded in the robes for the purple kilts and were glistening in the more than warm sun. Looking around, they liked what they saw.

Neither had any issue adapting to the strangers. It seemed easier this way. The newest Aardians weren't used to the fact that no one was focused on sex while they lived in various stages of undress.

Kelsey leaned close to whisper to her friend. "This kinda turns me on, Syl; everyone's glistening, healthy, strong, and looking good. I don't think either of us looks too bad. Why do you think no one is interested in us new girls?"

Sylvia got it. She whispered back.

"I think it's conditioning. They are used to being half-naked."

"I hope it doesn't mean we lose the urge. I don't think I could survive without the skin-to-skin ballet."

Sylvia grinned. "Better not lose the urge. I ain't goin' down without a fight. You seen any likely dancers?"

"Haven't thought about it yet. This subject is going to take some study."

Shiv looked back at me and chuckled. The girls broke off their whispers with giggles that made the rest of the party chuckle. A few yards ahead, Shiv grinned. The girls were happy.

"Ya gotta love happy girls."

As we sat around the cooking fire, Kelsey and Sylvia had questions. I chipped in where necessary but left most of the answers to Shiv and Stacey.

Sylvia opened the conversation. "Who's the boss in this camp? Do you call the shots, Shiv?"

They had already caught the fact that Shiv was leading the trek South. I was impressed with Shiv's answers, even more so as Stacey and the guys chimed in.

"Don't you ever fuckin' call me boss."

This caught everyone's attention.

"We're a democracy and don't need a prison warden telling us what to do. We all take the lead when we are the best for the task that needs doin'."

Stacey followed up. "Shiv is a natural warrior, scout, and guide. I am a farmer with a good eye on what we can and can't eat. I don't take orders, but I do take suggestions and questions. Mutt is probably our best archer and hunter. Pete is magic with tools, building, and inventions."

Kelsey smiled. "Cool. That's how we work... not that we are experts at anything useful here." She looked at Sylvia with a smirk.

"Wait a minute... I was a pretty good farmhand back in Chugwater. I think I could be kinda helpful to you, Stacey. I know how to plant, rake, mow, harvest, and separate grain." Sylvia was adamant. She wanted to make her way.

"I don't have any useful skills. I quit school to get away from an asshole. My superpower so far has been fighting off pimps and pushers who wanted to suck me into their stables."

Kelsey was a lot less optimistic about her ability to contribute.

Shiv leaned into Kelsey until his nose was within inches. "Don't sweat it, Kels. What I see is a blank slate. Let's have this conversation again once you have gone through boot camp and see what your new tribe needs and what you would like to rock."

I liked his approach and felt I could add to it. "Kelsey, I spent some time getting to know you in Seattle, and you were invited to Aard because I saw a warrior.

The way you handled yourself was rare. I will be very interested in what unfolds for you two as you acclimate and see your opportunities here, particularly in this tribe."

For the first time since I joined this troop to the South, Kelsey looked me in the eyes.

"What the hell happened to your nose?"

I laughed. "Does it look that bad? I was talking when I should have been listening."

Mutt laughed, too. "Dad... Is that you?"

Now everyone was laughing. Our noses did look a bit alike.

***

Shiv started us across the delta early and held to a track along the beach for a few miles. He reasoned that the tide would quickly wipe our traces away despite challenging beach travel.

Soon enough, we were up a twenty to thirty-foot grassy berm. The grass was still shoulder-high for the tallest of us.

As far as we could see, it waved like the ocean from the steady gusts coming off the water.

The air was much cooler here in the morning, but the marine layer had burned off early, so it was warming up.There was little conversation as we broke new ground, but by midday, Sylvia and Kelsey were getting tired and started verbalizing what they were absorbing.

Again, it began with Sylvia. "Should we be watching for the food we are used to gathering? I saw some of that celery beside that old driftwood log back there."

Stacey said, "Great observation, Syl. I've noticed a few clumps, particularly on the higher ground near a windbreak. That log is a perfect example. Notice it's only growing on the South side of the log.

That tells me the wind brought the seeds from the South, and they lodged against the log, germinated, and sprouted. I'd say that means we should find more of it to the South."

"Whoa, that's cool. I've also noticed that the grass has a great grain head. Still green but should make some great flower or cereal at harvest."

Stacey smiled again. "You're going to be good. Adelphi has already been harvesting this grain to test it for that purpose. Now that she's going on adventures, we can use some help in that area."

This science was an interesting topic to the crew, and Shiv got the message. "Ok, tribe. See that clump of trees inland? Stud and I were out here last year, and I think that is the entrance to a great campsite.

I'd say it's about an hour... whatever an hour means now, till we get there.

Now that we are away from the sound of the surf, I'd like you to stand still for a moment and listen. What do you hear?"

The trekkers grew serious but quiet. Kelsey's eyes widened. "I hear a woman screaming far away... Women. There is more than one... Wait... are those the Screamers you talked about?"

Shiv nodded. "They like to ride the winds that hit the far mountains and push warm ocean air up to the colder elevations. They smell prey of all kinds in those winds. They know we are out here somewhere. You will learn how we deal with them."

Everyone was deep in thought now.

"Are you all good to wait till we get to the cover of the trees before we take a break? We still don't know what might be out here, walking with us. Some of the Screamer's prey could be predators to us."

I smiled. The tribe got his message. The shelter was the priority. The conversation died down a bit as we ate up the distance.

As we got closer, the clump of trees turned out to be the face of a row of small hills, which began a cascading set of rolling hills. These were not like the heavy evergreen forest at the delta.

Instead, they were a patchwork of grassy hills framed by treed ridges and draws. This environment produced small, fresh rivulets that ran out in meandering journeys to the sea.

We saw that the rolling hills became more prominent as we got closer. They became taller and became the foothills of the familiar mountain range to the East.

We followed one of the small streams into the hills to a comfortable little campsite at the top of the first hill. We found the ashes of an old camp in a circle of stones tucked under the tree canopy.

There was a mix of coniferous and deciduous trees and shrubs here, but they weren't the size of the trees back in Freedom, the canyon, or the Tower Giant's camp. They were, however, tall by Earth standards.

"Welcome to 'Vue Mer.' As Stud called it. Sea Vista in English."

Shiv pointed west to the ocean swells in the distance. "This is a good jump-off place to go fishing at the sea, a trip to Freedom, or harvesting parties down in the grasslands."

He pointed at the next, much taller hill to the East. It was grassy and smooth but ringed by treed ravines, and we would need to cross one of them to get to it. "Just beyond the top of that hill is a beautiful grove of nut trees. The grove makes for a secure little village.

These ravines are thick with Humpbacks and some other game, much of the same vegetation we have been eating at Freedom, and Stud said he found berries on the back side of that hill. Not quite as big as the ones in the pass and tower, but still as big as your fist. More like a sweet tomato."

The beauty of the views struck everyone, but we were also hungry.

We broke down the packs to get our dried meat, vegetables, mushrooms, and berries. Shortly, everyone was happily eating and pointing out new features of the hilltop perch.

I looked around to a full round of smiles. One smile was a bit hollow, though. Kelsey still had much on her mind.

As we struck camp to make the rest of the way up the hill, I noted that Pete was particularly helpful in getting Sylvia packed up and ready, so while they were chatting, I asked Kelsey if she would walk with me. She didn't say anything but nodded.

As Shiv started the trek down the ravine to a crossing of a small creek, then the start up the other side, we all fell into single file, and I took the rear. Once we were up and out of the ravine, the climb up the hill was less steep and not so daunting, so we could walk in pairs again.

I spoke softly, "Kels, what's on your mind?"

Her eyes welled up when she looked at me, and she talked through gritted teeth to keep from crying. "Mac, I don't know what I'm doing here. I don't know how to be part of this village, but I need to belong somewhere."

I stopped and hugged her closely. "Kels, you do belong here. You simply don't know how much yet." She cried softly against my shoulder for a moment.

"I need to get to know who my dad is. I think I need to figure out who I am before I go to find out who he is."

"That's exactly why I thought this trek would be a great idea for you, Kels.

You won't find better mentors than Shiv and Stacey, but more than that, you can become known as Kels instead of Paul's daughter or one of the Sutlers. You have a blank slate."She wiped her eyes and smiled bravely, "I don't know where to start, but I'm pretty sure they don't need a hooker in the team."

***

Chapter 40

Three Questions and a View

"Let me ask you three questions, Kelsey. Take your time and think about them as we walk. Answer when you are ready."

She looked at me quizzically.

"First, what did you want to be when you grew up? ... when you were ten years old?"

We climbed the bald hillside behind the rest of the tribe for a while as she thought this through. I used an age that I hoped resonated with her despite her situation at home. Finally, she spoke.

"I used to escape my life with movies and my favorite singers. I wanted to write books, illustrate them, direct the movies made from them, and write and perform in the musical scores for them. My heroes were artists because they created worlds where I could be anyone I wanted to be."

"Sounds like you found that world."

Kelsey swung her head around to stare at me. In a moment, she responded with, "Maybe I did."

"Okay, second question. Now that we figured out what you would have become if the world hadn't come crashing down on you, what direction did you take when you got out of school?"

She was silent longer this time, and I let it rest. We almost reached the top of the hill before she answered.

"I ran away from home every few months from the time I was twelve because of the shit going on in that house. The only things keeping me within reach were my English teacher and my music teacher in middle school. When I no longer had Mrs. Bennet and Ms. Lavinsky, I had no use for high school, so I left.

I suppose I would have stayed if I didn't have to live with my mother, but at sixteen, the only option I could see was a boyfriend. His parents disapproved of me, and he was staying in school, so it was on to the next boyfriend. That is where my 'career' started. I was officially seventeen when I went into the business."

"That's where I found you?"

"Ya, three years of staying one step ahead of the pushers and pimps who didn't allow owner-operators in their territory. I'm unsure what my next step would have been if you hadn't shown up. Our block was heating up."

I decided to break the mood. "Want to hear something funny?"

"After that story, sure."

"Your dad has begun journaling our adventures on Aard. He is our first writer."

For the first time since I had met Kelsey, I saw the flash of glee in her smile.

"No shit!"

"No shit. Okay, third question."

This time, she smiled as I asked.

"Now that you have revisited the dreams you had as a child, we discovered what it took to build you into the woman I'm talking to today, and we have a glimpse of your future tribe... What do you want to be when you grow up?"

She laughed. "I'm going to try on every role in the camp until I figure them out. I will document it to make it easy to pass on the knowledge, and then I will open a boot camp to train others.

I will write about it, paint pictures, sing, and build musical instruments. One day, we will have music, art, and literature in all our villages. Maybe even theater."

Now I laughed. "What have I created?

The tribe turned to look to see what all the laughter was about. We noticed and remembered we had to be quiet.

When the trekkers saw the mood at the back of the pack, everyone grinned and quickened the pace. As we cleared the crest of the hill, the sun reached its pinnacle. The nut trees were all that Shiv had promised and more.

The ravine curved downhill to the South. The trees got thicker and, toward the next hollow, provided dense cover around the crest of the hill. The cover spread up to a small lake behind the ridge.

The nut trees continued around the base of the next towering hill, which changed into a coniferous forest of blue timber. Wildflower meadows stretched upward from the lake to fade into the tree line.

To the North, the hill sloped downward in a less treed vista that looked over miles of waving grassland to the tree line of the forested hill where we had fought the Screamers on one occasion and the giants on another.

We could not see the detail of that hill, but we could see the coastline disappear beyond the edge of the grass and the curvature of the planet we now called home. As beautiful as it was, we all knew we were still within range of the giants and the raptors should they come to know we were here.

"Come look at this, tribe." Shiv had found his landmark in the trees, just South of the small lake. Beside a house-sized volcanic stone, he waved his arms around the scene. "Where would you like your hut?"

No one had a problem with him calling dibs on the location. The truth was, there were many spots just as attractive. I walked to the South end of the lake and noted the clear water trickling happily down the hill into the shallow ravine.

I liked that the cooking fire would be below the mountain's crest, on the South side, and not readily evident from the North or at sea level at night.

The camp soon became a building zone as the trekkers constructed the beginnings of their village. They began food preparations and marked a semi-circle of hut footings around the village core.

This plan began with four huts. Building began on one hut for the single guys, one for the single girls, another for Shiv and Stacey, and a spare for me or any other guest coming through before the settlement grew.

***

I smiled as I saw Shiv and Stacey planning for a porch like Willow had back in Freedom. While Sylvia joined the camp activities, Kels and I spent some daylight searching for an antenna for the transporter Sirih didn't get to place.

Shiv pulled us to a spot on the shore of the lake. "Mac, not sure if it's what you need, but look just to the right of that rock bluff about 30 feet above the flower field across the lake."

It took a few moments to focus on the bluff he was talking about, but just to the right was a metallic yellow glint from the sun. "I think I see what you mean, Shiv. Yellow?"

He nodded. "Ya, Stud and I noticed it when we were up here last time but didn't have time to check it out. Wasn't expecting anything shiny up here."

"I'll bet it's gold." Kelsey laughed.

"Let's find out, kid." We grabbed bows, quivers, and sacks and headed around the bottom of the lake. A few minutes later, we were climbing through flowers, and for the first time, I noticed insects. We found pollinators the size of butterflies but with wings similar to bees for hovering.

Kelsey couldn't resist stopping to study them momentarily as they moved from blossom to blossom. They didn't appear interested in us, so we gingerly made our way between them.

The undergrowth was a little thicker in the forest, but we could follow animal trails that looked like Humpback tracks to the base of the rock formation that made the bluff.

There was a hidden cave at the bottom. There didn't seem to be any recent traffic in or out of it, so we continued to the right.

The wildlife trail rose to the base of the flashing vein of gold, polished by the wind-born tree branches. They guarded both sides of the smooth, golden trough. We noted a small stream running down the center of the vein, to pool slightly at the bottom before dropping down into the flower field and onward to the lake.

The water had worn a deep path in the soft metal, but it wasn't always in this path. In the past, it came down either side of the vein and had sometimes carved out pockets where the water had pooled.

The water had washed out dirt pockets embedded in the gold as well. About six feet from the bottom, we found a small chamber that originated deep in the gold channel that housed the transporter nicely.

My bag also carried the tools I felt I would need, and a chisel and hammer were all I needed to set the transporter. I charged it with its diamond fuel, connected it to the golden antenna, and fixed the small stainless-steel button to the box just out of the weather.

With Kelsey doing the configuration, I had her set the transporter for Willow's Cathedral. I had her tweak the settings to include paper.

I left her with the written instructions to adjust the settings to include tools, clothing, and other materials she may want to include. I then made sure she had the basic settings for simple human transfer.

When we were both comfortable that Kelsey could manage the transporter, we headed back for the camp. On the way down the hill, I suggested setting up a mail stop with her dad. At first mention, she stopped in her tracks momentarily and looked at me as though I was from another planet.

Before she verbalized her reaction, she thought about it and smiled.

"Yes, I think it's time I wrote my father a letter... 'Daddy dearest'..."

I wasn't sure how to react until she followed with a laugh that caught the crew's attention on the other side of the lake. As we heard the laughter coming back to us, we looked up to see the most spectacular sunset I had seen on Aard. The pinks, purples, and gold of Pegasi's light show were astonishing.

We pointed, and the work party in the camp looked back to the West as awestruck as we were. Then they pointed back beyond us, so we looked back as the sun struck the golden overhang and stood out like a gold tooth to the village.

By the time we got around the lake and into the camp, the sun had dropped below the water, and we could hardly see the yellow streak in the mountainside.

There was much to discuss around the fire that night as the new village bonded.

Pete and Sylvia had struck up a friendship as he talked through how they were going to build huts from nut trees.

Shiv and Stacey were busy plotting out the camp and planning for expansion. Mutt had gone hunting and, in the dusk, came back to camp with some freshwater fish. Mutt had confirmed that the ravines had a soft blue mushroom glow.

I introduced the camp transporter engineer, and Kelsey affirmed her desire to study and master boot camp. She had also captured a couple of notepads and pencils from Willow's Cathedral and would request more.

Over the evening meal, the new village discussed the name of the new camp. Many ideas were fronted, involving the vista, the golden tooth, the nut trees, and the hills. The discussion was still fluid when Alpha and Beta took to the skies.

The beauty of the camp was inspiring in the twin moonlight. As he watched the flickering embers rising from the fire, Mutt noticed the reflections from the moons hitting the gold pillar across the lake and reflecting two separate golden paths across the lake. They looked like twin tracks on a bridge.

"Look at the Moon Bridge." He pointed to the lake.

The village was named.

"Well folks, I'm heading for Willow's Cathedral and my little hut at the old Landing tomorrow, but I can't wait to tell the family back there about the beauty of your new home. Kelsey is starting a mail delivery service when I'm gone, so don't forget to write."

51 Pegasi - Black Mac

On that prompt, Kelsey started writing in her notebook in the light of the moons and the fire. I felt that this transporter might become the busiest one on Aard.

In the morning, I was off to the Cathedral, and as soon as I landed, Kelsey sent her first letter to her father. It was time for me to go to the Landing Pond and spend a little time with Willow. I needed to prepare.

***

Chapter 41

Time Out with a Ghost

Life was exciting at Willow's Cathedral and Freedom. Popeye and Jewels introduced a new dentist from Chicago, a business manager from Napa County in California, and two armed forces veterans.

One soldier was from New South Wales, Australia, and one from Utah. Tiffany and her crew had brought new folks in, too. The recent influx of immigrants brightened everyday life, courtesy of the Landing Team, Tiffany, Adelphi, and Jesus.

The village was buzzing about the scout's latest adventures. At first, they set up shop in the dark rainforest beyond the Tower Giants camp to the Northeast. With the Berry Warren and the grasslands burned off, their choice was a brazen cold camp right on the doorstep of the giants.

In just a few raids, they saved over a dozen people from the giant's cooking pots and escorted them North. For the first time, I didn't know everybody in our camps. The raiders used the Northern pass they found on their last run to get them to Willow's Cathedral and Freedom. Processing the immigrants led to a split delivery between Freedom and Moon Bridge.

Popeye and Kelsey were working on the transport.

This influx was good because they successfully broke people out, but they pissed off the Giants. "We are no longer a surprise to the Sasquatch tribes. They are constantly reminded that we are intelligent now. We have long outgrown the cute pet status. Humans are now being hunted methodically and with deadly intent on the East side of the mountains." was the report.

The escapees weren't followed this time, perhaps because of the change in direction and maybe because they lost some key players in their last attack on Freedom. We had eliminated Thom and Hempler, but more of a blow, they lost a few leading giants.

Tiffany was planning to explore the South in search of her old friends, the Pass Giants. It would be good to show a presence in other places so the Giants would not focus on Freedom. Everyone agreed that we needed a wider footprint.

This time, Adelphi would stay behind at the Moon Bridge camp to help Stacey and the team build up the food and medicine inventory tailored to the local environment. Interestingly, Princess wanted to be part of Tiffany's adventure. She had become one of the highest-caliber weapons experts over the last year. I believe she also had her eye on Jesus. I did a circuit of hugs, met some new folks, then headed for the old Landing to chat with Willow.

I sat on the cane bench and found that I still wept, looking at her burial site, still finding it hard to accept the loss. I still struggled to live a meaningful life without Willow. I couldn't yet see my future or how I would get over losing her.

The pond reflected only the mist and fog that hung over everything here.

I looked for her reflection in the water, hoping some magic or twist of the imagination would show her there, smiling. I talked to her through the afternoon as if she could hear.

I shared my hopes and fears, unburdening everything that had filled my heart and mind so heavily.

I decided that this place would be my permanent home, to build a cabin here and live out my days to be laid to rest at her side. I had little appetite but ate mushroom jerky and fell asleep as darkness settled over Willow's Memorial.

I dreamed she was there in the fog, smiling at me. She understood.

In the morning, I woke, my cheeks wet with tears. I had decided what to do and said my goodbyes to Willow for now.

I made my way back to the Cathedral and came in through the vent tunnel. It was early, so no one noticed. I set my coordinates for Seattle, left a note for Popeye and Jewels, and pushed the little stainless button on the wall.

Dad was home. When I stepped out of the transporter closet, he was busy at his desk in the packing plant.

"Hi, Son. 'Was hoping you would drop by soon."

He looked up and noticed my mood. "You look like you need some good news, Son. Are you okay?"

"Hi, Dad. Ya. Just been thinking a lot about Willow.

I needed to change the subject. "What are you up to?"

"Just connecting some dots. That off-world supply chain seems to be in some turmoil. It seems there have been some leadership changes. The lab in Portland shut down, but I think it opened again in Europe."

"Well, we did have a run-in on Aard, and some of their people didn't survive. A few of the giants didn't survive either.

We took quite a hit from the elements and those clowns at the same time."

Dad pointed at his laptop. "Well, son, I have a spreadsheet I've been working on with the names and locations of a group of transporter operations headquarters. To give you an idea, one is from here in Seattle, one is in Portland, one is in Tucson, with many more in the US and around the globe. Depending on where they find interest, they have built an underground network of local groups in midsize and sometimes smaller towns. Do you see a pattern here? I also have Detroit, Atlanta, Stillwater, Oklahoma... See where I am going?"

"I do, Dad. You and Tony sent me to Stillwater to get Jewels. It sounds like you found a list."

"We did, Son. Before the lab left, we got some names and addresses."

"Dad, do you have any details on Oregon? I may need to go check that one out for you."

"I thought you might. Let's get you some tools to work on Earth for a while. Your phone, clothes, credit cards, ID, and overnight bag are in the next office. There is a fueled-up, late-model Dodge Charger outside. Do you remember how to drive?"

I smiled and nodded. "Dad, I may need to go back a few years."

"Be careful, Son. I must remind you, don't mess with death, but a transporter is in the trunk. Leave a time-stamp trail if we need to come to find you. I have an Air tag under the carpet in the car."

"What the hell is an Air tag?"

"Modern tracking device. You have been away for a while."

***

I stopped for a haircut and shave to make myself presentable. I also defined my hairline, removed sideburns, and had the barber etch in a part. My beard became a cultured goatee. My goal was to change my appearance as much as possible to blend in and look different from the Mac that Willow meets later in the rainforest.

I liked GPS. Global Positioning System was probably the best accessory for a car I had ever seen. By evening, I was walking through the Indian Casino where Willow used to work. The next day, I overheard a dealer call the name of someone on Dad's list. I watched from my slot machine as a middle-aged, balding man joined the dealer for a quiet conversation. The information in Dad's file gave me a lot of insight into the man.

In particular, the file led me to the Global Main Street Revitalization Organization or GMSR. Gerald O'Reilly was named as the principal of the Mid-Oregon chapter. He was now doing the job Willow had been doing when she disappeared.

It turns out Sharon Rowlands was quite a legend in the company. They still talked about how she simply disappeared.

I checked in with the cashier to say I would be back later and asked about turnover at the casino, as if I may be looking for a job. I mentioned meeting a dealer named Sharon a few years ago, who inspired me to consider becoming a dealer.

The cashier told me Sharon's legend, but she wasn't the only disappearance. She had only been here a year and hadn't personally known Sharon, but a bartender and a waiter had vanished the same way over the next few years.

She mentioned that the turnover at the lower levels was high, but these were different. All their belongings were left behind. She pointed to an old newspaper clipping in a frame behind her counter. Willow's image stood out in the middle of a small group at the top of the story.

I returned to my room, connected to the internet with my phone, and studied Gerald and his organization. I wasn't surprised to find that Howard Thom was listed as the global CEO of the organization, but there was a note that his position was being updated as he had retired. I found it interesting that the organization made no mention of his disappearance.

I looked up and noted Sharon Rowland's last address. I had one more critical task while in Oregon. I hung my do not disturb sign on my hotel door and configured my transporter for the little cemetery next door to her apartment address five years ago.

I included clothing, electronics, and personal effects like cash and ID. I tucked the transporter under my arm and pushed the button.

I could see the neighborhood had not changed much. I took the shuttle bus back to the casino, gingerly bought fifty dollar's worth of chips, and sat at a slot machine in a busy section near a poker table. I was relieved the cashier was not the one I had met in the future.

I was down slightly more than twenty dollars when my heart jumped at the sound of a voice at the poker table. I turned my seat somewhat to watch the table from the side and almost had to leave as emotion rolled over me. A young, vibrant, confident version of Willow stood at the table.

In high-end makeup and a black linen business suit with a white, frilly blouse, Sharon Rowlands took a question from the dealer, made a slight gesture to a couple of robust 'ushers,' and walked to the next table.

At this table sat Gerald, with a bit more hair, dealing cards. He asked a question, and as she walked away, I could see he was unhappy with her answer.

Willow walked to a cashier window on the far side of the room and had a jovial conversation with the cashier before walking up a flight of stairs to a bank of offices with one-way windows over the floor. After a couple of wins that put me up twenty dollars for the day, I went to that cashier, cashed in my chips, and asked where I could get a quiet pub dinner, away from the crowds, later.

"I know what you mean. We have great food here, but the staff likes to get out of the din after work, so we have a few spots to hang out and chill. Canyon Creek Tav is old school. Down the highway, a mile and a half Southeast, is one of our favorites if we want to get away and settle for appies.

Depending on the shift we're working, the casino has Stix, though, and it is pretty good. We get a discount, and it's on the first floor but out of the way of most of the noise. The day shift ends at 5, so we often hit Stix for dinner." I noted the shift change time.

I went to the tavern for lunch and noted the standard tavern snack fare, so I decided to try the Stix for dinner. It was a good choice. The Stix had a much better menu and a lively atmosphere. I ordered a beer and a menu and found a seat at the back before the dinner rush. My plan paid off. Willow, two other ladies, and one well-dressed gentleman came in and took seats against a wall across from the bar.

My waitress came by with a glass of water and my beer. I thanked her and ordered my dinner. She left with the order, and I played with my phone as I quietly observed the scene over the rim of my beer glass. Sharon and her group ordered drinks and meals and chatted quietly about their day.

Willow was a bit distracted and quiet as the rest of the party chatted happily. Gerald came in shortly after, made eye contact with Willow, but found a seat at the bar. When their meals arrived, Gerald, who had not ordered a meal, walked over with his drink and sat at the table next to Willow, which had just been cleared.

He cupped his hand around his mouth and leaned toward Willow's ear to tell her something the rest of the table could not hear.

She looked at him with anger.

"No."

Her voice was not loud, but even I heard the one-word answer. He waved the waiter over and motioned to his drink. The waiter nodded and headed for the bar. Gerald turned back to Willow, and I could hear his whining question this time.

"Why am I always being passed over? I deserve that open table supervisor position?"

"Gerald, I don't make that decision and am off the clock. Book a meeting with Matt. He can give you the career advice you need."

"He listens to you, Sharon. Everyone knows you really make the call."

"I don't. Gerald. Take this to Matt and HR. Let me enjoy my meal."

The gentleman at the table stood up and faced Gerald.

"Go back to the bar, Gerald."

Gerald looked over everyone at the table. "Things are going to change around here."

He stood and walked back to the bar, dropped some bills, and walked out.

The bartender came to their table. "Buzz, Sharon, want me to eighty-six that ass?"

Buzz reached up and put his hand on the bartender's shoulder. "Looks like he did it himself, Bill. We don't want to stir the pot much. His brother-in-law is the head bartender for the casino. He's your boss and mine. If this goes any further, we can take it to HR and let them deal with it. We may all be working somewhere else next year."

Bill looked toward the door. "You're right, Buzz. Let's have a good night. Sharon, 'you, okay? She smiled and nodded. "Make mine a double." Everyone chuckled, and the evening improved.

The hardest thing I ever did was to pay my bill and walk out. I knew, however, that one word from me would probably mean I would never meet Willow. The vision of Sharon Rowlands in this setting drove home the image in my mind of Willow explaining how much she loved Aard and how her goal was to one day rest forever there.

Willow was where she wanted to be.

I left with mixed feelings about Gerald. I would have never met the woman who made my life worthwhile if not for his evil. I would, one day, sleep with her because of his evil act. Still, I need to meet him again. He and those like him must be stopped. I transported back to my room and time.

I slept well with sweet dreams and woke up needing to see Tucson.

***

Chapter 42

Global Main Street Revitalization Versus Old Friends

The drive back to Seattle gave me a lot of thinking time. I would have to watch for Buzz when I got back to Aard. I also needed a copy of my father's spreadsheet.

I wanted to see the name of the Tucson member of GMSR. I had a feeling I would know the name. It was time for me to check in on Lisa. I was a little worried about the business now. I was anxious to get to Tucson, but first to Everett.

Dad and Tony were at the packing plant when I returned to Seattle. I turned the key fob for the car over to Dad and sat down at the desk where they were discussing their work. They now had a database that covered the street cleaning cartel. Tony passed me an iPad with a sticky note on it with login instructions. They had a bookmark in the browser that took me to the front end of the database. I couldn't believe all the work that went into this data.

"Where did you find the time to build this? Your information framed the scenario that sent my Willow to Aard."

There was a little age in Dad's eyes as he looked up at me.

"Son, I've been working on this almost as long as you've been alive.

Our connection to 51 Pegasi is new, but this organization is older than I am. Not many people on Earth know about this. It is not healthy knowledge to have."

"What if everyone had it?"

"It depends on what you want Aard to be. You have seen the beauty of the communities built by outcasts. By people who recognized their second chance. You have also seen people with greed and nefarious intentions interact with and against those communities."

Tony added, "We hold the most beautiful secrets. With beauty, our ideal is to share. However, if we are to share, we share with humans who do not filter. We share the good and the worst of human nature. Are you ready for that?"

My family made a very good point.

I had to counter, though, "The weight of deciding who qualifies is heavy. We are human, too. We make mistakes."

My father followed with a statement that explained the age in his eyes. "One day, soon, Earth will know of Aard, and they will come. Just as the English, French, and Spanish came to the Americas. As I see it, we have only two ways we can affect the outcome.

We must continue to shut down the GMSR and build a culture we can be proud of in our world of second chances. But we must do this as quickly as possible to set a foundation to build on. Tony has the best view of the second option."

Tony leaned across the desk. "I have a theory I've been working on. I want to publish the proximity of people on that list to those who have disappeared. You just met the man responsible for sending the love of your life to a human farm.

She was not his only victim."

Dad nodded. "Tony's plan can work with my plan. I suggest both."

"That's a good plan, Tony. How can I help?"

"Just like you did in Oregon. Connect the dots and capture some proof of proximity at the time of transport. Fill up our database."

"I like it, but this will draw a lot of attention to us. It will speed up the discovery of transportation to Pegasi."

Dad said, "Let me take care of it. I know how to cover tracks in electrons. The dark web has some advantages."

I looked at him with a new respect. Whenever I saw my father, I learned a spectacular new fact. "I'm heading for Tucson. I have a feeling they need me." Bruce Abbot just came to mind.

"Can you please look up the name 'Bruce Abbot' on your program?"

A few taps on the keyboard and Dad read, "Bruce Abbot – Principal East Arizona Chapter."

"Yes, I need to get down there." I started configuring my transporter.

"Take a moment to breathe, Son.

You just drove from central Oregon to Seattle, and I have no idea when you ate last. We're going to grab dinner."

"You're right, Dad. I just noticed; I'm starving."

We had a fine family dinner at Lake Union. Then, Dad introduced me to a spare bed in the packing plant.

I dug through the phone I had used the last time I spent on Earth and found the number for Lisa Mortensen. It was time to attend to a promise for dinner. I called the number.

"Mac!"

"Lisa! It's so good to hear your voice. Are you in Everett?"

"I sure am. I have a nice old heritage place on Grand, between 11th and 12th. I can look down at the port."

"Any good places you would like to go for dinner tomorrow?"

"What would you prefer? A boisterous pub or a quieter atmosphere?"

"I'd like to be able to talk and catch up."

"Okay, why don't you come to my place? Then we can go down to Anthony's Homeport on the water. I'll send you my address so you can plug it into a GPS."

There was that GPS again. 'Not too different from the transporter configuration.

I used the evening to research GPS and its future. I found a lot to read.

51 Pegasi - Black Mac

After Lisa hung up, I noted that she didn't mention Richard and she didn't mention the company. I had a feeling all wasn't well, so I decided, while I was reading, I'd do a little research on Mac's Logistics and Supply before our dinner tomorrow.

My heart sank as I saw that most of my old leadership team had sold their shares and left the company. Lisa was one of them that had left. It turns out Bruce Abbot and his company had almost as much equity in the company as I had.

I'm sure they were badgering my accounting team to buy my trust. They wanted to talk with me and thought I couldn't be produced. Someone insisted I was dead and wanted to deal with my estate.

I called Andrew to tell him I was alive and said I would drop into their office in a few days.

***

Lisa came out of her house smiling wide as I parked the Charger behind her little white Tesla and opened my door.

"Lisa, you look amazing. Your hair, your blouse, jeans, cowboy boots. You've been making changes." I could tell she was happy.

She beamed. "Suddenly becoming single is motivating. My diet is much better, I've learned about hot yoga, I've got a five-mile jogging habit, and I'm happily back in my church."

I smiled as I stepped out and pointed at her Tesla. "Wow, nice car!

"Just trying to do my part.

Better than that big ol' oil burner you pulled into my driveway." She laughed as she made it clear she was grinding my gears.

"It's a loaner!" I laughed. "Ready for a ride in it?"

"I must. You've got me blocked in."

I met her at the front fender and hugged her as she came down the steps. "No Richard?"

"No, the 'ol' Dick' doesn't live here. Long story."

"Sorry…"

Lisa waved it off, smiling and headed for my passenger door. "C'mon. Our reservation is in 10 minutes."

In a few minutes, we were parked and walking up the steps to the restaurant. The Hostess met her there. "Ms. Mortensen. Your table is ready."

As they sat us overlooking the marina, Lisa raised her eyebrows and said, "You are looking spectacular, Mac. Fresh style, haircut, shave… A lot different than the last time I saw you. Must be a woman in your life."

She momentarily noticed the life drain out of my face and started apologizing.

"No, it's okay. I have a long story, too, but here we are. Two great friends, having dinner and catching up after far too long. First, let's catch up with you. Last I heard, you were expanding the company, and you were on fire. Things are different now, so fess up."

"Folks, here's some water and menus. Can I get drinks started for you?"

Lisa was anxious about the interruption as she gathered her thoughts. "I'll have a tall vodka cran, only one shot, please."

I looked up at the pleasant young waiter. "Could I have a light Mexican beer, please?"

"Pacifico?"

"Yes, that would be perfect. Thank you."

"Lime?"

"Yes, please."

Lisa was ready. "Mac, two years ago, we lost our daughter, Suzan, to a malignant brain tumor. We found out about it two months before she died. Within a month, her husband moved to Philadelphia with our only grandson. We haven't heard from him since."

Although she was shaky, it looked like she had been practicing this conversation, so I stayed quiet while she finished.

"The stress was horrible. Dick started drinking and staying out later all the time. He had retired from the fire department. When I moved to Everett, it was a make-it-or-break-it move. I didn't know that he was already having a fling with one of the EMTs from his old fire station.

He filed for divorce, moved in with his girlfriend, and bought a place on the Sea of Cortez. A little village in Sonora. They live there half the year."

"I'm sorry, Lisa. That's a huge change in your life."

"Mac, after losing Suzan, losing Dick wasn't a big deal. I already had the move in motion. We sold the place in Tucson. Half went to Mexico, and half came North to Everett. Frankly, after Suzan, we had little that kept us together."

She sipped her drink for energy, then said. "Now, about the company. Abbot has been buying our legs out from under us. Most of the old team is gone, and after retiring, I'm under a lot of pressure to sell my equity. The new board told me my board position was eliminated last month. Abbot offered me a better deal than if I sold my shares back to the company. Mac, they are offering more than it's worth. I can retire for good."

Take it, Lisa.

I'm heading down there tomorrow to talk with my trust managers. I have a bad feeling for the future of my old company and of Abbot, but I'd like Abbot to own that future rather than the tried-and-true family that had invested in that company.

I have something much more important that needs my attention, and I'd like to talk to you about it... Don't worry. I won't ask you to sell Amway or timeshares."

We were giggling as the waiter came back for our order. Of course, we weren't quite ready, but he was patient as I speed-read the menu; Lisa had her favorite, and I settled on the daily special to make it easy. He left, and we went back to our updates.

"Lisa, my life for the last few years has been so far from the mainstream that you are not going to believe most of it at first. So I'm going to save that story for the car ride back to your house because you are going to need to focus on what I say and it won't work well here.

Not in a restaurant with the waiter checking on us."

"Mac, I trust you with my life. Are you in trouble?"

"I don't think so, Lisa, not now, but I have seen some trouble I will discuss later. What I can discuss, however, is that I met the most wonderful lady and loved deeper than I have ever known. Then, I lost her to a terrible act of nature. I have loved and lost more than I could imagine, but I gained from it. I gained a much deeper respect for life and grew to know myself much better. I am stronger now, and I have a purpose."

"I'm so sorry, Mac. But I am so happy to hear you found that kind of love. If I can be honest, I was not fond of Margo. No need to go into detail, but I know you could have done better. I envy that purpose. I need some now."

I nodded as our meals were delivered. Lisa raised her glass for a toast. "Here's to life with purpose."

I clinked glasses with her, and we got busy with dinner and small talk. On the way back to her house, I said. "Lisa, I'm not sure how to explain this without freaking you out, so I'm going to give you the opportunity to hop out in your driveway to go in your house alone to absorb my story, then call me if and when you want to know more.

On my dash is a post-it note. Please grab it, read it, and keep it. She picked it up and read it out loud. "Society for Scientific Exploration by Elisabeth Rauscher and Russell Targ "The Nonlocal Universe."

"Now I'm going to tell you I have been on another planet. Literally. I have been living on a planet in the Pegasi solar system. I've been involved in space and time travel.

I will let that sink in as I take you home."

She was silent for a few blocks, and we were approaching her house.

"Mac, a few years ago, you came by the office, and I helped you get some clothes to go to Northern Canada. You were fiddling with a box. You told me it was a transporter... Was that the truth?"

I nodded. "Yes. I have one in the back seat, and I'm going to use it tomorrow to go to Tucson."

***

Chapter 43

Lisa goes to Aard

"Do you have time to show me how it works?"

"Of course. If you feel you are ready."

"Come on in."

I took the transporter and button in and set it up in her living room. Lisa watched carefully as I opened the box and exposed the controls. I connected a short cable with a thin steel shish-ka-bob skewer and plugged it into the ground port of an electrical receptacle behind her kitchen counter.

"Where would you like to go, Lisa? What would you like to see?"

Lisa had been preparing a pot of tea, set a couple of teacups on the table, and waited for the kettle to boil. She sat down at the table and looked down at her hands around the empty cup for a few pregnant moments. "Mac, I want to see your planet."

I stopped what I was doing, sat down beside her, and said, "I need to tell you a few things about that planet before I take you there. Let's talk about it over tea."

On cue, the teapot started whistling. Lisa got up, grabbed a couple of saucers for our tea bags, and pulled a pair of mint teabags from a drawer. "No need for caffeine at this time of night."

I laughed. "Good point."

She poured our steaming water and sat down. "Okay, I'm all ears."

"Lisa, this technology has been in use for a few years now, but it was launched first by some bad guys, sending people they didn't like off to this other world. Like any innovation, the science didn't start out being bad, but one of its principal scientists and his posse found a use that suited their needs and made them very wealthy."

I had Lisa's complete attention, so I took a moment to sip my tea, and she followed suit.

"When I first disappeared, it was because someone sent me to that planet. They wanted me out of the way and made a tidy profit by doing so. I, and a few other captives, escaped a terrible fate on that other planet despite the unfathomable partnership between these bad guys and some rather large citizens of that planet. The planet is beyond beautiful and habitable, but it has its dangers, as any planet does. Luckily, it is very compatible with human life."

I stopped again to sip my tea. Lisa took a sip again, then gave me the "come on" gesture with her hands, so I continued.

"Our little band of refugees escaped to a beautiful place but could not leave well enough alone because we knew we escaped a gruesome death.

There were far more people in that pipeline.

Just as Mac's Logistics and Supply is a critical link in the American supply chain, this ungodly partnership provided a supply chain to this giant race of creatures. Lisa, we were food."

I saw the shock in Lisa's eyes now, and her mouth dropped open with understanding. I felt I needed to get more out before I turned her loose with her questions.

"They started sending homeless from the streets of the world's cities and towns but gravitated quickly to people in their way. Lisa, my friends, and I have been fighting this regime on that planet and here on Earth. We have done a lot of damage to their systems, but they have a lot of money and are quick to fight back."

She finally found her voice. "Oh, my lord... Abbot?"

I nodded.

"I want to help."

"First things first. You need to know that we are all transported naked at first. The giant creatures did not need our clothing, and it is much easier to transport a human without clothes. Without extra elements in the transport. Lisa, the combination of shedding centuries of taboo and conditioning and the pleasant atmosphere where we now live on this planet have resulted in villagers who are usually naked from the waist up and dressed more like Amazonian tribes from the waist down."

She was silent again.

"Lisa, we call this world Aard. We have a few locations now, villages.

We have Freedom, Moon Bridge, the Landing, and Willow's Cathedral. If you visit, we can give you a full-length toga robe, but it will get hot during the day as the location is tropical. You will see a lot of skin but with no sexual connotations."

We were silent for a few minutes while I stopped to finish my tea, and she took time to absorb.

Finally, she looked up bashfully, "It's a good thing I've been working out. Mac, I must admit, this is a stretch of my comfort zone. I have always considered you more like the son I never had. I'm not sure how I will react yet, but I have been praying every night for God to give me a life to live for. God works in mysterious ways."

I grinned and said, "More like a big sister. You always got me out of scrapes and listened to my ideas. It will be hard on my conditioning, too, but I have challenged a father to accept his adult daughter in that environment, so I must follow my own advice."

Lisa stood up. "Okay, just for an introduction, then right back, right?"

I laughed. "Exactly. I need to be in Tucson tomorrow."

"Okay, do I take my clothes off here?"

I laughed again. "No, the transport will take care of that. A pile of denim and linen will be waiting for you when we return. I'll go first to ensure a robe is ready for you. In about 5 minutes, you push the button, and we'll be ready for your short tour." I stood up and pushed the button.

***

Jewels welcomed me at the Cathedral.

With a quick hug, I asked for a medium-sized robe to be ready for a visitor, and for this visit, I could use a kilt. "Welcome home, Mac. A kilt and robe are on the shelves along the wall."

"Of course. Thank you.

The lady coming has been a very close friend of mine for a long time. This experience will scare her, but seeing you when she arrives will be most helpful." I wrapped myself in the kilt and laid the robe on the bench. "Where's Popeye?"

"He's on his way back from the Landing. He just installed a transporter at the request of Shiv and Tiffany. The villages are getting bigger now, and sometimes we need to move multiple people and sometimes freight, so we need a wider target."

"Ahh, that makes sense."

The unmistakable hiss of the transporter made us turn, and Lisa opened her eyes to a colossal arctic cat rug.

"M...m...Mac?"

"Welcome, Lisa. Please meet my very good friend, Jewels."

Jewels smiled and helped her to her feet while wrapping her in the robe.

"Welcome, Lisa. Mac tells me you are a close friend, which means you are my new close friend, too."

Lisa's wide eyes belied her statement, but she said. "Nothing to it, Mac. How did I do?"

We laughed, and I hugged her again. "Lisa, you never cease to inspire me. You adapt to insanity much faster than most. Please step out into the main chamber. I want to introduce you to Willow's Cathedral."

"Mac, you just saw this old lady naked, and now you want me to walk about in a thin robe. Normally, I'd be freaking out, but somehow, I knew I had left normal back on Earth, and I'm okay with this. I'm not even blushing... much."

I chuckled, and Jewels hooked arms with her. "C'mon, Buddy."

At the back of the vaulted hall, Julio was kneeling at a small shrine he had set up. Lisa strode barefoot over to kneel beside him. He turned slowly and smiled.

"May I pray with you?"

Julio smiled wide and opened his hand to a small mat beside him. They kneeled quietly for a few moments in their silent grace.

Lisa returned to Jewels and me when she finished praying, where Popeye joined us. Julio followed.

"Julio, Popeye, please meet Lisa. Lisa was the backbone of my company in Tucson for most of the company's life, and she protected me over the years like a big sister."

Popeye nodded and shook her hand. "Welcome, Lisa."

In turn, Julio took her hand in both of his, nodded his head, and said, "Bienvenida a Aard, Senorita Lisa... Welcome.

"Gracias, Julio."

Lisa had misty eyes as she looked up at me.

"Mac, you didn't tell me how beautiful this place is."

"I may be biased, Lisa, but this whole world has amazing beauty. It also has its dangers, but beauty is in the eye of the beholder, so everyone here has their own idea of what is beautiful. To me, the dangers are part of the beauty."

She walked over to the Western opening and watched the sun heading for the horizon over her view of the sea. "I bet that is a beautiful sunset."

"It is, and depending on how long you want to stay, there is much more to see."

"I have a lot to think about, Mac. Let's go back home and talk a bit, and I'll know what I want to do very soon."

"Of course, I don't want to rush your decision. You have a lot to consider, but I will need to take care of the business in Tucson, and I'm not sure how long that will take. Please let Jewels or Popeye know when they can drop in at your place to answer questions and make plans with you if you wish to join us here."

I gave Jewels the coordinates, and Lisa asked Jewels to drop by her house at this time in four days. Julio followed us to the transporter and said, "Come back soon, por favor."

We headed for Everett. We quickly dressed in Lisa's house, and she made another pot of tea. It was getting rather late, but I knew Lisa needed to talk.

"Mac, I want to start by saying I thought you were up to something special when I saw you in Tucson.

Then I knew it was special when you came to me for your supplies. Tonight, you showed me something I could have never imagined. You took me to a place I didn't know in my soul. Tonight, I learned more about myself than I did about Aard."

"Lisa, this visit would change everything you know about the world. Willow, Jean, Shiv, Popeye, Jewels, me, and everyone else who took this journey found their calling. Discovering, both by their will or against their will, they found a purpose to the lives they had lost on Earth."

She poured our tea as she listened.

"Life with the people you met tonight gets to be more intimate than any relationship you have had on Earth. I think it is because we have become a tribe, not separated by electronics and distractors. Our groceries come from the world around us, and we count on each other for our lives."

"Mac, I have spent a lifetime building for a retirement I had not planned. I have enough money, particularly when I sell my company shares, but I never thought about how I wanted to spend the rest of my years. My health has held up for the most part, but menopause has begun my decline. I can feel it. I want to spend what I have left contributing, but I do have things I'd like to do here as well."

"You may find the mushrooms in our diet on Aard produce a nice surprise concerning menopause. Lisa, I have an idea. I may literally have the best of both worlds for you. Why don't you join me for breakfast in Seattle tomorrow? I'd like you to meet my dad and my brother. You see, Aard is going to need supplies. I need someone I trust who can keep a foot in both worlds.

I may know how to keep Mac's Logistics and Supply's North office alive."

Lisa smiled and clinked teacups with me. We finished our tea, and I headed for the canning plant with a busy mind.

***

Chapter 44

Foundation for the Future

Tony arranged breakfast at the Station, a quirky little coffee shop with breakfast sandwiches on Beacon Avenue. Lisa got to meet Tony and Dad for the first time. She had heard about them over the years, but they had never visited the office in Tucson. We kept the conversation light, and the family learned how critical Lisa had been to the success of my company.

Lisa even found a yogurt cup with some walnuts in a mason jar that made her feel good about a coffee shop breakfast. Tony asked her several questions about the freight load she had delivered to the cannery for Aard. We paid and headed back to the office to talk business.

The conversation deepened when we circled the big steel desk in our main office.

"Dad, I'm heading for Tucson to sell my shares in the company to Abbot. There isn't much of the old culture to save, and with Lisa out, most of the company's pioneers have moved on. The only ones left are the rank and file that Abbot will need to keep the machinery running.

If I read your plans correctly, Abbot may see a lot of trouble soon."

"That's very true, Son. You could keep the company, but it sounds like it has been infiltrated to a high degree, so it could get messy for you and your equity, too. There are no guarantees.

Abbot could escape with it all if everything doesn't land correctly, but his recent activities will probably cost him personally. His company may take off without him if the company isn't implicated in what he has done. I have almost enough now to turn my findings over to some friends in Interpol and the FBI."

"Wow, you know some top-level people."

"I've worked with them all my adult life."

"Why doesn't that surprise me? I'm not digging any deeper because I expect there are things you can't or don't want your family to know."

"You're right."

"Okay, here is what I'd like to do, and I'd like your blessing to ensure I don't step on your plans. I have all the Mexican connections I need to start again, and Lisa has Canadian and Pacific Trade Zone contacts. We have an office in Everett.

I could negotiate to keep it, or Lisa and I can partner with you in a new enterprise out of this building. My purpose would be to supply the communities on Aard. If your plan does what we hope, the GMSR and people critical to its charter mission will go away. For some time at least, we will stop the human trafficking to Aard.

I believe this will make it much easier for the new villages to grow and prosper."

"That's true. I have already been promising global organizations, trained to keep the deep stuff away from politicians, that I would have names and addresses for them. I have also promised the connection to missing people. It's their job to connect the missing person to the GMSR agent through their processes. Our database makes it much easier for them."

Tony and Lisa focused on the conversation. When Tony spoke up, he was addressing Lisa. "Lisa, would you bring me on board and train me in this new business? I think Dad and Tommy will be tied up."

Lisa was nodding vigorously. "Yes! I see where this is going, and I feel I have found what I want to do with my next fifty years. Mac, I want to visit Aard and get to know the people. I want to study the communities and help them build by supplying what they need."

"Thanks, Lisa. I was hoping you'd be inspired when you heard what we were up against. I'll update you on the details and schedule when I return from Tucson.

That leaves you and Tony a week to plan the best use of the building here or the office in Everett if we decide to keep the quieter port. Dad, do you need anything from me before you launch the database to your network?"

"Only one thing, Tommy. I have what I need as far as the trafficking cartel goes. Do your chores and let me know when the sale is complete. I want you all to understand that a few high-security people will know about Aard.

At some point, it will become public, but just like UFOs. It will take some time to separate fact from speculation."

"Okay, I'll take my spare transporter to Tucson but get a hotel room, and I'll rent a car to fit in better while I'm in town. I'll take a cell phone so I can communicate. "

"Why don't you simply send a paper note to the transporter here to communicate? Cell signals are not very secure."

"Leave it to Dad to add another layer of security."

Lisa laughed. "Listen to your father, Tommy. I get a kick out of your family name... I may need to use it more."

"I may be sorry I introduced you to my family, Lisa. This is beginning to sound like a bad idea."

Everyone got a chuckle, but we were ready to get to our tasks. Lisa began describing her warehouse in Everett, and Tony was anxious to go with her to check it out. I grabbed a wardrobe suitable for Eastern Arizona. I still carried my wallet, ID, and bank cards from my Oregon trip. I touched up my shave and called my accountant.

"Andrew, this is Mac. I understand there is some pressure to sell my equity in the company."

"Mac... 'Great to hear from you. The only way I know you're around is when I see your transactions going through. How was Oregon?"

"It was most informative, Andrew. Can I get on your schedule to talk business?"

"Sure; web call, or when will you be in town?"

"I'll be in Tucson tomorrow."

"Well, you're hard to nail down, so does 10:00 work for you?

I can move my morning around because the rest of my day can adjust easily."

"I'll see you then. Please have any communications from Abbot handy."

"Already stacked and assessed, Mac. See you in the morning."

***

I dressed up for the morning meeting. I wanted to make it clear that I was healthy and clear-headed. I sent an early email from my iPad requesting names and contact information for the negotiating parties from Abbot and the lawyer or lawyers Andrew recommended to speak with on behalf of my equity trust.

He was quick to send the names back. I forwarded them to Dad to see if he had background on any of them. I explained that I was going to my discovery meeting at 10 a.m. Knowing who to invite to the next meeting and in what context would be nice.

Dad was surprisingly quick with his reply. One of Andrew's lawyers was associated with Abbot through a shell company. Interestingly, Abbot's lawyer appeared to be neutral. Bruce and his lawyer were the only communicators on the request.

Dad sent me a name to give to my accountant to represent my business in the negotiation. He said he had primed him and was waiting for my call.

Randal Dupree would meet me today or tomorrow to discuss.

I felt I had what I needed when I went into my accountant's meeting to be prepared for the first step. He met me at the door and ushered me into a small boardroom.

His business seemed personable and comfortable for a business office. Official but friendly.

I reached out for a warm handshake. "Hi, Andrew. I want to thank you for everything you have done for me. It's been a strange few years, and you have kept the wheels on the bus turning."

He smiled at the relaxed opening and visibly relaxed. "It's good to see you, Mac. You look a world healthier than last we met. In fact, you look like life is treating you well."

"I can honestly say, Andrew, I struggle to keep up with my life. It has been demanding but in a very good way."

"If you don't mind me saying, Mac, it looks like you have been living large. Has your nose been broken? Tell me to back off if you like, but that colorless shirt, smart blazer, natural glow, and educated nose make you look like a force to reckon with."

I laughed. I had meant to dress for success, but I forgot about the deviation in my nose line. "I keep forgetting, Andrew. You are correct. I have been living large, and sometimes that means smoothing the rough edges. I am doing well. My life is speeding along and dragging me with it. That is the main topic for today."

"Right, let's get to it. Coffee, Water?"

"Thanks. Water might hit the spot."

He opened a mini fridge in the corner and pulled out two water bottles. It reminded me of our plastic-dependent world, but I had an agenda to keep.

"Andrew. How much does Les McNeal know about my account?"

"Les??? Uh... He approached me a month ago about corporate mergers and buy-out law. 'Just dropped his card and sent me an online brochure. I haven't shared anything with him yet, but he has signed an NDA."

"Can you bring up his law site on your laptop?"

"Sure... Give me a moment to flash it and share it on our boardroom screen."

In a few moments, he had the website on the big screen.

"Can you check his site footer to see if he has a client list or marketing page that tells us who he has worked for?"

He had a significant client list, and Abbot Logistics was at the top of the alphabetical list.

"Mind if we remove him from this deal?"

"Mac, I'm sorry. I had no idea."

"No problem, my friend. I have a little insight. Tomorrow, I will introduce you to a lawyer named Randal Dupree." For an hour, we planned for a meeting with the Abbot reps scheduled for two days from now. I shook his hand and left for my hotel.

Later that evening, I had a drink with Randal Dupree.

He was a striking man, about my father's age, with longer hair than I had imagined a legal statesman would carry. He extended his hand and said, "I'm pleased to meet you, Thomas. I've heard some amazing things about you."

His measured baritone removed any doubt of his powers of persuasion.

"Well, you're one up on me, Randal. Dad hasn't told me anything about you, but the strength of his recommendation means you come highly qualified."

"Let me see if I can solve that. I understand most people call you Mac. My friends call me Randy or Frog, depending on how many drinks they have had or how long they have known me."

"Great. I'll start with Randy, and please feel free to call me Mac. It's been a long time since anyone called me Thomas."

The waiter asked for our drink order and headed for the bar. We sat at a small corner table. Randy got right to the point.

"I've worked with your dad for over two decades. I'm the guy who will lead the presentation of the case on the GMSR to Interpol and the FBI. Part of the case is a portfolio of hostile takeovers like the one on your company that resulted in disappearing business owners and key shareholders."

"Abbot will appreciate me because he will think he got a deal, but he will give up the rights to your company name and anything else you desire to keep. He will pay top dollar for the assets, building, vehicles, customers, and goodwill."

He will also agree to a substantial annulment fee. That means, if the State, FTC, or DOJ disapprove, a bond with that fee transfers to you and the rest of the shareholders in your company."

"Nice. I see you have a history of closing loops."

He nodded. By the time we finished our drinks, we had a plan for our meeting with Abbot, and in it, I would mostly keep my mouth closed.

***

Chapter 45

Dealing with the Devil

Bruce Abbot arrived at the meeting with his financial officer and his corporate lawyer. The CFO carried a laptop and a projector, and the lawyer packed a briefcase. Abbot brought his best compassionate façade. Andrew suggested they wouldn't need the projector and offered an HDMI connection to access the boardroom screen that wouldn't need the local network.

The meeting started with Bruce suggesting it was great to see me doing well and asking if everything was okay. We hadn't been in the same room with each other for a decade, but he knew, probably better than anyone else in the meeting, what I had gone through.

"It's good to see you, Bruce. A lot has happened since we last spoke and even more, since we met face-to-face. I'd like you to meet Randall Dupree; you already know Andrew. It's been a rough few years since my wife died, and I've also been through some more personal trauma, but that's over now, and I'm looking forward to a much happier chapter in my life."

"I'm glad to see you are on your feet. Good to meet you, Randall.

Please meet my CFO, Mike Bradley, and my legal counsel, Mitch Shapiro. How would you like to proceed?"

Our host opened an agenda on his screen for all to see. The title read Abbot – Mac Logistics Proposal. "Gentlemen, there is a small fridge at the back of the room with water and sodas. On the side buffet is a coffee urn with cream, sugar, and sweeteners. You will also see some bakery goods, fresh fruit, and power bars for anyone who missed breakfast."

Randy took over. "Andrew, would you mind going to the agenda, please? We can discuss and agree on the agenda, the objectives, and the preliminaries as we grab drinks and snacks. In the meantime, I'll pass out these printed copies of the NDA, and everyone in the room can get a copy signed to protect all our interests in these delicate negotiations." He handed copies of the document to each seat in the room.

Mitch studied the document and nodded. "I also brought a version, but it is much the same as this one. He nodded to Abbot and Bradley and spoke. "We can use this version."

The first bullet point on the agenda was "Abbot Proposal."

Bradley connected his machine to the screen while everyone settled at the table. Once set up, we watched a twelve-slide presentation on the benefits of the Abbot acquisition of Mac's Logistics and Supply. The production clearly referred to the fact that Abbot already had over thirty percent of the company stock and was negotiating another ten percent.

I knew that ten was Lisa, and I had advised her to sell. I still had forty-two percent through the deal I had made with the company to buy me out.

Twenty percent was in my personal portfolio, and twenty-two percent was in the purchase trust that Andrew and his company managed. I had the final signature on both. The first offer was twenty million and thirty million in Abbot stock.

Randy took the reins. "My client has made it clear that should he sell, he wants to remove himself from the industry, as it would be too hard to watch what he had built go in a different direction. He will not want to be part of Abbot's future."

Abbot's team asked for a recess to discuss a counteroffer. They suggested they would need only a half hour. Randy and Andrew agreed, and we watched them leave the building. They were back in seventeen minutes.

Abbot looked at me as he said, "We understand the emotional stress. We will offer forty million for the remaining shares in your control, including all company assets, buildings, building contents, vehicles, tools, and goodwill. You or your shareholders must not post negative press of any kind."

Randy ignored the fact that Abbot had addressed me. "Forty-two million, one million per percentage, as well as the same offer to anyone else holding shares worth one percent or more, and a five million break-up fee, should legal or compliance issues block the sale in federal, state, municipal, or any other source."

Bradley responded. "Forty-two for your shares, but negotiations will be separate for other shareholders, and we all lose if the deal doesn't go through, so no break-up fee."

Randy expected this. "Gentlemen, my client has been through hell for over five years. His company was run as a family.

He knows his employees' kids; he has helped with their education and is the godfather to some of them. This is a hostile takeover in a warm blanket and those hurt. The last offer is the last offer."

There was silence in the room for a few moments, then Abbot said, "Let's go. Nothing more to say here."

We all stood up. I went to pull a bottle of water from Andrew's cooler, but I noticed Abbot's lawyer had picked up the blank NDAs.

"Have a nice day, gentlemen." Our host led the Abbot crew to the door.

At the door, Abbot turned and said, "We'll be in touch."

I didn't hear malice in that comment, so I expected he might have more to say after all.We sat back around the table and discussed what had just happened. The accountant asked, "So, Mac, what's the next step? Would you like to buy back shares to gain more control, sell on the open market...?"

Randy stopped him. "They're going to take the deal. I'd wager you'll get a call today to set up our next meeting. I'd like you to remember we don't need this deal."

I smiled. I was impressed. Andrew's phone rang.

"Hello? ...Sure, would ten AM work? Great. See you then." He looked at me. "They're coming back tomorrow morning." We all smiled.

***

We went for lunch near my old office.

I wanted to do a walk-through to get a handle on the mood, the status of my old business, and mostly how the employees were doing. The attitude at lunch was positive. Randy said, "Mac, I'd like you to come in late for tomorrow's meeting."

This surprised me, but he explained.

"I want them to understand that you are disheartened and worried about your employees. I want them to think you may be considering plan B. You may be considering rallying the troops or taking the poison pill route that ruins the goodwill and the company's profit from the takeover."

I was in awe. Randall Dupree knew corporate strategy. Andrew was taking notes. I could tell he was impressed. I knew the accountant carried an MBA; it was in his signature line, and I knew he had a lot of experience, particularly in the accounting end of the business spectrum, but Randy was teaching us all.

I went to the office and had to show my ID to get in. The reception staff were all new. Finally, they reached Miguel Garcia, who had been the manager of the import broker team. He was now the leader of the company. After a hug and warm welcome, he called the rest of the functional leaders to a meeting in my old boardroom.

Only four of my senior leadership team were left. Several had moved on with the sale of their stock. Miguel was the only one of the four who still owned the store. The head accountant, Linda Rodrigues, was at the table, but she had sold her shares and was weighing options with her husband.

"Welcome back, Mac. As you can see, much has changed."

"Welcome to the world of corporate drama, folks.

This is not how I thought the future of Mac's Logistics and Supply would roll out, but here we are. I would suggest you were the best in Arizona at this business. That is the only way you get the kind of attention a hostile takeover brings. Understand, folks. I hold no ill will. I love you and this company as I always had. This is no fault of yours... or mine. I won't lay any blame in this meeting, but I am here to find out what you will be doing with your future."

Linda responded, "Well, Mac. I took their offer. It was more than fair, but they insisted I stay on, at least for a year, to ensure a smooth transition. They promised me a healthy bump in salary to sign on the day the deal finalizes."

"Good for you, Linda. If anyone can keep it smooth, I know you can. Miguel also loves our customers more than his kids... sometimes."

This comment broke the tension, and the table loosened up. Jerry, our marketing manager, had also sold but would be moving to California when the deal goes down. Pam, our head of sales, would move on when the transfer became final. She had family in North Carolina but wasn't close with them. She had been buddies with Lisa, but when she moved to the Northwest, Pam had nobody left and wasn't sure what she wanted to do next.

The room full of leaders filled me in on the front line. They all expected to be kept on by Abbot as the work they did every day must continue if the venture were to succeed. As in any buy-out, they expected cuts when the two companies merged with some redundancies.

"Remember, team, don't burn any bridges.

At least three layers of government and a couple of regulatory boards must sign off before they can call this done. Sometimes, the paperwork can drag on for a long time. Sometimes, it gets a rubber stamp. It all depends on how this move affects customers and taxes. It can also depend on who Abbot knows, frankly."

I left the office feeling a lot better about the folks staying behind.

Andrew called me in the morning, just after 10:30.

"Mac, could you join us at my office by 11:00?"

"Yes, Andrew, I'll be there. See you soon."

I folded my iPad case and climbed into the rental. Andrew's receptionist handed me a bottle of water as she escorted me to the boardroom. The same crew was in place. This time, Randy sat directly across from Abbot's lawyer. They both had paper copies of an agreement with pencils in hand, and a copy was presented on the screen. The glass walls of the room were covered with drop-down privacy screens.

Andrew met me at the door, shook my hand, and indicated a chair at the head of the table. "Thanks for coming back, Mac. I think we may have a path forward."

Abbot stood and shook my hand as I passed, but Randy was engrossed in the document, as was Abbot's attorney. I waited a moment as the two legal reps discussed a few finer points of the language in the agreement.

When done, Randy looked at me briefly and then at the document. "Mac, Abbot Logistics is ready to accept our terms, but they have one request.

They want a global non-compete clause."

I had just sat down but stood back up.

"No handcuffs."

Abbot stood, too. "You said you didn't want to be part of the industry again."

"I don't, but life is about change. I will not be locked out of future opportunities by the subjective interpretation of that clause."

"We just don't want you starting a business next to us and using your name to compete with us. I'm sure you understand the ramifications that would have on goodwill. How about just the USA."

I could see Abbot thought I had escaped the off-world adventure and may want my old business back. "I'll give you Arizona. This is the only place my name has that strength in the market. Do you plan on using Mac's Logistics and Supply?"

"Okay, you have a non-compete in Arizona, and we have the rights to your company name in the US."

I looked at Randy, and he nodded.

"Okay, give me the office in Everett, Washington, well out of your way, and write it up."

***

Chapter 46

Interstellar Logistics and Supply

The papers were written up, signed, and submitted by the next day. The day after that, I was back in Seattle. Within two weeks, the governing bodies approved, and by the end of the month, Lisa and Miguel were millionaires.

Another interesting note was that Interpol and the FBI used the newspaper article from Oregon to launch their investigation into Abbot, GMSR, and hundreds of names in the database they obtained on human trafficking.

Names, locations, and missing person reports were triangulated, and people with shaky moral compasses began to turn on each other. Like electrical synapsis in the brain, a network of corruption became a lightning rod for exploding dominos, and the human supply chain dissolved into dust. The only thing that hit the media was the downfall of several wealthy companies around the globe. No one said anything about off-world transportation or 51 Pegasi.

However, I was sure some high-level government officials had new briefs on interplanetary exploration. I was not about to ask anyone about it.

I hoped it would take as long as UFOs and ETs to open to public view.

I told Lisa about Pam, and she reached out. Pam changed her plans and moved in with Lisa after a summer vacation in Everett. And, of course, an unbelievable education in interstellar travel.

Randy visited Dad and me, got to know Tony and Lisa, and helped us draft the new Interstellar Logistics and Supply company. It seemed like a lifetime, so my urge to return home was intense. Lisa wanted to come along, but Pam, who also came away with a nest egg, was more interested in setting up the new company's financial arm. She was spending more time with Tony as they gravitated to the controlling roles in the new enterprise. Perhaps there was more to the partnership.

Tony's grammar had improved, and I noticed he was much smoother in his delivery than I had ever seen. His stoic personality appeared to be softening. Lisa noticed changes in Pam, too. She told me her friendship had grown with Pam over the years, particularly after Lisa knew her marriage was ending. Pam had been alone most of her adult life, and the two bonded as they both needed company. Pam's focus, now, was on helping Tony restructure the packing plant.

It turns out Lisa and Dad had much in common. They enjoyed each other's company, but both liked their space. Dad had always been a tumbleweed, and Lisa's life had just opened to Aard. Nothing would keep her from spending quality time on the distant planet. I had to smile as images of unthinkable changes descended on our lives.

Lisa called me aside to discuss the trip to Aard.

"What are you going to do on Aard, Mac?

What's on your agenda?"

"Well, I first want to say hi to Willow at the Landing, get moved back into my little Landing hut, and explore the area. As much as I have traveled through it, I never spent enough time getting to know the plateau. I also need to catch up with the tribes. I need to know how Willow's Cathedral settled in and how the citizens of Freedom or Libertad rebuilt. I need to get out to Moon Bridge to see how they are doing. But at the top of my mind, I need to find Tiffany, Jesus, and their tribe to see what they noticed about the Giant's supply chain."

I looked at Lisa and saw she was visualizing everything I said.

"What are you going to do on Aard, Lisa?"

"Mac, I know it's not all fantasy. Some of life on Aard is challenging, even dangerous. I really want to know the world. Know the life that people live there. Ultimately, I want to supply them with what they need, but I will do that job better if I understand their lives and people's goals and visions. Mac, I want to go native."

I was impressed. "Lisa, that's a big step. This isn't about anyone that lives there, is it?"

She laughed. "Well, I would like to know Julio better. Mac, he intrigues me. He is of retirement age. He could be comfortable on Earth, but he prefers to live close to the Earth, and his accent...."

It was my turn to laugh. "Should I tell Dad to watch that Julio guy?"

She smiled coyly, "He knows. We have had some long conversations. Neither of us is ready for commitments."

I nodded. "Yes, with my dad, I understand that well. I've never known him to hang his hat on the same peg twice in a row. I'm a bit shocked by your change of direction, though. You spent most of your life working for one company, living with one man, and now you are opening your sail in uncharted seas."

"Isn't it amazing?" She scrunched up her nose with a little girl grin.

"Yes, Lisa, it is most amazing. When will you be ready to go."

"Tomorrow. I just need to ensure Pam waters some plants and clears the mail from the floor under the door slot. Someone needs to watch for the power, internet, and water bill."

The next day, we all gathered at Tony's favorite little coffee shop for small talk over coffee and then on to the new Interstellar Logistics and Supply headquarters.

We laid down the plans, but Randy counseled us to leave room for the assets of Mac's Logistics and Supply because he felt there would be a fire sale once the FBI and global police unraveled the delicate threads that made Abbot wealthy. We decided to move slowly on rebranding the Everett office, even though that came with me as part of the deal. Lisa was the only employee there, so Pam and Tony were beginning plans for the new organizational structure.

Lisa sat me down for some preliminary plans for her visit. "Who do I need to get to know on Aard?

I must pull together the needs of the communities and develop a distribution system for the freight and supplies they need. How do we plan to pay for the supplies? How could we make the deliveries to Aard pay for themselves and become sustainable?

I laughed. "Whoa! Which question should I answer first?"

"All of them. I've got work to do."

I laughed again. "Lisa, Julio, and Dan will be your best contacts on Aard. The planet has a lot of precious metals and gems that are easy to get to and an easy conversion to pay for any supplies they will need for the next century. We need to go slow for now, though. Aard will be a gold rush when word gets out, and we need to use this time to build a sustainable and planet-friendly foundation.

Have a meaningful conversation with Randy on what Earth markets will need to recognize the raw materials we bring from another planet. Regulators need to know the origin of raw materials. 'Especially precious metals and gems. We can't simply start shipping in mining equipment and shipping out gold. I'll introduce you to folks on both ends, and you can begin discussions with the villages. Everyone must be able to add their thoughts."

"Wow, I never thought of any of that, but I see it now. All I have to do is think back to the gold rushes and land rushes in Earth's history, and I can see the terrible things that go with humans finding treasure."

I nodded. "We have some delicate work to do."

51 Pegasi - Black Mac

Lisa was happy.

She had a better grip on the challenges but was also excited to have a mission, and with that focus, we went to Aard.

***

This time, Popeye supplied Lisa with her robe. This revelation took her back some, and then she watched me arrive and was taken back again. I quickly but casually wrapped in a toga, and she wrapped in her robe.

"This will take some getting used to, Mac. It will take me a while to get used to seeing my boss... my business partner naked."

"You'll be surprised how quickly it gets normal, Lisa. We have begun designing top clothing for the ladies based on needs rather than modesty. Think sports bra, pockets, chilly weather, and things like that. Welcome back. Welcome back to you, too, Professor." Jewels had just walked in, and she was wearing only a kilt.

Lisa did a double take, looked at me, back at Jewels, and back at me. "Professor?"

"It's a long story, but we can fill you in as we gather some folks for you to chat with. Popeye, I think you two, Julio and Dan, will be most important for this discussion. Any idea if we can get you folks around a table?"

Popeye pointed his thumb over his shoulder. "Julio was just at the Shrine. I expect he will return to Freedom soon, but I just saw him a few minutes ago."

Jewels said, "I'll go get him. He'll be excited.

He's been talking about Senorita Lisa since her last visit."

Popeye nodded as Jewels ran out. "Dan and Sirih were coming over this afternoon to set some coordinates for a trip to the Northeast. Tiffany wants to create a jump. I expect them soon."

"Excellent."

We stepped out into the main cavern as Jewels and an excited Julio trotted in. Popeye led us to an adjoining chamber the team fitted with tables and benches.

"Welcome to our mess hall," Jewels waved a dramatic arm over the furniture.

We sat down and started to discuss Lisa's mission. Julio supplied one of the coveted notebooks and a pencil.

"This takes me back to my roots," Lisa chuckled at the paper solution. "We'll need lots of these."

Echoing voices rang from the main chamber, and Jewels escorted Dan and Sirih in. Oliver was tagging along with them and joined as a bonus.

"Right on time, folks."

The two were still trying to figure out what she meant as she ushered them into our meeting. Sirih was the first to find her voice. "So, this is Lisa." She hugged her. So did Dan, and Oli shyly followed suit.

Then they made their way to me, and the process started over.

"There really is no stigma, is there...." Lisa was smiling but in shock.

Dan saw the reaction first, "Oh... I'm so sorry. We should be using Earth etiquette."

Lisa was quick to counter. "No, just the opposite. It's wonderful. I hugged two half-naked men and a woman I had never met, feeling a release and aura of welcome I could not have imagined. If they're free, I'll take another."

Dan laughed and hugged her again. This time. Like an old friend. With everyone settling around a table, I introduced them to the concept of Interstellar Logistics and Supply. I also updated everyone on our work to crash the organization supplying the giants with humans.

This news turned out to be a dramatic and emotional revelation. Julio made the sign of the cross, pressed his hands together, and looked to the heavens. Dan and Oliver hugged, and Oliver sobbed openly on Dan's shoulder. Sirih misted up and smiled through tears, and the effect rolled over the rest of us until we were all emotional.

I decided I had better change direction and pointed out that Lisa was to become their conduit for supplies needed in the villages of Aard. This changed the mood as Lisa took over. Her history magnified her office management skills as the vice president of expansion in her last job.

"Folks, you'll see a lot of me in the future, and I need a guide. I need to know the villages, the people, and what everyone needs to be successful, grow, and prosper in the manner you want to see and for Aard to become the home you want it to be." Lisa had their attention.

Julio answered first, "Senora Lisa, I am that guide. I manage our storerooms and will take you to meet the people."

Dan added, "Lisa, Popeye, Jewels, Sirih, and I can move you around Aard to the people you want to meet and get to know."

Lisa was glowing now. "I want to live here some of the time. Where should I live? I want to fit in. I think I want to wear a kilt when it is suitable. It's already stifling in this robe. I may need to work at it, though. Dressing like you is a challenge for a woman in her golden years.

Jewels took over. Lisa, when I came to this world, a wonderful lady named Willow was my guide. I hope to honor what she taught me by passing it on to you. Let's help Dan and Sirih get the configuration done, and on the way, we can head down to Freedom with Julio to get things started."

The configuration setup was quick, and Dan was off to meet with Tiffany. Sirih stayed back to keep one transporter expert at home. Lisa and Jewels headed for Freedom with Julio, Popeye stayed back to man the transporter, and I headed for the Landing to visit Willow. It was finally time again for me to reflect for a while.

***

Chapter 47

The Colony Takes Hold

Willow's memorial was in great shape. I could see her friends had tended to the site regularly. The cane bench and cane chair were showing signs of age.

In the bad guy's lab notes, I found that Aard had a slightly bigger oxygen content than the atmosphere on Earth, so oxidation moved quicker here. They were still solid and sound. The furniture simply created the illusion that humans had been here much longer than we had.

I had a long conversation with Willow's grave. I updated her on our breakthrough against the bad guys back at their source. I knew that would please her. Suddenly, my cheeks were warm with tears, and my eyes burned. For me, Aard, Freedom, and the wonderful people gathered on this distant planet all became one with her spirit. For me, Willow was Aard.

My mind flashed back to the awkward moment we met in opposing cages. It continued through even more embarrassing moments as we learned who each other was while mating. Then, my mind rushed ahead to the escape with Jean and the heroic efforts of an ex-con to save us.

Our life-and-death challenges bonded us as a team and connected us to a wild and beautiful life with nature in a second chance on a new planet. None of us could ever be happy in our old lives.

The spirit of Willow lived in everything I saw and did on Aard. With that realization, I set up my hut and camp for an extended stay and set out to gather my dinner. I was home, and I was at peace. This would be the core of the rest of my life. I had tried several times to live here, but finally, I felt content.

I spent the afternoon updating my arrow stock and cleaning a Humpback for dinner. Even though I had some stainless-steel pots and a couple of cast iron pans, I built a stomach pot around a fresh willow stick to keep my skills sharp.

I prepared a few plateau seed pods and carved up a new handful of mushrooms. To balance out the meal, I harvested a couple of stocks of the apiaceous-style plant that reminded us of celery.

By evening, I had a small cooking fire and relaxed with my first Aardian meal in quite some time. I relished how much better I felt about this meal than the fluffy food I had been eating on Earth. I had just finished cleaning up and started sipping my local tea when the camp's silence ended.

"Yo, Mac. You home?"

Tiffany, Jesus, Shiv, and Stud walked into the camp, followed by Popeye and Jewels.

There were hugs all around.

Shiv said, "The word around town is there was a celebrity in town, so we all gathered to get our time in with him."

I smiled wide and pointed at the Humpback stomach simmering high over the fire. "Lots of tea water there, folks.

Even some left-over Humpback and mushroom in the cellar. " I pulled out a stack of tin cups.

The crew shook their heads, and Shiv said, "We ate, Mac. Thanks."

After she filled her cup, Tiffany came to sit next to me. "Mac, the cages are empty. What did you do?"

I leaned toward the fire a little to address everyone. "Team, it was mostly my father who broke their supply chain. He built a database that connected the dots between the human trafficking cartel and missing people. He identified kingpins in that organization from around the world and identified many of them as connected somehow to people who disappeared."

I let that sink in for a few moments. It probably seemed too simple, but I hadn't mentioned my father's years involved in global nefarious organization hunting. Honestly, because of his role, I wasn't privy to most of what he knew.

I continued. "In my case, they connected a company and its founder, who was a competitor of mine in Arizona. It appears he was directly responsible for me landing on Aard."

This perspective was beginning to sink in.

Shiv spoke up first. "Does that mean you know who sent me here?"

"I think we could give you a name or two, who you would probably recognize, Shiv."

He was momentarily lost in thought but finally said, "I may want to send them a thank you card."

That brought a chuckle from around the fire.

"I think I know who sent me here," Tiffany said softly.

Popeye said, "I think we all have some idea. I'm not sure I want them to know I'm happy and healthy here. I'm better off if they think I'm dead."

Stud had been quiet, but he was thinking of others when he spoke up. "Mac, the villages will want to hear this message from you. You have led and inspired the colonization of this world. You have instilled a sense of family, community, and respect for each other and the planet that will live on long after we are gone. Regardless of how we live through the dangers and challenges on Aard, we all owe you a debt of gratitude for the second chance you have offered each of us."

I was amazed at his English. His accent was pronounced, but his grammar and delivery were uncanny. As I thought about it, I noticed it in everyone. Not just language but attitude and drive had been a wholesale change. Even my brother on Earth was evolving his approach to his world.

I looked down at my teacup, humbled by his statements.

"Stud, I was just doing what I felt was right for me, and you all ran with it. About the word colonization, humans have a horrible reputation in that regard. We need to look deeply into what we are doing on Aard and draw something much different than colonization into our constitution."

The team was silent for a few moments, but all nodded in agreement as they thought.

I felt Willow's smiling presence. Stud continued. "Still, Mac. We need to have this talk with everyone."

"Agreed, Stud. Perhaps we can get Julio to lead a family reunion at Libertad... What do you think?"

"First annual," smiled Jewels.

We settled the matter and spent the rest of the evening with stories from those who came to Aard of their own free will and those who simply woke up here. The stories were upbeat and optimistic. We smiled, even though we remembered and honored those we lost along the way in warm stories of their accomplishments and successes.

From our first loss, Randy, through Willow and Kia, there were warm memories of survival and achievement along with those tragedies. Our deep losses made life on Aard sweeter. Everyone who decided to stay loved their current life, and no one desired transport to Earth, even for a visit.

***

I transported to Moon Bridge with Shiv to let the growing tribe at Moon Bridge know about the reunion, and everyone was in. I no longer knew everybody but made it a goal to meet them. Most knew true freedom because of Tiffany, Jesus, and Princess.

I learned some interesting news while at Moon Bridge and took a short walk with Kelsea to see if she was ready for this.

"Yes, Mac. I'm happy. I can't wait to meet my father in this new environment, get past the past, and tell him the news."

I smiled wide. "This is what I've been hoping for."

I took the next transport back to Willow's Cathedral and had a short chat with Popeye and Jewels.

"Popeye, Kelsea is going to be here for this reunion. Are you ready?"

"Ya, Mac, I sure am. I've had months to think about this, and I want to be in my daughter's life more than anything. Jewels, too; she talks about it often. Mac, they're damn near the same age."

"Well, Buddy, that's a double-edged sword. She may relate better to Jewels than her old man." We all laughed at that.

"Popeye, she has lived a lifetime since she got here. She is no longer the angry young woman that flashed through the Cathedral when she arrived. When you meet her, you will meet a new friend with a three-dimensional life. Take the time to get to know her before coming to any conclusions."

He nodded. "I learned a lot the last time we had this conversation. I've grown up too, Black Mac."

His reference to my street name made me understand he would be fine. This gathering of the clan would be critical to setting the culture we wanted to nurture as we carved out a world for humans on this distant planet. I joined the migration to Freedom.

I sat with Julio, Stud, Hilda, Ann, and Lisa, who were growing as the leaders of Freedom. They discussed a regularly scheduled market day they wanted to propose to the rest of the tribes. The goal was to share supplies common to the environments of each village.

Perhaps, even more importantly, these gatherings would unite people to ensure they kept the family bond.

Julio had brought up the point that humans tend to descend into an us-against-them mentality when bonds withered.

I agreed. "Finding ways to stay related will be critical. Freedom is a hub in many ways. Bonding can be a priority for that hub."

Lisa said, "Julio and I have been discussing this, Mac.

We have a presentation to make to the assembly when everyone settles in. We want to introduce culture as a bonding agent and a form of community expression. We have found a strong interest in music, art, and even theater. A stage with curtains may produce a positive outlet for expression and culture."

I could see Lisa was good for Freedom. Her arrival did not involve as much drama as most others, so her approach was beyond survival. I felt her positive contribution to Aard, and I could see Julio was thrilled. I also noted that Lisa had taken up a kilt and stored the robe for evenings. She didn't appear to be self-conscious at all. She was no longer the long-time office manager I knew most of my business life.

"I think the theater should have a roof. We must protect it from the elements. At some time, maybe a roof for the audience, too. Often in the rain, we need entertainment." Julio was excited.

Ann was excited, as well. She was planning. "Vera and Penny have been harvesting Screamers.

We used to have to depend on the Pass Giants, but our hunters have learned a lot from their plateau hunting and have turned the tables on the Screamers. I have been building curtains."

The next day, we gathered at Freedom. Moon Bridge and Freedom had grown considerably, so the gathering at the rockface was enormous.Popeye, Jewels, Dr. Tim, the new dentist I had yet to get to know, Maritza, A fully healed Marus, and Sirih came into camp on the trail from the Cathedral. I had yet to meet a couple of new citizens that were with them.

The atmosphere began to turn festive as people started to gather.

Dan, Oliver, Hilda, Penny, and Vera had enlisted another pair of new citizens to help set up snacks and water for a large gathering.

As I watched Popeye, Jewels, and the crew from Willow's Cathedral merge into the growing crowd, I noticed another tribe coming down the trail from the teleporter at the Cathedral. Shiv and his expanded village were arriving.

I made my way to Popeye and Jewels. I hugged Popeye, looked him in the eye, and said, "Paul, Shiv's village has some big news. Are you ready?"

He nodded, but his lower lip was quivering, and he didn't trust his voice. Jewels hugged him tight, and I pointed up the trail over his head.

His daughter was at the front of the troop and was walking hand in hand with Mutt.

When they got close, Mutt pointed at Popeye, and Kelsey broke into a run. Mutt had to step it up to keep up. She ran to her father, hesitated momentarily, teared up, and threw her arms around him. The two silently sobbed in each other's arms for a few moments. Jewels stepped around them and hugged Mutt. "Welcome home, Mutt."

Kelsey grabbed her father's arms and drew back far enough to look up at his face. "Dad, would you and Jewels go for a short walk with Mutt and me? We want to talk a little before the festivities."

Still struggling to speak, Popeye nodded, but Jewels took the initiative, took Mutt by the arm, and started walking toward the mineral tubs. Kelsey took her father's arm and fell into step behind Mutt.

They disappeared down over the bank into the delta bed. I noted that neither father nor daughter seemed affected by the lack of shirts.

***

Chapter 48

The Villages of Aard

I knew what they would discuss because of my last visit to Moon Bridge. This day would be a massive milestone in the history of humans on Aard. We would also hear from Tiffany, Adelphi, Jesus, and Princess.

They had shared some of their news with me but had not yet opened some excellent news for the colony. The last few days, they were exploring North of Freedom, along the coast, and were due back for the gathering.

I reminisced with friends on the adventures of Aard while I watched the citizens reconnecting. A semi-circle pattern of huts had formed around the rock face. Aceraceae-type trees dotted the landscape, along with a Plantain-related tree that produced a smaller, rounder version of a banana the camp was experimenting with.

These were somewhat starchy, not sweet like a banana, but were rather handy when boiled or fried. The camp was calling them tree potatoes. Also common between the huts were stubby little tree ferns with thick trunks that rarely grew over 12 feet.

These fluffy umbrellas provided the best shade with a full crown of fern fronds that ensured cover from aerial eyes.

Tables and stools made of local wood and willow cane rested strategically in the shade of many of these fern trees and next to local huts. Stud and Pete, in particular, had become skilled at building furniture. I noticed some of the new folks had also taken up the trade. With a little direction from Julio and Lisa, people gathered in small groups to reconnect and introduce new citizens. They would then move on to the next table and repeat the process.

Popeye and Jewels, with Kelsey and Mutt, had returned and sat near the unlit cooking fire near the rock face. Their conversation was animated and happy. I took the opportunity to join them.

"Mac, I'm happy you have joined us. I told my dad the news." Kelsey was jubilant as she jumped up to draw me to a stool in the group. I reached for her belly. It was just beginning to show. "May I rub it for luck?"

She nodded happily, and as I looked around the group, I noted that Paul Sutter didn't miss a beat. He took his turn, cradling her puffy belly, and kissed her softly on top of her head.

"Congratulations, family. Your news will highlight this gathering when Shiv calls you up to tell the Aard-nation. How are you doing with the news, Popeye?"

His voice was back now, but he didn't need to say it. His broad smile said it all. "Mac, I couldn't imagine better news. I'm going to be a young grandpa. I'm going to have decades to spoil this child."

"Popeye, you're not that young," I laughed, "Just think how Jewels feels about this. She becomes a gramma."

Jewels squealed and hugged Kelsey tight. "This is awesome. We're the same age, and we get to share so much. I can't wait."

Kelsey giggled and hugged back tightly. "We'll be a team. How long till you go off the mushrooms?"

Jewels blushed. "Uh..." was all she could say.

I looked at Mutt, who was quietly smiling in the background. "Mutt. How are you with this wonderful news?"

"Mac, I had given up my dream of one day being a father, husband, and having a family. Meeting Kelsey was the best thing that could have happened to my life. I will be the best husband and father you have ever seen."

Kelsey smiled up at him from where she had sat. "Billy is the most amazing man. He is so tender-hearted but tough as nails. My man is protective but allows me to be me without judgment. He asked me to marry him, and I said yes... We need to find a preacher."

I looked at Mutt. "Billy?"

"You didn't think my mother named me Mutt, did you? I earned that name. Mom named me William but called me Billy. When I started school, the Mutt name started. I don't know why, but it stuck." He laughed at that, and we all joined.

"Kels was the first person since grade school who called me Billy." Kelsey smiled and pulled his fuzzy arm to her cheek. "He may be your Mutt, but he is my Billy."

"Would you like the rest of us to call you Billy?" I asked.

"Nah, I like the fact that Kels makes it special."

Expanding the moment, I said, "Folks, you may want to talk to Julio about the preacher topic. He married people as a judge, and he has a Catholic background if that is of interest. At the very least, he could help you decide how to achieve your goals. Lisa may have ideas, too, but be careful. She tends to take charge."

Mutt smiled. "We can start with Julio."

"By the way," I interjected, "I understand you two may not be the only ones in this program. Where are Sylvia and Pete?" I had seen them walking rather closely as their tribe approached.

"They went to find Jesus. He's kind of a big deal to Billy and Pete. He helped to save them, and he brought them to Freedom. Syl and I want to ensure he knows how much we also appreciate him. It's his fault I found my knight in hairy armor, and Syl found her farm boy."

I looked over to Julio's sign by the rock face. Freedom-Libertad said it all. Every last citizen was energized and happy as I surveyed the growing crowd under that sign. I could not see a wallflower anywhere. Even Vera happily engaged with the hunter team.

That's when I heard Tiffany's Tarzan yell and turned to see her and her scouts entering Freedom from the Landing trail. They had extras. The looks of happiness on their faces as they broke into a trot made me feel like we had made it.

No matter what our future would bring, I felt this band of humans would flourish.

They came directly to the central fire and reached for hugs all around. Adelphi and Jesus were packing long silver-green shoots out of their paperboy sacks. She said, "Excuse us for a few minutes. We're going to plant these near a backwater in the delta. We will be back in less than an hour."

"Bamboo?"

"Very similar. We think it will flourish here. It may be a mixed blessing, though. It has good food, great cover, building material, and great pulp for paper...but it spreads like wildfire. I think the terrain will control it to some degree."

"Well, I think your timing is perfect. The afternoon is getting long, and I think Julio and Lisa have a full program for the evening."

Adelphi and Jesus headed for the delta flats, and Tiffany and Princess joined the conversation at the cold firepit. Because of their proximity to the subject, Tiffany and Princess learned the news before the big reveal.

***

As Pegasi approached the horizon, a mighty horn rang out. Marus had created a Conch-like shell horn that made Tiffany's Tarzan yell sound like a whisper. Julio then produced a crude megaphone that carried his voice handily over the village. He called attention to a small platform near the rockface and called it the stage.

He announced a short agenda where he would have representatives from our related groups come up on his stage.

They would announce the news from each group. He surprised me by first calling me to the stage to open the ceremonies. He had me opening with news from the old world.

As I walked to the stage, I noticed Lisa grinning from ear to ear as she watched me approach, and I had my answer to the surprise. In a robust voice, I took my place without the megaphone and asked if I could be heard from the back. I got a positive response.

I looked over the crowd for a moment as they became silent. It was apparent they expected something from me. As any speaker knows, you usually come off as genuine if you hit a stage unprepared. Unprepared, unpolished, but real.

"For those of you who are new here. I am Black Mac of 51 Pegasi. Known to my friends as Mac, but those who know my secrets call me Black Mac."

I waved my arm over the village, "This is my family. We love each other. Like any family, we have conflicts with each other and the world around us, but we have bonded through danger, love, laughter, and heart-wrenching tears of loss when we lost family members."

I looked around the gathering at the close friends I had made through our trials and tribulations.

"Tonight, you will meet many heroes. Being here tells me you have met some of them already, but you should take the time to get to know them all. They will help you become heroes, and this world needs you. Life here requires you to have our back and us to have yours."

"I have good news for those who woke up naked in a cage."

I surveyed the crowd for a moment to let that sink in. "I will leave most of this story for Tiffany and her crew, as they have experienced the reality of this news. However, I am also related to a couple of heroes on Earth, and they have broken the human supply chain that has been delivering humans from Earth to the Fur-Giants on this planet."

I could hear the community exhale as though they had been holding their breath since they got here.

"This means that, at least for now, the cages won't be gathering new captives. Some may still be left to save, but Tiffany can update us. If you haven't met me, please prioritize looking me up and saying hi. One more thing before I turn the stage back to Julio.

Someone thanked me earlier for leading the colonization of this planet with humans. I'm honored by the kudo, but the word 'colonization' struck me as negative. Humans have a poor history with the term." We did not come here to colonize. Our earliest citizens were abducted and transported here against our will. Since then, we have survived then thrived. Now, we are growing and spreading out.

At this point, I want to point out that Giants, Screamers, Rainbow Lizards, Humbacks, and Aardvarks are citizens like we now are. We must build a constitution that enables us to live with each other and them, not eradicate them. We are equals; we are now in the food chain and making changes to the planet we now choose to live on.

Finally, these species may be food, predators to us, or prey. They may see us as a threat, but they are not an enemy. The giants are not inherently evil, as we see with Chuckles, but the humans who engaged with them first, are. In the same theme, we must ensure that our villages are one.

As we get distance between us, we must ensure we stick together in spirit. The transporters should make our villages more like neighborhoods of the same city. I now turn you over to Julio and Lisa, who are fully qualified to show us how."

Through applause, I stepped down as Julio waved to Tiffany and the team to give their update.

Tiffany introduced Jesus, Adelphi, and Princess, then confirmed they had visited three known cage centers. "The cages at the tower, one to the Northeast and a further one to the Southeast, are now empty. After our last rescue missions, the Giants have repurposed these cages as nesting cages for captive Purple Screamers."

This statement got a thankful murmur from the audience.

"We know there are other camps of escapees. We have seen signs: human footprints and old campfires. We have also found a few who have not made it. Some, perhaps, didn't know how to survive on their own.

We have found another great homesite about three days North, on the coast. It's mountainous, evergreen trees and canyon rivers crashing to the sea. But hidden in that rugged land is a beautiful high valley. A trail from the plateau at the landing goes almost all the way to this rocky headland.

It is thick with Aardvark critters that Penny and team have been bringing home, but with the prey come screamers. They come out to the sea there. The cover is critical, but that is also where we found bamboo, or something like it, in the lowlands of the valley foothills. Although Freedom will always be our hometown, we plan to make this valley our Northern home and leave in the morning if anyone wants to join us."

She had all our attention. "We want to start a village there as well. We'll have more to share once we have time to explore it better. Julio, who's next?"

Jewels stepped up next to give an update on the landing at Willow's Cathedral. Next, Popeye let everyone in on the expansion of Willows Memorial to include markers for Kia and Randy.

This news received a lot of applause as Popeye handed the floor to Dr. Tim and Maritza for their updates.

They had a regular clinic set up now and referred to the transporters as easy transportation for check-ups. They also introduced their new dentist partner.

Dr. Tim turned the floor over with one last comment. "We now have a few people experimenting with removing the mushrooms from their diet." Before anyone could ask for details, the team stepped down from the stage.

Next up was Shiv and his village. Shiv, Stacy, and two young couples took the stage. He waited for the stir caused by the doctor's statement to die, then said, "Freedom, and the people of Aard, we would like to announce that in about seven more Earth months, the first native Aardians will be born amongst us."

Freedom roared. The agenda dissolved as the stage was rushed. Congratulations rang through the village as Kelsey and Sylvia took ownership of the event.

I watched as Shiv and Stacey backed away from the excitement, smiling at each other, but there was something more... I figured it out when I saw Shiv pull Stacy close in the shadows, kiss her tenderly, and rub her belly. What was in the water at Moon Bridge?

There were other updates throughout the evening, but they played out in one-on-one interactions. Aard was about to be transformed into the second native planet for humanity. An evil undertaking replaced by organic human expansion into the stars.

This one small step at Freedom was the new "biggest step for mankind."

Suddenly, I needed to be with Willow, so Alpha and Beta escorted me back to the Landing, Willow, and a bed in a little hut where I dreamed of the caramel-skinned angel smiling in the sunlight on a warm 51 Pegasi day.

***

Chapter 49

The Tour

Life was good at the Landing cabin... for a week. Willow kept telling me in my dreams to get off my ass. I went down to the Cathedral to tell Popeye, Jewels, and their little tribe I needed to explore.

I decided to get to know our planet firsthand and check in on the other villages as I toured. I headed North to visit Tiffany and her crew first.

I could have taken the transporter, but my goal was to get to know Mother Aard. I did, however, send her a note via the teleporter to watch out for me. She quickly replied with a pencil map on a sheet of notepad paper. The trek was uneventful as I traveled North, close to the sea, but I noticed the Screamer's calls were getting closer. Perhaps a bit too close as I got to the mountains. I thanked the local fauna as their trails kept me deep in the evergreens.

The map was vital because I could not have found the camp without it. I literally had to find a cave that proved to be a narrow tunnel to the hidden grassy valley Jesus had found for the tribe.

Not far from the entrance I saw a dim light in the distance.

I counted six caverns off the tunnel that would have taken me astray if not for the milestones on the map.

As the light at the end of the tunnel grew stronger, I found a large cavern, well utilized and stocked with dry goods. The village had ample shelter, storage, and protection when needed... I also met someone I didn't know.

"Hi, you must be Mac." A tall, red-headed woman with a broad smile waved at me.

Taken aback, I stammered. "H... hi."

Her smile grew even wider, "I'm Rita, one of the new citizens Jesus and Tiffany saved. I was storing some of our dried fruit and was on the lookout for you."

She hugged me tight and said, "I've heard so much about you. Let's get you to the village." She turned on her heel and headed out of the cavern. I nodded to her freckled back and followed.

As was her habit, Tiffany had designed her village to sit deep in the forest, but it had a magnificent Eastern view of the valley, with a winding, small river disappearing through a crack in the rocks just to the North. I spent two well-spent weeks getting to know Rita, Matt, Jen, and another Ann. They had already started to pair off.

Rita was not in a hurry to pair up. She said she would be a 'free agent' until she met the other villages. Matt and Ann had already bonded in the cages, and Jen quickly gravitated to Vera.

Vera was a little slow to respond to romantic hints because she was still grieving Kia. The two had already bonded as friends, and Vera flourished as a mentor for the small-framed, new citizen.

Princess and Jesus turned into an item, focusing on exploration and trekking. All were happy with their lives and the trend for imigrants continued. No desire for Earth.

Tiffany informed me the Giants were hunting humans for sport on the other side of the pass, so it was good that they didn't have to travel with large groups of refugees anymore. Jesus and Vera occasionally made quick trips through the pass to look for escapees. She felt it necessary now to build a sustainable village and harvest Screamers when they got too close to ensure they stayed back.

I joined Jesus and Vera on their next trek. I wanted to review the old Tower Giant's territory to look for changes and ensure they were still focused on a different food supply. We found another couple of men looking for a home. They seemed skeptical of our story but admitted they had nothing better planned. With a small discussion on the side, Patrick and Marcel felt a community might be a good step for now.

While they were discussing, I suggested something didn't add up, so we may need to keep our guard up. Larry was still fresh in our memory, so Jesus and Vera escorted them home with some guarded caveats. I took my time heading South through the jungle and rainforest.

With my prized binoculars, I spotted a Rainbow Lizard before it spotted me so that I could give it a wide berth, but I noted that they lived inland.

Working through the territory, I had another element for my safety checkbox.

The Giants were busy. They were now chicken farmers, with a stock of young screamers growing in cages. That was good news.

I also saw the berry warren growing back, bigger and fresher than ever. I found a man and a woman living in the new briar patch, and they were more than willing to have an escort to take them to a safe village. They had scrambled into the forest when the warren burned, so they were happy to join Shiv and tribe.

I got to know Bob, a carpenter in his previous life, and Sandy, a dentist. We now had two dentists. The trek led me to a great visit with Shiv and his village. I got to see the growing bellies of the new moms and was happy to get confirmation of the third belly. Stacy was going to be a mother, too. Shiv was excited to show me his set of caverns above Moon Bridge Lake. They now had good shelter from the monsoons.

***

I took my leave after a couple of weeks and headed South. I wanted to explore the shoreline and work my way East to the tower we identified on our lab maps from a raid before the organization crumbled. A few days South, I could see the crest of an island far out to sea.

There appeared to be a small plume of smoke from where I could see, so I assumed I found a far-off volcano. This knowledge and the hot springs at Bitter Waters suggested we were near volcanic faults. I filed that away for our next gathering.

I fell into a pattern of looking to see what was beyond the next hill, through the next forest, and across the next river. I carried a notebook and mapped my journey. I came to larger rivers a few times and had to go inland for a few days until I could find shallows, fallen logs, or bolder fields the river ran through, but I always wound my way back to the sea.

One river looked very interesting as it flowed from a wide pass. I made a note to come back and follow it East.

I lost track of time but made a tiny mark on the back cover of my notebook every day. I planned to count them one day when I was back at Freedom. Every night, I thanked Willow for guiding me, and I had no doubt she kept me safe.

The monsoon season passed, but it felt shorter and milder at this latitude. The heat was oppressive, and I wore a wide-brimmed fern feather hat to protect myself from the Pegasi sun. I found a new, smaller version of the Humpback and flocks of small raptors that appeared to be the missing link between chickens and dinosaurs. They had scales instead of feathers, ate insects, and tasted like chicken. Really... like chicken.

This is where I noticed insects to a greater degree. A couple of their species noticed me. I found I needed to be in the open more, in the wind, to avoid the welts they were leaving on me. Of course, this made me nervous as Screamers were a daily sight. Finally, as the second monsoon season approached, the wind came up, the insects disappeared, and I came to an inlet. I could not see across this inlet, so I had to turn East or return the way I came. I needed to learn more, but that Eastern path would have to wait.

I chose to retrace my footsteps, and by the time the second monsoon season hit, I was well up the river that had fascinated me earlier and into a shallow but challenging pass. This is where I found Chuckles the Giant, who had befriended Tiffany. Rather, he found me.

I woke up in the morning, rolled off the Screamer hide, and he was sitting with a companion, cross-legged, waiting for me to wake. Of course, I broke into a short panic. He didn't know it was me until I pulled my blanket off. He grinned then and signed two digits and the wave of his small finger on the right hand. I replied, "Hi." Then, I used the alphabet to spell out 'Chuckles.'

He chortled, and that made me glad. He signed. "Friend, you are far from home."

I began to sign faster as American Sign Language started coming back to me, so I told him about losing Willow and how I was exploring the world. He told me two days' travel would take me to a dangerous Giant's camp. They were angry that their food source had stopped and were hunting escapees. They had started a breeding program like the Tower Giants had tried, but it was much too slow, so humans were now just sport.

He suggested I return to the coast and Bitter Waters to be safe. If I went forward, I would find only desert. I'd be in sand dunes and wind. No water. The river source was these mountains, but I would soon be on flat ground.

"Are there any humans living nearby?" I signed.

He nodded. There was a small camp up a tributary a short distance back from where I came and to the North. He would take me there if I liked.

This time, I nodded, and he gently picked me and my gear up. Chuckles and his buddy carried me for about an hour and a half, setting me in the middle of a camp. As he did so, I saw a few people scurry for the bush. We talked some on the trek, and I asked him if his tribe would be open to trade.

I made it clear I wanted to build a cooperative relationship with his species to put in the past our original reason for being on the planet. He liked that idea and suggested I come back when we were ready, and he would know we were here.

I smiled. I assumed that meant he could smell us when we were close.

He signed, "I go now." He smiled a Giant smile and was gone.

I called out to the camp. "Folks, the Giant is gone. You can come out now."

I got to know Sam, Theresa, Phil, Donna, and Bridgette for the next month. It took half that time to convince them that Chuckles was friendly and we could communicate. Once they got to know me and I relayed the information Chuckles had given me, it was not hard to convince them to come to the coast. Only Phil had any objection, but when none of the rest of the tribe wanted to stay, he agreed to come along.

We grew close on the trail. In that Aardian month, we fell into a pattern of building, breaking camp, and covering new ground. Shortly after my third monsoon on the trek, I had deposited five more residents in Moon Bridge. The growing village was alive with people, and the sound of toddlers chasing each other through camp brought the community to a new dimension.

51 Pegasi - Black Mac

Shiv took over the new citizens and assigned them mentors to find their niche.

***

I was tired and road-worn, so I took the transporter shuttle back to Willow's Cathedral. No one was in the landing room or the main hall, so I went to my cabin. It was, more than ever, home.

My first order of business was to sit with Willow. I sat on the ground, staring absently through the rungs of the old cane bench with my focus in the fog. The ghost of Willow smiled back at me, so real; I could smell her skin as though she was lying against me. She was talking to me, and more than four years of my life since the lightning bolt hit, melted away.

I hadn't been here at the Landing for a long time, but the pond was as I had left it. The new cane chair that replaced the one with the broken leg was still solid as it had been when placed, and the matching cane bench Popeye had built looked strong, but both looked older than their age.

I knew how they felt. I felt the curve of my broken nose. I tried living at the Landing three years ago but could not. Willow had left a much deeper hole in my soul than I expected. I feel she convinced me I had to explore. Many years ago, life in Seattle had been a waste of time if not for the Sutlers. Pegasi 51 had changed that. Willow's arrival had made it all worthwhile. Then...

The tickle from the tears running down my face was the first indication I was weeping. I stood. I focused again on the Landing, the pond, and the bench. I knew what I needed to do.

As I was in the habit of doing at Willow's Memorial, I kissed two fingertips on my right hand, touched them gently to the old seat, and turned to leave the apparition in the fog. I had news for Popeye, Jewels, and the camp.

Jewels saw me come around the pond into the landing cabin opening. She ran to me with open arms and hugged me tight. "How ya doing, Uncle Mac?" Jewels greeted me softly as I hugged her back. She knew what to expect because she knew where I had been.

The 'Uncle' title meant more than I ever thought it would. I nodded to the cooking pot. "Humpback smells mighty good Jewels; I hope there is some extra. I think I worked up an appetite".

"You know it, Unc. Anne and Siri are on an overnight trip to the Freedom Tubs, but I'm expecting Paul in a few minutes, and we'll fill up and trade some stories. We're so relieved to see you come back.

You've been gone three years... Ardian years, but still a very long time. This is the longest you have been away. There has been a lot of change here. We are dying to hear about your travels".

" 'Can't wait to spill the beans and show you my map. I don't suppose you have any bark tea. My old bones are beginning to tell on me".

"The water is just now coming to a boil. Bark is hanging in the pouch on the porch".

I walked over to pull the small sack of inner bark from the peg on the cabin wall.

Then stepped back to the fire and measured the ground potion into the Humpback's stomach hanging high over the fire. Tangy steam wreathed around my face with sweet memories as I poured. I went into the cabin, pulled three cups from the shelf, and walked back out to the table as Paul walked, grinning, back into the camp.

We three friends sat down for homecoming over a savory meal, warm willow tea, and warmer smiles. They insisted on giving their update first. Willow's Cathedral had its first baby. Paul and Jewels had welcomed Baby Mac Sutler three months after Mutt and Kels had delivered their baby.

Baby Mac was on an overnight sleepover with little Willow, Stud, and Hilda's two-year-old. After dinner, we retired to wicker rockers on the new, larger porch of the landing cabin.

***

Chapter 50

The Only Thing Constant...

The ground exploded.

We were horizontal in the dirt as the porch evaporated away and the cabin crumbled to debris. Everything, including us, vibrated on the ground like water drops hopping on a hot skillet.

"Jewels!" Paul's scream filled the drama as he grabbed in vain for anything solid. Large gashes grew like demonic black lightning bolts across the camp yard, and the evening light became a shaking slash in the blackness as I fell into the earth.

Paul missed Jewel's hand as they swiped toward each other, but he caught an ankle as she spun past him in a horizontal pirouette. He rolled to grab her with his other hand and hung on with all his might.

The world came to a stop in silence as though afraid to breathe. Sound came back far to the East, where Screamers were going crazy. Their cacophony grew louder as they approached in the darkening sky. Wild in their fright, they were fleeing their mountain roosts.

Paul and Jewels also became aware of the low rumble to the Southwest.

Boiling orange and red underbellies and lightning lit up the angry ash clouds as they expanded to the East.

Jewels sat up and scrambled into Paul's arms.

"Mac! Mac, are you alright?"

My muffled response came from the gash in the ground. Paul rolled around until he could peer into the gap. I scrambled, climbing a root system from a fallen tree. I was almost within reach. Paul had no way of decreasing the distance, but I was determined, clawing out of the darkness. Finally, his adrenalin-charged tug on my elbow helped to pull me back to the surface.

In moments, the three of us clutched each other around a vertical tree as Aard rose and writhed beneath us again.

We were knocked to our stomachs as the skies lit up. A mountain of exploding steam and lava rose from the sea in the Southwest as the new volcanic island grew off the coast, and three matching pillars of fire lit up the East in the Purple Screamer Mountains. To the South grew the angry, boiling steam and ash cloud blanketing the land, sea, and sky. The Eastern volcanos produced three more plumes, all leaning East. There was darkness to the West and North, but we could still see stars in that direction.

The ground grew silent again. The Screamer's noise was far over the sea now, perhaps near the Island of the Bleeding Flower. This time, we could stand. I pointed to the Southwest.

It looked like shooting stars were spreading from the new volcano.

"Quick, we need to get to the caverns." The two moons blurred by the smoke now, but the glowing mushrooms made for enough light to dodge and jump cracks in the earth carefully.

We entered the first chute into the caverns as an ominous whistling grew loud. Then, the explosions of catapulted lava and boulders hit.

Many of the underground paths were impassable, but we did manage to get to the cavern overlooking the sea. To our relief, the Cathedral was intact, and the transporter was untouched. The heat-rounded ceilings appeared to protect us from loose rock falling.

The light was dim now, but I needed to check the calibration to ensure anyone transporting in, would land where they expected to land. Popeye lit one of the wall torches with a sliver from the central hall fire. Once we had light, I was relieved to see the location settings had not changed via the GPS sensor.

We found a paper note at the transporter landing.

"We are safe. Please respond - Tiffany."

I set the transport to send to Tiffany and responded.

"Willow's Cathedral seems safe, but we are not all accounted for. I will update when it is safe to join us – Mac."

Above us and out to sea, the whistling culminated in explosions top side as red-hot boulders, boiling mud, and burning debris tore through our homes at the landing.

Huge plumes and fountains of steam exploded from the sea as molten boulders hit cool water. We had little to say. We were as safe as we were going to get for now.

We knew what was happening but didn't know to what extent it would change our lives, and our thoughts were on Freedom, Anne, and Siri, who were between us and the exploding volcano.

The proximity of the volcano would change everything about Freedom. Shiv and his tribe would be on the other side of the volcano but probably not far enough away from it to be safe. I hoped Tiffany's tribe wouldn't suffer anything more than minor shaking from their location.

Any more reaction was futile now until Aard finished the spasms. There would be no sleep in this area of Aard tonight. Just as my mind went to Willow and the memorial at the landing, the chambers at the Cathedral began to echo with panicked voices as Dr. Tim, Julio, Maritza, and Lisa arrived from the lower chambers.

Several others started to gather outside the transporter room. With them came Sandy, the dentist I had met earlier on my travels, and a man who looked familiar.

Popeye introduced them. "Mac, meet Sandy, our second new dentist. She's working with Dr. Tim to set up shop at Willow's Cathedral and Buzz, whom Jesus dragged into camp during a scouting trip with Tiffany. These two hit it off and now live in Freedom but spend much of their time in the Cathedral."

Sandy nodded, "Hi again, Mac. It's great to see you back in the village... or at least, it would be if the world would hold still."

Buzz reached out his hand. "Haven't we met somewhere, Mac? Maybe the village up North?"

I looked at him in amazement as my memory came flooding back. "Hi, Buzz. We have a couple of mutual acquaintances. When we get through this emergency, let's sit down and talk about Sharon Rowlands and Seven Feathers."

I watched as the light came on for him, but as he was about to speak, Dr. Tim said, "Ann..., Sirih...." I grabbed his arm as he headed for the lower entrance to the sea.

I pointed at the sea. It was gone.

"Dr. Tim, Sunami. The water has pulled out and will rush in at any moment. We need to get into the upper chambers. A vent chamber now!"

We scrambled upward.

***

The blast of air hit us with a force that shoved us against the rocks of the vent tube. We tumbled upward until we could grip a boulder or edge we could hold as sea spray and wind buffeted us like a hurricane.

In moments, the direction changed, and dry, smoky air flowed downward over us to remind us of what was happening on the plateau above.

"Hang tight, folks. This will repeat a few times as the tidal waves die down."

Once we saw the worst was over, Buzz commented, "I feel like we just run through the full cycle at the laundromat."

We needed the chuckle, but we were all eager to get back down to assess the damage, and when we were all accounted for and made sure there were no broken bones or serious bleeding, we climbed carefully back down to the central hall.

Thankfully, although damp, the main hall, the medical room, the storage, and the landing room were unharmed.

More people were climbing down out of a vent tube. Jewels screamed and ran for the newcomers with her arms out. Young Mac and Willow were presented in the arms of Jean and Hilda. Hilda ran to Jewels, and they hugged around the children. Paul and Jean wrapped their arms around them all.

Jean turned to me. "Mac, we heard you were home and were on our way to visit you at the landing. We are so happy you are all here."

We looked around us, thankful for the miracles in Willow's Cathedral.

The same couldn't be said for the lower chambers. They were flushed with seawater and strewn with driftwood, seaweed, and sea life of all kinds. We arrived as an eel, sea worm, snake, or something of that nature was slithering back into the sea. The size was shocking. It looked much like the sensational images of massive Amazonian Pythons I'd seen.

There would be much to clean up.

Dr. Tim was ready to find Ann and Sirih.

"The eruption seems to have subsided, Doctor, but the sea is probably not friendly right now. I can see by the cave openings that we are nearing daylight. Let's go topside to see what the plateau looks like."

He nodded, but I could tell he needed to do something, and I know the rest of us felt the same.

"Who lives in Freedom these days?"

Jewels said, "Stud and Hilda live there with several new folks, and of course, Julio and Lisa spend most of their time there. Of course, Marus, Ann, and Sirih seemed to rotate back and forth between Freedom and Willow's Cathedral."

Stud said, " Luckily, many are hunting on the plateau, North toward Tiffany's village. Some are in the South with Shiv. Freedom was quiet as many were elsewhere tonight.

He looked around. "Marus is missing. With Ann and Sirih, Marus is another.

We headed back up the vent tube. By the time we reached the surface, light from the North had illuminated the hellscape under the ash plume. Ash was still falling like light snow, but there were no longer flaming boulders. There were a few small fires, but the land was wet enough that the fuel was not tinder. Monsoons were due, so the current fires would not last long.

When we got to the landing trail, I wanted to turn left to see if Willow was okay, but we needed to get to Bitter Waters. We traveled in warm ash, up to our ankles, but the worn trail was visible, so we made good time off the plateau. We were all relieved to see activity in the dusty village of Freedom.

The village was mostly intact, but a few smoking boulders sat amongst the ash. We found some made it to the storage caverns, but for Marus Ann and Sirih. They hadn't heard from them, and the delta was awash from the tsunami again. They had been out since the eruption ended, calling and searching.

51 Pegasi - Black Mac

Dan and Oliver had been on their way to the tubs when they felt the quake and saw the volcano, and the coastline recede, so they hurried back to the village to get everyone to the highland up the trail.

The flood water hadn't reached Freedom this time, but they hadn't had time to return to the hot springs shelf, so we headed there now. There was no answer to our calls, and the hot tubs were covered in mud that looked like wet concrete. Without luck, we combed through the delta's barren gravel bars and backwaters for most of the day. We found many of our fishing canoes and rafts but no people.

The day quickly darkened mid-afternoon as a black wall built on the Western horizon. The Monsoon was on us. We hurried back to the caverns at Freedom. Stud and the village began working feverishly to prepare for the onslaught of driving rain, and the rest of us headed for Willow's Cathedral to do the same.

Popeye and I moved on to the landing and the memorial when we got to the vent tube. It was intact. Willow was still safe, but the bench and chair had burned. A large boulder sat next to their ashes.

The pond was gone. The ragged crack that almost became my tomb had swallowed the peaceful pond. Half the tree I had climbed out on was underwater. The crevice was still filling from the stream that had fed the calming pool. The huts would need to be rebuilt, and it seemed we would need to expand the memorial, but those tasks would wait for the Monsoon to pass.

I looked at Paul Sutler, and the pain in his eyes reflected mine.

"Let's let the Monsoon wash the landing clean, my friend.

Roger Haller   499

It appears that even on Aard, the only constant is change. We will rebuild every time. Every time, there will be a new chapter, and every chapter will be beautiful."

He smiled through his tears, "Yup."

Lightning blinded us momentarily, then overpowering thunder chased us to the vent tunnel. We hurried down to the safety of Willow's Cathedral to find Jewels with a note.

"I hope this note finds you safe. We have escaped to the South, out from under the ash. We will be all right but need to build in the rain. - Kels"

***

About The Author

Roger Haller

Roger Haller has always been facinated with the interaction of characters in challanging environments. From the Native North American stories publshed in his first Novel, 'Guaridan of the One' in 2008, through the stories that were published in the global anthology, 'Saterica', also in 2008, and 'Garage Angel', published in the Spec-Fic Anghology, 'Thank you, Death Robot', in 2009, the vivid characters driving his stories have been his trade-mark.

Roger was born in Tillamook Oregon, then raised in a Native family in South British Columbia timber and cattle country. Since 2000, his home has been Western Washington and he currently resides with his wife Joni, on a small hobby-farm in Monroe, Washington.

Now, with the retirement from day to day working in the tech industry, watch for several new titles from Roger and Cowboy Logic Press.

Cowboy Logic Press Books

By This Author and Others

'Guardian of the One' Imagine the universe as a single entity to which all things are attached. Follow a Native American legend as the new Guardian of the One begins the task of bringing the world back to this understanding. Many powerful entities can not let this happen. Watch Gadge and Sammy, his Dreamer, as they unravel the mysterious links of the soul. Are they in time to save the wobbly cycle of life?

'Satirica' A post acolyptic speculative fiction anthology by **Cowboy Logic Press**. Editted by **Dudgeon** and written by these fine global writers:

Joshua Allen	Bill Housley
RJ Astruc	Dan Kopcow
Jaspn K Chapman	Dan Marcus
Gary Cuba	Paul Mannering
Lawrence R Dagstine	Thomas L Martin
John Parke Davis	Edward Morris
Steven J Dines	Mike Philbin
Dudgeon	Anden Sharp
Victor Giannini	Kevin Spiess
Roger Haller	David Thorp

Finally, **'Into the Dark,: Escape of the Nomad'**, a YA Sci-Fi the whole family can read, by Bill Housley.

www.ingramcontent.com/pod-product-compliance
Lightning Source LLC
Chambersburg PA
CBHW051935020726
47501CB00001B/130